Bruecke to Heaven

Timothy D. ___

Prov 3:6

CHILDREN OF THE LIGHT

Timothy W. Tron

COVER ART CREATED BY TIMOTHY W. TRON

WESTBOW
PRESS
A DIVISION OF THOMAS NELSON

WestBow Press books may be ordered through booksellers or by contacting:

WestBow Press
A Division of Thomas Nelson
1663 Liberty Drive
Bloomington, IN 47403
www.westbowpress.com
1-(866) 928-1240

ISBN: 978-1-4497-5656-7 (sc)
ISBN: 978-1-4497-5658-1 (hc)
ISBN: 978-1-4497-5657-4 (e)

Library of Congress Control Number: 2012910860

Printed in the United States of America

WestBow Press rev. date: 07/24/2012

First of all, I would like to dedicate this book to my Lord and Savior, Jesus Christ.

During the struggle to maintain the Word of God throughout the ages prior to the Reformation, I hope that the countless lives that were lost will be lifted up in the passages of this text so that their efforts would not have been in vain.

I want to thank the writer's group led by Sims Poindexter at Goldston United Methodist Church, the church community, and the staff at the Goldston Public Library for their encouragement and support that inspired me to go forward with this endeavor. I would also like to thank Nancy Cope for her work in performing the historical review of the book, Gary Gaddy for providing an additional editorial review and my sister Johnna Tron Conner for the final galley review and spiritual support.

I also want to thank my aunt, June Tron, without whom I never would have started this journey. I wrote this work thanks in part to her genealogical research. I also want to extend thanks to our extended family and the Heimat Museum in Walldorf, Germany. I would also like to thank the wonderful folks in Valdese, North Carolina, for creating the beautiful Waldensian Museum and Trail of Faith.

Finally, I want to dedicate this book to my wife, Sheryl, who has supported my many endeavors through our nearly thirty years of marriage, and to our two adoring children, Jonathan and Mary, for providing me with the happiness of spirit and creativity to flourish in our nurturing Christian home.

For you were once darkness, but now you are light in the Lord. Live as children of light.

—Ephesians 5:8

Introduction

AND AUTHOR'S NOTES

After these things the Lord appointed seventy others also and sent them two by two before His face into every city and place where He Himself was about to go.

—Luke 10:1

Not long into Jesus's ministry, he realized he needed to expand his discipleship beyond his original twelve. He recognized that to reach the multitudes of humanity, he would have to enlist others to help spread the word, so Jesus chose seventy more disciples and empowered them with the same abilities and gifts as the original twelve. Then he sent them out into the wilderness.

This historical fiction novel is the story of a people who received the Word of God directly from the newly commissioned disciples. It describes how it transformed their lives into something more—something greater than they would have ever imagined. Their isolation in the remote Cottian Mountain valley that lay between Italy and Switzerland, which they had known since the beginning of time, provided them with the perfect setting to develop their knowledge and gifts over multiple centuries, unknowingly growing in spirit and power with each passing generation. There they remained virtually obscured from reality until late in the twelfth century, when a series of events unfolded to change their lives forever.

What the reader will find in this story is purity of faith. This faith was untouched by the external forces that existed well beyond its original delivery unlike any other place on earth. This word had not been obscured by the biases of mankind. It had been memorized word for word and passed down from one generation to the next, preserving not only the mere lines of Scripture but the ultimate spiritual power it possessed in its infancy. Regarding this "Word," the Bible reads in John 1:1-5,

> In the beginning was the Word, and the Word was with God, and the Word was God. He was in the beginning with God. All things were made through Him, and without Him nothing was made that was made. In Him was life, and the life was the light of men. And the light shines in the darkness and the darkness did not comprehend it.

Yet in truth, there were some who did recognize the Word and the light, and this is their story.

—Timothy W. Tron
2012

Note: The character names in this book are fictional and do not represent any real persons responsible for the actions or real events in history that correlate to the subject of this writing. Any correlation is only consequential and not intentional.

Chapter 1

FIRST CONTACT

And it will be when you say, "Why does the Lord our God do all these things to us?" then you shall answer them, "Just as you have forsaken Me and served foreign gods in your land, so you shall serve aliens in a land that is not yours."

—Jeremiah 5:19

The young boy sat on the outcropping of rocks and watched the sheep grazing below. The breeze was strong today, and it washed the rich alpine grass in swathes of motion like waves on an ocean. The air was crisp and cool as it blew Jakob's thick black hair into his face. He pushed it aside with his hand as he leaned back on the cold, hard granite that made his seat. The sun warmed him as he watched the clouds filtering through the pass below and blocking out the lower reaches of the valley he and his family had called home for as long as anyone could remember. A sheep bleated softly, and somewhere over his shoulder in the direction of the sun, a hawk cried his lonesome wail. It echoed off the canyon walls below, making an eerie reply, as if beckoning a foreboding to come.

Jakob closed his eyes and tried to refresh his thoughts with a quote of Scripture his grandfather had tried to make him memorize that morning at their daily devotional over breakfast.

He thought, *And it shall come to pass, when . . .*

"Hmm," he said, thinking out loud, "come on, Jakob, think."

He closed his eyes again. The hawk cried once more, and Jakob thought of the raptor soaring above closer to God. Again he thought, *And it shall come to pass, when ye shall say, Wherefore doth the Lord our God all these things . . . unto . . . us? Then shaaa . . . llt? Thou answer them, like as ye have forsaken me, and served strange gods in your land, so shall . . . ? So shall . . . we . . . no . . . ye . . . ?*

"Yes, that's it! *Ye serve strangers in a land that is not yours.* That's it!" he said, "*So shall ye serve strangers in a land that is not yours.* From the book of Jeremiah chapter five, verse nineteen," he said proudly to himself.

At that instant, the hawk cried again, and several sheep bleated as two figures emerged below out of the cloud bank on horseback, like ghosts from a dream. Jakob's eyes widened at the sudden sight of strangers. He felt hauntingly responsible for calling them into view, as if something he had just said had caused them to appear.

Their distance from him was far enough that Jakob could run and warn the others if he thought they meant harm. He had been taught since he was a small child about the unique gift he and his brethren possessed. The elders continually warned them to be on the lookout for outsiders who might come looking for them to try to destroy them because of their unique gifts.

While Jakob watched the riders, he desperately reached for his sling. It was the only thing that was available for him to use as a weapon. The strap of leather was aptly made for slinging a rock the size of his fist at a target with such velocity that it could stun or kill most prey. To a fully armed knight, it was nothing more than a nuisance. Jakob had used his sling only for the protection of his grandfather's flocks from wolves and even once a mountain lion. He knew how to protect himself against animals, but in this case, he would be no match. He could not defend himself against two grown, armed men. As they drew near, he looked to see if they were carrying any weaponry or for other signs of danger and an avenue of escape.

Jakob edged slowly and quietly out of their sight as he continued to scrutinize them. They did not appear to be moving in a threatening way.

Instead, they were approaching with caution and ambivalence, as if they wanted to be seen and acknowledged. Jakob still kept low, watching for any hint of a change in their mannerisms. As he watched, he leaned over and reached for a rock that was near his feet, just to be safe.

*   *   *

Marik rode a magnificent black stallion his master had given him for the journey. It was a pure-bred Arabian bought in trades his master had made on one of his many journeys to the far-eastern countries of the Persian Empire. As the magnificent steed stepped in a slow cadence, Marik saw the small flock of mountain sheep that were seemingly alone, without a shepherd, but he knew better. Somewhere nearby there would be someone who had already spotted them who was either off to warn the villagers or was close by, ready to strike if he felt endangered. Marik unstrapped the handle of his sword, just to be safe, as he cautiously rode up the increasingly steep grade of the mountain pass.

"Prepare your sword if you haven't already done so," he instructed his riding companion, who quickly answered, "Already done, sir."

*   *   *

As they drew closer, Jakob watched. Suddenly, he felt a shiver run the length of his spine. His mind rushed back to darkness and pain.

He froze.

He'd had this feeling once before in the not-so-distant past. It all came rushing back to him. He had visited this vision before in his nightmares. His grandfather said they were visions from God and were to be welcomed. His mind began to wander. As a fog comes over a lake and blankets its shoreline, so did his thoughts begin to blur and evaporate his focus on the moment at hand.

Jean Paul had reluctantly taken Jakob to the upper pastures at the request of his father. He liked giving his little brother a hard time, but he also enjoyed seeing Jakob learn and copy the things that Jean Paul took for granted. But taking Jakob along would slow Jean Paul down today and give him more trouble than he felt it was worth. At times he felt like a father since he was in charge of training young Jakob to take his place in the fields.

"You've got to start training your little brother to work the herds so you can start working with the stones like the men," Kristoff said to his oldest son as he walked from the barn to the house with the early-morning sun casting long shadows on the ground before them.

"Now take him and go. You need to go and get back before the afternoon since there are storms brewing in the west."

As they moved the herd to the upper pasture that morning, they could see the dark cumulus clouds gathering in the west. The clouds were far away, though, and quickly lost to the thoughts of the young boys who, once they reached their destination, began playing around and throwing rocks down the mountain stream's falls that bordered the pasture.

As the day wore on, they grew tired of games, found a soft patch of grass near the falls, and lay down to rest, as was customary, since by natural habit, the flock would do the same.

Jakob was awakened first by the low rumble of thunder echoing up the valley below. He sat up, looking over at Jean Paul, who had also fallen asleep. Then he heard the lamb crying down the crevice of the fall's ravine, and without thinking, he jumped up, grabbed his staff, and ran toward the sound of the young sheep's bleating above them.

*   *   *

Jean Paul awoke shortly afterward when another, yet louder, thunder clap shook the ground. He sat up and instantly missed Jakob. He jumped up and looked down the valley, but he saw nothing except the flock, which also had been stirred by the storm's grumbling and seemed to become nervous with the fast-approaching storm. They huddled in a mass with their backs to the wind, which had just picked up.

Jean Paul then heard the lamb and realized where Jakob had gone. "Jakob," he yelled as he ran in the direction of the crevice by the falls.

"Jakob!" His voice echoed off the canyon walls, but the response was cut short by another thunder clap, closer than the one that had awakened him.

In the distance he heard a faint, "What?" over the sounds of the rushing torrent.

Jean Paul ran faster, and when he reached the corner of the pasture, he could see above him the crevice that opened up to allow the furious mountain stream to flow into the gorge below. There on the edge of the rim stood Jakob, lamb in his arms, walking toward him.

*   *   *

Jakob saw his brother coming toward him and was about to say something when he felt the hairs begin to stand up on the back of his neck. It tickled him, and he giggled to himself. As he looked down at the lamb, he noticed something strange. The lamb's hair began lifting up toward him. He giggled again, out loud this time, at the funny sight of the fuzzy lamb.

Fuzzy lamb, he thought. *Fuzzy little lamb.*

Then heat, a roaring light . . . and nothingness.

*   *   *

Jean Paul watched in horror as he suddenly saw a blinding flash and then heard the angry sound of air splitting, torn by the force of the mountains. A violent river of electricity rushed past him. He stood stunned and dazed, as if in a dream. His eyes were momentarily blinded. There was no sound—just the feeling of wind and the odd smell of ripped air.

It started to rain.

When Jean Paul could see again, the picture above was nearly white, but the image was faint. He squinted through shadowed eyelids. Jakob and the lamb lay on the ground at the edge of the crevice. They did not move.

Jean Paul ran now with all his might, his ears still ringing as he yelled at the top of his lungs, "No! No! No!" he panted, "Jakob!" his breath was short, "Jakob! Talk to me," nothing but emptiness, "Jakob!" He yelled but he still could not hear himself. The rain came down now in sheets.

As he reached his brother, he saw that he and the lamb lay motionless.

Then a wave of sound slowly erupted, and he could hear himself crying as he stood over his apparently lifeless brother. He knelt down and gently picked up Jakob as water ran in little streamlets off his face and onto Jakob. Lost in time, he felt as if he were running in slow motion down the mountain toward their home, barely aware of the pain the lack of oxygen was creating in his limbs as he carried his only brother.

Tears fused with the rain, blurring his eyesight as he ran. It seemed as if his legs moved in slow motion. Jean Paul prayed and began chanting over and over as he ran, "Our father, who art in heaven, hallowed be thy name, thy kingdom come, thy will be done on earth as in heaven."

* * *

In a whirlwind of motion, Jakob could hear sounds and then nothing. The smell of his mother's fresh-baked bread seemed to permeate his awareness, and then suddenly, he blinked and heard someone say, "Praise the Lord!"

Jakob slowly opened his eyes and tried to focus, but the lamplight was dim. He could barely see, but because of the smell of his mother's bread baking in the hearth, he knew he was back home.

He fully opened his eyes and then saw his entire family, grandparents, neighbors, and Pastor Jeanne all gathered around the table he lay upon.

He began to sit up, and a pain like fire shot from his waist to the top of his head.

Jeanne grabbed his shoulder and said, "Rest, my son. You have been spared by the grace of God."

This was followed by the others reaffirming his statement with, "Thanks be to God."

Jakob lay back down and exhaled slowly while trying to feel his fingers and toes, which all seemed to be in working order. Then he tried to recall what had happened, but the only thing he could see was the flash and then nothingness.

His head throbbed with pain. With his eyes closed, he listened to the comforting voices around him as he slowly drifted off to numbness and sleep. The last thing he heard was his father saying, "God has reached down to touch my son without taking him home, and for this I am grateful."

Then he slept.

*   *   *

The shadow of the rider passed over Jakob, causing him to snap out of the trance. It startled him and caused him to jump, which caused the horse to rear. The rider had to wrestle with the horse as Jakob dashed up the rock face of the canyon wall behind where he sat.

The rider called to him, "Stop! Wait! We mean you no harm." He repeated the words in several of the dialects they had studied in preparation for their journey, knowing the people they sought could quite possibly speak a language unknown to any of them.

Jakob paused, standing on a small ledge some twenty feet up the wall, looking down upon the riders. He thought it was odd that the man kept repeating the same words over and over. He looked down from his vantage point. He was curious now.

"Why do you keep shouting, 'Stop! Stop!' over and over again?" he asked in the last tongue used by the intruder.

Marik, now confused, looked at Steffan, who returned his questioning glare with a look of shock. The boy had just returned their question with one of the oldest languages they had studied, not to mention that he had apparently understood the others as well. Marik thought it was ludicrous, so he replied in their common Frank language just to see.

"We . . . are . . . looking . . . for . . . a . . . special . . . people," he said slowly and carefully to see if the boy understood the modern Frank language he now spoke.

"Why do you come to our valley?" Jakob asked the strangers in the same tongue Marik now spoke.

Marik gasped, as did Steffan. It was not possible. A very young boy in the middle of nowhere was speaking the ancient tongue of Jesus' time and the language of their own time. It had to be the altitude, the countless days of riding the tiny trails along ragged cliffs, the lack of sleep—it was all catching up to him. Surely it was only his imagination.

Trying to brush it off, Marik continued in his native tongue to see if the boy truly understood, "We come in search of the Apostle Speakers. My name is Marik of Lyon. We come in peace on behalf of my master, a wealthy merchant in Lyon."

Without hesitation, Jakob replied, "I have never heard of the Apostle Speakers. What do you speak of?"

Marik was astounded, but something inside him wanted to test the boy further, so he replied in the language of the Catholic priests, "People who have the ability to quote the books of the apostles from memory," Marik replied.

"You mean like, 'For God so loved the world that he gave his one and only Son, that whoever believes in him shall not perish but have eternal life'?" Jakob quickly rattled off in perfect Latin. "Anyone can say such things. Why do you search for such a thing?"

"My God in heaven!" Steffan gasped, drawing an agreeable look from Marik in return.

Marik pressed on now, feeling driven to hear more. "Yes, but the entire book of John, not just single verses," he continued in Latin.

"Oh, like the elders, you mean?" Jakob replied. Now he felt his skin turning red as he quickly realized the error he had made. The blood rushed to his head. He feared the worst from this childish blunder, revealing so much.

"Yes, exactly," Marik said loudly now, going back to his native tongue and with such excitement he nearly lost his mount. It was almost too much for him. This child's linguistic skills along with his biblical knowledge was all too much.

Sensing the boy's sudden cause for alarm, he quickly softened his tone and continued, "Excuse me for being so overjoyed my son," he said, now almost in a whispering tone. "But you see, this is . . . you are . . ." *No, he is heaven sent,* he thought to himself. "Something truly remarkable," he continued, nearly breathless now, "something heaven sent. You have a talent that God has bestowed. Do not feel afraid. You have not betrayed your people. Forgive me for my moment of elation, for we are not the enemy who searches you out." Marik's eyes began to water as he spoke. "We are here to help spread this Word—the Word God has sent down for us all to hear."

Both Steffan and Marik were stunned from the sudden realization of what they had finally found, yet it was so much more than they had imagined. God was at work here more than they could have ever known. As Jakob watched, true, raw emotions begin to pour from both Steffan's and Marik's eyes. The boy somehow felt calmed. Marik's words began to ring true, and the pounding in his chest eased to a pulse of contentment as the words began to sink in. He still didn't understand why Marik had repeated the commands, for to him, it all sounded the same.

The two sojourners had finally found them after months of searching. They had traveled from one valley to the next, searching, asking about, and hunting these people until they finally reached this remote Cottian alpine region. It was early in the first century following the new millennium. Mankind had yet to experience the worst of times that would come to be known as the Dark Ages, when death and despair would become a way of life. The Crusades were in full swing, with Christians battling Muslims. Control of the church was becoming centralized and protected because of fear of outsiders and nonbelievers. The written Word of God was copied by hand, one page at a time, and it was usually guarded by Roman Catholic priests. The Word was protected and kept close to Rome. Spoken or written Scriptures outside the realm of the Holy Roman Empire were considered blasphemy.

Yet the legend of the Apostle Speakers had reached far and wide from the people who kept the Word of God alive in the villages where no papacy could reach. The desire for the Holy Spirit was passed down verbally from generation to generation. The fact that no written Word was available to the masses yet complete books had been kept alive was not only miraculous but divine, much to the chagrin of Rome.

Jakob had climbed from his perch down to a boulder overlooking the riders, still keeping a safe distance between them. He sat as they spoke further, now consistently using Marik and Steffan's native tongue until Jakob felt somewhat more at ease—enough so to feel safe enough to lead them to his village in the valley of Rora.

Nothing would be the same again.

Chapter 2

THE REQUEST

We get our bread at the risk of our lives, because of the sword in the wilderness.

—Lamentations 5:9

Arktos sat under the low apple tree sharpening a blade on the spinning, wet stone wheel he peddled with one foot. Sparks flew from the blade as it ground against the stone. He watched the sparks fly, and his mind drifted to the image of the heavens at night with the multitude of stars that shone above. He thought of Kristoff and how he would be among those stars.

He tried not to think of his son too much. The pain was still fresh.

Kristoff had died only a couple years earlier in an expedition of men who were trying to clear the La Croix pass that connected Queyras with Pellice. Kristoff had been the leader of the team that was to scout the area and make preparations for a larger work detail that would complete the project later that year. A freak storm had hit on the day the party reached the summit, causing an unseasonal blizzard that threatened the entire crew. The story told was that Arktos's son had saved the team by lowering them down on ropes to the cliff face below so they could reach an escape route.

Since there was nothing to tie the rope to, Kristoff lowered each man to safety below. As each man descended, the freezing rain pelted the mountain warrior. Undeterred by the elements, he continued on, ignoring the numbness in his limbs from the cold. Finally, when the last man was safe, he searched for an escape route for himself. He had climbed these treacherous peaks many times and knew their hazards all too well.

After finding a foothold in an ancient crevice, he began to work his way toward his brothers below. The ice had accumulated to a point where there was no place left unfrozen. The man inside the body stretched every fiber of his being to connect each hand-hold, each foot-hold, knowing his life depended upon each placement. He focused all of himself into one moment. Years of living at this altitude, years of climbing had created a body that was so hard, strong, and pliable that seemingly nothing could break its will—yet fate was unchecked for the humanness of the soul.

It happened before he knew it: the slip.

His body gave way. Nothingness . . . grasping . . . air.

Those below only saw his face as he passed the slim precipice where they clutched for dear life as his body fell past. None would ever forget the look. A gentle peace was all they saw on the face of a man who could only have been Kristoff. They all wanted to reach out to catch him, but none could. He died alone.

His body was broken and frozen far below, never to be found, but with one unselfish, heroic deed, he had saved the lives of his Vaudois brothers.

He died a hero.

The old man would have rather had a live son than a dead hero. Arktos's heart ached for the day when they would meet again. Darkness enveloped his life. If it weren't for his faith and his youngest grandson clinging to him for comfort after the loss of his own father, he surely would have died from a broken heart.

He thought, *For to me to live is Christ, and to die is gain.*

His thoughts wandered until he heard the horse. Looking up from his work, he saw the approaching riders, with Jakob leading them on foot, driving the flock of sheep before him. His foot stopped peddling, and the sparks ceased. Wiping the sweat from his brow, he sat up, placing the knife under his leg just to be safe.

"Grandfather, we have visitors," Jakob said, speaking in the same rhythm he had just used with the visitors.

"Yes, my son, so it seems."

Arktos immediately noticed the pattern and changed his speech to match. The elders all understood the gift but kept it to themselves, knowing that someday they would have to divulge the talent that up till now was unused and unknown. He knew Jakob had no idea and made the translation as naturally as breathing, which he continued to do as he drew near his grandfather.

"They come from Lyon, Grandfather, and they seek the Apostle Speakers," Jakob said in a shaky voice, fearful of how his grandfather might react.

Arktos shifted on his seat, moving the knife back into the belt behind his back. "Go and put the flock away."

While looking back over his shoulder at the visitors and his grandfather, Jakob moved the sheep into a holding pen behind their home.

Arktos sat watching silently as the riders approached. It was obvious his young grandson had given these men a reason to believe there were Apostle Speakers to be found here. Not knowing their true intentions could mean life or death.

His mind raced. "What do the good people of Lyon want with the Word of God?" he asked.

The pair heard him and immediately understood that the elder was speaking their native tongue.

The two were a few yards from where Arktos sat under the tree. They dismounted together, slowly and with considerable caution. Arktos scanned the pair, noticing the broad swords in their saddles, but he saw no other weapons. Their demeanor was not threatening, which left him with a sense of ease, but he was still concerned.

Jakob returned from putting up the sheep and moved to stand behind his grandfather as they spoke.

"My lord, we were sent by a wealthy merchant in Lyon," Marik began, "in hopes of finding the people who kept the Word of God in their hearts and not in their purses."

Jakob looked down at his grandfather and saw the knife stuck in his belt behind his back. He noticed that Arktos's hand was on the polished bone handle.

"We have searched for many months in many valleys, hoping that someday we might find the people who have become legendary because of their heavenly talents. We come seeking your wisdom and want to hire you to help spread the Word of God, using the talents that God has blessed you and your people with."

"Do not the good people of Lyon have the Roman Catholic Church to help them keep the Word of God?" Arktos asked with a hint of sarcasm in his voice.

"Good sir, you must know as well as I that the church does not want every man to have or to own the Word of God other than what the church *says is* the Word of God. We come asking for your help in going beyond the church and help give to man what God has given to you. Jesus died on the cross so that every man could inherit his kingdom. God gave us his only Son so that every man could be free from sin. Because of this giving, do you not feel a certain obligation to share this talent with mankind? God has given you this ability for a purpose, has he not?" Marik asked, knowing full well that if these people admitted to anyone from the Catholic Church what their knowledge or talents were, they would be considered heretics.

Arktos sat silently. His thoughts were of the true purpose he and the elders had spoken about—the reason they had been given this ability so many ages ago. Was this finally the sign they had been awaiting? Who was he to question God? The thought rattled around in his head.

Arktos felt the smooth, round grip of the blade behind him. He knew in one fell swoop, he could easily take the first rider, but the second might escape. There were centuries of human existence, centuries of keeping the Word alive, one verse at a time; all of this was at stake. His heart beat in his ears, pounding out the sounds of the rushing breeze across his stark white beard.

Arktos grunted and turned toward the house, calling to his daughter, "Julia, make us a place at the table. We have visitors."

Turning to the men, Arktos said, "We should go inside and break bread together and talk further. I have much weighing on my mind and must know the truth of your intentions before I can agree to anything outside of this valley."

"Thank you, sir, we are much obliged," Marik responded, bowing slightly as Arktos rose and motioned to them to join him inside as he drifted safely behind. Arktos knew this would buy him some time, and at best, someone would notice the steeds and bring help.

The home was an all-stone structure, with roofing made of massive slate sheets that overlapped. The walls were perfectly crafted stones cut to fit snugly together, making them airtight. The masonry work was astounding. At this altitude, wood was a scarce commodity, so the stones from the surrounding mountainsides were the only abundant building material, and these people had learned to carve them to perfection. The house was above the stables on the second floor. The stables, where the animals were wintered, was on the first floor. They were partially built into the mountainside, as was the top floor. The heat from the animals helped to keep the inhabitants above warm in the winter, which, at this altitude, was brutal and life threatening if not taken seriously.

As they approached the house, the warm smell of fresh bread encompassed them, and Marik realized how hungry he was. It had been days since they had eaten a real meal. They had been living off salted pork rations, which were nearly depleted at this point. Arktos showed them to the door and followed them as they entered, with Jakob close behind him.

Jean Paul was just returning from stone mason's school farther down the valley. He had just rounded the curve in the trail where he could see their house when he saw the party entering. He could see the horses tethered outside and saw that they were not militia, but they were still strangers with swords tied to their saddles. Instead of continuing toward the house, he retraced his steps and went to gather others in case there was trouble. He did not know the cause for the unannounced guests, but he certainly didn't want to risk the safety of his family.

Jakob's mother, Julia, his grandmother, Maria, and his two sisters were inside the house when they entered. The girls and their mother were seated around a large table and had been working on a large quilt that they had been sewing. Their grandmother had been kneading bread at another low counter in the kitchen. When the men entered, the women excused themselves into the next room. Julia came back to help her mother carry the drinks and fresh, hot bread to the table where they sat.

Arktos motioned for everyone to sit, which they did. As they sat, Julia brought the drinks to the table, setting them down in front of the men. Jakob sat next to his grandfather on the bench at the head of the table. As his mother set Marik's drink in front of him, she glanced quickly at their unexpected guest.

Her large, light blue eyes, the color of the summer sky, and beautiful, smooth, pure white skin caught Marik's gaze momentarily. He instantly thought he felt warmth in her gaze. She was caught off guard by his weathered yet handsome exterior. She was still mourning the loss of her Kristoff, but she was only human. It had been a long time since she had been with a man.

She instantly realized what she had done and quickly moved away, apologizing as she withdrew. Marik was also a bit ashamed and looked down. He did not want to cause any further issues, not knowing the marital status of the lady he had been immediately attracted to.

Sensing the awkward moment Arktos said abruptly, "Let us pray."

Arktos began a prayer, and Marik would have sworn Arktos was reading from a book. He recited from memory various passages of Scripture and gave thanks for the many blessings God had shown to his family. He also gave thanks for the good intentions of their sudden visitors, of which he was still wholly unsure. The prayer seemed to last for a while, but so much was said that its length was not unwelcome.

Finally, Arktos closed with, "In his holy name we pray, Amen," at which point they all repeated, "Amen."

Then Marik thanked his host for such a marvelous blessing. He began to introduce himself and his traveling companion as they passed the warm bread around, each person breaking off a piece and passing it onto the next person.

"Sir, I am Marik of Lyon, and this is Steffan. We come to you on behalf of the house of the wealthy merchant, Peter Waldo of Lyon."

The old man's heart froze. "Peter Waldo, you say?"

"Yes, my lord," Marik said with a bit of hesitation. He was well aware of the sudden change in his host's disposition.

"Do you know, my young guest, ·of the legend of St. Peter of the Vaudois?" Arktos began with an anger that began to well up inside him that threatened to spill over into pure rage. "Do you?" he asked in a louder voice with clenched teeth.

Marik and Steffan sat stone-faced, afraid to speak as the light softly flickered in the lamp overhead.

"I thought not!"

The gall of some men, raged the thought in his mind.

"This, this Peter Waldo of Lyon, does he know the true origin of the most honorable name he uses? I wonder! I truly wonder!" Arktos said. He paused as he angrily bit off another piece of bread and chewed furiously.

"He was one of the first to leave our valley on a mission to evangelize our Word to the world. Like the apostle he was named after, he risked his life to share the Word and the belief in the Christianity held true by all our ancestors gone before. He was eventually taken prisoner and burned at the stake for trying to speak out against the teachings of the Catholic Church. He was labeled a heretic and accused of trying to start a cult. Because of what happened to him, there has never been another to do the same." He paused to gather himself. "And now, this coward of Lyon hides behind the name of a saint. What is his real name?" the old man demanded as he watched the visitors with angry eyes, rising to his feet.

"Augustus Pizan," Steffan quickly retorted with no hesitation.

Arktos glanced at him, a bit surprised. Since they had arrived, Steffan had spoken not a word, and now he answered immediately. "Ah, I see our shy friend speaks. Nice. How nice."

"Sir, please allow me to explain as humbly as I may," Marik quickly responded.

"What!" Arktos angrily interrupted. "You want to explain to me how this coward hides behind a real man's name—a man who left the safety of the valleys and put his life on the line to spread the faith to save as many souls as he could before his own life was taken in spite of his grace!"

"Please, please sir, allow me."

"Yes, do go on. This should be entertaining."

"You have to understand—today things are different. The papacy is stronger and more dangerous than in the time of St. Peter of Vaudois. It is even stronger than when Claudius, bishop of Turin, was burned at the stake for his passionate protests against the medieval church here in the Vaudois. The mere mention of Augustus's plan to the Catholic clergy would lead to his public execution by the archbishop of Lyon. Thus, he uses the name of Peter Waldo, which, as you wisely deduced, came from the Vaudois name."

Arktos's attention was now piqued as he began to ease back in his seat. Jakob could see his grandfather's temples throbbing as he sat quietly watching and listening, prepared to race for the door at a moment's notice if need be.

"We are on a mission to find the Apostle Speakers, and once we find them, we have been instructed to ask for their help and pay them whatever funds necessary to get them to return to Lyon with us to begin the transcription of the Bible into a written format for its distribution to the common man. It will be written in the common language so all will be able to read its precious message. Our master has obtained materials from the Far East upon which thousands of Bibles can be written affordably—a material known as paper. We have teams of scholarly scribes assembled to assist in the transcription once we return. With the Word of God, this paper, and our scribes, we will spread the Word of God as it was intended."

At that point, Arktos raised an eyebrow as he nodded for Marik to continue.

"We have reason to believe that you, my lord, and your family are members of the secret society known as the Vaudois Apostle Speakers," Marik said.

"What makes you believe this?" Arktos asked, squinting as he chewed.

19

"God has led me to believe this," he said.

"Oh, how so?" Arktos said with a questioning look on his face.

"I don't know," Marik remarked. "It's only that I somehow sense this to be true, and I pray that I am correct, for Steffan and I have been too many places in these remote valleys, and now, having met you and your grandson, in just this short period of time, I can honestly say I feel the presence of the Lord."

"Are you clergy?" Arktos responded.

"No sir."

"Then what authority do you have to hear, speak, or discern the Word of God?" Arktos said sternly, banging a fist on the table and causing Steffan to jump. It disgusted him even to consider the mere implication that Marik might somehow have put himself closer to God than his own people had always been led to believe they were.

"By the fact, sir, that we are here because we feel he has led us here," Marik said softly. "We don't have to have the Catholic Church tell us what God is saying, but we don't pretend to hear God either. Sir, we firmly believe that God leads every man and not just those the church says are allowed to lead."

Arktos nodded in agreement but remained silent. His demeanor had slowly begun to soften as he listened. There was a moment of more silence.

"Go on," Arktos finally said.

"Sir, we have put our lives on the line to find you. Please say you will find a way to help us," Marik said passionately but softly. "If you are not the Apostle Speakers, then please help us find them if you know where they exist."

Arktos was mute again, neither agreeing nor disagreeing.

They all sat around the table in silence except for the soft shuffle of Julia's feet on the floor as she quietly moved around the table refilling their drinks.

Arktos picked up his wooden mug and took a long, slow drink while he peered at the others over the top of it. Then he slowly set it down, raised his head, and looked into the rafters of the home as if he were being spoken to from above.

Suddenly there was a knock at the door.

Jakob looked at his grandfather. "Go ahead, Jakob, answer the door," his grandfather said with his eyes closed and head still leaned back.

Steffan glanced toward Marik, who had bowed his head with eyes closed, as if praying. Jakob ran to the door and opened it to find Jean Paul standing there with his sword in hand.

"Tell them to come outside now," Jean Paul said sternly in the language of the Vaudois.

Jakob rushed back to his grandfather's side, whispering in his ear. Arktos rose and motioned to Marik and Steffan to step outside as they stole glances toward each other. As they stiffly walked out of the dimly lit house into the bright sunshine, it took a minute or two for their eyes to adjust, but when they did, they were shocked at the scene about them.

Jean Paul stood only a few feet in front of them with sword in hand, but behind him and surrounding them from all angles were men with bow and arrows drawn and aimed at the two strangers.

"State your purpose and where you are from, or we will not hesitate to let the arrows fly," Jean Paul said with an air of authority Jakob had never heard from his brother before.

Marik stood squinting at the armed mountain warriors who surrounded him. He had no idea what was being said. This dialect was nothing he or Steffan had encountered in their studies. He could pick out pieces of languages he knew here and there, but the tone was obviously hostile. For now, that was all he needed to focus on. Had he reason to feel threatened? He knew there would be no chance of escape, but for some reason, he was not afraid, and neither did he intend to fight.

Marik decided now was the time to be as true to himself as possible, so he spoke in his native tongue. "I come in peace and in the name of our heavenly Father, God almighty," he said, as he turned, looking at them through their armed sights.

Steffan was not as fearless as his traveling companion. He did not know the temperament of these people and just knew this would be his last day on earth as he stood there, knees shaking. A cloud passed overhead, and a breeze blew softly.

Steffan, now fearing for his life, began chanting an old gothic hymn his mother had passed down to him as a child. His head bowed, he chanted, eyes closed, knees shaking, and praying his end be quick. He began, "Give ear to my words, oh Lord, consider my sighing. Listen to my cry for help, my King and my God, for to you I pray."

As he sang, the song seemed to grow in him, reaching the warriors, who slowly began to lower their bows.

Julia had come to the door of the house after the party had left the table and peered out cautiously from inside. When the young man, apparently scared out of his wits, began the ancient chant, she recognized it from their own Scriptures they had memorized and passed down. She couldn't help but feel moved. A tear came to her eye as she watched, and suddenly she felt compelled to move closer. She came outside from the house and began to sing along with Steffan, "In the morning, oh Lord, you hear my voice; in the morning I lay my requests before you and wait in expectation."

As they now sang in harmony together, she moved closer to him so she stood just behind him when she finally stopped. They continued singing, "You are not a God who takes pleasure in evil; with you the wicked cannot dwell."

Then others began to chant along, softly at first but then slowly growing in crescendo in the same dialect and voice as Steffan, joining in the Psalm, "The arrogant cannot stand in your presence; you hate all who do wrong. You destroy those who tell lies; bloodthirsty and deceitful men the Lord abhors.

"But I, by your great mercy, will come into your house; in reverence will I bow down toward your holy temple. Lead me, oh Lord, in your righteousness because of my enemies—make straight your way before me. Not a word from their mouth can be trusted; their heart is filled with destruction. Their throat is an open grave; with their tongue they speak deceit.

"Declare them guilty, oh God! Let their intrigues be their downfall. Banish them for their many sins, for they have rebelled against you. But let all who take refuge in you be glad; let them ever sing for joy. Spread your protection over them that those who love your name may rejoice in you. For surely, oh Lord, you bless the righteous; you surround them with your favor as with a shield."

As the song ended, silence prevailed. The echo of a hawk's cry beckoned in the distance. Marik could not believe what he had just heard or seen. The entire war party had just chanted an ancient hymn together without a hymnal or song book, word for word, in the language of the Franks. He had never witnessed such a thing or felt such an awe-inspiring feeling lurch through his soul.

"Praise God," Marik whispered.

"Yes indeed, Mr. Marik, praise God indeed," answered Arktos.

Jakob leaned against his grandfather as the old man placed a hand on the boy's shoulder. He felt moved inside by the song, yet he couldn't understand what it was. His grandfather's hand felt warm on his shoulder, but another hand was there as well—one that had touched him once before and that was about to use him in ways he would never understand or believe possible.

Arktos called to Jean Paul, "Send word to the elders. We need to have an emergency council on the next Sabbath."

Marik felt a weight lift from his shoulders. Steffan passed out and fell to the ground in an exhausted heap at Julia's feet. Jakob looked up at this grandfather, who smiled back at him.

Soon their journey would begin.

Chapter 3

NOT THE FIRST TIME

After these things the Lord appointed seventy others also, and sent them two by two before His face into every city and place where He Himself was about to go.

—Luke 10:1

Later that evening, the men sat in wool-covered chairs around the hearth in the corner of the room with the rough-hewn dining table they had sat at earlier. Marik and Steffan watched the firelight flicker in the darkness. The smell of wood smoke and sound of the crackling fire caused their eyes to grow heavy. The two weary travelers sat and warmed themselves by the roaring fire of the massive stone fireplace. This was the first time in many months they could finally feel at peace.

Earlier in the evening, Arktos had Maria and Julia prepare a bountiful meal for the two men. They ate their fill and then some. It nearly brought them to tears to have a home-cooked meal presented to them in this fashion, like an honorary banquet for some heroic deed performed. They did not feel worthy, but the sheer hospitality of their hosts helped to melt their uneasiness away, and they spoke freely, openly sharing their recent adventures that had brought them to this remote valley.

More than once they had faced the pointed end of an arrow. Once they had been chased out of a valley with spears being tossed after them. Steffan lost his first horse in that escape, nearly losing his life with his steed's. Another time they spent several days trapped by a snowstorm in a mountain cave, surviving on boiled leather strips they cut off their riding gear. However, every time they faced what seemed to be certain death, they were delivered by what felt like the guidance of the hand of God.

The farther they traveled, the greater their despair became of never finding the Vaudois Apostle Speakers. Now here they sat, finally having reached their intended destination. The orange glow of the fire created warmth in the room that felt like the comfort of a familiar blanket on one's bed. Sleep beckoned them.

Suddenly, as if summoned to speak, Arktos began, "Do you know you are not the first to come?"

"Sir?" said Steffan since Marik had dozed off in his chair.

"You are not the first outsiders to come to our valley," he repeated.

"Marik, wake up!" Steffan nudged him with his foot.

"A long, long time ago, back when the mountains were young, they came."

Marik stirred with his eyes barely open, listening as if in a dream to the story Arktos was beginning to tell.

"Back many, many generations ago, the elders tell stories of the first Apostle Speakers who came—the original Apostle Speakers."

"You mean the apostles?" Marik uttered in disbelief.

"So the story goes," the old man continued. "They came as you two, as a pair, but on foot and dressed in robes. We were leery of them at first. Word was sent to our warriors to come at once. But then they did something that changed our hearts and minds. At that point that it became evident they had been sent by the Lord our God."

Marik straightened in his chair, now fully awake. "Caught in a small valley with nothing but the mountain at their backs and many of our mountain warriors surrounding them, much like you experienced today, they began to speak the Word of God. Mind you, we could not understand one word since they spoke in a different tongue, a tongue from the east. But as tensions grew, something miraculously occurred. In a flash, a lightning bolt from the blue hit nearby, and suddenly it was as if our ears had been exchanged for new ones. Everyone began to hear them speaking in our own tongue. The warriors dropped their weapons and knelt to the ground, praising God for delivering the two apostles."

His voice grew more solemn. "When they saw our reaction, they began to pray a prayer—but this was not just any prayer. They thanked God for delivering them to this remarkable place and thanked him for showing them the premonition. You see, apparently they were waiting for a sign—something out of the ordinary to tell them where and who they could entrust with the precious words they carried, as if it was a treasure to be hidden and protected for the centuries. When they realized they had found the people they had been searching, they told our people of their mission.

"They called themselves Olympas and Herodian. The two apostles had traveled vast distances, yet they did not seem weary. They were as strong and vibrant, as if having just started out on their mission. We learned that Jesus had sent them out in pairs to teach and heal, just as Jesus and the original twelve disciples had done. Realizing this could not be done alone, Jesus appointed seventy more men to become apostles who would have the same powers and abilities to teach as the original twelve. They were sent out in all directions, which eventually led the two to this valley. Olympas and Herodian were followers of Peter, the disciple Jesus taught first hand, so they intimately knew the magnificent power and glory of God from having studied under Peter.

"So our ancestors soon began trying to learn God's holy Word. They spoke of the Son of God who they had learned the Scriptures from. Their teachings were straight from the Master himself. At first our people felt overwhelmed by all the knowledge that had to be learned, but as the two apostles spoke, somehow God enabled our people to keep the word in their minds. He expanded their abilities to learn beyond normal capacity, and from the very beginning until today, the Word has been passed from person to person, mouth to mouth, word for word."

Arktos thought to himself. There was something else he didn't want to share with the visitors just yet. He thought about the power of the Word itself. It was something he had experienced only a handful of times, yet it was something his elders had talked about. Some of their people might possess this power. Nobody could know in advance who they would be, but the ones who learned to use it would be able to do extraordinary things.

Marik waited to speak during the pause, wondering what was going on inside the old man's head. Finally, he could wait no more, "You have the Word of God passed down straight from the apostles, then, don't you? In your head, you keep this Word?"

Arktos nodded. Steffan and Marik looked at each other and then back at the fire. They had definitely found the treasure they had been seeking. The firelight danced on the walls, and they watched as the images danced in the flames. Their minds raced with questions and thoughts about all the things they were about to learn.

Arktos finished his history lesson with a sorrowful ending. "Olympas and Herodian left our valley and traveled to Rome, where they were reunited with Peter. They began to preach to the growing Christian community in Rome when they were seized by the Roman soldiers. Nero was so angered that he vowed to make a public spectacle of the three apostles. He had them publicly executed. Olympas and Herodian were beheaded while Peter was hung upside down on the cross. It was about the year 66.

"We never will be able to thank them enough for the glorious gift they bestowed upon and entrusted to our people before they were so horribly taken out of this world. We remember them each year on November 10, the day they were martyred for being Christians as the Roman faithful cheered on. That is why, when our Peter left the Vaudois, he became a saint to us, since he was trying to carry on what the original apostles had done."

The old man hung his head down to his chest and closed his eyes, seeing in his mind the awful scene he had just described. He softly said, "May God have pity on their souls." Then he was silent.

He sat in this way for some time, lost in the past and thoughts of his ancestors. Arktos slowly drifted off to sleep.

Only the occasional crackle of the fire and Arktos's gentle snoring could be heard as Marik's and Steffan's minds reeled from the revelation Arktos had presented to them. They watched the flames of the fire dance on the ancient stones.

Somewhere outside, the faint hoot of an owl called in the night. As the embers glow began to fade, so did the two weary travelers. They soon retired to their pallets on the floor. They found it hard to fall asleep at first, but soon their bodies' weariness pulled them into sleep, where they could not escape, like the journey they were already entwined within.

Like this one, there would be no escape either.

Chapter 4

TIME TO SHARE

I will bring the blind by a way they did not know; I will lead them in paths they have not known. I will make darkness light before them, and crooked places straight. These things I will do for them, and not forsake them.

—Isaiah 42:16

Early the next Sabbath, the elder council met to discuss the matter of the two men from Lyon and the possible ramifications they faced by exposing themselves as the so-called Apostle Speakers. The sheer acknowledgment of such a statement could at the very least bring the pope's militia down upon them.

Up until now, they had been able to remain unseen, hidden away in their mountain valley, memorizing, preserving, and worshipping. They were the epitome of apostolic virtues. Yet, with this potential change, they would face challenges and hardships like never before. They would find a world that was not accepting but polarizing in its beliefs such that their world would be become threatened to its very extinction.

Lifting the veil off of their hidden treasure would then open the Pandora's Box of scrutiny and retaliation they had for so many centuries been able to avoid. However, spreading the Word in a form that would reach a multitude of souls versus the singular audience would be reaching out as God had intended. However, the consequences of such a decision could be martyrdom at best. When the emergency meeting was called, it was not taken lightly, for this one decision could mean the beginning of the end of their homeland as they knew it.

They met in the secret location that only the elders knew existed. Each seat of the enclave was filled by each of the heads of families in the Rora Vaudois (valley). Each member was required to select a successor to his seat, which would be filled upon his death. Then and only then was the new member notified and escorted to the secret location.

It was an early-summer morning. The sun had yet to rise, and the dew was still thick on the high mountain pastures. The mood around the torch-lit stone table was somber but curious. They had been gathered in an emergency meeting by brother LeTron. Everyone was keenly aware of foreign intruders who had recently arrived in the Rora Vaudois, but the actual intent of their visit was still a mystery. This led to untold numerous possible theories and speculations that had already spread through the breadth and width of the valley. No matter how sinister the rumor were that had been spread, no one could deny that they also had heard of the chanting incident and the profound effect it had on all those at the scene.

Knowing that time was of the essence before the general populace would work themselves into an unwarranted frenzy, the council had to act swiftly yet wisely as to any actions regarding the two parties in question.

Elder Albert Jourdan stood and called the meeting to order. "Let us bring our hearts and minds together as one. Let us pray."

The stocky elder Jourdan, dressed in his provincial mountain clothes, was easily distinguishable from the next elder by the unassuming purple scarf he wore around his neck. His other distinguishing feature was that most men of his age normally had a thick beard and a receding hairline of snow white hair. Albert was one of remarkably few who chose to keep a clean-shaven face.

"Heavenly Father, we ask for your guidance and leadership in the decisions we humble servants here below are about to make. We ask that you give us the patience of Job and the wisdom of Noah. We know our decisions can and will have far-reaching conclusions that only you can know that are part of your master plan. Lord, speak to us as your will would have it, for we praise and give you the glory. In Jesus' heavenly name we pray, amen."

The remaining elders answered, "Amen." Albert motioned for them to be seated.

The chamber they occupied was an ancient cavern formed many millennia before when the earth was young. Human inhabitants over those many eons rarely left more than a brief mark on its walls—until the most-recent inhabitants. The entrance was small and easily guarded, with boulders blocking the view of the mouth so that one could easily enter unseen. The first cavity was long and narrow, and it opened up into a small, atrium-like chamber with various wings branching off from it leading to small grottos, one of which the members now occupied. Farther past the atrium, the cave opened up into a large, cathedral-like room that rose several hundred feet above to the stalactite-laden roof. Up at the farthest reaches of this roofline, there was an opening to the mountaintop above. Light filtered in through the crevice that had been formed over centuries of erosion. The sunlight lit the chamber with a reverent glow that shone on the stone altar below. Carved into the stone were the simple words, *"Lux lucet in tenebris,"* the mantra of the Apostle Speakers. They were taken from the gospel of John and meant, "Let the light shine in the darkness." Here in the cavernous chamber with the outside light filtering in lighting the altar with these words, the power of the Holy Spirit encompassed all who set their eyes upon it.

The meeting continued. One by one the elders spoke of their concerns and the relevance of their actions would have for their people. They had managed to keep and preserve a few handwritten parchment Bibles that had been transcribed from the Word they received so long ago, using them to recall Scriptures as they continued to teach their family members. These few Bibles came at a great cost. It could take up to three hundred sheep to make enough skins to produce one Bible. Then there were the countless hours that were necessary to transcribe from memory the spoken Word onto the precious pages. But now, with the pressing issue at hand, their small yet precious cache would be threatened as well, as their physical beings. Somehow, they must move forward. All the elders agreed that doing nothing would not be following the path God had chosen for them.

As the order of speakers moved around the table, it was eventually Arktos LeTron's turn. All fell silent as he sat with his head bowed.

Brother Albert spoke softly, breaking the momentary silence. "Brother, we look to hear your words."

Arktos kept his head bowed, unresponsive. His hands were resting on the massive stone tablet of a table. Unnoticed at first, a twitch began to appear in his hand and slowly gained momentum until it was noticeable by all. With his head still bowed, both of his arms and legs began to tremor as his head began to sway gently back and forth. Then, with a sudden jerk, his head flew backward, his face toward the heavens. His eyes rolled back in his head, and only the whites were now visible. The other elders sat in shock as a voice began to emanate from his wide-open mouth.

"Fear not," the voice boomed off the granite walls, echoing farther into the recesses of the cavern, "for the Lord your God will prevail so that your enemy's bones will become ashes in the soil."

The other members sat with wide eyes, their mouths froze open in the moment.

"There will come one who shall lead you from this valley and protect you through me. Many will know of their talents, but there will only be one who will have the ability to control the talent and use it for my will."

Arktos jerked at each audible announcement. It seemed as if his body was a vessel being used to pour out God's words. Sweat dripped from his brow onto the table, making little pools.

The voice continued, "You are the chosen. You must carry on. Follow the one, and make my will your own!" The thunder of the words shook the room, and suddenly a dove flew in from the mouth of the cave entrance, landing on the table near Arktos, who, at that instant, fell face forward onto the table, collapsing in an exhausted heap.

The elders paused as they watched the enchanted dove. It slowly flew up now, as if in a dream, up and out of the cavern through the crevice that lit the ancient altar. They rushed to surround Arktos, laying their hands on him and comforting their dear friend, fearing the worst. As he lay there silently, unmoving, Albert knelt and began to pray aloud as the others fell in with him, all kneeling around the table.

The torch light flickered off the walls as their voices softly resonated into the voids of darkness. When they finished, they remained on their knees.

Arktos slowly raised his head and then opened his eyes, trying to regain his focus as he looked toward Elder Jourdan. There he sat, his head on his hands, murmuring something.

"Brother, are you all right?" Albert quickly spat out as the others quickly stood and gathered around.

"My head, what happened?" Arktos asked.

"You've had a vision, my brother. The Lord speaketh through you."

"Water," he said, his voice cracking. "My throat is parched."

One of the other elders quickly left the chamber to retrieve some water from a spring that ran just a short distance from the mouth of the cave.

"Don't you recall anything you just said?" Elder Jourdan asked.

"Ohhh, no!" Arktos moaned, running his fingers through his snow-white hair as he sighed in stunned anguish. "All I could see in my mind was a blinding light." He continued on, obviously frightened and bewildered by what had just transpired. "Ohhhh my head." His elbows smeared the little pools of perspiration that had drained from his brow moments earlier.

The brother returned with the water in a gourd and handed it to Arktos, who drank greedily. The brother had a concerned look on his face, though, as he caught Albert's eye. Albert noticed the change in the brother's countenance when he returned.

"What causes you concern, brother?" Albert asked.

"When I went to get the water, I thought I heard something from the valley below." He paused, looking back toward the entrance before continuing, "But I'm not sure. I have a grave feeling there is an ill wind blowing."

Albert looked at Arktos, who now suddenly seemed alert, and as their eyes caught one another's gaze, they could feel the low rumbling of a thunderous herd. Ice ran through their veins.

Everyone but Arktos raced to the entrance. This was God's will; their path had been chosen.

Arktos looked toward the sky-lit altar in the other chamber as a dove lit upon the inscribed stone, and he felt a hand on his shoulder. His strength was suddenly restored.

"Go. Be strong," a voice whispered as the pain in his head abated.

Arktos rose and walked toward the morning light, reaching into the cave's entrance. He looked at the valley spreading out below. He paused and leaned against a rock. He felt a renewed spirit, yet he felt a purpose pulling him. He knew deep down this was his time.

A dove flew by as he began to descend into the rumbling chaos below. The air began to stir, and the clouds danced across the peaks of the mountains. The time of change was upon them. Their path had been chosen. They would now begin their journey that had always been. God's will had begun.

Chapter 5

THE ONSLAUGHT

The Lord gives voice before His army, for His camp is very great; for strong is the One who executes His word. For the day of the Lord is great and very terrible; Who can endure it?

—Joel 2:11

akob had been sitting with Jean Paul in the stables that morning. They were going over their Sunday-morning lessons after they fed the animals in preparation for their usual Sabbath services at church when they heard the sound. The first thought that instinctively came to their minds was an avalanche, which was common in the winter months, but this was summer and the snows on the upper peaks were not deep enough to cause this alarm. This was a low rumbling that quickly caused fear in their hearts.

Riders! Lots of them!

Jean Paul raced for their only stallion and quickly threw a saddle pad on the horse. "Hurry, go get the women. Get them to safety. Tell the other two they are on their own. I'll try to find Grandfather after I've warned the others."

With that, Jean Paul shot off toward the village in hopes of sounding an alarm before his worst fears became true, all the while praying it was not too late.

As Jakob raced for the house, his mother met him at the door, already aware something was wrong. Steffan and Marik were not far behind her and looked on as Jakob spoke.

"Mother, Mother, go to the safe place! Jean Paul says riders are coming. Girls, Momma, get your things! Let's go! Hurry! Riders!"

A flurry of activity began. Almost as if it were their second nature, they gathered a few belongings and bare essentials—enough to help them survive an extended stay outside the home, for how long they didn't know. At this point, survival was their only thought.

Marik and Steffan rushed to their horses, which had been taken to the stables, and hurriedly began preparing their mounts. They too had no idea what was about to transpire. Should they flee to safety with the women and children, or should they stand and fight? They both felt an obligation to their gracious hosts to stand with them in this hour of impending doom. They moved quickly and did not speak.

Jakob grabbed his satchel and sling and then raced for the barn. As he crossed the yard, he looked down to the farther reaches of the valley and saw an image that caused him to pause in fear. He looked back to the barn just as Marik and Steffan were emerging from it. His mother, grandmother, and sisters had just disappeared up the hillside and over the ridge. Marik and Steffan froze as they saw Jakob fleeing toward them. They looked over his shoulder down the slope of the mountain, and what they saw in the distance caused their hearts to race.

A multitude of armored riders had invaded the valley like a black cloud of locusts swarming a field. The mounts carried various armaments of destruction, with banners indicating their allegiance to the Holy Roman Catholic Church waving behind as they drove upward, shaking the earth as they came. The mass of flesh, steel, and sanctity moved with purpose toward their destination, where the will of one greater than any terrestrial army awaited.

Jakob now realized the magnitude of danger approaching and redoubled his speed, preparing to flee up the back trails beyond the farm to the safety of the ridges above their farm. Marik quickly mounted and drove his heels deep into the beast's side. The horse leapt, and before he knew it, Jakob was being lifted into the air as his legs still ran below him. Steffan followed behind as they drove their horses to higher ground, with Jakob directing the way as they went.

Jean Paul reached the outskirts of the Rora village where the majority of the Vaudois's inhabitants lived. He had not approached unnoticed, and a small crowd began to gather. His mount, lathered from the hard ride, panted with fury as its rider jumped from the mount in front of the village meeting hall. Others gathered as he jumped upon the front steps and began shouting, "Riders approach! Gather the warriors! Riders approach, hurry! They have already reached hanging rock pass!"

As he shouted, some ran off to spread the word. Others raced to gather weaponry. Some just stood there, frozen in horror. They had all been warned by the elders that someday outsiders might come to take them away to punish them for their Apostle Speaking abilities. None could imagine, however, that this would ever come to fruition until now. Here they stood.

"Where are the elders?" someone from the crowd shouted.

Jean Paul had not noticed before now, but he suddenly remembered Grandfather holding the emergency enclave that morning and that he had yet to return.

"They are off on a special enclave as we speak," he replied with an air of frustration in his voice.

Worried glances passed back and forth between the few remaining villagers gathered in front of the meeting hall.

"They surely will be returning shortly, but for now, we must prepare to fight if need be," Jean Paul continued.

Several mountain warriors suddenly appeared around the corner of the street on horseback. They wheeled their mounts in front of Jean Paul as the others looked onward.

"Mount up! Let's go! We've no time to lose!" the leader of the band shouted to Jean Paul.

"What about the elders? Should we act without their consent?" Jean Paul asked.

"If we wait on them, we may have nothing left to defend."

Jean Paul jumped to his horse while the others turned their horses in the direction of the oncoming invasion. They dug their heels deep into the sides of the animals, jolting the animals to drive their tendons and muscles into immediate action. Dust, leather, and sweat flew as they sped off toward the outskirts of the village's limits to buy time for others to mount a defense—a defense they knew they was no match for what they could feel approaching.

There was no time to consider the intent of the approaching force. There was only time to react, as they saw it. The elders normally did the thinking. These young mounted soldiers acted out of fear and passion—a volatile combination when unchecked by wisdom.

They took the only course they knew of at the time. There was no regard for compromise and no time to contemplate discussion—only time for action. They did not realize that a possible slaughter might be preventable if they openly discussed things with the invaders, as an older and wiser man would do. The ones who took this charge were nowhere to be found, so the youth went, as youth will do. The Lord looks over those who know not what they do, and these few misguided young men would soon learn from this deadly experience they were about to encounter. The results, regardless of their actions, would quickly alter the path all the Vaudois's residents would have to endure for future generations.

As the main flank of heavily armed militia began their ascent into the valley, they were instructed to be on the lookout for attacks from any and all angles. As they rode up the narrow passages, their ranks began to file into smaller but longer columns.

They had been sent to the valley to search out and destroy a sect of heretics that had been reported to the regional baron in Turin. They were to use as much force as was needed to get the inhabitants to decide upon an ultimatum: either pledge their faith to the Roman Catholic Church or face death. There were reports of possibly small armed bands that were disorganized and untrained. Nonetheless, the overwhelming show of strength would certainly be a deterrent.

The papal crown, in its religious realms, wanted to minimize the destruction and carnage if necessary. This army of the papacy was not much concerned about maintaining any public image, but the crown wanted to be perceived as holy arm of God that was capable of preserving Christianity by force if necessary. Most, but not all, of the men in this force had for so long raped and pillaged in the name of the papacy during the first Crusades and other smaller wars that they had become accustomed to such vulgarities.

A few of the men had joined the papal guard more recently as a means to make a living, giving little thought to the purpose they served. These men merely wanted to feed their families back home; however, they were significantly outnumbered. Some of the men in the army were youthful spirits searching for danger and adventure, while others were mere vagabonds bent on nothing more than plundering all that came across their path. As such, for the most part, the wicked vastly outweighed the moral, creating a force that represented a battle-hardened, cold-hearted lot of souls who actually took pleasure from such destructive onslaughts as they were hoping they would encounter today. A good day of swordplay and mayhem would make for a good night of raping and pillaging, they figured. It was all done in the name of Christianity, of course. Why else would they be put here? It was all in a day's work.

As the elders descended from the secret mountain bastion they had just left, their worst fears were soon realized in the vista stretching out below them. The massive army approaching the village from below was so massive that the rumble of the cavalry could be felt up the mountainside. The ebony swarm of death crawled up the ridge toward the only place the elders had ever known as home: the Rora, the Vaudois. This place, which was so precious and unstained, would soon be contaminated by a cancerous force of humankind intent on holding true their purposes of faith based on human greed rather than the real Christian virtues they claimed to uphold. The valley would soon be forever stained in its purity by the bastardy of evil that had spread forth from Rome. The invaders' tenets would only curse all those who would not conform. They would persecute those who truly were the guardians of the real faith that was established by the apostolic virtues passed down through generations. Their faith was tested by time, tempered by the human spirit, and buoyed by the essence that was linked to the heavenly host through spiritual bonds yet to be realized and foreseen. With these heavenly gifts, they would someday reach beyond the mere boundaries of the mountains in which they were born.

The elders raced to reach their armed protectors to try to dissuade them before they became martyred as a result of a seemingly fruitless action in the face of the overwhelming odds they could see quickly approaching. Their aged bodies could not cover the ground as quickly as they once could. Living at these high mountain elevations tended to keep the body in a physical shape that would maintain youthful vigor well beyond the normal aging years, but still, age always won and would take its toll. As the elders ran, they soon realized there was no way they could reach their warriors in time to stop them from rushing into the mouth of the serpent that now slithered up the narrowing passage, inching ever closer to their homes and families.

Realizing the inevitability of the situation, they began marching together as well as they could, considering the terrain, and began chanting Scripture as they marched. With only the Word of God as their weapon, down the mountain they came.

Up the mountain evil surged, with the spirit of youth the only thing between the two titans of faith. These youths had yet to live to become the future generations of what had been so long passed on. They appeared to be facing a totally brutal massacre, wasted lives, and unforgiven sins unless something miraculous transpired on this day of the beginning of the end.

Only something miraculous could save them now.

The front lines of the papal force could see the village now. They had not encountered the first obstacle and still rode along unchecked. As they cleared the high, rocky cliffs, the trail opened up into a large, panoramic pasture that sloped upward from their current position. The idyllic valley sat before them. The pastures were green with the early summer grasses, some cut and piled into shocks already, others with grains growing in small patches.

They had not yet seen a soul, but they had expected that since this day was chosen to attack for a reason: it was the Sabbath. If they were lucky, they would catch them in their house of worship and have them caged, trapped all in one place, making their job all the more easy. The complete elimination would be an effortless campaign.

"Prepare swords!" came the command from the sergeant at arms.

Leather straps holding down large broadswords were loosened. Shields came up as they prepared for the unexpected, just in case they weren't totally able to launch a surprise attack. They didn't care much about the element of surprise, but if they were able to accomplish it, the day would go all the easier.

Jean Paul and his fellow Christian rebels had ridden hard to reach the higher ground, where they now watched. Their blood chilled to the bone at sight of the insurmountable force below. They dismounted and circled around the brink of the canyon wall that overlooked the valley through which the army had just passed. They had missed the chance try to slow the army's approach; now they could only mobilize their small force at the rear flank of the ominous force that had now halted as it prepared for the final push into their village.

They had the high ground, but their weapons and numbers were obviously no match for what was below. Undeterred, they sat and planned for what would surely be a suicidal attack. There was nowhere to turn and no place to hide. These people would not go down without a fight, or until they could breathe a last breath of the pure but thin mountain air. They were indeed the true Christian warriors.

Jean Paul silently pulled his arrow on his long bow, as did the others, knowing deep down this was not going to halt the approach of the apparently demonic force between them and their people. Then, through his aim, Jean Paul saw them. He slowly eased back down and motioned to the others to follow as they watched.

Way off in the distance, dressed in their enclave robes, arm in arm, marched the aged leaders. Were these old men crazy?

The elders marched in unison now. They reached the upper stretches of the village, quoting Psalms as they strode, "Yea thou I walk through the valley of the shadow of death, I fear no evil." Death lay before them.

When they reached the last curve in the trail, the lead guard stopped and signaled for those behind him to halt. As they pulled up even and filled in the ranks, which were some one hundred riders wide, they faced a steep, picturesque mountain village on a ridge above them that was sitting just past an upward-sloping, pasture-covered hillside. The sergeant and his comrades all felt the pangs of altitude on their foreheads. They breathed this air, which was so cool but so thin, heavily, as did their sweat-laden steeds, who suffered mightily under their armored loads.

Jean Paul looked at Lorenz, the oldest of the armed Vaudois men. He met Jean's gaze and nodded in approval, for this was their only opportunity to strike at the force below. They wouldn't win, but they would at least buy some time for their fleeing families and possibly take out a few of the black-souled devils who stood in a mass below their vantage point. Jean Paul raised up just above the point to where he could take aim and drew back his long bow again, as did the other warriors, in preparation for the beginning of the end once more.

A small whirlwind kicked up in front of the lead guard, turning leaves and small specks of earth into a spinning mass that grew into a funnel-shaped tiny fury as it swept past and danced toward the rock face of the mountain to their left, above which the small band of warriors prepared to launch their missiles of death. Once the tiny tornado passed, there was only a slight remnant of sound remaining that could barely be heard. It sounded like something rhythmic but faint. The lead guard's horse's ears perked up.

Jean Paul was just about to signal for the men to fire when he caught the sound on the faintest drift of current: the elders. Now not only could he see them better, but he could also hear them. They were loudly chanting verses of Scripture.

"What are we waiting on, Sergeant?" called the captain, who was holding the right flank of the deadly force.

With that, the sergeant drove his steel spurs into the ribs of the brute he rode and yelled, "Charge!"

The papal satanic force took off toward an unseen enemy in a roar of hooves, clank of armor, and scream of a destitute horde of mindless rage with weapons drawn. They were looking for any and everything possible that they could strike down with the fury built from days on the road to a destination with no sense of purpose.

Jean Paul and his brethren let loose their projectiles, which took down several of the rear of the marauding hoard. Some turned and looked to retaliate, but then they saw the vantage point and simply spun to catch up with the rest of the horde. They watched in horror as the mass drove beyond them to the village they had just attempted to save in what fragility of purpose they had shown.

Arktos saw them approaching, papal banners flying and displaying the symbol of the cross. He closed his eyes, redoubling his prayers as did the others with whom he was locked arm in arm, chanting as they strode, knowing that any minute they would be reunited with their loved ones who had gone on before. Soon their end would be the beginning of glory.

The lead lines were at full charge now, sweat, earth, fury all boiled into the rage that mixed with the wind that began to roar in their face.

Their heads pounded.

Their vision began to blur.

Suddenly, long, dark tunnels . . .

The air was hard to find, their breaths stabbing their chests as they drove forward.

Closer now . . .

Just a few more yards to go.

The elders were clearly visible now, as was the chanting, the insatiable chanting, ringing like sirens in their ears—the pain.

The darkness . . .

Arktos heard the crashing sound of flesh and bone before him, with metal and stone clashing, as if there were great armies colliding.

The front line melted into the earth as if driven down by an almighty hand, forcing them to plow themselves into the sodden earth they had just ridden upon. Great shards of earth plowed before the mighty warrior steeds, sword into horse, bone into flesh. Blood flowed over vast swathes of green grass, turning the field a morbid palette of gray ooze mixed with horror and screams. The subsequent ranks of riders crashed into the front line that had run into an invisible wall where the air no longer existed; their heads were ready to explode.

Jean Paul and his compatriots watched as the hand of God worked upon the evil force that had seemed before to be unstoppable. The few figures that lay below them, some still twitching as the life seeped from their bodies, were a small fraction of the force that now faced an unseen army that they could not battle.

As if in slow motion now, the bodies, man and beast, began to wrestle with the realization of what could not be. Some began to gather themselves and regroup, falling back.

Across the valley from Jean Paul, a loud alpine horn sounded, and on cue, a large force stood shoulder-to-shoulder across the entire length of the ridgeline that bordered the valley chasm below. Archers, mountain warriors from the surrounding valleys who had been summoned by riders sent out by what now seemed like eons ago, stood in formation.

"Fire!" a voice boomed.

The ones who had the sense of mind to begin falling back suddenly looked to the sky. It turned dark with the whispering sound of death reaching an arc and then beginning to race toward their demonic targets below. Screams echoed off the canyon walls. Shrieks of horror were heard as waves upon waves of arrowed death launched, with Jean Paul and his band adding to the flight.

A few of the invaders were able to find cover and retreat toward the chasm where the stream crashed to the precipices below as they raced for their lives. Some leaped to their deaths. Only a handful were able to escape.

Arktos watched. The elders had seen the mighty power of the Holy Spirit. Earthen rubble, weaponry, cross-laden shields scarred from collisions, flesh entwined with bone, pain, and anguish stretched out across the valley before them. They could see arrows as thick as blades of grass at every angle in every possible entry into their victims. Their enemy had been brought to near-total annihilation.

The few who were lucky enough to survive the raging torrent had a story so unbelievable to tell that many would discount their recantation, leading to doubt and further speculation. But for now the victory was with the Vaudois, with the people who still held close to their chests the very Word they now knew was threatened.

Now they knew the future was upon them, and the challenge was at hand. It was up to them to embrace it and go forward as God intended.

As God intended. Indeed, this was their plan.

Chapter 6

HELL ON EARTH

The hand of the Lord came upon me and brought me out in the
Spirit of the Lord, and set me down in the midst of the valley; and
it was full of bones.

—Ezekiel 37:1

Marik, Steffan, and Jakob watched the surreal battle from a
vantage point above the valley below, having fled the home
site in advance of the invading force. They stood in silence,
dumfounded by the indescribable scene that had just taken place before
them.

The once-daunting army now lay in ruin, shattered, broken, and still,
except for the few who lay in agony, slowly dying, crying out for their
mothers, some praying loudly. They could see the elders still standing
in the tall grass of the pasture at the edge of the village with heads now
bowed and hands folded in prayer. The wind was blowing their long
robes around them, whipping their hair in tufts of white.

The warrior force that had assembled from the neighboring valley now
approached them on the narrow trail that followed the ridgeline where
they stood. The lead rider, a strong, stout, but aged man, nodded to
them as they approached. They returned the gesture. Behind him a
force of mountain warriors, hardened by the high altitude, followed,
bows hanging over shoulders, some with broadswords mounted on their
saddles while others had battle lances on their sides. These were the
Vaudois militia—the warriors who protected the ancient valley's people.
They rode short but stocky mounts with large, hair-covered hooves,

which aided in stability on these treacherous mountain passages. These were men who would have been the same age as Jakob's father.

"Are you the stranger we've heard about from Lyon?" the leader of the warriors said to Marik.

Marik hesitated as he glanced down at Jakob, who stood quietly watching the rebel troops amass.

"Yes, I am Marik of Lyon Gaul."

"Where is Jean Paul?" the leader asked.

"We thought he rode to alert you," Marik answered.

"Yes, Jean Paul sent for us. We come from the neighboring valley. We are the protectors of the faith, but we never saw him. We only received word that he needed our help." Then the warrior leader paused as his steed shifted the weight on its back. His brow lowered, he asked, "What brings you here, Marik of Lyon?"

Marik felt his neck redden, but he kept his composure as he responded. "We are here on a quest. We were sent to find the people who can help us write the Bible into common language for every man to own. I guess you could say we are on a mission for God. We had no idea we would be witness to one of the most unthinkable, unbelievably lopsided battles ever fought."

The warrior leader nodded at that. "God has delivered us from them this time. However, I fear after witnessing the importance the church has placed on our Vaudois today, that the future will only bring more death to our mountain home. You know they will only come back to revenge this loss." He paused, studying the two. Then he looked back down at the obliterated mayhem of carnage below and continued, "Nonetheless, today we live to honor his holy name another day."

With that, the warriors turned and began their descent to the valley below toward the village. Jakob looked up at Marik, as if to ask what to do.

"Let's go down and see who we can find and pray the Lord has protected your family, son," Marik said.

As the last of the mountain force trailed off toward Rora, Jakob and his newfound friends followed closely behind.

*   *   *

Stoically the elders faced the horrific scene scattered before them and then suddenly, as if being instructed from an unknown command, bowed their heads and fell to their knees as one. As Arktos knelt on the ground, his head in his hands, he felt the presence of others. If his faith had not been what it was, the scene that had unfolded before him and the elders would have been all but unbelievable. As he bowed before God the almighty, he began quoting the twenty-third Psalm again, as before, but now with even more vindication, for the Psalm lay before them in all its gore and hopelessness.

"Yeah though I walk through the valley of the shadow of death, I will fear no evil."

The other elders, still kneeling before the mass of flesh, humanity, and brute carnage that lay strewn before them as a witness to the holy power, began to speak as one along with Arktos. "The Lord is my shepherd, he will lay me down beside still waters."

Arktos felt so insignificant in the face of this power that now seemed to press them farther down to the ground. They felt as they could not be low enough to warrant their praise to his holy being. He began to weep for all the generations of struggle that had brought them now to this point. They had reached a point of no return. His chest heaved with strained emotions. Passions that had been held in check for so long now lay open upon the face of the plain of death, bearing all before the raw savageness that now lay tamed and still in death and agony before them.

Arktos felt his sixty years weighing upon him. He felt the entire Vaudois relying upon him. He seemed to nearly fall into an abyss of darkness when suddenly, like the first tinges of light on the horizon at dawn, he could softly hear the sound of an ancient hymn. Ever so slightly, he heard it raise its corona through the bitter fog of night, reaching out to his heart. The closer the song, the lighter the weight became until he felt his throat begin to vibrate with the sound of music, and he began to sing. It was low and guttural at first, but just as the snow begins to thaw in the springtime and trickle from tiny rivulets to become a stream, so did his voice find its legs and begin to run.

As the warriors approached the elders, who now knelt with their faces skyward, singing together in unison a song of praise, they couldn't help but be struck by the moment. Elders, old men, kneeling and singing praises to God! Beyond them, in piles of broken bones, flesh, and stains of crimson upon the earth, lay utter destruction. The contrast was unspeakably horrifying and inspiring at the same instant.

Marik's eyes watered. They had just found this jewel of a valley, only to have it transformed now in the presence of the distraught evil that had seemed to follow them. It would never be the same, and yet, it was somehow something that was inevitable.

Marik turned to Jakob and looked down at the boy, who now seemed to be old beyond his years, and said, "We must go now. We must go and make this Word available to the rest of the world. We cannot wait for evil to try to take it away forever."

Jakob nodded. He too, even at this young age, could easily read the lesson God had given them this day—a day that would never leave his memories. This day would be written in the minds of generations to follow.

This day would become a monument to others of what can become and what to expect from the darkness that lives in the hearts of mankind who cannot fully accept the Holy Ghost into their hearts—hearts that are brazen against the will of God and seek only their own gain.

Chapter 7

DEPARTURE

For you see your calling, brethren, that not many wise according to the flesh, not many mighty, not many noble, are called.

—1 Corinthians 1:26

It had been decided by the council that Marik and Steffan would escort Jakob and his grandfather to Lyon, where they would meet with Peter Waldo and begin their transcription of the Bible. They didn't feel comfortable with the idea of allowing one of the few valuable handwritten Bibles to leave the safety of their Vaudois, but with Arktos as part of the mission team, they knew the task could be completed, although it would be a long and arduous task on the part of Arktos. He was possibly the most knowledgeable of all regarding the memorization of the Scriptures, a feat not mastered by many. Having committed so much Scripture to memory had been his lifelong ambition, driven even more since the loss of his son. He and Jakob would finally begin the evangelistic journey, for which they had apparently been chosen.

"You will take proper care of my son, Mr. Marik," Julia said as she stood with her hand on Jakob's shoulder on the morning of their departure.

Looking down at the boy, Marik smiled, and with a fatherly gesture, he reached his hand toward the boy, "You can trust I will guard him with my life, madam."

Jakob looked at his mother, who gently wiped a tear from her cheek as she knelt to bid him farewell. As she hugged him, he wrapped his arms around her, smelling the sweet fragrance of wild flowers she had woven into her hair, and he felt the warmth of home. He felt a knot grow in his throat. He wanted to cry, but he tried desperately to choke back the tears.

She whispered into his ear, "Go and make your father proud."

Now there was no holding back the flood of tears he had been hiding. Through the wave of emotion, he saw Marik move toward him and put his arm around him. He felt comfort from this new friend, and his sorrow began to ebb.

"We had better get moving if we are going to make any headway today," Grandpa growled as he stood near the horses holding a rein in his hand, watching the touching scene. "Before we go, let's have a word of prayer," he said.

With that, he knelt. The others followed, and he began, "Oh blessed heavenly Father, Maker of heaven and earth, blessed be thy name. We ask you today to continue to watch over us as you have done since the beginning. Dear Lord, keep watch over our family and home. Keep them safe, Lord, and I pray our journey would be fulfilling in your eyes, for we live to serve only you. I pray that our escorts know you, Lord, and have accepted you into their hearts, for our people's lives are at their mercy. We are about to walk into the lion's den and awaken the beast in this journey we are about to take. We pray that you are with us each step of the way, for we knowingly live each day at extreme peril to preserve and cherish your holy Word. You are the only true living God, and in your name we pray, and in Jesus' holy name, Amen."

Julia paused as she still had her arm around Jakob. He stood and began to mount his horse, and she reached for his hand. As she stood looking at her youngest son, she could see his father's eyes in his face. "Jakob, I want you to remember we love you with all our hearts."

"I know, Mama."

"And Jakob, don't forget your songs."

"Yes, Mama, I'll keep singing them and think of you when I do."

"Please take care of Papa." She paused now as the emotional flood was nearly beyond her control. "He's old, but he can be terribly stubborn sometimes."

"Yes, this I know too," he said with a smile.

"Jakob," she said, her voice now in a whisper, "be safe." As she tried not to weep, she said, "Live for God." The quiet sobs came now, unwanted, but she continued on through them, "For I love you as he loved his only son." With that, she turned her head, trying not to show her tears as she backed away from Jakob's mount.

Marik gently nudged his horse, and the others began to fall in line as they started to ride off, Arktos falling in the rear, with Jakob in front of him. Jakob looked back as they slowly began to descend from the valley. His home became a distant spot on the mountainside. This was the only place he had ever known—his home, his family, his Vaudois. Fear of the unknown had not gripped him until now.

His mind drifted back to when he was a child. His father was with him in the pasture as they walked among the flock of sheep. It was a day much like today, with high blue skies with barely a cloud. His small hand was in his father's large, strong, calloused palm.

"Father?"

"Yes, son?"

"How long have we lived in the Vaudois?"

"All our lives, son." He paused before replying, "Why do you ask?"

"Was I born in a barn?"

"A barn?" Kristoff let out a loud laugh.

"You know," Jakob said meekly, "like Jesus?"

Kristoff smiled as they walked. "No, my son, you weren't born in the barn like Jesus," he said, smiling down at the precious child. "Just above it though." Jakob smiled back.

"Were there angels there when I was born, like with Jesus?"

"I'm sure they were. I know they were smiling on me."

"Do angels talk to you also, Father?"

With that, Kristoff stopped and bent down to Jakob's face. He held his face with both hands and said softly, "Yes, my son, the angels speak to us often, and with our hearts in the right place, we can hear them. Never forget to keep God in your heart, for if you don't, you will find the day you quit hearing them speak to you."

"I won't, Father. I will never let God out of my heart."

"I know, son. You are from the Vaudois; you can't."

They both sat down, and as they did, the flock of sheep grazed around them, unthreatened and peaceful. A cloud's shadow passed over, racing across the ground.

"Father?"

"Yes?"

"Do you hear angels singing too?"

Kristoff looked at him with a curious look. "I'm not sure that I have heard them singing."

"I do."

Kristoff looked at his young son. The warmth in his heart overflowed with joy, for these were the moments he would cherish forever.

Blessed are the meek, he thought, "Son, I'm sure you do. Sing something for me, will you?"

And with that, Jakob began singing a tune, something he had never heard before, yet something enchanting—something that sounded older than the child's years.

As Jakob sang, Kristoff closed his eyes and let his thoughts travel with the wind on the tune of the song. In his mind, he could see Jakob being born and afterward, his beautiful wife and son lying together. Then there was the family sitting in church on Sunday afternoons like today, spent with everyone enjoying the Sabbaths. Then suddenly whiteness, blurring, and a flash of a scene came to his mind—a scene of a cold, freezing struggle, shouting and crying, others being lowered on a rope somewhere on a mountain, and freezing cold. He began to shiver. Then he saw a bright light. He had a feeling of complete calmness and then numbness.

He jumped up. "Stop it!" he shouted, scaring Jakob to death in mid-sentence of song. The boy began to cry.

Kristoff realized his error and sat back down next to him. "I'm sorry, I didn't mean to frighten you, but the picture in mind—it was so real, so frightening."

"I'm sorry, Father. I won't sing again."

"No, no, that's not it. The song was beautiful. It's just . . ." he searched for the words but couldn't find them.

"Just what, Father?'

"I don't know, but never mind. Let's get back to the house. It is getting close to supper, and your mother will be worried."

They stood and walked back, hand in hand again.

It was one of the last times Jakob could remember being with his father before the tragic day. How he missed him.

Jakob looked back at his grandfather, who smiled encouragement toward him. Way off, his mother stood, watching and waving. He could feel her with him as the distance between them grew. That gnawing fear of the unknown seemed to be comforted by what his mother had said: "Make your father proud." The knot came back to his throat. He turned and faced forward, toward the other riders, and watched as they began to ride down the trail, down the mountain. The team passed the meadow where Jakob first saw Marik and Steffan ride into their valley. Now they were leaving together.

God knows best, he thought to himself, and he began to sing a little song as they rode, humming softly, making himself feel a little closer to home, even now as they rode away.

Softly the green grass of the pasture swayed as the sparse clouds drifted overhead, throwing shadows across the snowcapped peaks as they flew by. The ruin of the battlefield scarred all that was of beauty. With time, it would return to its grandeur; with time it would heal.

He would not forget this place. He knew in his heart he would return, but when was unknown. One thing he knew, without ever having left, was that he would be changed. He didn't worry how. His grandfather was there, so he felt safe. His innocence was far beyond his years, for the dangers ahead were far greater than any of them could know at this point. The battle they had witnessed days earlier was still a nightmare that had yet to sink in. Somehow, the gruesomeness had yet to reach their hearts; somehow the spirit of the Lord was leading them on a purpose much greater than the evil that was awaiting them.

With each step forward, they were stepping into the future.

Chapter 8

AWAKENING

For I say, through the grace given to me, to everyone who is among you, not to think of himself more highly than he ought to think, but to think soberly, as God has dealt to each one a measure of faith.
—Romans 1:11

Their journey to Lyon was for the most part uneventful. They purposely tried to maintain a low profile and were careful not to mention when stopping what their purpose was. Before leaving the Vaudois, Marik instructed Arktos and Jakob on how they should act and dress so as not to draw attention to themselves. They wore clothing of the time period but not distinctive to the Vaudois. Marik made it clear that they should not engage in open dialogue in public; rather, they should wait until they were in private to speak on matters that pertained to the purpose of their trip.

Marik also provided information to the Vaudoisian people on what the Catholic Church had recently considered heresy and what mannerisms and customs they considered indigenous to the Vaudoisian people, which would make it easier to identify someone from that region should they choose to travel outside of the valley for any length of time or distance. This information, along with the events that transpired during Jakob's journeys, would someday be the basis for instructions by which the school of Barbi would operate when they were evangelizing outside the Vaudois.

Early each day, just before sunrise, Arktos rose and recited volumes of Scripture to himself while kneeling in prayer. No matter where they camped, he would perform this ritual, regardless of the environment around him. Often Jakob would awaken to hear the murmured chants of his grandfather and find him kneeling on his robe in prayer.

After his morning ritual, Arktos would instruct Jakob on the text he was learning. Intrigued, both Marik and Steffan began sitting in on Jakob's lessons as well, finding Arktos's biblical wealth of knowledge so impressive that it could only be a gift from God. No man they had ever known could quote so much Scripture from memory. It was unnatural to the point of being spiritual.

They noticed that with each passing day, Arktos seemed drained more and more from each of the sessions with Jakob. At last, they realized they would need to stop somewhere with better accommodations and take a badly needed rest.

They found a small village in the foothills of the Alps, Chambery, where they checked into a small but well-kept hostel. Steffan took the horses to a nearby livery stable. Jakob helped his grandfather climb the stairs to the room they had reserved. The ancient oaken door was engraved with curious carvings Jakob had never seen before. His grandfather was so weary that he barely looked up from the floor as they crossed the threshold into the room. Jakob helped him lie down on the bed, and then he too collapsed in pallet on the floor next to his grandfather's bed.

Jakob had never traveled beyond the cathedral mountain walls of the valley, and to him, this was the trip of a lifetime. As he lay on the bed of feathers, his grandfather's snores rumbled through the room, reminding him of the falls near their home and the magnificent rumbling they could make. He remembered the high, snowcapped peaks and his family. His heart ached as homesickness wound its way into his thoughts. He tried to push it back, but it kept coming into the foreground of his consciousness.

He thought of his sisters and mother, and he wondered what they might be doing right now. He missed his older brother, Jean Paul. Now, with him and Grandfather gone, they would need help from other families in the valley. Jean Paul alone could not run the farm and keep up with the chores that both he and Grandfather would normally take care of. However, in the Vaudois, helping other families was expected and not something unusual. Everyone helped each other, in sickness or in health. Everything was a community affair, since all were brothers and sisters in Christ. Living in such an isolated location forced them through years of hardships to work together as one. Their unity and faith had made them strong.

That strength was what Jakob had to rely on in the coming weeks. At this moment, he felt so vulnerable, so helpless, and so alone. At moments like this, he truly missed his father. As he lay on his pallet on his back with hands behind his head, he closed his eyes and began to drift off. Then he could hear the song he used to say were angels singing to him come back to him. He softly began humming the tune to himself. As he hummed the song he didn't know by name, his mind could see more clearly into the past.

He was walking again with his father; he could almost reach out and touch the sheep in the flock, feel the gentle alpine breeze, and hear the waterfalls nearby. He hummed on, and soon he was in a dark cavern someplace he had never seen before. As he was growing up, he had heard of the secret place the elders met for the council, but nobody other than those on the council had ever seen the inside of the secret enclave. But now he was there, as in the pasture with his father. He stood looking around and could see a large rock slab, like a table. There in the middle of the table, sitting in a shaft of light, sat a snow-white dove.

A thunderclap erupted, and the dove flew off. In an instant, Jakob sat straight up, being ripped from the trance to the present as Marik burst into the room. "Get up, get up! We must leave immediately!" he shouted.

Jakob looked over where Grandfather had lain, but he was gone. Marik looked at the empty bed and then to Jakob. "Where's your grandfather?"

"I don't know. I . . ." he stammered as he tried to wake up, "I must have fallen asleep."

"You've been sleeping for over two days. Of course you fell asleep! While you were in your sleep coma, Steffan went to check on the horses at the livery stable. There was a couple of the pope's guard there, a couple who had escaped from the massacre in the Vaudois. Hurry now, get up. We must go."

"But Grandfather, we can't leave without him."

"He'll be fine. We can find him later. You are in danger here. We must move and quickly. The guard I was talking about followed Steffan from the stables. He tried to lose them and did for a while, but now they are back. We don't know why, but we believe they might have recognized us from somewhere."

"I'm not leaving without Grandfather!"

Suddenly they could hear shouts in the street down below. They ran to the window to find Arktos on the street below surrounded by the two guards who had noticed Steffan earlier. The guard recognized Arktos. They had evidently survived the massacre and were hell bent on enacting revenge upon the old man regardless of the fact that he was only guilty of praying at the scene of the battle.

Arktos was an old man, but he was exceedingly spry from living his lifetime in the rough, rugged terrain of the Alps. Being outnumbered by only one guard was not much of a problem for him, but being worn down from days of travel took the edge off of his full abilities. He had homemade knives in each hand.

The guards, one with a saber and the other with a hatchet, were trying their best to disarm the mountain man. The guard in front lunged, just missing Arktos's chest, cutting a slash in his upper bicep. Blood began to trickle down the old man's arm.

Rage erupted from the old man that Jakob had never seen—an anger that caused him to begin shouting Scriptures as his eyes became red with fire. He lashed out at his attacker, who had barely missed his mark, driving the blade deep into his back as he swung past, puncturing the aortic valve and dropping his assailant into a death heap before he hit the ground. As he spun to drive the blade into the first guard, he caught the tip of the axe of the second guard with his other arm, flipping it up while swinging his blade underneath, catching the stomach of the second guard and ripping open his abdomen. As the guard bent to grab his stomach to keep his bowels from escaping, Arktos drove his blade into the back of the guard's neck, severing his spinal cord. The guard never knew what hit him as he fell lifeless to the ground.

Arktos stood over both his beaten adversaries, breathing heavily, spattered in blood, head bowed. People began to gather around to see the spectacle that had just occurred.

Fearing the papal authorities would be alerted, Marik shouted down at Arktos, "Stay right there. We'll be down in a second."

Arktos didn't move. He stood still, back hunched over, blood dripping from his right arm, and began quoting Scripture. Arktos had not felt this omnipotent power overwhelm him in many years, and it scared him. This was not the first time. The last time he could recall was when he was a much younger man, so the strength that came with the unworldly power he had just come out of was taken for granted as adrenaline driven, not from a divine source. But this time was different. Arktos was still shaking from being released from its electric hold. He prayed for forgiveness. Death was lying at his feet—death caused by his hand.

"God, what have I done? Was this your will?" He prayed, "I have lived as you have wanted, done your will." He struggled to subdue the fear within that now coursed through his veins as he tried to continue the prayer. "Now to become like a savage beast?" He continued to pray for answers with head bowed. He was shaken, confused, and now wounded.

Marik grabbed Jakob, and together rushed down the stairs. Steffan, aware of the confrontation, had already retrieved the horses from the livery stable and was coming down the street toward the site of the skirmish.

Someone shouted, "Here comes more of the guard."

Farther down the street opposite from the direction Steffan was coming, a small detachment of papal guards was heading swiftly on foot toward the scene. Marik and Jakob landed at the bottom of the stairs at the same time as Steffan arrived, and they quickly mounted their steeds, getting Arktos onto his horse.

Marik was becoming frantic since the old man was in some sort of trance and he could not get him to mount his horse. Finally, in an act of desperation, he shouted at Arktos, "God said let there be light."

Arktos stared at him and smiled. "God is gracious indeed, Brother Marik. I guess we better flow like the river." Then he jumped to his mount and drove his legs into his horse's side. The horses bolted under their drivers' legs as the guard shouted behind them.

Blood had been shed. Jakob had seen a side of his grandfather he didn't know existed—a powerful side that could produce a rage so potent it could slay another human being with only the blade of a knife. He looked at his grandfather, who now looked his age, tired, and weary, as they rode hard out of this village.

How could he have slept for so long when it only seemed like a few minutes? Then he remembered humming along to the song in his dream. More questions began to flood into his mind. It seemed that every time he thought of the song, something strange happened. Or was it more? Was it every time he sang the song something happened? More questions than answers flooded his mind, and right now, they were riding as hard as their horses could go.

If it were true that he had slept for two days, then at least Grandfather would have rested for some of that time.

Suddenly, from behind, they could hear shouts again. Around a bend in the road from behind, they could now see the papal guard riding hard toward them, apparently gaining on them with fresher steeds. With only Marik, Steffan, and Grandfather, they would be no match for half a dozen or so guard that now were trailing them, ever more closely.

Then the song came back to Jakob. "What if?" he thought out loud.

He began singing words from a Psalm to the sound of the song—words he had never consciously put to the melody before now.

"God is our refuge and strength, an ever-present help in trouble. Therefore, we will not fear, though the earth gave way and the mountains fall into the heart of the sea, though its waters roar and foam and the mountains quake with their surging. Selah."

Jakob stopped singing as a thundering roar suddenly shook the earth. From behind, the quickly gaining guard suddenly disappeared from their sight as a gaping hole opened up in the road, as if it had devoured them from sight. They were gone. Jakob pulled the reins of his horse and stopped.

The others realized what had happened and slowed their horses, turning them back around and walking back to where Jakob sat on his horse, looking back at where the papal guard had disappeared.

Then he continued to sing in a soft voice, "There is a river whose streams make glad the city of God, the holy place where the Most High dwells. God is within her, she will not fall; God will help her at break of day. Nations are in uproar, kingdoms fall; he lifts his voice, the earth melts. The Lord almighty is with us; the God of Jacob is our fortress. Selah, the Lord almighty is with us; the God of Jacob is our fortress, Selah."

They all sat in silence. Jakob looked back at where the soldiers had disappeared. The others looked at Jakob and realized that something remarkable had just transpired before their eyes. This boy was remarkable, his grandfather unique, and together, they were from a place on earth that, as the days passed, it was becoming apparent was unlike any other in this world.

"So much for laying low and not standing out," Marik said to Steffan with a wink.

"Ah yes, but the Lord is on our side," responded Arktos, "and if anything, the ones that might have spread the word to more guard are now gone. Others might talk, but that word will not spread as quickly, and hopefully we will reach our destination before it does."

"Let us continue on then, brothers," said Marik.

Then they silently turned their horses toward the direction of Lyon and continued on their journey.

Somewhere behind them the sound of a hawk cried, but there was no echo, for this was not the Vaudois.

Chapter 9

REFLECTION

I call to remembrance my song in the night; I meditate within my heart, and my spirit makes diligent search.

—Psalm 77:6

A couple of days passed, and they finally reached the outskirts of Lyon. Marik and Steffan had kept constant vigilance for any signs of the papal guard. It was imperative at this point that they remain elusive and not be detected for fear that they be followed to Waldo's secret compound. The Catholic Church had not yet declared Waldo a heretic, but once the transcriptions they were going to be working on became published, as was the plan, all that would change. Remaining out of sight and out of mind was crucial at this point. To the public eye, Peter Waldo was still a wealthy Lyon merchant and an upstanding citizen. His calling to the Lord had yet to be revealed.

Since there was a danger they would be detected, Marik decided to move into the city under the shadow of darkness, so they made camp well outside of the city and waited for nightfall.

Early on as dusk began to fall, they sat around a low fire. Arktos, who still had a gaping wound that had started to become infected, was being attended to by Steffan. Jakob sat next to them, watching the operation that was being performed on his grandfather with concern. Steffan was able to clean Arktos's wound and cauterize it with coals from the fire. The smell of burnt flesh permeated the air, but Arktos grunted with satisfaction at the operation.

"You are blessed with a talent, my son," he said to Steffan, who had quietly but efficiently worked on the old man and then withdrew back into the shadows from the light of the fire.

"Thank you, sir."

"Where did you learn to do that? You are obviously trained in the medical arts."

"I had some medical training while attending the academy of arts in Lyon."

"Really now," said Arktos with eyebrows raised. "You have been professionally trained in the arts?" he questioned again, for this was another area that Arktos had longed to provide for his people—proper education that could be used to benefit the Word of God.

"Yes," replied Steffan, again meekly for fear he had done something wrong, especially after seeing what Arktos was capable of doing to his adversaries. He did not know what to expect next out of the elder Vaudoisian.

"Hmmm," grunted Arktos again as he sat with his elbows resting on his knees, with his chin resting on his hands in a thoughtful repose.

There was a long silence. Only the crackle of the fire was heard as a slender column of smoke wisped into the chilly night air. It was an unusually frosty night for late summer. The crispness of the air reminded them that fall would soon be approaching. It was providential that they would soon be in the safety and protection of the compound where they could focus on their work that lay ahead. Marik was concerned for the elder and the effect the days of travel might have had on his powers of memory. At least he was certain the rest at the compound would do him good. However, since the confrontation with the papal guard at Chambery, Arktos appeared to be regaining his strength, and if nothing else, he was appearing more vigorous with each passing day.

These two chosen ones of the Vaudoisian we have escorted from the Rora are more perplexing the more we get to know them, Marik thought to himself. *Surely Master Waldo will be well pleased with my discovery.* Up to this point, Marik had not thought of the monetary reward, but at that instant, the thought did pop into his head. *I wonder how much the master will reward me for such a find, for in and of itself, I have already been blessed beyond compare.* To Marik, the monetary reward was going to be miniscule in comparison. With all they had witnessed up to this point, all they had learned, there could be much written on this alone.

Steffan, the scribe of the group, had tried to keep up the log of the journey since its inception. There were some minor gaps in his writing, but overall, he had managed to capture the heart of the expedition to this point. Arktos aided him at times when he would ask the elder for advice on this or that item he had written. The elder Arktos was glad to help since he realized this was to be used someday to help in the spread of the Word of God. They were merely pawns in the grand Master's plan, and they all needed to cooperate to make the ultimate goal a success.

"Steffan, what have we written lately?" Arktos piped up again after the long silence.

"Nothing sir, not since . . ." he paused now out of fear of inciting something in Arktos that might set him off, "well, nothing since our incident back Chambery." At this point he winced at the words, half expecting a roar from the old man.

To his surprise, Arktos responded calmly, as if nothing had happened, "Get out your tablet, and let's put something new down."

"Yes," Steffan replied. Then he went to retrieve his writing tablet and writing instruments from his riding satchel.

"Jakob, did I ever tell you about how the Apostle Peter came into our lives in the Vaudois?" Arktos asked.

Marik, who had been nearly asleep laying back on his bedroll, sat up at this. Steffan rushed back, opening the tablet and inking up his quills.

"No, Grandpa, I don't remember it if you did," Jakob replied sleepily from the near darkness of his bedroll.

"A long, long time ago, long before my time, the two apostles, Olympas and Herodian, entered our valley and began their teachings to our people. They were students of Peter, one of Jesus' original disciples. The beginning was not easy, but with the hand of God on our people, Olympas and Herodian soon became like one of our own. Legend has it that the longer they remained, the more miracles seemed to happen every day. God was truly working with those heaven-sent evangelists. At the same time, the talents that our friends here, Steffan and Marik, have now seen firsthand were being bestowed upon us. To this day, we still are learning what extent our abilities are to be used and how.

"Olympas and Herodian kept telling us that someday their master would visit us. Now we knew from their teachings that Jesus himself would someday come back, in the glorious return, but our ancestors were unsure at that point what Olympas and Herodian meant. They often spoke in parables, as did Jesus, and when questioned, they would only repeat the parable, as if to say, 'God's Word is not to be questioned.'

"Then one day, he appeared, walking like any other man up the trail leading to our Vaudois. Up the trail came Peter, one of the original twelve disciples. How blessed was that day!

"Olympas and Herodian met him at the edge of the village and welcomed him in, introducing him to everyone. They told Peter of the first encounter and the miracle that allowed them to speak the same tongue. Peter up to that point had not spoken in the Vaudois tongue, but after the instruction from Olympas and Herodian, he began to speak in our dialect.

"The entire village met Peter there that day, and they all knelt at the edge of the Rora and prayed in unison. The elders spoke of that day as the day that everything became stronger in our faith. Everything became clearer, and our purpose as a people was then written in stone.

"However, Peter was not able to stay with us for long. After a couple of glorious days, he said he would have to leave. The Romans sought to arrest Peter. He was concerned for our wellbeing and did not want to give them the chance to find our Vaudois and destroy the delicate bloom of spirituality that had been started here. Knowing that our safety was at risk, he left us, leaving Olympas and Herodian behind to finish their teachings. Before he left, he gave us a memorable gift. He said it would forever remind us to be fishers of men."

"What was it, Grandfather?" asked Jakob, his curiosity piqued.

Arktos rose up from his seat, leaned in toward the fire, and pulled something out from underneath his tunic. Tied on a leather string that hung from around his neck was a bone fishing hook. Arktos raised it in the light of the fire for all to see.

Marik stood and walked closer, and Steffan wrote furiously in his tablet.

"You see, to this day, the council passes the gift from Peter on to the elder of the council who is most elevated in mission toward our spiritual goal, and at this moment, that is me."

Marik was in awe. Here in their midst was an ancient artifact, passed down from generation after generation to this day, something the one of the original disciples of Jesus had given someone. It was a real bone hook, now centuries old, something that literally tied them back to the actual apostles—something that made what they were doing all the more real. Marik sat down next to Arktos, bewildered and still in shock at the revelation.

What else will this elder do to surprise us? he thought as his gaze moved from the ancient fish hook and back to the fire.

Jakob touched the bone and smiled as it hung from the leather necklace his grandfather held up for all to see, causing it to sway gently back and forth. Arktos carefully placed the artifact back in its safe place, close to his chest, and laid back in his reclining pose.

The fire cracked again. Night birds sang in the woods nearby.

"When do we leave?" Jakob asked Marik, who also now retreated back to his humble bed.

"Hopefully, if all is safe, we will leave in the wee hours of the morning after we've had some rest. Steffan and I will scout out the roads in a couple of hours. We will wake you when it is time to go. Your grandfather will be with you until we return, so sleep well, my young Vaudoisian."

Jakob lay back, eyes closed, thinking of the apostle Peter and what the Vaudois might have looked like back then when the famed apostle visited. He soon drifted off to a deep weary slumber, dreaming dreams of glory.

Soon all was silent . . .

Chapter 10

FULFILLMENT

Therefore we also pray always for you that our God would count you worthy of this calling, and fulfill all the good pleasure of His goodness and the work of faith with power,

—2 Thessalonians 1:11

They had arrived at Waldo's estate before the sun touched the horizon early that morning. One of Waldo's sentries, Gabriel, met them just inside the large wooden gates that protected the compound from the outside, which was part of an earthen block wall that fully surrounded the entire outer area of the compound. Waldo had many servants and workers under his employ, several of whom had just risen from sleep to see the commotion at the gate.

Marik hugged Gabriel, as was customary of comrades that had long been separated.

"My friend, you return to us safely, and with guests I see," Gabriel said to Marik, smiling broadly while holding him out at arm's length after their greeting.

"Yes, my brother in Christ, we are abundantly blessed."

Gabriel's gaze shifted to Arktos and Jakob, who were still on horseback. Jakob's eyes were wide with wonder as he took in the complex structure they had just entered. Arktos nodded in acknowledgment at the sentry's attention. He was also impressed but weary from the journey and his recent injury. He was anxious to find a resting place where he could get some badly needed recuperation.

"Come, come, the master has prepared a large meal for our special guests. We had word of your impending arrival," Gabriel said, moving to lead the horses farther into the compound.

"Oh really?" Marik responded, walking his horse behind. The comment caused Arktos's eyebrows to rise.

"No need to worry, my friends," Gabriel said, since he noticed their immediate alarm. "We had people waiting on outposts for any signs of your passage who were to send word. The skirmish at Chambery was seen by one of our scouts and reported back to us shortly afterward. We were ready to send support if needed, but you were not followed, from what we were told, so there was no need to intervene at that point. There is no doubt the papacy will receive word of the event and more patrols will be sent, but for now, we are safe."

Marik thought to himself at that point that they obviously had not seen nor heard about the miracle that happened shortly after the skirmish outside of the town, when the papal guard was swallowed by the earth. Although he was disappointed, it might actually be beneficial that this was not known by others. He still didn't understand what had happened, and until he did, he would rather it was kept quiet.

After they reached the corner of the courtyard and dismounted, a servant came and took their mounts from them. They were escorted to the entrance to another walled courtyard, still lit by torches on either side of the entry. The lights flickered in the early-morning predawn glow. Gabriel gently rapped on the door with the large iron ring that hung there for that very purpose. Immediately the door opened, and they were shown inside.

A fountain flowed in the center of a lush garden. Nearby there was a table with two figures seated, a man and woman. Their faces glowed from the light of the candles that sat in the center. The sound of the gurgling water echoed off the ancient stone walls.

"Welcome!" boomed the man's voice. There was the sound of chairs being pushed back as the pair stood. "Welcome to my home, dear friends."

Gabriel motioned for them to continue forward as he stood in place near the doorway.

Arktos moved first, reaching Peter Waldo, who now stood with arms outstretched. Arktos extended his arm to shake hands, but as he drew close, Peter grabbed him and hugged the elder Vaudoisian with a full embrace. Arktos, slightly caught off guard at first, gingerly returned the gesture.

Peter, releasing him, stood again at arm's length, holding both of Arktos's arms as he spoke. "For so long I have waited for this day. I can't tell you how much of a blessing your presence here means to us all," he said as he glanced toward the woman. "This is my wife, Gwyneth." She politely nodded at Arktos, who returned the nod with a slight bow of his head.

"And this, is the young man I have heard about," said Peter, now looking in the direction of Jakob, who stood in the shadow behind his grandfather. He now peeked around his grandfather at the mention of his presence.

"Yes, my grandson Jakob," Arktos responded proudly, politely backing away and putting his arms around Jakob.

"Wonderful indeed," replied Peter, "positively wonderful. God could not have blessed us more. I am so thoroughly overjoyed. Our prayers have certainly been answered. We have much work to do and much to learn from you. First, I know you have to be weary from days of travel, so I have prepared lodgings for you here in the compound. I hope you will make yourselves at home. If there is anything you need at any time, please let my servants know and we will make your accommodations as pleasing as possible. Gabriel."

"Sir," Gabriel responded, still standing at the doorway of the entrance into the garden.

"Notify Doctor Koblenz. I want to have Arktos's injury looked at tomorrow."

"Sir, yes sir," he said, and he disappeared quickly.

"Marik, you and Steffan may need to take some much-needed time to recover as well. Once you feel ready, we will get a full report of your journey. As I said before, we have much to learn and much to do."

"Yes my lord," said Marik wearily. Marik had suddenly felt the many miles of his journey begin finally to catch up with him. Now, back in the safety of the compound, he was at last free to let down his guard. The muscles in his back began to relax, causing the many miles of travel to wear on him like the heavy clouds on the mountains before a storm. "That would be exceptionally gratifying, sir," he said, bowing his head in respect to the offer.

"I hope that you won't mind that I have taken the initiative and had our chefs prepare a sumptuous meal for everyone. I want you to be fully sated so you will be prepared for the arduous work we have ahead of us. When you are finished dining, you will retire to your respective chambers for some sorely needed rest."

He turned and gently held Gwyneth's hand as they left the garden together. Servants immediately appeared, rearranging the garden furniture to its original position and showing the weary entourage toward a dining hall just off the garden.

Inside the hall were heaping mounds of meats, cheese, and fresh fruits and various pitchers of drinks. Jakob's mouth dropped in awe at the sight of the bounty of food—enough to feed their entire village—for just the four of them. Marik and Steffan found seats but waited for Arktos and Jakob to take theirs first before they too were seated. Everyone paused as the elder bowed his head to pray. Everyone followed suit.

"Oh gracious heavenly Father, we lift up our hearts to you, giving you thanks for the many blessing in our lives. We pray for our families, both here and at home. Lord, we ask that you show us your way in the coming days and lead us where you would have us go, for the grace of God cannot keep us where the will of God does not lead us. I pray you provide this glorious bounty to the nourishment of our bodies. In Christ's name we pray, amen."

The prayer was followed by a collective, "Amen," from the others, and they all began to eat ravenously since this was the first real meal they had eaten since leaving the Vaudois.

As they eagerly devoured portion after portion, Arktos watched his grandson eating his fill. He felt comfort at the sight. The scene reminded him of holiday times in the Vaudois, when a plentiful bounty was shared with all the families in the community's banquet hall off the church in the middle of their village. The hall would be decorated with thick evergreen boughs that were sprinkled with red berries from holly trees. Scented candles burned, giving off beautiful aromas that mixed with the smell of fresh breads and foods spread across the thick-legged tables burdened under the heavy edible loads. Everyone would eat their fill while talking about recent events or family members' health. It made Arktos warm inside thinking back to those days.

However, now, everyone ate in silence, weary from their travels. The food quickly brought on the feeling of a need for sleep till their eyes became heavy. With their stomachs now full, each retired to his respective chamber for rest and recuperation.

Arktos and Jakob retired together. They found a large room with a high window that was now allowing the growing morning sunlight to filter in, lighting the room in a soft glow. There were two large beds, each covered with feather-filled mattresses and silky linens. Jakob ran and jumped onto the bed nearest to the wall with the window, disappearing into the billowy softness. Arktos laughed as Jakob giggled with glee. It was the first time in a long time that he had heard the boy laugh like a child again. It was almost as if he had forgotten that Jakob was still a child, yet to reach his teens.

Jakob rolled into a sitting position, removed his dusty mountain boots, and then lay back with arms outstretched and sighed loudly. Arktos, amused by the boy's actions did the same. They both laughed.

"Grandpa?"

"Yes, my son."

"Is this what heaven will be like?"

Arktos smiled before answering and paused before speaking. "I would have to believe it might be, my son." He pulled a pillow close to his face and embraced it. Then he continued, "The clouds might be as soft as these pillows. Don't you think so?"

Jakob smiled. "Yes," he said softly. Then the food and weariness from the road began to pull him down—down into a deep, restful slumber. Sleep overcame them both. As the morning sun rose, Jakob and his grandfather slept peacefully. They had reached their destination, their destiny—the place where they and the others who were with them would soon reshape the face of mankind with their gifts.

They were here to do God's work, but for now they slept, elder and grandson. Together they would return to mankind one of God's greatest gifts that had been greedily withheld by men who were bent on controlling the Word of God—the Word that no man alone should own but that all should share.

As they slept, angelic hosts watched and waited; an eternity was on their side, and time would soon come for things to change.

Chapter 11

BREAKING GROUND

But you be watchful in all things, endure afflictions, do the work of
an evangelist, fulfill your ministry.

—2 Timothy 4:5

The knock at the door was sudden and rushed. Julia quickly
rose and walked to the door, looking through the slot that
afforded her a view of the visitor outside. Lorenz, one of the
local militiamen, was hurriedly rapping at their door this early hour.
Julia cautiously opened the door.

"Yes, what is it, Lorenz?"

"Morning, my lady," he said, slightly out of breath as he stood with
his horse untethered, holding the reins ready to ride. "Is Jean Paul up
yet?"

"He is already out tending to the sheep, why?"

"I need to speak to him immediately," he said with a serious countenance.
"What pasture do you think he went to?"

"Is there trouble?"

"I can't say, but we need to get our militia organized immediately.
Word has reached us that another assault from the papal army is being
planned, and we need to prepare."

"He's in the upper pastures today."

With that, Lorenz turned and mounted his horse in an instant. His bow was slung over one shoulder, and the quiver, packed with arrows, was mounted to his saddle.

"Please ask him to see me before you take him away," Julia said.

He nodded and then turned his horse and dashed up past the house, leaping over a low rock wall and up through the pasture behind the house that led to the upper pastures.

Julia sat down at the table, head in hands, and sighed.

One of Jakob's sisters came out of the bedroom to find her mother sitting with her head in her hands crying.

"Mother, what is it?" she asked softly.

"Don't worry, child," Julia said with a troubled tone. "No need to worry. Get back to your chores. We've work to be done. Winter will be here before we know it, and we'll be wishing we had such beautiful days like today to waste away. Hurry now and go help your grandmother finish the knitting. I have a feeling we'll need the warm clothes this year."

The girl turned and left her mother alone.

"Lord, please give me strength to carry on," Julia said, wiping her face with her apron, rising, and returning to the pile of potatoes she had been preparing. She looked out the window that faced the mountain behind her home and could see the horseman disappearing over the next ridge as he rode off to find her lone remaining son.

"Lord, please watch over us all, for now more than ever we need you here with us," she said and shoved her hands back to work, trying desperately to forget her immediate world and immerse herself in her work. She hoped and prayed that everything would be all right, that everything would someday return to normal. Someday they could worship their

Lord as they were taught to do so, so many centuries ago by the two apostles. Someday glory would return.

*   *   *

Lorenz crossed the ridge just as a gust of frigid air blasted over, stalling his descent on the other side and momentarily blinding him, causing water to well up in his eyes. Below, Jean Paul stood, staff in hand, surrounded by the sheep he was leading to a nearby grazing spot. From Lorenz's blurred vision, there appeared to be two Jean Pauls below, one holding the staff while the other stood off to the side away from the flock walking with him. He shook his head and tried to wipe the excess moisture from his eyes to clear his vision that was obviously messed up from the blast of cold air in his face. When he looked again, the other figure was still there. It turned and looked toward him and then was gone.

"What in the . . . ?" he asked himself. He pinched his thumb and forefinger together at the bridge of his nose and squinted his eyes closed, trying to regain his composure. He opened his eyes again.

Jean Paul stood still now, looking back at Lorenz, who now had been detected by the sheep, who had alerted Jean Paul to the approaching rider. Lorenz looked again, but the other person was gone. He could have sworn the other figure looked like Kristoff, Jean Paul's deceased father, but with the recent events surrounding the family's tragedy and separation, he thought it best not to mention to the boy of what he had just witnessed.

"Jean Paul, good morning," he bellowed down the mountainside.

"Good morning, Lorenz," Jean Paul echoed back. "I'm guessing you're here early to brighten my day," he said jokingly.

"Ah yes, you are as sharp a whit as was your father once was," Lorenz said, now approaching and grinning down at the young man. Lorenz felt Jean Paul was like his own son. He was nearly the same age as his own boy who had died in an avalanche two winters ago. Lorenz had been extremely close to Kristoff and was supposed to go on the scouting party with him on the fateful trip that led to Kristoff's death, but Lorenz's wife became ill and was pregnant with their third child, so he had to remain behind. He still felt guilty even to this day for not going along since he felt he could have helped prevent the tragedy.

"We, unfortunately, have militia work to do," Lorenz said, now in a serious tone.

Jean Paul leaned on the staff now as the sheep began lowering their heads, no longer in alarm, and began grazing contently.

"Why, what's wrong?"

"We've received word that the papal army, including the central contingent out of Rome, has learned of the massacre of their regiment and want to enact a revenge attack."

"And what are we to do—throw sticks at them when they come marching up our valley?" Jean Paul said mockingly as he lowered his head, shaking it in despair. "Maybe we can have the elders pray us up another miracle."

"You are too ambivalent in your beliefs, brother; you should know better."

Lorenz thought of the image again he had seen as he topped the crest. He thought about mentioning it to Jean Paul, but again, he decided against it.

"Yes," Jean Paul sighed, knowing Lorenz was right. He shouldn't discount the miraculous defeat the previous army had received at the apparent hands of God since their own militia had only performed peripheral attacks on the flank forces once the majority of the army was immobilized.

"We need to get the others together and prepare what defenses we can so as not to be caught totally off guard as we were before. Maybe this time we won't have to call down the angels on them and we can run them off on our own." Lorenz half-heartedly chuckled, which elicited a laugh from Jean Paul as well.

"Yes, give me till noon. I've got to get these sheep fed and bedded back down, and then I can leave for the rest of the day."

"All right, that sounds good. We'll all meet in the village at the hall."

"Alright, see you then."

Lorenz turned his horse and raced back to the summit of the ridge, turning and looking back over his shoulder as he was about to plummet back down the opposite side. There again was the second figure! It made him catch his breath. He started to pull up the horse but kept going. *I pray, Lord, you are sending this boy an angel because his family surely needs you,* he prayed silently as he rode toward the village to prepare for the inevitable return of evil.

Jean Paul watched Lorenz ride to the ridge and thought it odd that he paused the way he did. Everything must have been acceptable since he continued on. Maybe he thought of something he had meant to say before leaving? If so, was it important? Probably not since he continued on. Or maybe he had something personal to say but couldn't. It puzzled him. Then a sheep bleated, breaking this endless loop of useless worry, and he turned back to tend to the flock he was supposed to be taking to better pastures—what little was left. The weather had been turning much cooler as fall approached, so the pickings were getting quite slim at this elevation. They soon would have to pasture the flocks farther down the mountain, and with the recent events, that might not be possible this season due to safety concerns. He began herding the sheep, tapping a couple of them on the flank to get them started moving. They jumped at the touch and scared others ahead of them onward.

The wind blew a gust. As the rush of air blew past his ears, it made a gentle roar. Then these words seemed to dance into Jean Paul's consciousness: "I'll be with you, my son." Then there was only the sound of the wind again.

He stopped. The sheep kept going this time. The wind blew again. He heard no voice this time. He turned to see if someone was there. Nobody. He looked up the ridge behind him. It was empty save for a few boulders that lined it. Lorenz was long gone; he had headed back into the village to prepare.

He began to walk again when the wind blew a gust once more. "Do not be afraid, for I am with you each step of the way."

"All right, who is this?" Jean Paul said, stopping again and this time slamming his staff into the earth while spinning around, looking in all directions. There was still no one, except for the sheep, who now had stopped at a lush green patch of grass and began grazing. He peered up into the sky as the morning sun, which was now well above the peak of Mt. Le Croix, directly shone into his face.

The wind blew his clothes around him, and his hair brushed back and forth into his face. He moved it back to see an empty, clear blue sky. The few blades of grass tickled the ground, but still he saw no one.

"I'm listening, if you are still here, whoever, whatever you are."

Nothing.

Suddenly a wave of emotion erupted inside him from the pit of his stomach. He felt his knees weaken as he crashed to the ground, head spinning. He held the staff upright between both hands, clinging on for dear life and support. His ambivalence toward praying had garnered him much grief from his mother since the latest attack. His mind could not erase the dark images he had witnessed that day. It was like an infection he carried, consuming the grace inside him, until he questioned everything he had ever been taught or known. Now he felt an urge to kneel to the ground and pray that was so strong, it was as if it was being forced upon him from some unseen hand.

Almost involuntarily, he bowed his head and began praying. At first he felt awkward, but then, like the movement of the mountain stream, the words began flowing. He began praying to God like he had not done in months. He asked for forgiveness for having been part of the killing that was done to protect the village in the battle earlier that month. He asked for forgiveness for doubting the wondrous power of God. He went on and on, begging for the Lord's forgiveness and confessing his sins aloud. He began weeping in prayer as he continued to feel the presence of someone, something heavenly that now was here to visit in some way.

As he wept, tears ran down his arms, wetting his sleeves. Little droplets of pain wetted the grass below him. He prayed for his grandfather and brother, for their safety, and for the success of their mission. The more he continued, the lower his body became until he was almost laying on the ground. Tired, weakened he had nearly cried himself out when again the voice came, saying, "Look up."

The reddened rims of eyes looked up from his pitiful yet humble position. There, standing with the sunlight at his back but with the light nearly shining through him stood an image—an image that looked like . . . Yes, could it be Kristoff, his father?

"Father?" He squinted against the sun, raising his hand to block its force into his eyes. "Father is, is that, you?" he asked so softly that the wind nearly sucked his voice away.

The figure said nothing and nearly flickered away to nothingness in the light. Then it said, "Be strong, my son, for I will be with you always." Then he flickered into nothingness and was gone.

Jean Paul sat down now, looking at the spot where the image had stood. He closed his eyes and tried to envision his father once again. It had been a long time since Kristoff died on that scouting trip. They were to survey the pass for the construction project that was supposed to make all their lives better. The new route they were to create would have opened up the pass for easier access to larger towns where they could trade goods as well as spread the Word of God. The tragedy led the elders to believe God did not want them to take the Word beyond their Vaudois—that it was not time. They waited, and time passed on.

But time had weakened his memories of his father, and it bothered him. Nevertheless, just now, he knew that was his father. The image so clear, so new, yet it was gone. He prayed again, without sorrow but with joy, for this was a blessing, even if it was only for an instant. To be able once again to hear his father's voice and to see him alive, healthy, and vibrant as he had ever been in his young lifetime was more than he could believe.

The wind blew by and swathed hands of movement across the mountainside as the young man, his head on his knees, prayed while gentle sheep grazed below. The sun was shining in the ancient sky and was rising for a new dawn, a new day.

Chapter 12

ROME NEVER SLEEPS

For I know that after my death you will become utterly corrupt, and turn aside from the way which I have commanded you. And evil will befall you in the latter days, because you will do evil in the sight of the Lord, to provoke Him to anger through the work of your hands."

—Deuteronomy 31:29

The papal guard's sergeant at arms called the room to order, "Attention!"

A red Persian carpet lay on a glasslike marble tile floor that ran the length of the golden, ornately decorated room. Humankind was embattled in its attempt to triumph in its spiritual will having just lived through the first of what would be several Crusades. It would soon be tested to its core when its total existence would be challenged by the clutches of death in the Dark Ages, but somehow, behind the veil of secrecy, the Holy Roman Empire continued to defy all the indecision and gruesomeness. God, in all his splendor, was the only one deserving of a throne room like this, let alone for a mortal figure many considered to be the incarnation of heaven on earth. Through false teachings and corruption, this holy sanctuary became tainted and lost its way in the search for the Word, the Spirit, and the way of the Lord. Now this force, stained with greed and corruption, using the feudal lord systems to control the bishops and cardinals in outlying provinces, was on a path of collision with the truth, with the real Word of God, for heaven would someday make things right.

The sentries nodded to the royal brass trumpeters to announce the arrival of the papal guest who was about to enter. They trumpeted a customary introduction, which was followed by the announcement, "Your holy Excellency, I present to you the head of the Northern Holy Roman Empire's Papal Army, General Lucier."

The guards in the magnificent cathedral room of the head of the greatest power on earth since the dawn of the Roman Empire, Pope Lucias III, stood in perfect attention as the papal guard general stiffly marched into the room, flanked by the papal palace guard. His Holiness sat with his head bowed, reading over some parchment as the party approached, obviously ignoring the pomp of the arrogant military guard, which was a necessary evil in these times.

They reached the bottom of the throne steps and stopped, snapping to attention and being announced by the papal announcer, "Your holiness, the head of the Northern Roman papal guard forces, General Tiberius Lucier."

He continued reading, and then, in his own due time, he finally looked up from his reading glass, paused, and observed the party at his feet. General Lucier was a highly decorated soldier with a lifetime spent in the military. He was dressed in his dress uniform, complete with knight's armor chest plate, which displayed his many medallion and ribbons from the many campaigns he had been on throughout his military career. He had dedicated a lifetime to preserving the sanctity of the Holy Roman Empire, striking forces down that opposed the ideologies or will of the church in the name of the Roman Empire, now under papal control.

"Yes, you request an audience with the papacy," His Holiness said with the demeanor of someone who was tolerating the interruption only because he needed a break.

"Your holiness, sir, I do, in the name of the Father, the Son, and the Holy Ghost," Lucier replied quickly and correctly.

"Well, go on then, I have many matters to attend to today."

"Your holiness, sir, I come to report to you of the recent events in our most northern province."

"The humiliating defeat, you mean," he retorted with a snort of agitation.

Lucier instantly noticed the inflection in the pope's speech and stood silent, delaying the remainder of his report, which had obviously reached the papacy before him.

"Well, have you nothing to say? Or rather, did you come all this way to interrupt me and then just to stand there and gawk?"

"Your holiness has already heard my report then?" Lucier said, straightening and becoming agitated that someone would forego his command and behind his back give word to his Excellency.

"No, not *your* report, but I do have my own connections in places so that Rome never sleeps when it comes to retrieving secrets from the masses. But please, continue on. I could certainly use some much-needed amusement this early morning."

Lucier continued now with a glare in his eye, "We sent a regiment when we received a tip from our scouts who were assigned to follow and investigate the Lyon merchant who searches for the Apostle Speakers after they had made contact with men from his employment."

He paused, but there was no response from His Excellence, so he continued on, "We did not detain them for questioning but had them followed instead. They eventually led us to the Vaudois, where they made contact with what we believe are the Apostle Speakers." Still there was no sign of approval, so he continued further, "The operation took many months to come to fruition since the Vaudois in which these people hide is extremely obscure and difficult to find, even for the Lyon men who had information as to where these people were to be found."

"Why do you say *what we believe,* General?" His Holiness interrupted briefly.

For centuries, it was known that there were small pockets of non-Catholic Christians, most of whom were spread throughout the remote reaches of the alpine valleys. Since there were so remote, their effect on the papacy and its control upon society up to this point in time as a whole was negligible. Thus, searching them out for destruction was considered more trouble that it was worth. However, as the legend of the Apostle Speakers grew, so did their effect on the beliefs and followings of the Holy Roman Empire and its subsequent papal reign.

Now, with the ongoing Crusades placing ever more emphasis on the control of Christianity and the possibility of God's Word being confused with a version that was unknown and unedited, the existence of the Apostle Speakers was becoming an identifiable issue the church had to address. The possibility of an unacceptable version of the Word of God escaping and being spread beyond the isolation of the mountains would certainly threaten the control of the papal grasp upon the people. That control could deteriorate or even be jeopardized. Time was of the essence to either convert or extinguish these people before their influence and beliefs stretched beyond their solitary confinement in the rock walls of the alpine expanses they inhabited.

"Sir?" He looked puzzled at the question that seemed out of context. "What do you mean?"

"You said that we believe they are the Apostle Speakers, did you not, General? Why do you make such a speculative statement after all that transpired?"

"Well, Your Excellence, because we never were able to question them there or afterward due to the defeat," he said, lowering his gaze at the mention of the word.

"So you are reporting that we had a defeat of a full regiment without confirmation that we were even attacking the right people, and even with that, we were defeated by a force that was overwhelmingly outnumbered and out armed." He was now beginning to show anger as the blood vessels in his royal temple began to pulsate. "How was this possible, General? Did you not send seasoned troops to exterminate these heretics?"

"Sir, yes sir, we sent some of our best troops,"

"Best troops, General," he interrupted again, this time with a raised voice. "The best troops, are that what you're going to tell me?" His countenance reddened with each passing word. "You're going to tell me that you sent some of our best troops to be massacred by a bunch of mountain sheep farmers?" He paused, growing more upset. "Is that the best we can do, General?" He was now standing, as some of the papal assistants became alarmed.

"Sir, the reports we have coming back are that they had some sort of secret weapon, your Holiness."

"Secret weapon," he said, laughing out loud. His voice rang off the ornately painted cathedral ceiling under which they now stood. Sitting down, he gestured to the papal attendant for a cup to drink before he continued, "Please do explain this, this secret weapon, General."

"Well, Your Excellence, we aren't sure, but we—"

"Aren't *sure*!" the pontiff now screamed. "The Holy Roman Empire loses an entire regiment and you're not sure, General? Maybe I could send the shoe boy here to find out what actually happened! Not sure! I can't believe that's what you came here to report."

"We were attacked by a force unseen and far greater than ours," the general retaliated. He knew this was an implausible fact, yet it was all he or his staff could glean from the few reports of the event.

The pope now sat, sipping the sweet elixir from his golden chalice laden with rubies and crystals, glowering down at Lucier. He was silent as he listened, strumming his multiple-ringed fingers upon the cup. Lucier noticed Lucias had calmed a bit, so like a seasoned swordsman who notices the slightest weakness in his opponent and knows when to parlay a jab with a return thrust, he instinctively felt it was time to continue further. "We only had a few survivors who escaped by throwing themselves into a raging torrent and nearly drowning, but they still managed to make it to safety. They reported an unseen force and a sound so loud it caused horse's heads to explode and the blood in their own heads to boil."

The pope chuckled now but waved his hand for Lucier to continue.

"There were archers posted on the canyon walls surrounding the valley who finished off those who were able to survive the invisible force that took down the front lines. They were pinned in with no protection and nowhere to run."

The pope now clucked, "Tsk, tsk, tsk," sipping complacently again at his chalice.

The general stood silent, seeing that he was being patronized by his Holiness. He tightened his chest muscles under his armor to force his anger to remain in control. He continued, "Sir, we lost a lot of good men up there."

"The Lord has mercy on the just and the unjust, but we cannot allow heretics to defeat the army of God." He now spoke in a soft voice, but suddenly, as if possessed, he shrieked, "Now *can we, General!*" He angrily banged his cup down on the arm of the throne, causing the remaining liquid within to go spraying all over his robes and the expensive Persian carpeting. He went into a fury of rage, tongue lashing those around him, spewing verbal threats at the party before him until he was nearly foaming at the mouth.

Seething the words through his teeth, he said slowly and deliberately, "I don't care how long it takes, but I want this mountain vermin hunted down and obliterated from the face of the earth!" He continued to speak the words with teeth clenched, "They are *not* the Apostle Speakers!" Again he slammed his fist on the arm of the golden gilded throne in rage. "There is no such thing, and I want *you*, General, to lead the next expedition, and I want it done right this time. Do we understand one another, General!" He now boiled with vengeance and anger.

"Yes sir, your Holiness sir," the general said, snapping his heels together and standing firmly at attention with all his might, as if to say yes with his voice and his body.

"Good day, General!"

With that, the military party spun on their heels and ceremoniously departed the papal chamber.

The chamber doors had not fully shut when Cardinal Augustus emerged from behind the long curtain in the shadows of the corner of the large room, walking up to within close earshot of His Excellence and ceremoniously bowing as he strode. Still holding his bowed position, he bent near the papal ear, whispering with full breath, "You know as well as I that if the Word they possess breaches those granite walls, our control of this empire will be at risk."

"Yes, of course," the pope responded, still fuming from the previous encounter.

"You must not rely on these military types alone. Allow me to send the clergy with them, for they will not be met with the same force as these bloodthirsty types. Besides, the Lord God commands it as he did at the Nicene council seven hundred years ago."

The pope nodded in agreement, and then he glared into the face of the most-favored cardinal, "I know full well the risks of this Word—the Word that we hold dear—carelessly being carried by these lay speakers. Yet, what bothers me most, Augustus, what keeps me awake in the blackest moments of the night, are what these innocent, ignorant souls would do should they learn that they can embrace the Word of God without the need of a clergy or worse, learn that they can accept Christ into their hearts and obtain heaven without penance toward the church." He glared sullenly at Augustus before continuing. "Do you realize the depth of this threat? That's not all. Then there are those words that we do not know, those words not accepted by the council."

He paused, leaning back and rubbing his ring-laden hand under his chin.

"You see, these words, my friend, any and all, they are like light to the soul. They can bring hope to those in the darkness or despair to those that are without." He held his pose, but his eyes fell upon the now-standing cardinal. "Are we the ones without, my friend? Or are *we* the ones searching for the light?"

Chapter 13

DAWN OF A NEW DAY

And the angel answered and said to him, "I am Gabriel, who stands in the presence of God, and was sent to speak to you and bring you these glad tidings.

—Luke 1:19

Jakob awoke to the soft, hushed sound of his grandfather reciting, "Many have undertaken to draw up an account of the things that have been fulfilled among us, just as they were handed down to us by those who from the first were eyewitnesses and servants of the word. Therefore, since I have carefully investigated everything from the beginning, it seemed fitting to me to write an orderly account for you, most excellent Theophilus, so that you may know the certainty of the things you have been taught."

Jakob rose up from his bed, leaning back on one arm and rubbing his face with the other, trying to clear the many hours of sleep from his eyes. He looked around the room that their honorable host, Master Waldo, had provided. The light filtered in as if it were still morning. He felt as if he had slept for ages again, but this time, he didn't awake to the sudden need to flee.

His grandfather knelt on an animal hide spread on the floor in front of the stone fireplace, which was burning a low fire. There he continued his biblical recital, with his eyes closed and his head bowed in prayer. "In the time of Herod king of Judea there was a priest named Zechariah, who belonged to the priestly division of Abijah; his wife Elizabeth was also a descendant of Aaron. Both of them were upright in the sight of God, observing all the Lord's commandments and regulations blamelessly. But they had no children, because Elizabeth was barren; and they were both well along in years."

Jakob's eyes drifted around the room as his grandfather continued on. The walls were dark and ornately trimmed with wood that led up the walls a considerable distance above their heads to the ornately trimmed ceiling overhead. An enormous candelabra hung from the ceiling, having been placed in the area of the room that required light after dark. There was sparse furniture, but the few pieces that did exist looked exotic in their construction.

Jakob's grandfather's face danced in the early morning firelight, half lit by the light filtering into the room from the morning sun, half from the fire. He looked refreshed and youthful. Evidently their rest had refreshed him with revived vigor. Sensing Jakob's awakening, he paused and turned, seeing Jakob sitting up in bed.

"Come, my son, let's pray together."

Jakob crawled out of the nice, soft, warm bed, feeling his bare feet hitting the chilly marble floor. It briefly took his breath away. "Ooh, cold floor."

"Come by the fire, it will warm you."

Jakob walked over and knelt down next to his grandfather.

"Are you ready?" his grandfather said, looking down at him.

Jakob nodded, and Arktos began, "Heavenly Father, thank you for the many blessings in our lives. Thank you for giving us the gifts we will share with all your people. We pray that you watch over the Vaudois, our families, and our hosts, for we know that we live only to serve you. Thank you for giving us your Son, Jesus Christ, who died on the cross so that we can live, free of our sins, if we choose to live as he did. Humbly, Father, I pray that you will bless us and watch over us, for it is in God's holy name I pray, amen."

There was a gentle knock at the door.

Jakob rose and quickly crossed the room to the thick-timbered door "Yes, who is it?" he said before opening the latch.

"It is I, Gabriel. I have come to invite you to the morning meal."

Arktos arose and nodded for Jakob to open the door. "Come in, my friend," Arktos said as Jakob slowly and cautiously opened the heavy door.

"That is fine, sir; I have other guests to invite, but thank you nonetheless."

"Yes, we appreciate you and your master's hospitality. We will be ready shortly."

"Just come down the hall and turn left. We will be serving in the dining hall."

"Thank you again, brother in Christ."

With that, Gabriel saluted them and quickly walked on to the next room. Jakob shut the door.

"Wow, another meal," he said, his eyes wide with excitement.

Grandfather smiled, pleased. "Yes, my son, this is exceptionally gratifying, but we must soon give thanks by giving back with the gifts God has bestowed upon us."

"Then let's practice, Grandfather, for I do not want to disappoint Master Waldo."

"Yes, my son, let us practice."

They returned to the fire and knelt, again this time both continuing in the book of Luke. "Then an angel of the Lord appeared to him, standing at the right side of the altar of incense. When Zechariah saw him, he was startled and was gripped with fear. But the angel said to him: 'Do not be afraid, Zechariah; your prayer has been heard. Your wife Elizabeth will bear you a son, and you are to give him the name John.'"

The fire crackled as they carried on quoting Scripture, enjoying the togetherness they now shared in this apparent haven of safety.

"Zechariah asked the angel, 'How can I be sure of this? I am an old man and my wife is well along in years.' The angel answered, 'I am Gabriel. I stand in the presence of God, and I have been sent to speak to you and to tell you this good news.'"

They both paused, looking at one another, both knowing they had just had the same thought.

"Gabriel? Grandfather, you don't think . . . ?"

Arktos did not answer, turning back toward the fire and silently staring into the burning embers.

"You don't think this could be that Gabriel? Could it be, Papa?"

The elder's eyes were now closed, his head again bowed. He replied as if speaking from somewhere else, "It is not up to us to judge or make assumptions based on things in this world, my son. We must accept what God has given us and welcome each day into our hearts."

Jakob felt a familiar tingle down his spine. He shivered at the feeling, and his mind instantly began to drift as he too turned back toward the fireplace, watching the dancing embers.

He could see Jean Paul running toward him on the mountainside. The rain fell on his face, but he felt the heat from the bolt burning through his body. His head swam. He could see the vast army below being crushed by the invisible force, as if a hand had stopped and pushed them into the earth. Then again, he was in the cave. This time the dove flew up from the stone table toward a shaft of light. His eyes now focused again as a wisp of smoke trailed up the chimney.

The knock at the door startled them both.

Jakob rushed back to the door, "Yes, we are coming," he said to the closed door.

"Yes sir," an unknown voice on the other side responded. "Our master seeks your audience; they are all waiting for you in the dining hall."

"We'll be right there."

"Fine, I will let them know, sir."

"Let us not keep our gracious hosts waiting," Arktos said, rising and putting his arm around his grandson.

Jakob looked back over his shoulder as they left the room, and for a brief instant he thought he saw a dove sitting on his bed. The door closed, and it was gone.

Things are happening too fast, he thought as they followed Waldo's servant to the dining hall. *Too fast. I'm just a boy. Why me?*

He felt the warmth of his grandfather's arm around his shoulder, and he felt comforted as they walked down the hallway to the dining hall. *Thank the Lord Grandfather is with me.* His thoughts of home weren't as painful with him here.

"I don't know what I do without you, Grandfather," he said out loud.

"Son, my world would not be the same without you either."

"Let's get this day started, we have much to do."

At that moment, they entered the dining hall, where Marik, Peter, and all the others awaited them and stood at their entrance.

"Ah, my esteemed guests," Peter announced as Jacob and Arktos stood at the doorway to the large hall. "I hope you found our lodgings acceptable?"

"Yes, my lord, we are very blessed."

"We have much to do. Come, let us feed our bodies so we can then feed our souls."

"Amen," Arktos responded.

Chapter 14

INCEPTION

Let our master now command your servants, who are before you, to seek out a man who is a skillful player on the harp. And it shall be that he will play it with his hand when the distressing spirit from God is upon you, and you shall be well.

—1 Samuel 16:16

They began to work in earnest after getting their fill at breakfast that morning. Waldo had a room prepared for the transcription process that was to take place, with Arktos quoting and several scribes ready to write the words down as they were spoken. They planned to work in shifts, with Steffan overseeing the operation. They would work throughout the day or as long as Arktos had the strength to continue.

Jakob sat in on most of the first few days of sessions, but as time went on, he found interests outside of the room as his youthful curiosity took control.

He began to explore Waldo's vast compound. Waldo's travels over the known world had resulted in vast holdings of good that were stored in various warehouses throughout the stronghold. Treasures of all kinds were piled in dusty rooms, some stored meticulously and others hastily stacked. They were all categorized and accounted for by the staff, who worked seemingly around the clock, packing and unpacking goods as they came in, though most of their time now was spent packing and selling goods. Waldo had determined to sell off his holdings and was using these sales to fund the transcription process they had now begun.

Jakob wandered in and out of the warehouses, sometimes finding something of interest to occupy his time. Oftentimes he found crates of goods that were unopened and uninteresting.

One late morning, he found a particular building, offset to the back of the compound. He saw a room he hadn't noticed before with the door ajar. He walked up to the door and pushed it open, wiping cobwebs away, as the door creaked open, he walked into a large room filled with a treasure trove of what appeared to be musical instruments. There were skins stretched over round rings and long cylinders, making drums of all shapes sizes. Jakob tried his hand at some of them, laughing at the amount of racket he could make. The dust stirred at each pounce on a drum, making him cough with laughter.

He continued on farther into the room finding other things, he could see how some might be used to make sounds. There were others he certainly couldn't see how they could be used to make any noise, let alone music. Such was the case when he came upon what appeared to be a broken-stringed instrument in the shape of a pear, but long, wooden, and with knobs at the top. It lay in a skin that had been apparently made to carry it in. He poked his hand into the skin, feeling around for whatever else might be lost in the back. His hand touched upon what felt like a stick. He hesitantly pulled it out, just to see why there was a stick in the bag. To his surprise, there was some hair on the stick, stretched from one end to the other.

Now what in the world, he thought to himself, holding it up and looking at it in the light that filtered in from the dust-covered windows that sat high on the warehouse walls.

The hair was a little frayed on the ends. Not many were left hanging from end to end. He had no idea what this stick with the hair was or what it was used for, but it obviously wasn't suitable for anything by itself. So why was it in the bag with the strange-looking, gourd-like instrument? He held it over the gourd thing, touched the hair on a string that was still somewhat tight on the instrument, and rubbed it.

A funny scratchy noise came from the gourd, with a hint of squeaking interlaced. The hairy stick didn't seem to do much, so he threw it back down on the furry bag. *What a useless instrument, if indeed that's what it is,* he thought to himself as he started to turn to leave.

"Did you like it?" came a voice from the doorway.

The sudden voice in the stillness scared him, causing him to jump. The figure was shadowed from the sunlight coming in from the door so that the face was hidden.

"I'm sorry, I, I was just looking around. I didn't hurt anything," he stammered in apology, worried that he might upset their gracious host—or worse, that his grandfather might find out and cause him to be disgraced in the eyes of their host.

"No worries, my child," came the voice again that was now more familiar. Jakob cautiously moved to where he could get an angle on the face of the speaker. "The master was looking for you. Your grandfather became worried since they had not seen you in a while."

"I'm sorry, I didn't mean to cause anyone to worry, I—" he started, but the voice cut him off.

"Do not worry, my child," replied the voice of Gabriel, which Jakob confirmed as he finally reached a point where the light shone enough on his face that he could see the speaker.

"Did you find the lira interesting?" he asked.

"The lira?"

"The thing you were rubbing the bow across."

"Bow?" The only thing Jakob knew as a bow was one of the best weapons possessed by the mountain militia in the Vaudois. They were taught to use the long bow in the rock school, along with other skills that were considered necessary to be a productive member of the Vaudois. They were all necessary to ensure their survival in the remote regions.

"Yes, the stick with hair," Gabriel continued.

"Oh, that!"

Gabriel now walked past the boy to where the instrument lay, picking it up and holding it in his arm while turning the pegs on the end, causing the strings to begin to hum as he tightened them into tune. With the lira in one hand, he reached for the bow and tightened it at one end, turning a peg so that the hair tightened—what little was left. He then positioned the end of the instrument away from the pegs toward his chest and held it tight against his body while moving his fingers on the strings as he began rubbing the bow back and forth across the strings, as if sawing a log in two. As he did this, suddenly, a noise erupted in the room that sounded like birds, choirs, and voices singing all at once.

Jakob stood motionless as the new foreign melody began to envelop him, circling him, dancing through his thoughts, tickling his toes, and causing his mind to race and his soul began to soar. It was nothing like he had ever heard before in his lifetime—nothing of this earth.

Gabriel stopped, looking at the boy, who now looked as if he had been put into a trance, eyes glazed over, mouth agape.

"Jakob? Jakob?"

His eyes flickered, and he momentarily shuddered, as if waking from a dream. "Aaah, yes, yes sir."

"Are you all right, my child?"

"Yes, yes," he said, now flushed with joy. "That was—that was like nothing I have ever heard before." He spoke now hurriedly and with emotion. "What is that thing? What were you doing?" he asked. Questions now flooded his mind, as if in a frenzy.

"Like I said before, it's a lira, from the Byzantine Empire."

"What were you doing with that stick you call a bow?"

"I was pulling the bow across the strings and playing it. Did you like it?"

"Like it! It was like being in a different world!" Jakob responded, with tears now forming in his eyes. "It felt as if you were speaking to me."

Gabriel put the lira into the fur bag, along with the bow, and tied it shut, picking it up and walking to where Jakob stood.

"Here," he said, handing the bag to Jakob. "I believe the master will want you to have this."

"But I—"

"No worries, my child," he interrupted. "I have a feeling this is something you will want to learn how to play," he said as if he already knew what to expect. "Besides, while your grandfather is busy getting the Scriptures transcribed, you'll need something to keep you from getting into trouble, and well, I've got time. I can teach you to play," Gabriel said with a smile as he put his arm around Jakob.

Jakob looked up at him and smiled but with a slight look of worry on his face. "Are you sure I can learn? That doesn't look easy. I made such a horrible sound when I tried."

"I have faith you will do just fine," Gabriel said, chuckling softly to himself as they walked out of the instrument warehouse and into the sunlight that flooded the large main courtyard they had entered on the first morning they arrived in Lyon. "I will let Master Waldo know you are borrowing his Byzantine lira. He will be glad to hear someone is actually using it instead of it collecting dust."

Suddenly, Jakob felt the now-familiar twinge along his spine. It was a cold autumn morning. He paused and looked up. Gabriel stopped and looked up to see what the boy had suddenly found so captivating above them. Shielding the sun from his eyes as he looked, he saw nothing but a clear, azure blue sky. Jakob still stood looking skyward, eyes glazing over as he stared into space, listening to the voice coming seemingly from above, "*Faith cometh by hearing, and hearing by the Word of God.*"

Gabriel softly put his hand on the boy's forehead, and he came to. "It will be alright. I understand."

Jakob realized he had another episode, but this time, Gabriel was there and brought him back. "You, you heard it too?"

He nodded. "Yes, my child, it seems you have done something pleasing in God's sight. Jakob," he said, quite seriously, "I am here to help you." He put his arm back on Jakob's shoulder and bent over, looking into Jakob's sky blue eyes. "You have nothing to fear, my child. The Lord our God watches over us all. Now let's go get a bite to eat and then get busy learning how this thing can make some music. Does this sound like a pleasant thought?" he said, patting Jakob on the shoulder.

Jakob grinned back. "Why sure," he said, feeling more whole again than he had felt in year. It was almost as if he were speaking to his father once again. "That will be great! Thank you, sir."

"No, thank you," Gabriel responded as they walked toward the kitchen, passing the room where Arktos and scribes continued working. The sound of Scriptures being quoted in slow cadence could be heard.

"Thanks be to God," Gabriel said softly as they strolled past. "Thanks be to God."

Chapter 15

COMING STORMS

The Lord is slow to anger and great in power, and will not at all acquit the wicked. The Lord has His way in the whirlwind and in the storm, and the clouds are the dust of His feet.

—Nahum 1:3

The shortened autumn days enveloped the alpine region as cold air began to claim its icy grip on the realm. The Vaudois people were used to the season and were preparing for the incapacitating days that would keep them inside but made their ministry of faith possible due to the forced isolation. During these long winter months, when travel was at a standstill and outside work was done on an extremely limited basis, the Apostle Speakers polished up their apostolic Scriptures and continued the never-ending task of passing them on to the next generation.

This time of last-minute preparations found Jean Paul and his mother, with the help of their fellow Vaudois brethren, putting the final touches on the hay and grains for the winter. The fellowship he was having with the others made Jakob's absence less painful for Jean Paul. In the meantime, both he and Julia kept busy working. The labor also kept their minds occupied on the task at hand.

Preparations were also being made in the event of another attack. The elders were certain word would have made it to Rome and the church would seek revenge. They had gone through the battle sight, burning bodies in massive funeral pyres, each one being a temporary monument to the insanity that now gripped an empire that was supposed to represent the holiest of holies, the embodiment of Christ on earth. Instead it wrought its will savagely upon those who were unwilling to convert and follow its doctrine.

Once the flesh and bone had been cleared, then the most valuable pieces of armament were recovered and repaired. They were stored in caches to be used in the inevitable future battles that would come. They found much-needed tack for their horses, which was a rarity here in the Vaudois. Here in the mountains, skins and handmade leather ropes were usually all that was available for riding gear. Now, with the gleaning of the battlefield, they for once had supplies that were rarely seen in this remote region.

Although it was gruesome work, the elders felt this was a mixed blessing. The Lord was providing for them, but then they truly did not want their differences with the Holy Roman Empire to come to all-out warfare. However, this was not in their hands, and if the Lord wanted them to fight for the Word they had been entrusted with, then they would prepare to the best of their abilities for what lay ahead.

In some way, they wished that the tragedy had never occurred. They feared the wrath of Rome might be worse than the outcome of the first onslaught might have ended in. They couldn't know that their total annihilation was Rome's ultimate objective in the first and all subsequent attacks. They were going to need all the help they could get from neighboring Vaudois and the fresh supply of armament they now collected in troves from the decimated battle site. However, nothing would compare to the power of God that had protected them previously. That power was all that stood between them and total destruction or capture. Everyone knew that capture usually ended in a tortured death, so to die in battle would be a gain.

Jean Paul had not seen the vision of his father again since the morning in the pasture when Lorenz visited him. He had not said a word about it to his mother for fear that it might cause her to fall into a state of despair. Having lost both his father and Julia's parents at such a young age had left him more skeptical than most Vaudoisians. This caused his mother concern, and she prayed for his wellbeing often.

Julia daily asked God to touch Jean Paul's troubled heart and to ease his pain. But now, with the recent tragic events and more looming on the horizon, Jean Paul had seemed to become more mature and accepting. Knowing this, she also took comfort in knowing that winter would prolong any further immediate papal attacks. The combination of the two put her heart somewhat more at ease, yet she sensed there was still something brewing in thoughts of her oldest son. She felt she needed to speak to Jean Paul because she feared he was drifting away from her. With this in mind, late one evening, after the girls had gone to bed, she sat with him by the fireplace. Somehow she would find a way to break through to him.

She was knitting a sweater as they sat together, mother and son. Jean Paul was silent as he sat and watched the flames, having just come back in from bringing in more logs for the fire.

"How's the temperature outside tonight?" she asked, trying to stir conversation.

"Cold," he answered abruptly, going back to his thoughts and avoiding eye contact by looking back into the fire.

"Did you get the load of wool taken down to the village today?"

"Yes."

"Good," she said, desperately trying to think of something else to say to elicit some type of conversation, but she was drawing a blank at every turn.

"Have you practiced any Scriptures lately, son?"

"No, I've been busy preparing with the militia."

"I know, but we must keep the Word of God close," she said in a hopeful tone.

"Would you mind reciting some now?" she asked hesitantly, knowing that if he said no, she might break down. "I would really like it."

She couldn't take another night of sitting in silence until he retired to bed or fell asleep in the chair, which was usually the case lately since he had been working hard both on the farm and with the Vaudois militia men preparing defenses and armor for the next inevitable attacks. In the back of her mind, she knew nothing would protect them physically other than leaving and trying to hide somewhere else, but this was where they started and where they would always be. Running away was not an option. She knew from the first attack that God had been on their side and was the only reason they were spared. Of course, the Vaudois archers helped to finish off the few soldiers who weren't killed in the first wave of death.

With that in mind, Julia felt keeping the Word of the Lord close to their hearts and minds was probably the best defense they could find. She pursued Jean Paul further. He had not spoken since her first request, but then he began, slowly and shakily.

He had not recited in a while, and the words were not coming to mind swiftly enough. He felt ashamed since this was the gift they had been given. To lose this would be worse than anything any of them could imagine, so he felt slightly angry at himself for allowing the other things to hinder his daily devotion. Feeling the redness on his neck from part embarrassment and anger, he continued on, speaking now so his mother could enjoy the words as she sat knitting.

"Then Jesus came from Galilee to the Jordan to be baptized by John. But John tried to deter him, saying, 'I need to be baptized by you, and do you come to me?' Jesus replied, 'Let it be so now; it is proper for us to do this to fulfill all righteousness.' Then John consented.

"As soon as Jesus was baptized, he went up out of the water. At that moment, heaven was opened and he saw the Spirit of God descending like a dove and lighting on him. And a voice from heaven said, 'This is my Son, whom I love; with him, I am well pleased.'"

He paused for a moment and saw his mother look up from her work and smile.

"Very good, son, thank you for making my heart warm with joy."

"Yes, Mother, I know, you are welcome. I'm sorry that I have not been more diligent in my studies lately. It's just that there is so much to do, now that it's just us."

"Yes dear, don't worry. I understand, and I am not upset. The Lord our God will protect us, and we should not forget. And like you said, as did Jesus, with you, I am well pleased."

He smiled and continued on until he reached the end of the book of John.

As the fire died down, he sat for a while after his mother went to bed and thought about all the many things that needed to be done and things he could not know that needed to be done. It overwhelmed him to the point that he was forced to slide out of his chair and onto the floor. Turning, he faced his chair and leaned on the seat with his hands in prayer and prayed, "God in heaven, our Father, Maker of heaven and earth," he paused, searching for the grace inside, "Lord I seek your guidance. I seek your wisdom, for we are doing everything we can to do your will. Please forgive me for when I digress and don't perform my devotionals daily as I should be doing, for the last thing on earth I would want to do would be to lose your Word, Lord." He lowered his head more until it rested on his hands, and he sat there praying silently until he unexpectedly drifted off to sleep.

Clouds surrounded him. It was as if he were floating. He then realized he was riding a mighty, stately horse, himself dressed in full battle armor, up a mountain. He rode the horse upward through the thick clouds until they reached an open area. Up ahead was a cave.

He dismounted from the horse and was walking up to the mouth of the cave when he heard what sounded like someone calling his name. He spun around but could not see anyone. When he turned back around to continue onward, out of the top of the cave flew a white dove. It landed in a spruce tree nearby.

The scene was surreal yet peaceful. The wind began to pick up, and the sky grew dark. He moved to remount his horse, but as he watched in horror, the horse's legs began to melt into the earth until it disappeared. He stood there, blood dripping from the sword he now held in his hand. He tried to move, but his legs felt like they, like the horse, were starting to melt in to the earth.

"God help me," he tried to call out, but his voice wouldn't work.

He tried again, "God please help me!"

"Seek the shelter of the cave," a voice whispered.

He looked, but again, he did not see anyone. He tried moving, but instead, he suddenly shot like a bolt to the entrance of the cave, as if flying, dropping his sword as it clattered to the stones below. He could see a dim light from within and started to enter when he heard a voice again.

"Jean Paul."

His father stood before him at the mouth of the cave, dressed in battle armor, gesturing for him to come. As if in slow motion, he tried to move, but again, he could not.

"Jean Paul."

His father stood now, sorrowfully looking at him in the bluish tint of light that was barely able to filter through the dark clouds that were now overhead. It was eerily silent. Lightning flashed, and then he was gone.

"Jean Paul, wake up!"

He felt a hand on his shoulder, and suddenly he jumped.

"You were lying face down in the chair," his mother said, standing behind him. "I didn't mean to alarm you. I only wanted to wake you out of the terrible dream it seemed you were having so you could get to bed and get some decent rest."

"Yes, Mother, I'm sorry. I was just praying and then—"

"It's alright," she said, stopping him, "I heard you making noises and thought you were hurt and came to check on you."

He put his hand on hers and patted it, saying, "Thank you, Mother. I love you."

She turned and went back to bed. Jean Paul retired to his side of the bedroom and laid back down in his bed this time, trying to shake the image of the cave and the light inside out of his mind.

What did it all mean, and who was talking to him in the dream? "God, please watch over us all, Amen," he prayed, and then he quickly fell into a peaceful slumber.

Chapter 16

CONVERSION OR DEATH

Then I will teach transgressors Your ways, and sinners shall be converted to You.

—Psalm 51:13

L ucier had left the papal meeting that day with a bitter chip on his shoulder. Here he was, in the autumn of his life, being reprimanded by his Holiness. *How demeaning*, he thought. *I'll be damned if I let a priest tell me how to command my army.* In the back of his mind, he couldn't help getting the feeling he was being watched. Just to be safe, a few blocks away from St. Peter's Square, he stopped by a local pub for a brief respite and rejuvenation of his soul before heading off to a meeting at central headquarters.

It was dark and gloomy in the tavern, even at this time of day. He needed time to regroup. He ordered his usual grog and sipped slowly at the bitter ale as it slowly numbed the pain of resentment that brewed in his heart. *God has put me in this position, yet I feel like I'm being used as a pawn for another's purposeful gain,* he reflected. Again, he tried to block the ill wind of thought that continually seemed to try to seep into his mind. Another pint later, he was remiss about the encounter and emboldened to carry on his mission, putting his conscience's sensitivities aside as a sign of being weak as he left the confines of the bar. "Toughen up soldier," he ordered himself as he bit his lip in anger as he walked toward the officer's legion headquarters for a meeting with his top commanders and advisors. "Time to make things happen."

As he crossed the threshold the entrance hall of the headquarters, the battle-dressed Roman guards snapped to attention. He stepped hastily past, saluting as he went. He found the conference room that was already occupied by several lower field generals in his command along with the central region's officer corps. In addition, there were papal adjuncts in attendance. He scoffed to himself, *The papacy wouldn't dare miss out on knowing what is going on.* Then he noticed the pope's key cardinal, Augustus, was already in attendance. He stood at the head of the table. Lucier's skin crawled, for he now saw this was not going to be a purely military briefing, as he had expected. He had sent his aide ahead to brief the room of his intentions; however, he had none regarding the papacy, yet here they were now in full force.

As he entered, several lower-ranking officers stood at attention. He curtly told them, "Stand at ease, men." Then he walked to the front of the room and up to Augustus, who now stood as if he were about to lead them all in mass.

"Cardinal Augustus, I didn't know that His Excellence was so bored that he needed to be notified of every little meeting held by our Royal guard," he said bitterly in the face of the cardinal, who smiled an evil sneer of a grin in response to the emotional statement.

"I am here to honor God and present an option that will," he paused ceremoniously to garner the full attention from the remainder of those present, just in case they weren't already paying full attention, "hopefully alleviate the unnecessary loss of our valuable guard."

Lucier's teeth ground in his jaw as he tried to restrain his anger. He could feel his temples beginning to throb. His military instinct was to crush this pompous, feeble, egotistical being in front of him, but fortunately, his officer training had prepared him for years to follow proper military protocol, as well as papal protocol, so he dismissed the urge to reach for his short saber and sever the head of this sickly, pale excuse for a human being who stood defiantly in front of him. The sickness that he represented, in all his regalia of the papal court, was the Holy Roman Catholic Church.

Lucier responded as best he could without raising his voice, but he spoke seething through his teeth. "Then please do tell," he started, trying to control his anger, "what have you in store for us, dear cardinal." With each word, he grew increasingly sickened at the sight of the pontiff's pawn standing before him. "Oh don't tell me, the papacy is now preparing battlefield strategies as part of their campaign to reach out to nonbelievers?" The others in the room erupted in nervous laughter.

Augustus stood, not amused by the retort. He calmly and icily waited, as the laughter ended to nothingness and then dread. "May I, General Sir?" he asked as he motioned to the chair at the head of the table.

"Please do, Cardinal."

The cardinal took his place, pushing back his robes and chair as he sat gently, placing his thickly sleeved arms with jewel-encrusted, ringed fingers folded on the table. He nodded a signal to the adjuncts to bring the prepared tablets to the front.

Unfolding the documents, he began, "His Holy Roman emperor and papal entity, Pope Lucias III, sends forth edict number 785.3, that all persons in the northern regions of the Holy Roman Empire must heretofore and at once cease and desist all previous forms of religion, succumbing to the only true form of faith in Christianity, the Holy Roman Catholic Church. Any other form of Christianity henceforth will be considered heresy and as such an abomination and subsequently a threat to the sovereignty of the Holy Roman Empire. Because there may be pockets of non-Catholic believers present in the northernmost reaches of our domain, we are announcing the creation of a missionary force to be sent out immediately as a forerunner to any further military operations. Once the teams have been dispersed and given a predetermined amount of time, allowing souls to be converted to the only true form of Christianity, then we will continue the brute force conversions that would require conversion or death as the ultimatums."

He paused, looking up from the scrolls. "Are there any questions?"

Lucier looked around the room, as most, if not all, of the military leaders present looked at him with raised eyebrows, as if to say, "All right then, this matter is out of our hands for the time being." This was fine with Lucier since this would give them more time to plan and prepare. And in essence, these missionary priests could retrieve needed information about the location and logistics of the heretics they were going to be fighting against. Not to mention the winter months would soon be upon the northern region and any military operation would be foolhardy and perilous at this time.

"You have prepared a team already?" he asked the cardinal.

"Yes, they are ready to leave immediately and only await our approval from this consulate to embark upon their journeys."

"Very well, give us a moment together alone, and we will provide you with an answer in the next few minutes," he said as he held his arm pointed toward the door, showing the cardinal and his entourage the way out.

"We will wait outside" the cardinal said, rising and nodding to his adjuncts to retrieve the documents that had been unfolded.

Lucier and his generals met shortly afterward with him, explaining the good fortune that this provided them. He explained that the additional time could be spent obtaining maps of the terrain on the area as well as giving them time to prepare troops for the high-altitude terrain. Before they underestimated this element, which may have been responsible for the detriment of the previous operation.

They gave their approval, which was merely a formality since the papal decision had already been proclaimed. Their approval was simply a sign of acknowledgment and submission to the seat of the pope, which was now the supreme command and apparent dictator ruling the entire once-illustrious Roman Empire.

Subsequently, the missionaries who had been preselected were notified and left for the furthest reaches of the Holy Roman Empire, where they prepared to try to convert as many poor souls over to Catholicism as possible, if for no other reason than to save their lives and souls in one fell swoop.

As the missionary teams headed north out of the city of Rome, cold northern winds wisped around them—a foreboding of what was soon to come. They were escorted with only a handful of papal guards—soldiers who were only there for the protection of the priests who would be traveling into potentially hostile regions. They were expendable forces but a necessary precaution since the roads were swarming with bandits, marauders, and murderers.

The snows had begun to fall in the alpine regions now. As the missionary contingent marched out of the holy city, the leaves of autumn fell silently, softly landing on the ground and making a blanket of color. The bitter air of religious reformation preceded their formations. As foul breath exhales from a voracious beast, so did they come to proclaim in the name of the Holy Roman Empire their will and religion upon the most loyal of Christian people who had existed since the time of Christ.

Painful days lie ahead, for all.

Chapter 17

A SONG FOR HOME

Hear now My words: If there is a prophet among you, I, the Lord,
make Myself known to him in a vision; I speak to him in a dream.
—Numbers 12:6

Days turned into weeks as the weather grew cold. Unaffected
by the weather outside, Arktos and the team of scribes led by
Steffan continued to compile verse after verse, chapter after
chapter of Scriptures from the remarkable old man's memory. At times
they would have to take breaks since the mental focus it required of him
was draining. The ability to recall the multitude of words—words that
had been saved for generations since the original words were spoken by
the apostles—was a miracle in itself. Arktos could feel a power that was
not of this world flowing through him during the sessions. Although he
was a source for the will of God, it tired him physically. Even though they
had been going nonstop for several months, he refused to rest. Eventually,
when Christmas was just a couple weeks away, he became so weak from
the magnitude of work that he fell ill, and they were forced to stop.

At the same time, Jakob was being tutored spiritually and musically by
Gabriel. They became quite close. The boy and his angelic guard were
nearly inseparable, which was helpful to Arktos, since he did not have
to watch over his grandson. Gabriel's help with Jakob left him free to
work. Jakob was becoming more and more proficient with the lira and
had now learned several songs quite well.

The day was cold and blustery outside, but inside their room, Jakob
sat with his grandfather, who was lying in his bed, resting, and trying

to regain his strength, which had been dragged down from the recent cold he had suffered from, as well as his work. Peter was worried that Arktos was pushing himself too hard and had ordered them to stop the work until after Christmas. Now Arktos rested peacefully, knowing he was not letting others down by not pushing onward. The rest was rewarding as well, since he had not spent much time with Jakob the past few months.

The fire felt warm on such a cold, cloudy day. Marik had stopped by earlier to visit and left with them some hot drinks, which they now sipped as they talked.

"Grandfather, have you heard any word from home?" Jakob asked.

He shook his head no as he sipped the dark drink, which was scented with mint but quite reviving.

"I miss them—Grandmother, my sisters, Jean Paul, and Mother," he said, trailing off as he looked toward the fire as he drank.

"Me too, son, me too," the old man said. He thought of his wife of many years. She was as strong a mountain woman as any. The years had bent her body down physically, but in his mind, he could still see the days when her stunning beauty would take his breath away. They spent many glorious spring days holding hands and walking along the cascading mountain streams. Love was young, as were they, free as the wind. It was a bountiful time in the Vaudois. There were several years of bountiful harvest so that the flocks were abundant, families grew large, and lovers could relish in the splendor of the beauty of everything that surrounded them. He could remember that they would often quote their favorite Psalms for one another. Then they would lay down in the soft grasses, the tender blades gently bowing to their caresses, the sweetness of her breath as his lips met hers.

They sat in silence, each in their own thoughts of home, of love. Flames from the fire made shadows dance on the walls as they sat wondering and watching as their minds drifted from one memory to the next.

Eventually Arktos broke the silence, "Play me something you've learned, will you, my son?"

Jakob looked up at his grandfather, smiling. "Yes," he said as he got up and walked over to his lira, which was wrapped in the protective skin in the corner of the room. He took a couple of minutes to tune the strings, as he had learned from Gabriel, and then tightened the bow and spread rosin on them, so the hairs could aptly flow across the strings.

"Do you have any special requests, Grandfather?" he asked.

"No, my son, anything, anything you play will be a blessing," he said as he leaned back in his bed, sitting his cup on the table nearby and closing his eyes in preparation.

Jakob had been learning ancient songs in his lessons with Gabriel—songs that were biblical in nature. Up till now he had not learned them with any words. He just learned the basic melodies, so their true meaning was unclear, but the melodies were rich and rewarding in their tone. When he practiced alone, he could play the songs while feeling his spirit soar with the sound of the music, vibrating into the midst of all that surrounded him.

Up until now, he and Gabriel had trained in a remote location of the compound so as not to be heard by anyone else. Even in Jakob's solo practices, he kept to himself and out of earshot of anyone, at the instruction of Gabriel. So now, here in the presence of his grandfather, this was his first performance for anyone else other than Gabriel.

Jakob began with a song, which Gabriel taught him from the forty-sixth Psalm, gently pulling the bow across the three strings of the lira, quickly losing himself into the melody as he went. His mind wrapped around the notes of the song, unaware of the world around him. As he played his grandfather lay still, his eyes closed, and was silent. He did not move, except for the slow rise and fall of his chest.

The music wrapped itself around the room and danced with the shadow of the flames around the walls. Jakob, now moving, his body swaying with the music, was still unaware of anything other than what the melody was provoking him to play next. He glided wistfully, as free as the wind. He was back in the Alps, his home, the wind blowing his hair, the fresh smell of mountain laurels blooming in the spring.

The notes touched his heart, warming his soul. He continued playing, free, unabated, touching warmth and feelings that tingled his soul. He was nearly to the end of the song, his mind effortlessly floating, weightless, his fingers, instrument, and mind one being, when his grandfather, suddenly and without warning, shouted "Stop, sssstop, *stop!*" He suddenly sat upright, eyes wide open, hands in front of him as if he were trying to prevent someone or something from performing some act that must have caused him alarm.

Jakob instantly stopped, feeling ashamed that he had done something wrong. As he did, Arktos, now aware of what he had just done, shook his head, dropped his arms, and began rubbing his eyes with one hand while leaning back on one arm. "What," confused, he grasped for words to describe it, "in God's holy name," he said as if in a state of shock, "was that?"

"What, Grandfather, what?" Jakob worriedly asked for fear the music had caused this violent reaction. "Was it that bad?" Jakob asked, now fully ashamed at what apparently seemed like something he had done wrong or played badly.

"No, no, my son," Arktos said, shaking his head, trying to regain his composure. "It, it wasn't that."

"What?" Jakob asked, now totally confused. "What do you mean?" he asked again, trying to gain some sort of foothold on reality now.

"I don't know," Arktos replied, again refocused. "No, I didn't know what was happening, but I was . . ." Now it was as if he were afraid to say it. "I was not here," he said, turning and looking at Jakob, who now had sat with the lira on his lap. He was terribly concerned about his grandfather's mental state.

"Do I need to send for Master Waldo? Do you need a doctor, Grandfather?"

"No, no certainly not. I'm perfectly fine," he gruffly replied, swelling up his chest at the mention of his health.

"But if you were taken away or gone somewhere else, but I saw you here the entire time, then," he searched for meaning, "well then, how—"

"I don't know," Arktos said, interrupting Jakob's stammering. "All I know is that I was not here. I was." He was trying hard not to believe the vision he had just had, but he couldn't. "I think I was back home."

Jakob now looked at Arktos with furrowed brows, in deep concern that something was truly wrong with his beloved grandfather. "You mean you dreamed you were back home?" he said, trying to reaffirm what he had just heard.

"No, my son, I *was* back home!"

"Grandfather, you were here with me the whole time. How could you—"

"I'm telling you, I was there! They were advancing on us, like before, only this time they weren't being stopped by the hand of God. They were marching straight into Rora, killing and burning everything in their path." He glared at Jakob, biting his lower lip in fear of what he had seen. Then he continued, "I was there. I could feel the heat from the fires, the sounds of the battle, and the . . ." He stopped talking and bowed his head.

"The what? You were saying?"

"Nothing, my son." He bowed his head now. In his heart, he knew the truth, "It was a vision. I'm sure God gave me a vision, that's all."

Jakob bowed his head as well. He felt guilty for something he was still unsure of, but he had to tell grandfather now what he felt. "Grandfather?"

"Yes," the old man said, now leaning back in his bed once more, reaching for his drink, still trying to blink the scene he had just seen from his eyes.

"Gabriel warned me."

He looked up, slightly startled. "Warned you?" he asked with a perplexed brow. "Warned you of what?" he asked now, interested and concerned at the same time.

"He said that my music would transcend souls and time and to be careful when and where I played it," he said, unbelieving of his own words.

Then, unaware of the source of the thought, the song Jakob had just played came back to him. Arktos began to sing the words to the song that neither of them realized until now that Jakob had just played. "God is our refuge and strength, a very present help in trouble. Therefore will not we fear, though the earth be removed, and though the mountains be carried into the midst of the sea; though the waters thereof roar and be troubled, though the mountains shake with the swelling thereof. Selah. There is a river, the streams whereof shall make glad the city of God, the holy place of the tabernacles of the Most High. God is in the midst of her; she shall not be moved: God shall help her, and that right early. The heathen raged, the kingdoms were moved: He uttered His voice, the earth melted."

Then he paused, looking at the boy who seemed now totally bewildered and blushed from emotions at the bewildering finding. "Son."

"Yes, yes, Grandfather?"

"My son, you are blessed by the hand of God."

Jakob looked scared at the powerful accusation. Arktos had spoken the lines of the song that belonged to the melody Jakob had unknowingly played. When the realization of the words, the melody, and the meaning of the moment hit him, it was like seeing the sunrise for the very first time. He wanted to shout for joy! He could barely contain his excitement for what he had just become aware of.

"My son, you have been blessed with a power, an ability that is so strong, it can evaporate one's mind and put one into another place and time," he now said, excitedly rising up out of the bed and standing, shakily but with purpose.

The boy now sat stunned and in silence as the fear of the unknown and the fear of what he had just done to his grandfather collided in his mind. He became pale with alarm. His heart told him it was worthy, but his mind was racing for explanations he could not reach in this terrestrial world.

"My son, you sent me to the future, to where our world would melt as God has said, by the hands of the unrighteousness that spreads across our home like a demonic cancer."

Jakob was numb with all the emotions of fear, joy, anxiety, and pain now spinning around in his head, to the point that he felt like throwing up. He felt nauseous as he leaned over, bending over his lira toward the floor.

"Stop, stop please, just stop talking, Papa," he said sickly as he placed his instrument on the floor beside the chair. "I don't feel well," he said, sliding out of the chair and onto the floor on all fours. The room spun around, and he gasped for air. He tried to hold on but felt himself slipping, slipping away. The last thing he remembered was the wool of the fur rug pushing against his face; then it was dark.

Chapter 18

CHRISTMAS LOVE

To the Chief Musician. On a stringed instrument. A Psalm of David.
Hear my cry, O God; Attend to my prayer.

—Psalm 61:1

For as long as anyone could remember, the Christmas celebration was a badly needed break during the cold winter months in the Vaudois. Special treats had been set aside and saved just for the time when friends, neighbors, and families would come together to celebrate the birth of Jesus Christ.

Julia, Maria, and the girls had eagerly prepared for the feast of the yuletide for days, baking breads, cakes, and pies. Fruits gathered in the fall had been preserved, some just for this particular feast. The banquet hall next to the church in the village was decorated in beautiful but Spartan splendor. Boughs of spruce lined with red berries, wreaths from bough of evergreens, lace, intertwined, with bows made from twine and grasses collected gave a fresh smell to the air. Hundreds of candles gently flickered, making the whole scene glow with beauty and joy.

The table where the food was placed groaned beneath the weight of the massive feast that lay prepared of which all were to partake. There were meats, cheeses, baked goods, and preserved vegetables in dishes, decorated into various formations. Large flasks of drinks of various kinds lined the length of the table so that there was scarcely a bare spot to be seen.

The entire Vaudois was here tonight for the feast, everyone in their best Sunday clothing, all here to honor God and to fellowship and celebrate the birth of Christ. To open the festivities, Pastor Jeanne led the congregation in prayer.

They all stood around the hall, encircling the tables, holding hands, and praying in unison, silently at first. Then the pastor spoke in prayer for all, "Heavenly Father, we all gather here tonight to honor the birth of your Son, Jesus Christ, whom you sent to us so that he may die for our sins. Lord, please watch over us because now more than ever we need your guidance. We are thankful for all the many blessings you have bestowed on us. We thank you for the miracles in our lives, for the precious life you have given us, for your miraculous protection of our people, and for your Word. Lord, help us to carry on your will. We pray for those of us who are not able to be here with us tonight."

Some heads turned while still bowed, looking in the direction of Julia, Jean Paul, his grandmother, and his sisters.

"We ask that you watch over them as they carry on the mission you have given us from the beginning of time, and Lord, we know that we may soon be tested to the length of our endurance, but we thank you for knowing that in Christ we live, and to die for him is to gain. Thank you for all the blessings you have bestowed, for the glorious feast, and for the hands that have prepared it, for in Christ's holy name we pray, amen." Then everyone in the room answered with one voice in unison, "Amen."

Jean Paul looked at his mother, her head still bowed. She slowly looked up at Jean Paul. He noticed tears in her eyes. He moved toward her to comfort her, but before he could reach her, others had also noticed and surrounded her with loving embraces. Jean Paul smiled and felt warmed. Such was their love for one another here in the Vaudois, their home, their sanctuary.

His sisters and grandmother stood off from their mother, so he walked over to them and helped them maneuver toward the banquet table to begin filling wooden plates that had been stacked at one end. He was the father figure now in the home and was doing his best to fill in during his grandfather's absence. He missed Arktos and Jakob, but he knew they were doing a great deed in their mission. He just wished he could be with them at times, but he knew he was needed here at home. With that thought, he continued to visit with friends and family. Tonight was about joy and celebration. The problems that waited were left at the door tonight.

Tonight the birth of Jesus was the celebration. Tonight all the past year's struggles would be momentarily forgotten so that life—the splendor of life itself—could be rewarded with a momentary lapse of fear and worry to be replaced with happiness and the joy of life eternal.

The candles dripped little pools of wax as the magnificent feast was slowly consumed. The stone walls of the grand hall warmed to the touch with the excitement that flowed throughout the evening. Conversation hummed, surrounding the room with warmth that only matched the glow of the candlelight. A comforting warmth—a feeling of considerable relief—came over everyone who was gathered in the banquet hall. They had a feeling that something greater than anything they knew was standing guard tonight—a feeling that God was going to make it all right. God would somehow keep the Word alive. Here in the Vaudois, tonight was about love.

Several hundred miles away, Jakob and his grandfather longed for home. They knew that tonight was the great feast in the banquet hall, and for as long as Jakob could remember, this was one of his favorite nights of the year. After the great feast, they would play children's games and sing ancient hymns.

Things were different now, though. Here in Lyon in the Waldo compound, Jakob was learning a lot while his grandfather was saving the Word of God for humanity through the support of the wealthy merchant, Master Waldo.

But Jakob was changing at the same time. Since the incident in their room, neither he nor his grandfather dared mention it to anyone else other than Gabriel. When they finally did mention it to him, he immediately became solemn and asked that they meet in private to discuss the matter.

He escorted them back to their sleeping chamber and shut the door, looking behind them to make sure they had not been followed. It was only a couple of days before the splendid Christmas feast, but even with the joy of the season in the air, the solemnness with which Gabriel confronted them suddenly erased any thoughts of merriment.

"Please, sit down my friends," he said, moving toward the fireplace and stirring the logs around with a rod that lay next to the hearth as they found their seats. Sparks flew up the chimney as the rearrangement of logs caused the light from the fire to leap into the room, making it brighter and suddenly warmer.

Arktos and Jakob looked at each other, both guessing in their own minds what they were about to hear from Master Waldo's mysterious guard.

Gabriel turned from the fireplace duties and faced them, arms crossed. "Brothers, I have asked you here this evening for a very special reason," he said with gravity in his voice that seemed to make the earth shake. "You both have obviously been chosen, yes, chosen by God, to do great things."

They both nodded in understanding.

"However, there are many things you do not understand and many things that will become clearer to you the more you become enlightened." He spoke softly now, moving closer to them. "You have a gift, each of you. Arktos, the one you possess you are more familiar with and are using now in God's will. The Word you possess is God's Word, not to be owned by any man. The fact that you and Master Waldo are working together to preserve this Word and to spread it to all mankind is entirely a part of God's master plan."

He then turned toward Jakob and spoke slowly and distinctly.

"You, on the other hand, young brother Jakob, have another gift besides the ability your grandfather has—one that is even more powerful."

Arktos looked toward Jakob, reaching out for the boy's hand, laying his gently on top of Jakob's to comfort his fears.

"You have the ability to change the world through music."

Jakob nodded but could not speak.

"You cannot blindly play music in front of people without knowing how to control your gift or else unwarranted things can take place."

Jakob looked at his grandfather, who was already staring in his direction when Gabriel said these words.

"Yes, brother," Arktos said, turning toward Gabriel, "so we have found."

"Jakob's power overwhelmed you to the point you were moved to a different place and time, did he not?"

"Yes, absolutely."

"You're lucky."

"How's that, brother?"

"You could have been killed," Gabriel said, now kneeling down next to Jakob. "My child," he said placing his hand on top of Jakob and his grandfather's, "you can change reality. You can move others' minds to places that have never existed and never will exist." He paused slightly. "You can literally channel into the power of heaven like a river, through which all the infinite spiritual realm can flow, with unprecedented results. You can literally become the hand of God."

With this, he stood up and walked back toward the fire. "But first we have much training to do, lest you make another grave mistake and this time, your poor grandfather may not survive to tell of it."

"So, now you must truly tell us," Arktos hesitated before asking, "are you the angel, the angel," taking in a gulp of air, "Gabriel?" Arktos finally asked.

Gabriel chuckled, "I know what you are thinking, and many thanks be to God, but I hope I have not misled you, fine sir."

"But you know so much."

"I only observe the obvious and listen when the Almighty speaks, as do you."

"I'm sorry if I have insulted you in anyway Master Gabriel. I—"

"No apologies, please. You are like brothers to me, and I feel most honored to know that you think so highly of me. All I can say is that I am inspired to live up to your expectations of me someday—someday soon, I pray." At this he stood and nodded good-bye as he swiftly and quietly left their chamber.

Jakob, still stunned, didn't know what to say.

"Praise the Lord," whispered Arktos.

"Amen," whispered Jakob.

Chapter 19

COMPROMISED

Remember those who rule over you, who have spoken the Word of God to you, whose faith follow, considering the outcome of their conduct.

—Hebrews 13:7

The fingers of Rome stretched beyond the known boundaries of its empire. The once-formidable Roman Empire had shrunk in recent centuries, with the Crusades taking their toll. But the weakening of the Roman politico allowed the Roman Catholic regime to become ever more powerful. The papacy's strength vastly overshadowed the emperor to the point that the position was merely a puppet for the pope.

Those talons reached outward at the behest of the papacy, working their icy clutches into the bodies and souls of the inhabitants of the regions in or around its control, as was the case in Lyon, where papal spies had been sent in search of any heretical activities. The missionary priests had spread into the northern region of the empire as far as the winter storms would allow. They had not yet reached the Vaudois of the Rora. Turin was as close as one group made it before a blizzard drove them into permanent winter shelter.

The spies in Lyon and other cities throughout the region were on the constant lookout for heretics speaking the gospel outside of the confines of the church. Someone having written language would be considered in contempt; someone actually creating manuscripts to be dispersed to the common man would be considered an enemy of the church. For someone to have the ability to be able to translate the Latin into common language would be plausible, but having someone transcribing the Word of God directly from the apostles would be nearly ludicrous.

However, it was indeed Peter Waldo's dream to have the Word of the Apostle Speakers written into a book that would be able to be read in the common language of the day; a layman's Bible. This Bible would consist of the Word collected from the Apostle Speakers, so its variation from Rome's version of the New Testament would differ based on what was actually given to the people of the Vaudois. This difference was of utmost importance to the papacy since any variation was considered inappropriate for literary consumption by the masses.

Of course, several of the writings not included in the New Testament (known as the Gnostic Gospels) had already been collected and archived by the Roman Catholic Church and were closely guarded. Then there were the apocryphal books, part of the Catholic literature, that were given to the congregations as was necessary for mass by the priests of the church. The only Word of God spoken was through the church's ordained priests. Any other Word spoken outside of this realm was considered heresy and considered an abomination to the church, its people, and society as a whole.

Waldo realized the danger he faced, but he kept the activities within the compound closely guarded, letting no one without the proper credentials or background checks to enter within its walls. With the sentries, who were led by Gabriel, there was little fear of their work being compromised. By the same token, Waldo also had his own network of informants placed throughout the region and more heavily dispersed in the Lyon area. It was through this network that he knew of the arrival of Jakob's party on the morning they arrived.

Yet evil was constantly trying to find ways to penetrate into the tender crucible of faith that kept humanity's soul from falling into an abyss of eternal darkness. The eternal battle between the forces of Satan and the heavenly host of angels was never at rest. The battle had now manifested itself on earth as the attempt by humankind and angelic hosts to preserve the precious words given to mankind by God. The forces of evil were doing everything in their power to end this Word and crush it out forever so that only the manuscripts owned by the Roman Catholic church would be left. Their ownership would be closely guarded and interpreted to the masses such that their intent and meaning could be manipulated to benefit the keepers of the word. This would give Satan a firm grasp on mankind, with little hope of salvation, and thus would cause eternal damnation, discounting the sacrifice of God's only Son, a travesty of the gravest consequence.

But darkness walked the earth.

Thus it was not considered out of the ordinary on the cold, gray January morning when a pale young boy dressed in papal garments that were tailored to fit his frail build made an entry beyond the sentry at the Waldo compound, saying he was a courier for the bishop's court and that he had a letter to be delivered in person to Peter Waldo. Papal couriers were not uncommon, since Master Waldo was considered to be an influential figure in the local community and was an active member in the Lyon chapter of the Roman Catholic diocese. Since today's courier was just a young boy, the sentry did not think it necessary to summon Gabriel on the matter and directed the boy to the location of Master Waldo in the compound, sending him on his way unescorted.

The unassuming face of the child, along with the importance of his errand, made for a complacent decision on the part of the humble guard. The boy was purposely sent to take advantage of the guard's optimistic opinion of life. Thus, the door was opened for darkness to enter through the window of faith and hope.

Jakob had finished his morning lesson with Gabriel and felt like he was spiritually walking on air. He had now learned several songs, but better yet, he was learning how particular songs might affect his listeners and when to use them. His youthful vigor for learning was only outdone by his growth-induced hunger, which had struck him now.

He was headed to the kitchen for a late-morning snack when he saw the boy standing in the shadows outside the workroom where his grandfather and scribes worked. At first he thought he was one of

Waldo's servant's children, and he called to him, "Good morning." The boy turned, startled he had been found, and froze.

The boy's odd reaction made Jakob realize something was afoot. The uniform of the papal court, which Gabriel had shown him pictures of to teach him the ranks and offices within the realm of the church, now came back to him in a flash. The boy was out of place outside the door of the workroom. Suddenly Jakob felt his skin begin to crawl at the realization of who the boy was and what he was doing here came to focus in his mind.

Before he could yell for help, the boy dashed off, and the chase began. Jakob pursued him, weaving through crates piled in the courtyard, in and out, seeing him, not seeing him, but still quickly gaining on him. Having lived nearly all his life in the mountains gave him great speed. He was close to grabbing the boy, starting to reach for the tail of his robe, but suddenly as they rounded another pile of boxes he was cut off by a merchant's cart coming through the front gate. The papal spy spryly slid underneath as it passed, escaping outside the gate.

Jakob started to pursue him further, but the sentry above in the watch station called for him to stop. He skidded to a halt just outside the front gate as the devil in the papal cloak sped away, weaving through the crowd and looking back over his shoulder as he ran. Jakob yelled at the sentry, "Why did I have to stop?" He was angry, knowing he could have soon caught the boy.

The guard, who had just finished checking in the delivery on the cart, was startled when he saw the boy running from Jakob. Before he could act, they had both run through the front gate. Fearing a spectacle outside the compound, he was forced to stop the one boy he could catch—Jakob.

"I had no choice," he responded soulfully." He then sounded the horn of alarm. Gabriel and the other sentries quickly arrived at the main gate to find the guard and Jakob standing dejected because of what had just transpired.

The sentry explained to Gabriel what had just happened. They could have gone out and captured the boy, but to pursue him in open daylight would only arouse suspicion of why grown men would be chasing a papal court errand boy.

It was inevitable. The Word would be known to all soon enough. There was the sense of urgency, and everyone knew there was no turning back. Word would now get back to the bishop stationed in Lyon and then eventually back to Rome.

Jakob felt responsible for not catching the imp. He had become soft living here in these plush furnishings. His strength from working out on the high mountain pastures was weakening. He stood with Gabriel and the other guards now as they discussed contingency plans on what to expect and what their next steps would be when more papal investigators came. They sent word to Master Waldo, who then summoned everyone into the main courtyard. He said he had something terribly important for everyone to hear and that he would give everyone a chance to get assembled before he started.

They were scattered about the large courtyard, some sitting on crates, others standing awaiting the news from their master. All feared something tragic had happened after the commotion at the gate and the subsequent alarm being sounded. A look of worry spread across their faces.

Waldo walked into the courtyard as if nothing was wrong. He reached a central point to most of the staff who members who were present, paused, and cleared his throat. He began, "My friends, staff, and servants, we are gathered here in this compound and have been so for the past few months in order to serve a higher purpose for the benefit of mankind." Everyone nodded in agreement as he spoke.

"Going into this mission from God, we knew there would be certain risks." He paused, looking around, his eyes resting on the sentry at the gate who had allowed the momentary slip in judgment that had resulted in them now being addressed by Waldo. "Let us not judge ourselves or others for whatever mistakes we think might or might not have been made that have now and most likely will alarm the local papal authorities as to our work being done here." The sentry lowered his head in apparent shame. "We can all be proud that we are doing God's will, regardless of what might happen in the near or distant future," he continued, now raising his voice slightly and more spirited. "You are making it possible for all mankind to be able to hear, read, and preach the gospel of Jesus Christ to every person alive."

Jakob turned his head toward Arktos, who had now arrived on the outskirts of the yard, sitting on a bench, resting, and then seeing Jakob, motioning him toward him to join him on the bench. "I want you all to know that Satan will do everything in his power to keep us from succeeding, even to the point of using children to do his work. It was only a matter of time before the news reached outside these very walls, for you see, my friends, I will soon begin spreading the Word of God myself using the Word received from our special guests, Arktos and his grandson." All eyes shifted to Jakob and his grandfather seated on the bench, each looking up and smiling in recognition of the acknowledgment. "It is our duty to take this gift of the Apostle Speakers and help them in their cause to continue to evangelize the Word of God to the rest of the world."

Waldo went on for some time with his uplifting, spiritual oration. When he was done, he walked to the sentry who had erred earlier, putting his arm around his shoulders, hugged him assuredly, and told him that all would be fine and God would make everything right. Waldo then beckoned for Arktos and Jakob to join him as he walked toward the dining hall.

"Come, my dear friends, let's go dine."

Rising from the bench together, Arktos more slowly than Jakob, they all walked together to the hall to eat the noon meal together. Waldo gave the entire staff the rest of the day off, saying that everyone needed to spend time in prayer, for the days ahead would be challenging. Now time was of the essence, and going back was not an option.

They all knelt at the grand dining hall table and prayed. The sound of the solemn words passed out the door, down the hall, and through the entire compound, including the sentries at the gate, and all knelt in prayer and prayed together as one. A shaft of light broke through the gray shadow of the day, hitting the uppermost point of the roofline above the hall where they all knelt in prayer.

A snow white dove flew out of nowhere and lit upon that very spot. God was smiling.

Chapter 20

INNER SANCTUM

For the Word of God is living and powerful, and sharper than any two-edged sword, piercing even to the division of soul and spirit, and of joints and marrow, and is a discerner of the thoughts and intents of the heart.

—Hebrews 4:12

Winter's icy grip now entombed the Vaudois, forcing its inhabitants to seek permanent shelter for long periods of time with little if any ventures out of their hibernatory confines unless absolutely necessary. Stores of supplies had been set aside for the long winter months that came each year, so spending weeks inside the safety of their alpine stone homes required a certain willpower combined with the ability to live within one's own mind. One's own sanity was at risk if not kept in check with an occupation during these solitary days.

Jean Paul and his mother, grandmother, and sisters spent many long hours practicing their Scriptures, going over each gospel carefully so they would not forget one syllable. In the afternoons, when everyone else worked on various crafts, Jean Paul found it too difficult to sit still, so he would steal away into the stables below and work on his swordsmanship, practicing in an empty stall while the livestock and horses looked on in ambient curiosity.

The frozen land that kept them isolated in their valleys protected them from forces that were totally impaired from entering the alpine regions at this time. Jean Paul did not give thought to the safety the elements provided. All he knew was that his brother and grandfather were away, doing God's work, hopefully safe, and in no harm. He knew Marik and Steffan were good men from their short time together, but he did not know this merchant Waldo or if he would be able to provide adequate shelter for his family. While he practiced, he thought about his brother.

He performed the moves his had learned from his father with his father's large, ancient blade that had been passed down for generations in their family. He remembered the day his grandfather gave it to him and how heavy it felt. Its weight matched that within his heart for his missing father. But with each year, the once seemingly oversized sword began to feel lighter as he grew. However, he knew without someone to spar with, he could only lunge and follow his own shadow on the stable walls. He needed a live sparring partner, but with the recent blizzards, there was no escape to even reach the village and find Lorenz, who he had become even closer to in the absence of his brother and grandfather. He could feel his strength growing with his age, but he had to wonder if Jakob too would be learning, if he was even still alive. There had been no word from them. Each day he practiced, studied, and planned in preparation for what in his heart he knew was coming.

Gabriel also knew.

Each day he worked with Jakob, not only on their instruments and Scriptures, but since the uninvited papal spy, he had also begun sword training with the young Jakob. The rock school in their valley also secretly doubled as a warfare training school, but Jakob had not yet reached the age requirement to attend. He very much wanted to go with his brother to train, both in trade and in blade, but now, being away, he had all but forgotten the school until now. The elders frowned on the training, but they all knew it was a necessary evil for them to be able to protect themselves physically as well as spiritually.

Jakob's work on the lira was reaching a certain mastership that Gabriel was becoming quite pleased with, not only in skill but also in his ability to control the power that came with it. Gabriel quickly found his musical student was just as adept in learning the blade. It was obvious that he had used crude weaponry, in that the sling and staff he had when herding had become secondary tools he had taken for granted, yet they proved useful as he learned the swordsmanship they now worked on.

"Stand ready," Gabriel instructed, "and prepare for what your opponent is about to do . . . try to anticipate."

Jakob stood with the wooden training sword ready for Gabriel's word.

He lunged toward the boy, who, with the speed of youth, dodged the lunge, matching the parry with wood to blade, easily avoiding the slow test move by his teacher. Gabriel spun, moving for the blind spot, but Jakob had anticipated this move, just having being caught the day before, and matched the downward stroke Gabriel sent toward his shoulder. Gabriel smiled. They worked in a steady stream of parries, turns, swings, and near misses, and all the while, Jakob was holding his own.

"You learn quickly," Gabriel said, smiling as they paused for a brief rest.

Jakob smiled in return. Pleasing Gabriel had become his passion. He wanted to prove to him that he was worthy of his teaching and his attention meant the world to him.

A flash of thought flew into Jakob's mind, and he quickly dropped low, coming in toward Gabriel, swinging in and upward at his abdomen, catching the ancient warrior momentarily off guard, but he quickly parried and caught Jakob on top of the head with the flat side of his sword, sitting the boy down with a great ringing in his ears. His eyes watered from the blow, which took him to his knees.

Gabriel held his sword on top of his head, with his arm outstretched, now looking down at the boy. "Always be prepared to expect a result from your actions, my son," he said, lifting the blade gently off the boy's head. He placed it gently under his downturned chin and lifted it so their eyes could meet. When Jakob looked up, Gabriel met his gaze with a fatherly smile that warmed him through.

"Yes sir," he replied through the tears. "I believe I like playing music more," he said with a smile.

Chapter 21

EVIL SLEEPETH NOT

For since the creation of the world His invisible attributes are clearly seen, being understood by the things that are made, even His eternal power and Godhead, so that they are without excuse,

—Romans 1:20

Since the report of the group in Lyon, the papacy had requested additional information from the bishop's guard stationed there. However, the security at Waldo's compound had been put on high alert, and no entrance inside the walls was unnoticed or mistaken since. The papacy was frustrated and becoming increasingly anxious since they could not penetrate the gate at the compound. If there was a militant force growing with heretical purposes in mind, they were failing to uncover it at this pace. The spy's reports of a concerted effort to produce some sort of writings raised even more concern, and thus the need for action was at hand. The fear of the Word spreading forth from the mountain regions was now becoming a reality—a threat to not only the hierarchy of the Catholic Church, but also on the grip of control it held over all its subjects.

Sergeant-at-Arms Armand led his column of mounted papal cavalry slowly through the early-morning fog that enveloped the streets that led to the front gates of the Waldo stronghold and dismounted, halting the cavalcade behind him. They had planned an early-morning raid, planning to catch the rebels off guard and make this mission a simple, quick, and easy task. Hopefully they would be back to the barracks in time for an early lunch.

He handed the reins of his steed to his corporal, who had already dismounted and was waiting ready for the task, saluting as he did. The mission was simple: confront the persons inside the Waldo compound, and then search for, recover, and destroy anything that was found to be heretical in nature. Armand's horse stamped his large black hooves at the ground, stirring up the dust. Armand motioned to the next two in line to dismount and advance toward the large wooden fortress doors of the compound. He then motioned for the others to prepare for an advance by force if necessary once the gate was breached.

The first two soldiers knocked on the door. The depth of wood sounded great as the echo of the knocking reported back over the wall.

There was no response. They knocked again. Again, there were only echoes . . . and nothing more except for the crow of a rooster in a nearby courtyard, welcoming the glow of the morning sun upon the distant horizon.

Armand ordered the sabers to be drawn, positioning a quarry of archers across the road upon a rooftop for a better vantage point. When they reached it, they reported no movement inside the compound. They moved a large battering ram forward through the column and positioned it at the door.

Armand called out to those who were apparently hiding inside with a hollow voice, not expecting any response to its call. He began to read from a prepared scroll, "By decree of His Holiness, Pope Lucias III, I have been ordered enter this premise to investigate reports of heretical dissertation . . ." His voice echoed off of silent walls.

He nodded to the battering ram detachment. They moved forward swiftly and with force. The blast of the first ram shook the walls, causing dust to lift off, shaking plants, and causing a large roar that echoed back down the street behind them. Curious bystanders came into the street.

The soldiers pulled back and ran forward again. *Boom* roared the ram, and again, the door stayed tight. A bird flew from the compound as if disturbed and now seeking shelter from this rudeness elsewhere as dust fell from the tops of the compound walls.

Boom, again the roar continued. Crowds began to gather in the streets. People looked through veiled windows, trying to see what was going on in their otherwise normally quiet neighborhood.

Finally, with one final serious blow, the door cracked open and the entrance was breached. The soldiers raced into the interior of the Waldo compound, prepared to be repelled by someone, their adrenaline rushing, the sound of the boom still echoing in their ears.

They were only met with silence, emptiness, and abandonment.

Their own shadows followed them from room to room. Empty cases welcomed them at each warehouse. Mice scurried away when startled by sudden appearances of soldiers in an otherwise forgotten rooms.

"Sir," reported Armand's corporal, "we have appeared to have been circumvented by someone warning them of our plans."

Armand nodded. "Yes, it does appear so."

They were standing outside the room where the scribes had been found by the young spy so many weeks earlier. Armand entered the room with the long, flat tables.

What could they have been doing in here that was so important that they would risk their freedom? he thought to himself. It bewildered him why anyone would try to create trouble for the church, especially supposed Christians. He walked from room to vacant room as his men searched everywhere for signs, remnants, clues as to where the previous inhabitants had gone. They had left many of their furnishings behind, apparently only taking the most essential items. The compound still appeared to be functional, although there were no supplies left in the warehouses and the rooms were void of any signs of activity.

Armand had known Waldo as a youth. They had gone to the same academy of the arts. He knew Waldo's family; they were all good Christian people. What on earth could cause them to become militants in this absurd cause to disrupt the Holy Roman Catholic Church? He was still shaking the thought around in his head when he walked out of the room and back to his horse that waited in the center of the main courtyard of the Waldo estate. *Why would someone put his entire life's work into jeopardy for something that was already available?* he thought as he leaned against his saddle, hands on his head, elbows pressed against his horse for support.

His head was spinning from the thoughts that churned inside his mind. Why? He knew he must talk to his priest right away and ask. This was far more complex than he could take in. He had a job to do. He had to focus.

"Sir." The corporal had followed him, curious as to what his sergeant was thinking since he had not spoken a word since his previous question. "Do you want me to go ahead and post the notice?"

"Yes . . . yes, go ahead. We still need to follow orders"

"Yes sir," he said, saluting and spinning as he reached for a scroll in the pouch of his horse's saddle bag. He walked to the front of the compound, just outside the main doors, and with a nail and hammer, he tacked up a notice to anyone who could read: "By order of the Holy Roman Catholic Church and all constituents thereof, this residence is now under the control of the church and has been confiscated for heretical, subversive, militant propaganda and activities therein."

Some of the braver bystanders had now wandered close enough to read the sign, with questioning and unbelieving looks as its meaning dawned on them. Off in the distance, the beautiful strains of a lira could be heard playing a mournful, sullen song that drifted on the mist that now glowed upon the morning light that beamed from the sunrise on the horizon. The rooster crowed, and then there was silence.

Armand and his regiment rode out of the compound in a swirl of dust after having secured the front gate with a timber and spikes from the outside. The notice posted earlier glared at them as they turned their backs to return to the garrison.

As they rode off, Jakob and Gabriel watched from their vantage point above from within the guard tower, where they had watched the entire spectacle that morning. Gabriel had Jakob begin playing his lira prior to the arrival of the troops. He played the song they had been working on prior to Christmas—the old song of the psalms that had no name. As he began playing, the entire compound became transfixed in time within the uncharted notes of the melody while they continued to work, study, and transcribe, unaware of the oncoming threat. The morning mist was eerily glowing as he played as Gabriel nodded approvingly.

"No matter what you are about to hear or see, keep playing until I tell you to stop. Do you understand," he said in a tone softly to Jakob that sounded like he meant what he said.

Jakob nodded in time with the melody he now played.

The power of his song drifted into every corner of the compound, touching the souls of all within, lifting them in spirit and mind to other places—places they all knew separately but wholly at the same time. They continued their tasks, but all becoming enveloped in the memories, thoughts, and dreams they fell into. As these thoughts became clearer in each mind, they drifted physically into the mist as souls leave bodies behind upon the final Day of Judgment. They left the compound behind without leaving its walls.

Gabriel watched over the scene as Jakob continued his mastery of song and power that came with his ability to connect to angelic hosts with the sound of the spirit that emitted from his instrument and heart. Jakob could see the Waldo compound members becoming transparent but couldn't believe his eyes. Gabriel touched his shoulder and whispered, "Keep the faith, my son, keep the faith . . . focus."

Meanwhile, the soldiers had busted the front gate open and began their search, not finding a soul within.

The power of the Lord was at work. The flow of spiritual power through the young boy and his angelic host blanketed all within.

Gabriel watched Armand as he appeared to become moved by the spirit and knew the song was reaching his heart and possibly, moving him to realize that what he knew as faith was all a lie. He would someday find the truth of the Word of God somewhere beyond his own immediate realm of faith.

He looked down at Jakob, who was still continuing to play; his young prodigy was growing stronger each day. He smiled as he realized his work here was nearly complete and that he would have to leave soon. Once the soldiers left, after barricading the front door from the outside, he knelt down in front of Jakob, who had been focused with his eyes toward the floor of the tower post, and looked into the boy's eyes.

"My son, it is done. You may now stop."

The notes ended, and as they did, the apparent mists of vapor returned the souls and bodies back to their previous form. All was as it was before, with only the recollection of each person changed to that of a daydream.

"Come, we have much to do before I go," Gabriel said to Jakob as they began to descend the guard tower into the courtyard below.

"Go? Where are you going?"

"My time here is nearly complete," he said as they reached the ground level. Gabriel reached for the boy as he descended.

"But why, why do you have to leave? Where are you going." Jakob felt abandoned at the mention of Gabriel's departure. "Why?"

"Hush my boy," he said, touching his fingers to Jakob's lips, as if to say, "Hush, all will be clear in time. I will always be with thee. Never fear." He patted Jakob on the head, and they both turned to walk inside as he looked back over his shoulder at the gate and motioned to one of the guards they had relieved to retrieve the barricade and sign from the front of the gate's entrance before retaking his position back in the tower.

It was clear that time was short for them all, and things would soon change for many.

Chapter 22

THE SERMON BEGINS

And my speech and my preaching were not with persuasive words
of human wisdom, but in demonstration of the Spirit and of power,
—1 Corinthians 2:4

The warmth of spring was beginning to emerge in the city,
along with the blooms, the sap rising in the trees, and the
birds returning from their winter migrations. The air was alive
with movement, aromas, and sounds. A young girl walked with her
mother, holding their empty baskets toward the market that morning,
anticipating fresh, young, tender vegetables fresh from the gardens of
the local farmers. As they neared the marketplace, they could see up
ahead a good-sized crowd had gathered around a speaker, who seemed
taller than all the others. As they drew closer, they could see he stood
on a leftover shipping crate, which was his stage for the moment. They
reached the outskirts of the crowd and stopped to listen. The market
often had street performers, minstrels, and other wayfaring strangers
trying to survive off the generosity of the shoppers. Today appeared to
be no different, with the crowd gathered around the speaker.

However, as they stood listening, they heard something altogether
different from performers in the past. This one seemed to be speaking to
them, as if he were trying to educate them and warn them of evil things
to come. But something that made him seem even more of an oddity
was that he wasn't trying to sell anything, and he wasn't asking for tips.
He was—could it be true?—yes, he was giving his words freely to all
who would listen. He emphatically proclaimed over and over again that
the people should listen, for the time was drawing near when everyone

could learn the Word of God on their own without having to wait for the clergy to tell them.

People listened with suspicion, for if what this speaker said was true, he could be found guilty of blasphemy and hanged, which was a common practice. One man turned as the speaker continued. He looked at the young girl and her mother and smiled.

"What is he talking about?" she said.

"He's saying that we can learn to read God's Holy Word ourselves and that he knows a way. He's saying we will all have the chance to do so in the near future."

"Reading God's Word ourselves," she scoffed. "He must be either half mad or on spirits."

"No, he's been quoting Scripture and speaking about the Word of God as if he has read it firsthand. He's quite entertaining." As he said this, around the corner of the far end of the marketplace rode a small contingent of papal guard on horseback. The speaker noticed their arrival, and at his pause, the audience also turned. As they turned to look, he seemingly vanished into the crowd gathered around him and was gone.

The audience, now apparently gathering for no reason, began to disperse as the guard rode up.

"Where is your minstrel?" the lead soldier said, looking down from his horse to one of the few remaining members of the former audience who had not yet left the area. The man he spoke to was elderly and dressed in ragged clothes. The horse shifted under the weight of the soldier's armor and weaponry.

"Don't know, sir," replied the old man. "He's apparently run off."

"Why did he hasten away so?"

The elder now appeared to be getting nervous with the questioning, and wanting to leave, he shook his head. "Couldn't say, sir." He paused, thinking carefully of the words he chose, for he knew that the charge of heresy was what they were searching for. He did not want to be found associating with this poor soul who had obviously reached a point in his life where he was willing to take the risk to spread the Word of God. He, on the other hand, had not, so he replied, "He was carrying on about God and such, a bunch of mumbo jumbo if you ask me." He started moving away. "I need to finish my shopping and get back to my home, if it's alright, sir. My dear old wife will be expecting me."

"Go on then, God speed."

"Yes, God speed to you too, sir," he said has he shuffled on.

"Spread out and keep an eye out for him," the leader said to the other mounted guards as they broke up into pairs and began fanning out throughout the marketplace, looking for the suspicious person who had sped away upon their arrival.

The old man turned the corner, removing the cloak from his head as he did, and smiled. Arktos loved being so close to danger, but he was glad he was able to move undetected now in public without being considered a suspect to the papal guard. Peter, on the other hand, was becoming well known for his growing popularity and was finding it more and more difficult to preach in public without being harassed or chased off by the guard. The local bishop was aware of the performances, but he was unaware that the person responsible for the rebellious proliferation of the gospels to all persons and the public speaker were one in the same.

For now, he enjoyed the anonymity of the occasion and was beginning to attract larger audiences and more quickly with each appearance. The word was spreading throughout the city that there was public preaching being performed by someone other than the Catholic clergy and that he was very knowledgeable of the Scriptures. He seemed to be very well educated and had a source of the Word of God unlike anyone they had seen to this point.

The excitement and fervor of his speeches was also drawing acclaim from his patrons, to the point they might be considered followers. The word was that he had been a wealthy merchant but had given away everything to be like the apostle Paul and go out and preach the Word of the Lord to the common man, regardless of his position in life. He dressed in humble clothing, often rags that had been tossed out or discarded by others. He also carried a Bible, from which he often read. It was said that he had a translated version of the Bible the priests used from which he spoke. Where or how he had been able to achieve this was part of the mystery of the man, who was becoming known as the prophet of Lyon.

As Arktos walked, he removed his outer garment. He rounded the next doorway and could see a staff leaned against the wall. He reached out with his garment as he passed the hidden doorway, handing his robe to a figure that took the robe and returned him another garment, of a different color and make, which he then put on. He did not stop as he did this but continued on his way. All this transpired in an instant, so that even if someone were watching he might have blinked and missed the transaction.

Arktos shouldered his new outer garment and headed back to the marketplace to pick up a few items before returning home.

Peter put on the robe Arktos had handed him, put up the hood, and followed the shadows back to their latest sanctuary to rest for the day. He felt led to continue his mission here in Lyon but it was only a matter of time before he was caught, and if he had not yet completed his goal, then all could be lost. Yet each day he seemed to be beckoned to venture out to share the Word, and each day he was safely delivered back home. He knew that soon they all would have to leave to continue the mission that had been started. The only place of safe refuge was where this most valuable resource was found; they must eventually go back to the Alps.

In just the past few months, they had made great progress, capturing nearly all of the known New Testament gospels, but more work still had to be done before their work was completed. There were those not known by the church—the ones that haunted the mysterious hidden corridors of the minds of those in power until it became a cancerous question that burned without end.

The more he learned from reading the words being written down each day, the more difficult he found it to sit idle and do what he felt was nothing while others did all the work. For that reason, he continued to leave the safety of their hideout to venture out and preach the gospels he had heard sometimes for the first time. Sometimes when he spoke, he could barely contain himself with the great awesomeness that hearing and knowing the Word would create in his heart. It was as if the dam of spiritual awakening had erupted and the only relief was to spread its glorious story to anyone who would stand long enough to hear.

But hearing the Word wasn't his only inspiration. There was also Jakob. Peter was captivated by the beauty of this boy and the many wonderful talents he had been blessed with, from the songs he had learned to play on his lira to his swordsmanship, all of which he had learned while being under Gabriel's tutelage.

Peter couldn't put his finger on it, but the feeling of the Word he was inspired to spread was only quickened by the notes he heard Jakob play on his lira. When he read the Word and heard the music together, it was almost as if he was transfigured into another state, unbeknownst and yet being connected to a heavenly realm. How could anyone sit still when this ultimate rush of strength and power infused into the soul, becoming manifested in the heart, blood, and lungs that are the physicality of the spiritual body, by which we are all tied to the earth?

This was the moment he had lived for all his life, and now he must be careful not to go too headlong into this river of spirituality and drown for sake of reaching the other side.

"Patience, patience, Peter," he would tell himself as he stalked along in the shadows. Soon he reached the hidden door behind the wall of ivy on a back street, into which he vanished from the light of day down flights of steps to a hidden, cavernous catacomb of tunnels below the streets of Lyon.

"You return with quickened pulse," said a voice from the darkness of the room he had just entered as he removed Arktos's garment.

"Yes and no," he said with a smile. "It's not what you think."

"Not from the hunt but rather from the joy?"

"Yes, my friend, absolutely."

Gabriel smiled and emerged from the shadowed corner he had been standing in, holding a large broadsword in one hand and its sheath in the other, into which he slid the long blade and placed it gently on the table in the center of the room.

"You know we must soon embark for the safety of the mountains," he said, still looking down at the majestic weapon.

"Yes." He paused pondering the move. "I know."

"Your wife and family are hiding in Venice, in the safety of the of your cousin's estate. Marik has taken them there and has them safely tucked away, so why do you hesitate?"

"The work here is not done. Steffan has told me they are working on the last book Arktos believes he has left in his head, so we can't stop now when the end is so near,"

"No, it is not finished, but it is now started and to a point where we can leave and manage from afar. Is not Steffan capable of continuing on his own, and what would it gain us to lose you now?" he said, stepping closer to the candlelit table. "Soon they will need us there." He hesitated. "Storms are brewing."

"Storms?"

Peter looked as Gabriel stood now, eyes closed, peering beyond the table, looking without seeing. His voice seemed distant as he spoke. He could not explain to Peter what he knew or felt, but he had to convey what he felt to him in a manner that would not alarm him. He was fearful the knowledge of what was to come might overwhelm him like a wave crashing over the bow of a ship and capsizing it and its crew.

Gabriel said after an eerie silence, "Evil grows more powerful day by day, and we have much work to do before it tries once more to extinguish the light."

"Yes, I feel an urgency as well. I've been—"

"Been preaching I know," interrupted Gabriel, "but the written work will become the voice of many. You alone will not make the difference. Your gift of wealth has made it possible now for the word to be spread to the starved and deprived masses."

"This is true."

"Besides, how many of the Bibles with the new books from the Apostle Speakers are there now?"

"At last count we have compiled quite a collection of new books to add to the Bible. Although Arktos continues to add to the number of books, with what we believe will be the final one, Revelation, being worked on at this time."

"Excellent!"

"Once he has completed this last book, we will depart. You will be able to establish all the necessary arrangements for the printing and compilation of the new Bible in your absence. Besides, this should be the precaution you have already taken, since any day now you could be captured and made prisoner or worse, killed."

"Yes, but . . ."

"But what?"

"What books do we include?"

"For now, we will transcribe them all and God will decide later. For now, keep all the Word preserved to this point alive, if it is feasible."

"I believe we might be able to do so, but it won't be easy."

"Nothing worth anything ever is, is it?" Gabriel smiled, turning and placing his hand upon Peter's shoulder.

"No, my dear friend, it is not."

At that moment, one of the servants knocked hurriedly on the outer chamber door.

"Senor Peter, Senor Peter," breathless he continued, "are you there?"

"Yes," he said, concerned.

"Come quickly. The boy has been taken just now, by the guard."

"What!" Peter yelled, rushing for the door, with Gabriel now on his heels, sword in hand.

He threw open the door. "Sir, we must hurry. They somehow laid in wait not far from our secret entrance, and when he approached, they rushed him, still unaware of our enclave." The servant had already turned to rush toward the upper streets, "We must hurry. They have just done this deed, and we may yet save him." He motioned for them to hurry, and they gave chase.

The light of day was weakening in the sky, but it was much brighter up here on the surface, so when they cautiously emerged, they had to shade their eyes at first until they could focus. From the blinding whiteness they could see the guard farther down the street, loading Jakob onto one of their horses. He was already in chains and being loaded face down, with his arms outstretched, tied to his feet from underneath the horse.

He made no noise.

They had not yet been seen, so Gabriel motioned for them to keep out of sight until they could get closer. They were now making their way up the street, keeping to the recesses of walls or anything that would keep them hidden from their quarry.

However, just as the lead guard called for them to mount and prepare to move, Gabriel motioned for Peter and his servant to stay. Peter understood. They had too much to lose if he were also captured. As quickly as Gabriel had made them stop, he vanished.

The guard unit began to move off, turning down a side street just up ahead, horses and riders paired, roughly a dozen total in the detachment, with the horse Jakob was tied to nearly in the middle of the unit. Peter watched them move around the corner, and as the last horse turned, he couldn't believe his eyes. There riding next to the other cavalryman, in full guard uniform, was Gabriel. As he turned the corner, Peter could have sworn to the heavens above he caught him winking. He almost laughed out loud.

"My friend, we need not worry," Peter said to the guard. "Let us go back into our sanctuary. The Lord has everything under control."

"Yes, Master."

"Besides, I am weary and need rest. It has been quite an eventful day."

At that moment around a corner, in the opposite direction from where the guard unit had left, came Arktos with a basket in hand full of market goods and groceries.

"Ahh, a sight for sore eyes I see," Peter said, relieved to see at least one of the precious guests still safe.

"You must surely either be ill or in dire need of companionship," Arktos responded, chuckling to himself.

"Yes, but for now, let us go repose in safety. Gabriel will return soon with Jakob, who has just been taken into custody by the guard."

Arktos paused.

"No, you need not worry, my old friend, for Gabriel is already well within reach of retrieving him, if not already."

Arktos smiled at this and nodded in agreement as they quickly disappeared from sight of the street.

Chapter 23

STORM CLOUDS GATHER

Then the multitude rose up together against them; and the magistrates tore off their clothes and commanded them to be beaten with rods. And when they had laid many stripes on them, they threw them into prison, commanding the jailer to keep them securely. Having received such a charge, he put them into the inner prison and fastened their feet in the stocks.

—Acts 16:22-24

Lucier had passed the winter months planning his next move upon the obscure valley deep within the remote regions of the Alps, where the Apostle Speakers kept vigil over the Word of God. The small contingent of priests and their escorts that had left Rome in the late days of fall had reached no farther than the foothills of the eastern Piedmont regions before inclement weather halted their progress. They took shelter within the local villages near Turin where the previous army had established a base camp. They set up makeshift churches from which they could operate on the local population, bring more souls into the great Christian juggernaut known as the Roman Catholic Church. The reports from the early subversive scouting parties parading as priestly missionaries had momentarily failed, but like a cancer, they would continue, unwanted or not.

Very little information about the exact location of the valleys the Apostle Speakers inhabited had been gathered, and in fact, those who had survived the tragic one-sided battle the previous year had trouble even recalling where they had been months after the event had transpired. Several of those Lucier had spoken with in an attempt to gather more information on the area had become sick or in some cases, they went into convulsions upon trying to recall details of the campaign. There weren't many who had made it home from that fateful day, so the pool of information was small to start with. With this supposed trauma they all exhibited, there was almost nothing known about the people within the mysterious valleys, other than the legend that continued to extend beyond the cragged peaks that protected them from the outside world.

Although no information had come from the alpine regions, there was word of a small contingent of subversives operating in and around the western Piedmont regions. The report that the Lyon bishop had filed had piqued Lucier's interest, since it was said there appeared to be an attempt by a wealthy local merchant to proliferate the holy Word to the masses through a common-language Bible. What piqued Lucier's interest in this story was the fact that someone was either translating the Latin from the Catholic Church's literature, which was a severe crime punishable by law in itself, or worse . . . could it be?

Could it be that someone had managed to persuade some of the Apostle Speakers to leave their sanctuary, venture out from their seclusion, and being spreading their Word? With this merchant's aim at marketing the Word to the masses, it could totally undermine the power base of the church if it were true.

Lucier hated any scourge upon the church. Many years ago, when he was a young cadet out training in the field, a band of Islamic marauders attacked his village in the darkness of night, raping and murdering all within. They set the buildings on fire before leaving so that those who were left barely alive died painful deaths in the flames that ensued. When his military detachment returned, all they found were the ashes and remains of the loved ones they had left behind.

Having lost all that he loved, Lucier became a voracious warrior, with no fear of death, for all he lived for was gone. Fearless is the warrior who is not afraid to die in battle, and thus he quickly rose in the ranks as his legendary fierceness in battle grew. He fought with the Christian armies that rode out to Byzantine to battle the hordes of Islamic armies that battled for religious and global supremacy.

He had too often dreamed bloody nightmares of the battlefield, only to see his wife and children perish before he could reach them at the end of a long, windswept field whose end he could never reach. Lucier had little room left in the chambers of his darkened heart for compassion for anyone who even whispered contempt for his Christian beliefs or the church that professed to encompass all of its beliefs in what was avowed to be a protective spiritual shell. The church was his only family that remained, and any sign, whisper, or action that attempted to harm it quickly joined the darkness in his heart.

It was with that concern and dissent of authority in mind that Lucier sent word to the bishop of Lyon that he would like to come for a visit and question the young courier who had reported the alleged activity. In addition, he wanted to speak with the sergeant who had led the search of the compound where it was thought the operation was based. Although it had since been reported to him that there was nothing found during the search, he couldn't help but entertain the thought of this potential threat to the papacy. Even the slightest seed of opposition had to be nipped in the bud before it was allowed to bloom.

His speculation about the sergeant's report was fueled by a clergy's report some days later of the sergeant coming in for an audience with the local priest. He began by asking for forgiveness of sins, which was not uncommon for soldiers under the papal regime, but eventually he began asking more questions. He had troubled thoughts about the church's authority over God's Word. The report read that he became so incensed by the answers that he left upset without actually making any confessions. This had disturbed the clergy who met with the sergeant so much so that it had been reported to the bishop's office. They felt it should be considered under the auspices of the issue of the compound search. They thought it could possibly lead to the corruption of mankind's soul.

Lucier found this disturbing, which made him wonder what was actually found in the compound that day. His suspicions grew with each passing day. The inactivity weighed on his mind as a heavy snow on a roof, so much so that he decided to take a small contingent on a quick visit to Lyon to speak firsthand with some of the witnesses. Although the winter thaws in the mountains had not yet begun, his inner fire grew hotter with the thought that each day they allowed to pass gave the disease another day to spread. If there was one thing Lucier knew well, it was that an enemy's front lines can only be fortified when the attacker lies quiet.

*   *   *

Jakob had been uneasy since his captors had bound him and thrown him, face first, on the back of the horse he now lay upon. They rode deeper into Lyon's fortified inner city, where the guard called home and where the notorious dungeons of Lyon existed. As the horse bounced along at a canter, Jakob's breath was constantly being knocked from his chest, making him more irritated the farther they rode. He tried to look around but was flanked on both sides by guards in front and behind his horse, with one riding aside the horse he now lay upon.

Jakob strained his neck and looked out toward the back of the cavalry column as they came around a corner and thought for an instant he caught a glimpse of a familiar face in the helmet of one of the last riders. He had to be imagining things to think that he looked like Gabriel. A guard smacked his back with the flat side of his sword when he saw Jakob looking, knocking what little wind he had left in him out and causing him to collapse back on the horse, deflating his hopes of rescue.

*   *   *

Gabriel's ire grew as he watched Jakob being manhandled. He felt responsible for the boy's capture. They had tried to keep a low profile, but the guard had evidently been lying in wait for anyone coming or going from their most recent hideout. The boy was an easy target, so he would also make for an even easier informant once they began putting him under duress in the torture chambers. He quickly overcame the last guard in the column, dispatching the lifeless body before the others realized what had happened. He switched his outer armor so that he now appeared to be one of the mounted soldiers.

As they rode, the sergeant in charge of the detachment looked back over his shoulder at the boy and smiled. They were quickly making their way back to headquarters with a splendid prize for the major of the guard, who had directed them to be on the lookout for the subversives, since they had received a tip from another tortured soul they had held captive in the dreaded hole in the bowels of the Lyon dungeons.

The Lyon brigade was led by Major Wesselow, who had made his way up the ranks through brutality and abuse of the citizens he was supposed to protect. He had received word from General Lucier to be on the lookout for possible Apostle Speaker subversives in his city. The sergeant in charge of this platoon knew that his major would be quite impressed and that this would make a great impression upon the general, especially if they were able to pull some much needed-information from this boy.

With each step of the mounted column Gabriel was thinking out his next move. He had the advantage now of the element of surprise if he needed it, but something was clouding his mind. He lost focus for a moment. The buildings kept causing a pattern of dark and light to flash into his eyes. The bell tower rang, striking five times. He had to focus. What would be the easiest way out? He felt something overpowering his mind. *Yes,* he thought, *I will simply volunteer to take the boy into the jail and escort him down into the dungeons. I never intend to make it all the way down, since I can easily move the boy into the shadows and escape.*

From the back of the column, he continued to struggle with his thoughts when suddenly he felt the hair on the back of his neck began to stand up. Something vile and demonic was near, and he could feel its presence.

A young child ran to the side of the road to watch as the attachment rode by. Gabriel watched the boy stand and salute as they passed. His eyes stayed on the boy as they continued farther until he almost had to turn his head to continue to see him. Then he noticed the reason for his sudden feeling of darkness. Voices of a distant past began to sing in his mind but were too far off to break the trance.

Twenty yards behind their column, another smaller detachment was advancing, more heavily armored, with a flag bearer carrying the seal of a ranking official of the guard. Gabriel turned his head away from the child and looked fully around now. Turning in his saddle to see more easily, he could see a general dressed in black, with a red cross on his shield depicting the sign of the papal guard and quickly gaining.

Something about this felt all wrong.

*   *   *

Lucier saw the detachment ahead and urged his escorts to catch them so they could enter the fortified inner city together. As they drew near, he could see they had a prisoner tied to one of the mounts. He also noticed it was just a boy.

Why would the guard be taking a mere boy into custody? he thought as they quickly approached the back two riders of the column.

The afternoon spring light cast long, dark shadows from the taller buildings they now rode between. Lucier focused his eyes from dark to light as they intertwined between the buildings now within sight of the inner city's walls. He also noticed the last rider on the right had for some reason not suited his armor correctly. It was not fully clasped. His eyes followed the undone side plate up to the hilt of the sword, which was also on the wrong side of his rider—a hilt with curiously encrusted gem work on it. *Quite fancy for a mere cavalryman,* he thought.

At that instant, Gabriel caught Lucier looking at him, and with somewhat a suspicious look, Lucier shouted, "Guard attention."

The entire column stopped, almost throwing Jakob off his steed, but he was caught by the rope that held him to the saddle. The sergeant at the head of the column quickly raced to the rear to see the reason for the command when he saw the general's detachment riding behind. Then he too stopped his horse, leaped to the ground, and saluted.

"General Sir, to what do we owe this honor?"

"At ease, Sergeant," Lucier replied with his return salute. "I have come to visit your fair city to talk to some people of interest. I need you to escort me to the major."

"Sir, yes sir, it would be my honor, sir."

"And Sergeant, what is the nature of your arrestee here?" Lucier said, now pointing to Jakob, who was now laying still across the horse, enjoying the reprieve from being bounced to death.

"He's believed to be associated with the subversives in our area, sir."

Lucier gently nudged his horse to ease himself alongside Jakob's position. He drew his ebony black sword and gently placed the tip underneath Jakob's chin, tilting it ever so gently upward and looking at the boy as he glared back.

He looked at Jakob with disdain. "Hmm, an interesting-looking little chap," he scoffed.

Gabriel had moved his hand to his side.

*   *   *

Jakob felt the cold steel under his chin. His heart was surely about to beat out of his chest. He felt the horse's pulse through his own as the beat rattled up in this throat. He wanted to cry out, but he didn't dare. This darkness that had suddenly come before him was nothing like he had ever witnessed before. He felt the burning sensation on his back again, and then he began to see the evil fade into the tunnel of black, and all was gone.

*   *   *

"He just passed out," said Lucier, laughing and dropping his sword tip but keeping it at his side. "Some subversive you have here," he said, shaking his head at the sergeant. "However," he suddenly turned and pointed his sword toward Gabriel, "arrest this one too!"

Had Gabriel been alone, he could have easily cut down the nearest guard, for they were clueless. But now that he had been pointed out, he was quickly surrounded and could not get to Jakob before they might harm him. So he sat, blood cold, as he looked through his helmet at the black eyes of the general.

"You thought you could infiltrate us an get your boy back . . . well, you might have if I hadn't chanced upon you," he said, now drawing closer to Gabriel, with his sword still drawn and pointed toward Gabriel's chest. "But you didn't know I'd ride up behind you and find your dress a bit disheveled, along with your Knights Templar sword at your side." He smiled at his own ingenuity. "Quite unusual for a regular cavalrymen."

Gabriel's skin crawled. "You're so observant," he fumed, "for a papal pawn."

Lucier's face grew cold and stolid. His sword, now touching the breastplate of Gabriel's chest armor, was prepared to be driven into the beating heart of his soul.

"I'd just as soon run you through," he said now through his clenched teeth, "but you will provide a valuable tool once we break you down. And if you choose not to cooperate, then we have your young friend here, who we can surely torture into a slow death that would certainly bring out the best of you."

Lucier smiled and motioned to the other guards as he backed away while they threw Gabriel from his mount to the ground and put the chains and shackles on him.

"Yes," he mockingly drew out the words, "would-be hero, you'll make a fine addition to my visit here to Lyon. Who knows, we might even have a little public torture just for fun. Oh what a trip this has turned out to be after all." Then he and his escorts rode ahead, into the gates of the inner portion of Lyon, into the dark shadows. Into the belly of the demon they disappeared.

The faint sound of a choir singing could be heard as the horses' hooves echoed off the cobblestones, fading away into the depths of the abyss known to all as Sheol Prison, hell on earth.

Chapter 24

FOREBODINGS OF DARKNESS

The utterance of him who hears the words of God, and has the knowledge of the Most High, Who sees the vision of the Almighty, Who falls down, with eyes wide open:

—Numbers 24:16

Jean Paul awoke from the dream with a sense of despair. Since the attack, he had experienced a recurring dream of being captured and taken away. This night's was no different except he had gone farther than ever before. He sat up in bed, wiping his brow with the back of his arm and leaning back on his arm, propping himself up. The room was still dark as the night was pitch black with the new moon. All was quiet save for the small sound he could hear being made by his mother and sisters softly breathing in deep sleep in their beds in the room next to his.

In his dream, what had not yet slipped beyond his purposeful grasp, he could hear the cries of anguish. It was horrible. He purposely tried to push it out of his mind, but the darkness kept pulling it forward until he could see the people who were crying, reaching for him through the bars with scarred, bonelike, filthy arms, asking him to end their lives or liberate them from this torture. He could smell the dankness of the depths of the abyss of humanity in some dungeon and the acrid smell of the few torches that lit entrances to cavernous recesses of hell filled with writhing, pale, macabre limbs. The limbs sometimes crawled into the dim light to beg for mercy, the haunted faces stretched tight, teeth bared, eyes sunken, hopes vanished, and souls barren of any faith left save for that small light that still shone in the faint darkness of the deepest recesses of their blackened souls.

Jean Paul felt as though there was something else there as well—something evil, something waiting.

Then, as he walked farther into the prison, he came to a chamber where he saw a young boy sitting with what appeared to be a soldier. The boy's back was to him, and he could not tell if he was crying or not. The soldier stood over him and was comforting him with a hand on his shoulder. The soldier paused, as if he heard the visitor, and turned his head slightly without removing his hand from the child's shoulder. He looked at Jean Paul and nodded, as if to say it would be all right, and then turned back to tending to the boy and his despair

The scene bothered Jean Paul because he feared the boy could be Jakob, but he couldn't seem to speak to tell him to turn around. He felt helpless, and then emptiness began to turn his stomach into knots. Then he realized his stomach was rumbling from hunger. He remembered the small meal he had eaten at supper and that it was not nearly enough to satisfy his growing hunger.

He had kept vigil over the farm while becoming the true man of the family. With his grandfather and brother now gone, he had been pushed into the role he had been putting off with his grandfather still around, leading the family. But now . . . he was all that was left. It was a struggle, but he accepted the responsibility.

He worked on his swordsmanship each day while studying his lessons and still keeping the farm running. It took a lot of energy. Some days seemed like they would never end, with wood needing to be cut for the fire, water to be hauled, meat to be butchered, and the many other chores that fell on him to handle in the absence of his brother and grandfather. The food supply had not been adequate for the entire community this winter because of the attack that had occurred that took away from the winter's normal preparation.

Fear of another attack was constantly on everyone's minds, regardless of the elders' preaching that the Lord would guide and protect them. They were short on hay for their flocks and low on preserved meats and other stored goods that helped them get through the long winter months. They had been through lean times before, but this time, the sense of fear that weighed on them was heavier with the pangs of hunger gnawing at their souls as well.

Now that spring was near, they would still suffer a while longer, but soon they would have new spring vegetables or at least be able to travel beyond the frozen passes to try to get out to trade for much-needed supplies. Safety would also now haunt them like the long shadows of the passes they would traverse to reach the larger villages with larger markets.

He quietly got up from his bed and moved to the kitchen area, which was slightly lit by the embers of the fireplace, which still glowed in the hearth across the room. He searched the counter, looking for a spare crumb of bread or cheese left over from the night's meal. He found the heel of the last loaf of bread made from the previous day and took a mug of water from the water bucket. He sopped it in the darkness, sucking on the taste of home in his mouth as he closed his eyes, savoring the juices that flowed down his throat, quenching his parched soul.

The faces returned from the dream. They had hollowed eyes in gaunt faces, many appearing to be others from the Vaudois, but older and in poor health. He opened his eyes again, trying to flush the thoughts from his mind, when he saw the dark figure standing by the hearth. The embers glowed red, causing the figure to appear to be dressed from head to toe in a dark-hooded robe the color of blood.

Jean Paul tried to speak, but with the bread and water in his throat, he could only make a slight gurgling sound, nothing else. He wanted to ask who the being was who was standing there in his home at this haunting hour. He tried to move to get up and possibly reach for his sword, which lay near his bed, but he found he could not move any more than he could speak. He felt cold, frozen, abandoned, and alone.

The darkness stared at him and beyond. He could feel it reaching inside him, pulling out what little hope and goodness he had left. The feeling from his dream of evil now overwhelmed him like the waves of a boat, and he felt suffocated. Again he tried to move, this time with all his might. Ever so slightly he could feel his leg move, but again, nothing else, and his voice would not come no matter how hard he strained to yell.

The figure now began to move, floating slowly toward him. The eyes glowed red like the embers in the hearth in the black ebony chasm of a face that lay shadowed within the dark, blood-colored hood.

He again felt horror and screamed with all his might. A gurgle arose in his throat, and he began to hear an eruption of sound come forth as he closed his eyes and pushed. The strain arose from his throat, and he felt the coldness of the room slap his mind into awareness. He opened his eyes in stark realization.

The figure was gone.

*   *   *

Jakob awoke with a start. He didn't realize he had drifted off to sleep, but he felt Gabriel's gentle touch on his shoulder and realized again with horror that they were still in the bowels of the Sheol Prison, the depths of Hades many had seen but few ever returned or escaped alive from. He tried to cling to the comfort he felt while asleep—comfort he had not known since leaving home. It was almost as if he had been back home briefly, but the essence of family still lingered in his mind as Gabriel spoke.

"Rest, my son, for we are here only for a short while. The Lord our Father will soon release our bonds."

Jakob smiled and looked up at Gabriel. He never seemed to be worried by anything. Even now, here in this horrible place that stunk of death and decay, he appeared to be at peace.

Suddenly there was a loud slam of the heavy cast iron door that was the entrance into this hell on earth. Then there were heavy footsteps and sounds of the metallic clank of armor and weaponry. A command from down the hall could be heard: "Guards to attention, the general is now in the prison."

For the first time since Jakob had known Gabriel, he saw something tense in him.

Gabriel could feel the darkness envelop the air as he also heard the commands and oncoming footsteps. The clearness of being became veiled, as if in a fog. He tried to see beyond, but there was nothing. He felt the hair on the back of his neck rise as suddenly the figure appeared at the small window that looked into their small, dank chamber that was their cell. They could hear the lock in the heavy wooden door turn and the hinges creak as it swung inward. The light of the torch blazed behind the figure as his dark shadow fell upon them. The flickering flame caused the shadow to dance as in an eerie, wicked display of taunting as the figure stepped into their cell.

"So you are the chosen one," he scoffed, now placing his hands on his hips as he spoke. The flame followed him into the small space that now became slightly crowded. The light engulfed the small chamber, illuminating the small boy and his protector. Their dark shadows danced on the rock walls behind them. They did not reply. Jakob just moved closer toward Gabriel, half hiding now behind his cloak but still peering beyond.

"So you have nothing to say for yourselves," Lucier said, pausing and expecting a reply.

Gabriel's face did not change in demeanor. He kept a constant lock on the eyes of the general.

Lucier, now becoming irritated by the lack of response and respect, felt his minions becoming restless behind him. He did not like the penetrating stare Gabriel seemed to hold on him. He wasn't aware at this point of the power he had over the unearthly being that now stood powerless before him.

He continued in a brazen tone, "Nonetheless, tonight we have you in our clutches and will find out how much you really want to rebel against the only true representative of God on this earth—the one I hear that you fail to recognize and that represents us all before God: the Holy Roman Catholic Pope Lucias III. We will see if you will confess your faith toward the pope, and if not . . ." he turned and motioned to one of the escorting guards to move forward who held up the chains of the burning cross in their direction, "we will then put you to the torch and let you burn in eternal hell fire so that your physical being will match your soul that is eternally damned." At that, he began laughing, and the guards joined in as they began to turn to leave the chamber.

Gabriel felt powerless to act and was still fighting through the fog when he heard the small voice beside him speak.

"We will pray for your soul."

Lucier turned back. The light now played on his face, which held a grimace that figured between pain and hate. "What?" he hissed between his teeth as he turned and beamed his sight at the young boy who no longer cowered behind Gabriel but was now standing in the middle of the cell.

Jakob spoke as if possessed by a power beyond his small frame, "May the Lord be with your soul, and in the words of Jesus Christ, Father, the hour has come. Glorify your Son, that your Son may glorify you."

Lucier swung at the boy to smack him with the back of his hand, but before his fist could strike the child, the arm of his protector shot out and stopped the swing in full stride. Without a pause, Gabriel swung and pinned the arm behind the general's back, knocking the torch out of the guard's hand. The room went dark, and the sound of muffled blows and strikes of skull against stone could be heard outside the door. Then quiet.

*   *   *

Jean Paul sat up in the bed again, this time wet with sweat from head to toe but vividly aware he had just had another nightmare. It had been more realistic than ever before. He felt drained and weary. He threw back the covers as he looked at the sword sitting by his bed. He rolled onto his knees on the cold stone floor and began to pray. The stones were cold, and they again confirmed he was back in reality. He had to gain some foothold on the only comfort he knew outside of this desolate, isolated realm they called home, so he looked to God once more for answer. Before his words came to mind, there was a voice so strong and loud that he opened his eyes for fear his mother and sisters might be awakened.

There was nothing but darkness and the moonlight filtering through the cracks of the shutters on the window across the room. He was almost afraid to close his eyes again for fear he might be still caught in the nightmare he thought he had just escaped. He purposely began to pray again, but now he spoke the words silently so they might have more meaning, with his eyes open. Then the voice pierced his body like thunder once again.

"You will lead the people," thundered the voice.

He now trembled with fear and collapsed to the floor, with his hands folded in prayer and his head bowed, touching the cold slabs of the floor. He felt so unequivocally humbled that he felt powerless in the presence of the Lord.

"Rise and go forth. Do not fear, for I will be with you always," the voice said.

Jean Paul felt as if he was losing his mind, falling into an abyss of helplessness, when suddenly warmth came over him like the hand of God. It caught him and lifted him up, erasing all his fears. It felt as if nothing else mattered. An unconditional love had enveloped his soul and wrapped its loving arms around his heart.

"You will find them in the darkness but lead them to the light, always, for you are the light in the darkness, always."

Jean Paul did not speak. He waited for more words. When there were no more words, he began praying fervently and as passionately as he had ever done in his whole young life. He felt God was there and was now listening. Since the death of his father, he had felt abandoned and jilted by God. He felt his prayers were just nothing more than himself talking into the face of the canyon walls, echoing back the emptiness he felt within. The recent events in his life, from the miraculous massacre to the mission his grandfather and brother had set upon, had left him feeling confused. Was he merely left to tend to the women and children while others were to do God's will, or was there something else he was missing?

Now it was clear. He had been asked by only the Great I Am himself, and it was clear what he had been asked. Jean Paul's mind raced as he continued to kneel in prayer until he lost consciousness deep in the night.

The next morning, as the dark of night dissipated into the grayness that predawn light brings, Julia awoke and found it strange that Jean Paul lay asleep on the floor next to his bed. The soft light of the coming dawn made his shape visible upon the cold stones. She gently raised him up, and as she did, he awoke, but only enough to take comfort in his mother's touch. Then he collapsed back into sleep in his bed, exhausted from the visit he had just experienced. His weariness was matched by a comfort that left him full within, sated to the point of total comfort and warmth from above that took away all his fears. He felt the love of a parent that was not bequeathed.

Before he drifted off, he whispered to his mother as she tucked the covers around him, "I've been called to lead us, Mother."

She smiled and patted his head lightly. "God calls us all, my son. Now rest. You did not appear to sleep well at all last night. I will feed the animals this morning; rest and take today off. You need a break."

In a nearby valley, an army amassed, preparing an invasion while those in its sights were fully unaware. This time there would be no protection from the onslaught. The people did not yet realize their potential or gifts that would someday lead them from this place. They would soon come to know the wicked edge of the sword and the spiritual test that facing the end would evoke from the very depths of the Scriptures they held within.

Now, like never before, they would need a leader. His time would come soon. For now, he smiled back at the gentle hand of his mother and drifted off to sleep

Chapter 25

DEATH REVISITED

And it came to pass when Israel had made an end of slaying all the inhabitants of Ai in the field, in the wilderness where they pursued them, and when they all had fallen by the edge of the sword until they were consumed, that all the Israelites returned to Ai and struck it with the edge of the sword. So it was that all who fell that day, both men and women, were twelve thousand—all the people of Ai.

—Joshua 8:24-25

Lucier had gone ahead with his plans to attack the valley of the Vaudois once again once the weather broke. Its exact location had been retraced, and after a few tortures of nearby villagers, they were soon able to secure its location. He had sent his command ahead to the northern army to bring as many of the inhabitants back alive to be incarcerated as possible, but they were not to hesitate to kill any who fought back or resisted their captors. The major in charge was a battle-seasoned soldier who had fought beside Lucier in the first Crusades and who would be loyal to his superior to death if needed. Lucier knew that while he was investigating the suspects in Lyon, Major Crowell would be quite adept at taking care of those in the valley. He had fully briefed him on the previous failed mission and what to expect.

The contingent of priests that accompanied them added weight to the fact that they realized a higher power was responsible for the defeat of the first contingent because they came armed in all aspects of spiritualism. Crowell's only hesitation was that he had been instructed to destroy everything in his path that resisted—including women and children.

This bothered him. He knew Lucier and that he could be ruthless at times, but never before had he known him to ask for anyone in his command to slaughter the noncombatants.

On what was to be the night before their attack, Crowell found he could not sleep, so he summoned one of the head priests who was traveling with them to come at once to his tent for consultation. Father Torrinto soon arrived, and his entry was announced. He found Crowell reading from his journal in the candlelight. As he entered, Crowell looked up and motioned for the father to be seated on the chair nearby.

"I hear you have need of the Word of God in this dark hour," said Torrinto in a sullen but sure voice.

"Yes, I need some reassurance." Crowell paused, rubbing his chin as he spoke. "You see, I've been given a mission to accomplish, but like none other before . . . and I'm bothered in my heart for what I am asked to now do."

"Does this something you speak of have to do with the eminent battle we face tomorrow?"

"Correct," he said, now pausing, as if reflecting on the mental images he could foresee.

"Go on."

"Tell me, Father, of the passage in the Bible where God asked the Israelites to destroy everything in the city that was so bad that God didn't want anything from it to survive . . . for the task I have been asked to do is similar in its demands."

The priest pulled from his robe a sheaf of biblical notes. He found the place Crowell asked about in the Old Testament book of Joshua. He translated, "When Israel had finished killing all the men of Ai in the fields and in the wilderness where they had chased them, and when every one of them had been put to the sword, all the Israelites returned to Ai and killed those who were in it. Twelve thousand men and women fell that day—all the people of Ai. For Joshua did not draw back the hand that held out his javelin until he had destroyed all who lived in Ai.

"Is this what you asked to hear sir?" said Torrinto, looking up from the page.

"Yes, yes it is," Crowell responded, nodding in agreement as he spoke. "This will not be the first time, so my conscience should rest."

"Yes, this is true," said Torrinto. "The Lord is with you and will guide you, for his will be done. Tomorrow the wicked, vile, twisted tongue of the devil is before you, and it must be eradicated so that God's divine power can go on unblemished and pure, in the Catholic manner in which he intended."

Crowell nodded in agreement as Torrinto spoke. They then prayed together, and Torrinto was excused. Crowell lay back on his pallet and breathed a deep sigh of relief. Regardless of what the Scriptures said, this was not going to be easy. Then again, it was good against evil, as the priest had instructed, and nothing bothered him more than something or someone coming between him and the Lord.

I'll just picture them as demons, he thought. Then he closed his eyes and slept.

*   *   *

Marik had escorted Waldo's family to his cousin's estate in Venice safely and was about to return to Lyon when he felt led to veer off of his scheduled course and alter his return route. As he rode the following day, he kept thinking about Jakob's mother and the people in the Vaudois. He couldn't help thinking that there seemed to be an unusual calm to the air as storm clouds were brewing over the horizon.

It was about midday when he came to a crossroads—one leading back to Lyon and the other onward north toward the valleys of the Vaudois. He started for Lyon when suddenly a blast of air threw a devil's tail whirlwind into his path, causing his horse to start and rear, nearly throwing him from his mount. The steed landed and jolted ahead. Marik pulled the beautiful black stallion back in but not before he had made a good distance up the route that led to the mountain valleys he had just been thinking of.

He chuckled under his breath and thought to himself, *God, if this is your will, then let it be done.* Then he rode on. Surely he wouldn't be missed that long, since his master and his guests were busy preparing the manuscripts and would not need him in the immediate future. Besides, this way he could give Julia an update as to how they were progressing and allow her an opportunity to send any letters to her son and father-in-law in Lyon. He felt a glowing warmth spread over his mind as he thought of her. Another excuse to see her again made him feel a comfort he had not known in long time. Perhaps there was something there he might have missed. He put it out of his mind for now, since there were graver issues at hand, but a thought will wander like the trickle of the melting snows, as did his as he rode on.

The closer he came to the Vaudois, the more circuitous the route became. The forced reduction in speed allowed him more time to think. As before, he would try to be careful and not ride directly to the valley. Unlike the first journey, this time he had an idea of where he was headed. Although he was sure of where the valley was located, the path that led to it was twisting and uncertain. Surely this uncertainty would aid in his obscurity, although it would slow his travel somewhat.

It was now going on mid-spring, and the weather was breaking, so the riding would be much more enjoyable. Haste was not an issue in his mind. The melting snows made every stream and waterfall he rode past gurgle with the essence of the purity flowing from heaven above. The smell of blossoming bouquets wrapped their sweet aroma around his mind, nearly making him feel intoxicated with their passions. Little did he know of the circumstances that faced both parties he had now become so intertwined with in this journey of faith.

Little did he know how things were about to change or that indeed the storm clouds were brewing and were just about to unleash their fury.

The beauty of God's creation he found on this day would soon be all he would hope to ever dream of having, if even just for a moment in time.

It would be all the hope he would need.

*   *   *

The darkness of the dungeon created an empty void inside the cell, but the door that was now ajar shone a sliver of light upon the bodies that lay upon the cold, dank floor. A hand pulled back the heavy door, widening the arc of light into the room. The torches on the walls lighting the hallway farther down the prison bounced and glowed upon the rock-hewn walls. Sounds of groans and muffled voices were all that could be heard. The hand soon emerged, followed by the body of a boy. Jakob stood in the light, looking down the hall. Gabriel, still behind him, was wounded and bleeding from the sword that Lucier had drawn. He waited for Jakob to move.

"We must leave at once," whispered Gabriel as the boy stood motionless.

The fog of darkness still enveloped Gabriel's mind and made his thoughts spin. He grabbed his temples and squeezed, trying to contain the pain from the pressure he felt. The blood dripped from his arm onto the floor below. He could hear Lucier still breathing. He lay against the wall, also gashed and bleeding. He was still alive but unconscious from the blow he had suffered from the head butt Gabriel gave him during the struggle.

"Jakob . . . did you—" He was cut short.

The boy stepped out of the cell and was immediately seen by the guard at the front gate, who began to sound the horn of alarm. Then Jakob let out a wail that came from beyond. Jakob's mouth was open, as if he were singing, but there was a sound so pure, so loud, and so awe inspiring that it reached through rock, body, and soul and drained the very thought of life from each person who felt the sound wave wash across his or her being.

The guard at the main gate dropped the horn and stood with his arms at his side. The sound continued to ring, and suddenly the earth began to shake, as if triggered by the voice that now shook the foundations of the crypt. Clanks of metal could be heard as voices uplifted in rejoicing began to erupt from the pits of humanity in the holes along the corridor. Doors flew open, and weary faces, bewildered but relieved, began to emerge, reaching for the voice that drew them forth. They rubbed the sores on their arms and wrists that had been created from the many shackles and chains that had kept them locked. They walked, stiff legged, toward the boy, who now began walking toward the main gate, followed closely by Gabriel.

The sound now turned into a song—one so ancient the words were unknown by everyone who heard them, yet they came from the small body from whence the voice continued. The sound emanated through the cells of their fiber, passing from flesh to spirit, diving deep into their souls.

The guard at the main gate fell to his knees and began praying. The door burst off the hinges and fell to the floor with an eruption of dust but no sound, save for the song that now encompassed all of the matter that existed in the pit of despair from which they arose.

As Jakob reached the head jailer, the jailer begged forgiveness and continued to pray as the boy reached out and touched him on the head. The song stopped. The prisoners and other guards, stunned, stood watching as the child blessed the head jailer, granted him mercy, forgave him for his sins, and then asked him to believe through the Holy Spirit in Jesus Christ. As the child stood, still with his hand on the head of the guard, the guard began to weep.

"Do you want us to stay?" he asked the guard.

"No, no . . . go . . . all of you go . . ." He motioned, and the entire multitude of imprisoned humanity began to flow past, including the other guards who were under his command.

Still with his hand touching the guard, Jakob continued, "Do you know the love of Jesus?"

The guard, wiping the tears from his eyes, shook his head no, and began to reach for his sword. Jakob withdrew, but the guard, sensing the alarm in the child, put out his arm and motioned. "No, no, you don't understand . . . I will be put to death for allowing this mass escape. I must die" he said as he prepared to drive the sword into his own chest.

At that moment, Gabriel emerged and said, "Do not harm yourself, as Paul said before 'Believe in the Lord Jesus and you will be saved, you and your household.'"

Unbelieving yet confused, he stopped. "What do you mean?"

"You see, all you have to do is accept Jesus into your heart and your soul will be saved so that you can walk in eternity with our Lord and God."

The guard replaced his weapon and began to stand. "I will, with all my heart and soul, for what I have just witnessed, could only have been possible because of the power of the Lord."

A groan from down the hall could be heard, and in the dimly lit hallway, from the cell in which Jakob and Gabriel had emerged crawled the figure of Lucier. "Guard . . ." he called hoarsely. "Guard, sound the alarm."

"Quickly, we must go before others come. if we stay, I will surely die, as will you my brethren."

"Follow me. we will stay to the shadows, going through the underground passages."

As they began to race off, Lucier's voice could be heard calling for help, echoing off the empty chambers that now held their captor, alone and abandoned.

Chapter 26

HOPE IN VAIN

They have envisioned futility and false divination, saying, 'Thus says the Lord!' But the Lord has not sent them; yet they hope that the word may be confirmed.

—Ezekiel 13:6

A rooster crowed in the early morning as darkness turned to gray. There would be no sun today. A thick, overcast sky blanketed the upper peaks of the surrounding mountains enclosing the Vaudois below. The daily routines began as they always have for centuries, with the morning prayer, Bible studies, chores, and then the meal. However, today, unlike so many others, would be a dark chapter in the story of the Apostle Speakers. Today would become a judgment day for the weary keepers of the faith.

As the army made its way into the lower reaches of the Vaudois, the alarm went out, but unlike before, there was no omnipotent protector to halt the onrush of the army. The few militia mountaineers who were able to reach their posts did little to stop the crush of weaponry that bore down upon the tiny village. Jean Paul was in the pasture with the flock when the onslaught began and had only reached the house to warn his mother and sisters when the first riders reached the crest of the ridge facing their home across the meadow below. He knew there would be no chance of survival for his mother, grandmother, and sisters if he didn't act. Julia took Maria and the girls and quickly began heading up the back trail toward the secret sanctuary. It would take them hours to reach it, but at least it was safer than staying behind. There was no time to saddle their sole horse, so they ran on foot with what little they could quickly grab and run with.

Meanwhile, Jean Paul prepared his bow and took aim at the lead riders. Several more warriors joined him who had just arrived from the village to help with the initial onslaught. This was very much like the first attack. Heavily armored soldiers on horseback were driving across the meadow, with foot soldiers following. This time they did not advance at full speed but advanced with caution. Jean Paul and his comrades let several arrows fly, some hitting their mark, others bouncing off the metal armor. No retaliation shots had been sent. It was as if they were merely spitting into the wind, with no impact. They quickly realized the futility of their actions and prepared to retreat to the next line of defense—the village wall, their last possible stand.

They fled Jean Paul's house and farm just as the archers set free a swarm of arrows that blanketed the yard, killing all the livestock that remained, pinning them to the earth as a seamstress prepares cloth to be sewn. The beasts bleated and moaned with anguish and pain, but the roar of the hooves of the horsemen soon drowned them out. They lay there writhing in the final throes of death in silence as the roar drove past them in pursuit of Jean Paul and the others.

They ran as quickly as they could, reaching the village walls, leaping over it and joining many others who had taken up the same position. Jean Paul looked around. The women, children, and elders had already fled the village to find safety in the sanctuary. What was left were mostly farmers, hunters, and craftsmen preparing to battle against skilled fighters who were seasoned in countless battles in previous Crusades. He knew this would be a losing battle. He had only time to bow his head and ask God for guidance. Nothing came.

How is this being a leader? Jean Paul thought as he opened his eyes, preparing an arrow for his bow and turning to see the first of the cavalry riders reaching the curve in the road that led to the village behind them.

He looked down the line. Others were prepared as well, arrows ready. Again he tried to listen, eyes closed. All he could hear was the growing roar of hoof beats approaching, pounding in his ears, matching time with the beat of his heart. He asked for forgiveness from God and stood. He turned toward the oncoming wave of slaughter and yelled to the others, "Arrows ready."

The others stood.

"Fire."

The oncoming riders continued their advance. A couple took hits between their armor, halting them, but the majority continued on, unfazed by the first volley. Then the archers from the advancing force returned fire, darkening the sky as the arrows flew toward them.

"Down, all down," shouted Jean Paul as the air whirred with the incoming projectiles.

He ducked behind the wall as the lethal rain of wood and steel began to fall. Brother Lorenz, who had been next to Jean Paul, failed to crouch far enough and took an arrow to his head, instantly killing him and splattering blood on Jean Paul as he fell forward, crashing his face into the wall.

The riders were now nearly to the wall as Jean Paul ordered them to shoot once more. "Arrows ready." The remnants of their force stood. "Aim for the knees," he yelled. "Fire."

This time their shots had more impact as the arrows took out the legs of the horses and they fell forward, causing several of the riders to be ejected from their mounts, some having their horses land on them, others merely being thrown free of their horses only to come up quickly to their feet and continue advancing on foot.

The army's front line reached the wall, and the few Vaudois fighters who remained began hand-to-hand combat. Some fled while others stayed to fight, which included Jean Paul. He was soon surrounded, as were all of the other warriors who remained. They fought gallantly but soon became keenly aware that they would all soon die. Jean Paul had only managed to wound his adversaries at best, since they were all heavily armored compared with to light armor that Vaudois men had confiscated from the battlefield from the previous battle. Even so, they were taking heavy casualties until the only ones who remained were Jean Paul and two others. They were completely surrounded, overwhelmed, and outmanned. Major Crowell rode up on the scene and demanded the fighting to stop. Still swinging when the order was called, Jean Paul's blade, reaching its mark, bounced off the papal knight's armor unharmed. So weary was his swing that he nearly fell forward from the sudden pause in action.

Crowell dismounted, handed the reins to one of his escorts who had also dismounted, and walked to the soldiers who now surrounded the three remaining brave warriors.

Jean Paul sank to his knees, as did the others when they saw him collapse. He began to pray the Lord's Prayer loudly enough for the other two to hear him, and they began to do so as well.

Crowell walked over to Jean Paul and pulled out his sword. This one appeared to be the leader. Jean Paul's head was bowed in prayer, and he was in the perfect position for Crowell to decapitate the youth and be done with it. Crowell grabbed his sword with both hands in preparation for the quick downward swing that would be necessary to cleanly sever his head when he heard him speaking. Could it be? Was he actually praying?

"Forgive our trespasses as we forgive those who trespass against us . . ."

Crowell's mind drifted off in hesitation as the conversation with the priest the night before returned. His concern about killing women and children had apparently been for naught, since they had already fled, leaving behind this ragtag force of an army. But what struck a chord was the fact that these demons were praying the Lord's Prayer. *How could they?* he thought. *Did the priest not say that they would speak as if demons, yet here they are speaking the language of the church?*

"Stop at once," he shouted to Jean Paul, coming back to the present.

Jean Paul finished with, "The power and glory forever, amen."

Crowell positioned the flat side of his blade underneath Jean Paul's chin and raised his face to meet his. "Do you know what you say?" he asked, unbelieving "Are you prepared to die?" he said, with his teeth clenched. He felt a rage inside him he couldn't explain.

He raised the blade above his head, ready to drive the steel through the youth's flesh, pausing once more, this time to ask the Lord's forgiveness for the act he was about to perform, when again, he heard the unfathomable. He looked down at the youth, whose eyes were closed in prayer, "The Lord *is* my shepherd; I shall not want. He makes me to lie down in green pastures; He leads me beside the still waters. He restores my soul; He leads me in the paths of righteousness for His name's sake. Yea, though I walk through the valley of the shadow of death, I will fear no evil; for You *are* with me; Your rod and Your staff, they comfort me. You prepare a table before me in the presence of my enemies; you anoint my head with oil; My cup runs over. Surely goodness and mercy shall follow me all the days of my life; and I will dwell in the house of the Lord forever."

Crowell's arm's buckled slightly. He felt queasy.

The words kept coming: "The earth *is* the Lord's, and all its fullness, the world and those who dwell therein. For He has founded it upon the seas, and established it upon the waters. Who may ascend into the hill of the Lord?"

The gravity of the moment weighed upon his body, and he dropped the sword, leaning on it for support as he looked down at the mere boy who did not waver but continued to pray aloud, quoting Scripture word for word, as did the other two who knelt under the raised blades behind him.

The clouds wisped over the peaks. The air was cold upon the soldiers' exposed flesh. Banners of the Catholic Church wafted in the gentle breeze, with crosses turning to and fro, as if nodding in agreement to the sound of the Word.

The other soldiers waited the command in silence, watching the strange behavior of their commanding officer. "Sir . . . we are ready," said one of the executioners who was waiting for Crowell's command.

In a brief second of inner anger at all that had been done or said of the vile people who desecrated the word of the Holy Roman church, he spit the command, "Down."

The sound of bone and flesh meeting steel could be heard behind him, followed by the gentle thuds of the heads dropping to the ground as a melon from a basket. There was no cry of fear before the sound, no wail of anticipation, only the silenced breaths of prayers that ended in whispers.

Jean Paul continued, unwavering, now resolved to join his Maker on the other side.

Crowell, now nearly sick with anger, raised his own sword to finish the task when a pain shot through his body, making him fall back, as if being shot. It was a flash of fire that caused him to drop the sword and crash backward, careening for the ground. The others quickly came to his side, with one of the other executioners striding to finish what Crowell had apparently wanted to complete.

Crowell tried to focus, but the pain was so intense he could barely raise his head. A dark tunnel formed his vision as he fought to retain focus.

The words of the boy kept flowing, each one stabbing his heart. He saw the executioner raising the blade in his place, and with the strength he could pull forth between the arcs of pain, he yelled, "Halt, stop at once."

Jean Paul also stopped.

Sweat ran into his eyes underneath the battle-scarred helmet he wore. He pulled it off, wiping his face with the back side of his armored forearm, sweat glazing the metal plates. "Let him be . . . we can use him," he said, now squinting between the throbbing pain that ran from his arm to his temples.

"Sir, are you all right?" asked the sergeant at arms. The executioner also backed away and watched the Vaudoisian with contempt.

"Sir, I can finish the job if you like," he said coarsely, as if he enjoyed killing.

"No, let him be . . . God has stopped me for a reason," Crowell said through the pain. "Get him up and bind him. We'll take him with us while we search for the others."

At this command, the executioner summoned soldiers nearby to bind Jean Paul, one on each arm, lifting him and throwing him face down, binding his arms and legs behind his back. When they were done, they lifted him up and bound him on the back of a nearby horse that had been prepared for the captive.

From the corner of his eye, Jean Paul could see the bodies of his brethren, some pierced with arrows, some with severed limbs, while others appeared to be merely asleep. Then there were the other two, Jared and Stephen, bodies were separated from their heads. This was not how he wanted to remember them. He saw them in the open field when they were boys, racing, arms outstretched, pretending to be horses as they ran, the wind whipping at their clothes as they ran wildly through the tall alpine grasses. He could see them all sitting under Grandfather's apple tree, hearing the Word of God together and enjoying the stories he would spin. They would all laugh until their sides ached with pain—pain now they would never feel again.

A soldier bent over to collect a severed head and grabbed the blond mane that belonged to the head of Jared, as if it were nothing more than an ornament. He grabbed it like a rag, stuffing it into a burlap bag. Jean Paul watched in horror as the remaining dead had their heads severed from their bodies. Other soldiers jokingly carried on as they placed them on poles and positioned them along the wall, as if some macabre decoration of death or conquest to warn any who might follow what they were to expect.

Jean Paul felt as if he would be sick, but he closed his eyes and continued to pray. The burning sensation of tears now blurred his vision. He was searching for any sign God was with him at all. What had he done to be delivered from death . . . or into the hands of hell?

His head spun as the horse began to move, being led by another mounted cavalryman. They continued onward through the village in search of the others who had fled. Some of the troops had continued onward at the start, trailing those who had fled on foot. Jean Paul prayed his mother and sisters would make it to the sanctuary, or for that matter, that everyone would safely make it. He feared that they might not have been quick enough to evade the eyes of the enemy and had been seen escaping up the trails that led to the remote cave.

He could see from his bound position scenes that caused him dark despair. His heart mourned as he saw body after body, fallen and slain along their trail. Men, women, and children were being slaughtered with no concern for life . . . He silently wept.

The tears felt hot as they dripped from his cheeks onto the leather of the strapping below his face that kept him bound to the horse. The wetness from his tears left dark streaks on the leather; together they melted into the sweat stains left from the steed that were created in the drive to the village from its onslaught that began the massacre.

The clouds that had enveloped the sun began to weep as well, until a driving rain started to fall. The cold drops only found numbness when the penetrated Jean Paul's body, for he was now resolved to escape. He was wrapped in the grace of God.

The soldiers pulled their heavy cloaks over their shoulders as they continued on, doing their best to follow the tracks of their quarry that were quickly being washed away in the torrential downpour. Jean Paul lost consciousness, and the darkness that overcame him was welcome

Chapter 27

FREEDOM

But now having been set free from sin, and having become slaves of God, you have your fruit to holiness, and the end, everlasting life.
—Romans 6:22

The darkness of the caverns they traversed through to escape the dungeons were often lit from distant torchlight that weakly shone down long corridors. Large rats scurried across their path, red eyes glowing in haunting grimaces as they passed. Water dripped and ran down the walls, creating a glistening sheen to the dankness they raced through, with the head jailer leading the way.

Gabriel felt stronger and more in control of his thoughts the farther they traveled. Now he realized fully the source of the drain on his strength earlier. Collecting himself, he put his mind more into their immediate situation and the person who was hopefully leading them to a successful escape. He was well aware of Scriptures that described the event that had just unfolded. Jakob too was aware. Neither escapee spoke a word as they quickly and silently followed their leader.

They emerged from a secluded exit from the prison, which was covered by overgrown bushes and low-hanging limbs from budding tree limbs, and the guard motioned for them to follow. Gabriel quickly caught up and matched the guard's steps.

"Your name, sir?" Gabriel asked.

"Joseph," he said, panting his response since they had not slowed their pace since starting their escape. The thought of the papal sentries following them caused a feeling of despair. "I must reach my family and find refuge for them, for surely Lucier will have them cast into the lot we have just departed."

Gabriel easily understood their fate. Anyone assisting in their escape faced death, as would his family. They did not hesitate to follow or match his fearful, hasty pace.

"Surely the Lord will find mercy on my soul for what I have done," Joseph said as sweat poured down his dark, concerned brow.

"Fear not, for the favor of the Lord is with you," Gabriel responded.

"What will I tell my wife and children? What have I done?" he questioned out loud. The reality of the situation dawned on him as they approached the humble, low building with a surrounding stone-walled yard that was the guard's home. In the vastness of the moment in the prison, there was no question as to what the right choice was, but now, with the coming dawn, here near his home, he realized what his choice meant. They entered through a wooden gate, which was covered with ivy, and quickly made their way through a series of doors and curtains.

"You stay here while I speak with my family," he said, motioning them to a small room with sparse, roughhewn furniture, which was obviously hand made.

Jakob sat on a small pallet of a bed and leaned back against the wall. He laid his head back, closing his eyes, feeling the weariness of the last few hours weighing upon him. He listened to the sound of Gabriel's footsteps walking out of the room. He was just about asleep when he heard the small voice.

"Hello."

He blinked his eyes open, half awake, seeing a young girl's head looking into the room. Her body was hidden behind the veil of the curtain separating the rooms.

"Who are you?" she asked, still hiding behind the cloth, as if she was afraid to enter the room until there was a satisfactory answer.

"Jakob," he answered wearily. "Jakob of the Rora Vaudois."

Over the past few months, he had often felt pangs of sadness for his homeland. Even though Peter's wife had tried her best to make him comfortable and treat him like her own son, he still longed to be held in his mother's arms once again, to hear the sound of his sisters' voices laughing and playing. It all came back to him now as the young girl now hesitantly entered the room. She was dressed in provincial clothing—a long tunic dress that was plainly decorated with a cord drawn loosely around a tiny waist. She wistfully moved closer. Her golden hair was tied with a small knot of cord and hung behind her.

"You and the other one come with my father from the prison . . . why?" She squinted as she asked the question, as if there were suspicion in the thought. Jakob didn't get the words out before they heard a heavy knocking at the front door. Quickly, she grabbed his hand and pulled him up and out of the room, whisking him away farther to the back of the compound.

*   *   *

Gabriel had been concerned about them being followed or worse, Joseph turning them in for a reward. He felt the presence of darkness nearing, so his concern was more for what their next move might be when he heard the horse's footsteps beyond the front gate. He knew they would have to make an escape out the rear of the compound if they were to evade capture again. He definitely knew he did not want to go back into the recess of that hellish abyss, with the presence of darkness all around. He didn't like the feeling of the fog that enveloped his mind, and he could now feel it approaching again. He must move quickly. The knock came at the door.

Gabriel moved back to the room where he had left Jakob, but the boy was now gone. How could he have not listened to his command to stay put? He felt a twinge of anger, but the need to flee overwhelmed it. He hesitated momentarily when the feeling of standing to fight took hold. *No*, he thought. *Mustn't now, it's too soon . . .*

The knock came again, and he moved, quickly now, finding Joseph and his family frozen in fear. He grabbed Joseph while moving, pushing him into action, and they all now began their frenetic departure. There was a stable at the rear of the compound, and they quickly mounted small but sturdy horses. There was still no sign of Jakob, but there was no time now. They could hear the shouts of the soldiers as they entered the house and the noise of furniture being tossed against the walls, breaking and crashing as they moved closer.

Gabriel told Joseph to meet them on the eastern edge of town near nightfall, where they would carry on their journey to safety. He spurred his horse to return back to the former hiding place from where it seemed it had been a century since they left. As he did, out of the corner of his eye he saw Jakob and another small figure dart through the alley and into another building. He knew the boy could find his way around the city, and if he was with someone else, then he obviously had help and would be alright for now. He had to return to Arktos and the others to notify them that the time was now for them all to move. The papal guard would be on high alert and would possibly round up any suspicious persons. They could ill afford another visit to the dungeons of Lyon, where this time they might not witness another miracle. The dark clouds of destruction were growing now, and distant thunder of horses' hooves drew near. The horse bolted underneath Gabriel, and he was off. The future was nearing, and soon a desperate people would find more of their kind joining their ranks.

*　*　*

Jakob and his new friend had heard the commotion coming from the compound and knew they could not go back. They saw the girl's family ride off toward the eastern side of town, and Gabriel raced off in another direction. Jakob instinctively knew he must make it back to their hiding place, for he felt that they would soon have to leave after their close encounter with Lucier. The girl with Jakob, Anna, was quick to lead him to safety, and he wondered if she too was angelic. He didn't know any more if he was being led by God or by sheer luck, but he felt he was definitely being protected. From his early childhood lessons with his grandfather, he knew deep down the help was from a divine source.

Anna was scared now. From the first moment she had awoken today, she felt there was something different in the air, but she had not counted on anything of this nature. She had instinctively, but with some degree of curiosity, led Jakob out of the room toward the back of the compound to show him around and find out more about him. Then all hell broke loose. Scared and looking for a safe haven, she took Jakob from one hiding location to another. As a child in the large city of Lyon, she had found many hiding places in play, but now they were a matter of preserving their freedom. She did not know the gravity of their situation. Jakob followed until it was obvious they were merely continuing to hide. When he felt there was a chance to move farther back to where he needed to go, he took charge and grabbed Anna's hand, pulling her behind as she struggled to keep up.

"We must hurry now," he said as he looked back over his shoulder as they raced along from alleyway to alleyway. Her eyes were wide with fear as her hair flowed behind her.

"Where to?" she asked, gasping as they raced.

"To a sanctuary, but only for a short time. Then we will probably meet up with your family later." He added the last part to try to comfort Anna's fears, which seemed to be growing with each passing street.

The farther they went, the more papal soldiers they could see beginning to come out onto the streets. They appeared to be looking for someone or somebody. They moved faster, keeping to the shadows. Time was of the essence.

They could smell the early-morning smells of the marketplace, which was near the sanctuary. Jakob knew they were close now. He kept the pace, even with Anna slowing him. They darted through a narrow passage between two large buildings—almost there now—and erupted into a side street, where several guards stood.

The guards were startled by the sudden appearance of a young boy fitting the description of the escapee and the young girl. They had positioned themselves near the area where they had first found the boy and suspected he might return. They drew their swords and daggers, quickly encircling the innocent pair, eliminating all possibility of escape.

Anna looked at Jakob with utter despair and horror. *What have I done to become a fugitive, and why does everyone appear to hate this boy?* she thought to herself.

Jakob could feel Anna staring at him, but this was not the first time he had been in this predicament. However, unlike before, he had planned on what he might do if it ever happened again. His only weapon was his gift. The countless days of practice with Gabriel had given him the strength and faith to do what must be done. His confidence was the only thing that had been left untested. He had to act. As the guards came bitingly close, Jakob began.

The shock of what Anna was seeing could not match what she heard. The battle-hardened soldiers who were put here in Lyon mostly disliked it because it didn't quench their thirst for bloodshed, was about to be sated. They suddenly shrunk in maddened fear. Agonizing wretchedness pulled masks of horror across their gruesome faces as their limbs began to distort and shrivel under the weight of a force unseen but heard . . . for Jakob started wailing. It was a pitch, an octave so unreal that it could only resonate from a godly source.

Anna saw the scene unfold before her, but for some reason unknown to her, she did not hear. It was apparent that there was a sound that was causing this, for the soldiers grasped at their ears, as if the pieces of flesh were crushing their skulls, trying to cover them to protect them from absorbing the punishment any further. One barbarian completely ripped off one of his ears and began to chew it in a grisly display of agony while he fell to the ground, writhing in painful numbness, matching his fallen comrades in arms.

Jakob continued, eyes closed, hands folded across his chest, pushing the sound outward while focusing on the images in his mind. At first it was a practiced sound he made, one that made the connection, but then suddenly, as if he was transported, he could see his Vaudois again—but something was dreadfully wrong.

He could see the blood and trail of death up the mountain that was unfolding. He could smell the horse and feel its bindings around his chest. He was bound but alive. His heart quickened, for death was everywhere. The village was being destroyed by the papal soldiers. The heads of fellow Vaudoisians, absent from their bodies, stood vigilant guard, watching in death while mounted on pikes and poles. He wailed the pain that smote his heart. He began to tremble with rage as tears filled his eyes. He could not stop. The smoke of burning homes and bodies filled his nostrils as gruesome scene after gruesome scene passed. He was fearful that at any moment he might see his family, but they were nowhere to be found. *May God give them safe passage,* he prayed. The water fell about him as the sky opened up.

Blood began to ooze from the fallen soldiers' orifices, as if their heads were being crushed in a grape press. The child's pain was being directly transferred to them and magnified to an untold level of grief. None of them could breathe, for their chests had been compressed beyond life support.

The punishment only ceased when, drenched in sweat, shaken, and exhausted, he stopped singing, falling to his knees, head bent in prayers, falling to his hands. The soldiers lay there dead. It was such an utterly horrific death that none would understand or believe the story the young girl would try to convey.

Anna stood, reaching down for Jakob, afraid to touch him but feeling the need to do so. She felt a connection to him somehow after witnessing the event that had just taken place. She knelt beside him and began to pray.

Arktos and Peter had just turned the corner, a few yards from the sanctuary door, when they saw the boy fall to his knees. Sensing something serious had just transpired and fearing the worst, they ran to his side. He was unharmed, as was the girl, who appeared to be trying to comfort him. As they approached, she looked up at them, helplessly whispering, "Please help us."

Arktos thanked God aloud as he hugged them both, wrapping his long arms around them and bear hugging them so hard that Jakob seemed to come back to his senses. They were unharmed, which was not the case for the soldiers, who now had become victims of their own sins. It was not difficult for Arktos to imagine what had happened because of the positions of the soldiers' bodies and the spot where Jakob and the young girl stood. Time was fleeting though. They needed to make haste. It was apparent the city was abuzz with fevered searching by the guards, who were evidently looking for recent escapees from the horrific prison. Apparently Jakob and Gabriel were involved somehow, because here Jakob now stood.

"We need to leave immediately," Peter said firmly but hesitantly. He did not want to stop the reunion but felt the need to preserve them for their own safety. He knew the dead guards would soon be missed and joined by others who knew of their presence.

"They're dying," Jakob whispered to his grandfather as Arktos tried to get him to his feet.

"Yes, my son, they are, but do not worry, for they were well deserving of their fate," he said as he looked down at the heathen bodies that were strewn about in their own blood and bodily fluids.

"No . . . not them."

Arktos stopped. "Who then?" he said, stopping before he knew he had said it, for if Jakob was not talking about here, then the only other place that mattered was surely where the boy was speaking of. A slice of cold water shot straight through his thick barrel of a chest to his heart.

"God the Father in heaven . . . not the Vaudois!"

"I pray it's not true, but the picture . . . just now . . . so vivid." Jakob began to fall back down, but Anna came to his other side, propping him up under his left shoulder while his grandfather grabbed the other.

"He saved us just now, sir," she said to Arktos as Peter led the way out of the street and back down to safety. "You must know . . . it was something like I have never seen before in my life."

Arktos nodded, for now his thoughts were beginning to turn to the few words the boy had spoken. He began to pray and ask for the strength he needed to keep in mind that God would take care of them, for it was all in his hands, even though he felt the longing to take care of things in his own strength.

Chapter 28

BROKEN HEART

A man who isolates himself seeks his own desire; He rages against all wise judgment.

—Proverbs 18:1

arik had ridden for several days now and was looking forward to the rest that awaited him in the Vaudois. He had been extra careful not to make his path obvious as he traveled, which caused him to take routes less traveled and more precarious through the mountainous regions he now traversed. He felt as if he were always looking over his shoulder on this trip, but since he was riding alone, he was able to travel more quickly and at his own pace. He had felt uneasy since making the turn onto the road that led to the mountains, as if something was amiss. There had been very little indication of any movement by the papal guard toward this direction. That was what had set him on edge. Something was odd. As he trotted his stallion through the narrow canyon in which he now rode, his mind was on the absence of the dangers when he rounded the curve ahead and his heart nearly stopped, as if cold water had been poured into his veins.

There in the bend before him were severed heads mounted on poles. The flies buzzed around the scene of death, adding to the macabre vision of stench and decay. Sullen faces looked downward as if praying in silence for an answer to the brutality they had faced in the final moments of their lives. The display of death was obviously placed where it was to provide the most shock possible to travelers who might round the bend. He could only guess why, but the perpetrators of the act were definitely trying to display a statement of their presence and what they would do to anyone who would stand in their path.

Marik regained himself and spurred his horse forward, now more cautious, moving his hand to unstrap his saber at his side. The heads were not fresh, but they were not very old either, since the blood was still coagulating around the ragged flesh that lay open at the necks of each head. His heart began to race as his thought flashed the faces of Julia, her children . . . Jean Paul . . . the old grandmother. Would they survive, or were they already gone? He rode fast now but watched every movement of every new space that came before him for any sign of the adversary he knew had already reached his sanctuary he had hoped would remain unscathed.

The fear that would normally cause him to hesitate was being suppressed by the sheer rush of adrenaline that pulsed through his soul. Fear and anger at what he dreaded lay ahead drove him blindly forward, with no concern for his own safety. He spurred the horse faster, careening around tight, narrow curves up the canyon. Gashes ripped into his leggings as the walls more than once came close enough for the jagged rocks to lash out at them as they tore past. Death could not cause him to slow, for now the moment at hand had awakened something deep inside that could not be dampened until the darkness that choked his mind was vanquished. His hand brushed the saber at his side as he and the horse surged forward up the steep mountainside. Flashes of bodies, dismembered pieces, and bloodied rocks passed by as they raced onward. Still no living being to either assault or to save came into view—only the vestiges of the evil that now blackened the soil where once only purity existed.

*   *   *

The soldiers stood over the body that had recently breathed its last breath at the hands of their fellow soldiers. They were greedily working at the boots they were trying to strip from the body when they briefly heard the sounds of a horse's hooves just before the hot, searing blade slashed through the flesh and bone of the neck of one of the looters. The other instinctively dove for cover when the sharp blade stung his back as he tried in vain to escape the rider's fury of death. Their slumped bodies joined their victim and added two more to the countless number who lay slaughtered around the village as the rider vanished as quickly as he had arrived.

*   *   *

Crowell had ordered his men to continue pursuing the few remaining combatants up the valley but not to go beyond the upper reaches of the village. The rain had ceased for now, but more storm clouds were gathering at the highest peaks of the rugged mountain terrain that surrounded the valley. There had been almost no resistance, and Crowell's fear was that there might be an ambush if they were to pursue the people farther into the narrow valleys of the upper Vaudois. He also knew that many would escape beyond that point, but for now, he was satisfied with the body count he had compiled. Several hundred lay dying or dead, and by this time tomorrow, the village would be utterly destroyed. With nothing left for the heretics to return to, he would have accomplished his mission, however small a step. At least it would be one less village left to resist and spread the heretical decrees of these Vaudoisian people.

As they moved upward, he continued to pull in his flanking troops so they would not be stretched out too far. In these remote valleys, a retaliatory strike could come from any angle at any moment. He was not taking chances. Along the way, he was having his battle-hardened soldiers collect and display the dead. They had learned this tactic while on the Crusades. The vicious display was meant to mentally challenge the most ardent opponents into having second thoughts about attacking, and if they did, the imagery would be difficult to forget.

He was still having difficulty breathing at this altitude. The pain he had felt earlier left him sore, and his head throbbed. The dull gray skies only added to the sullen demeanor that engulfed his thoughts. He would be glad when this mission was complete. The fact that they were attacking their fellow countrymen rather than totally alien Islamic infidels was unnerving. He tried to keep such thoughts at bay, especially while in the midst of a battle, but now that the fighting had all but stopped, the lull was provoking his conscience to the forefront.

He dismounted from his horse and stood at the foot of a large boulder that separated two buildings while he watched priests who had been embedded in their ranks provide last rites for the dead. Torrinto and other priests were merely going through the motions since they knew they could never minister to all the dead, and besides, these were the heathens who had turned their backs on the church and in the priests' beleaguered minds, God as well. Administering last rites to beings who they felt were morally and spiritually equivalent to animals was more of a nicety than anything. Besides, it gave the younger priests plenty of practice, which was part of why they had been brought along. There would plenty more in the future to practice on—both in forcing conversions and if not taken, then last rites.

As Crowell watched the pitiful display of church ritual, a column of soldiers moved into view, some mounted and others walking their steeds. Toward the rear of the train were the wounded. They pulled up to the major and stopped. The lead sergeant reported.

"Sir, we have secured our flank and retrieved our dead and wounded. And major, we also have one of theirs," he said, standing stiffly at attention while he spoke.

"One of theirs you say?" Crowell asked while rubbing his chin. "Show me."

The sergeant led him to the rear of the column where the body lay across the horse, strapped across with his hands tied to his feet underneath, as if his body was a saddle.

"I didn't know we were taking prisoners," Crowell said, walking around to the side of the horse where the head of the prisoner hung limply.

"Sir, with all due respect, this is the one you ordered us to bind and—"

"Oh yes, yes, that's right," he said, interrupting the sergeant. He suddenly felt the pain in his arm again as he lifted Jean Paul's chin. Jean Paul had still not yet gained consciousness.

Crowell studied him as one might the carcass of a successful hunt. *The clergy would have you believe these people are demons,* he thought to himself as he studied Jean Paul. This youth looked to be reaching early adulthood, yet Crowell recalled from his encounter with Jean Paul earlier in the day that he carried himself with character well beyond his years. His features were weathered but youthful. Even with the many cuts and blood splatter scattered about his face, he bore a handsome visage. He dropped the boy's chin and backed away.

"Keep this one under close guard, Sergeant," he said, pointing his chin at Jean Paul.

"Yes sir, Major, sir" replied the sergeant.

"We'll have a little chat with him later this evening and see what he knows. Put him under house arrest over there." Crowell pointed to the community house where Julia and the children had spent the previous Christmas festival. Now it was merely a cavernous shelter, with no signs of the beauty that once lit its walls. "Put him under guard, and have the priest attend to his wounds. I don't want him dying before I have a chance to be entertained."

With that he laughed a smirking laugh that erupted into a deep, raspy cough he had to pause and catch his breath from before continuing.

The rain began to come down again in icy sheets. The major pulled his cloak up over his head, trying to protect the back of his neck from the seemingly freezing moisture. The others hurried about their arduous tasks and sought cover in what remained of the houses that had not yet been set on fire. Crowell's eyes followed the sergeant at arms, who continued on with his team and trailing wounded and dying soldiers, while a guard took Jean Paul and the mount to which he was bound to the community house.

Crowell turned and walked back to his horse. He needed time and a warm, dry place to sort things out before they continued. For now, the tasks at hand would keep his men and his adversaries busy. He needed time to regroup and plan for the next move. He knew he was a stranger in this barren land, and he could not rest until he was back in the safety of their home barracks. Strange as it seemed, this was war.

*   *   *

Three lone footmen remained behind at the wall where Jean Paul had made his final stand. They did not see the rider approach as they bent to the task at hand. The larger of the three was digging the grave with a pick, as the other two laughed while leaning on their shovels. There had only been a handful of casualties on their side, so it was fitting that they receive a proper Christian burial. The men at work had only recently joined the guard, and as such, they were the first to be chosen for grave detail.

"This ground is nothing but rock," said the big man from down in the hole he dug.

"Oh get on with it," cracked one of the onlookers.

The other one chuckled, "We don't want to be all night digging"

"We? I don't see *we* digging," he shouted as he swung the pick down into another solid stone.

Just then the weight of a body falling upon him knocked him to his knees. As he looked up, he could see the horror in the face of the remaining soldier, who now dropped his shovel as the end of the saber penetrated through his body toward the hole. The sword vanished, and he slumped to the ground, revealing the warrior who had wielded the weapon. The big man could see retribution written on the face of the man. He wiped the blood of the fallen soldier off on his black cloak with the back of the hand that was not on the sword, which was now pointed point blank at his throat.

"Are you ready to die like those slaughtered sheep you so ruthlessly murdered?" he said through his clinched teeth.

The big man stood, knowing the man above had full advantage over him with the height and superior weapon. He did not shrink from the threat, though. He had been in worse predicaments and come out alive—maybe not unscathed, but alive.

"May God spare my soul if it not be my day to do so," he replied. The man's face instantly changed.

Marik realized he had become the horror he had witnessed and vowed to never return to again. He felt the rush of anger drain from him, but now here he stood over a man who was prepared to battle for his life.

"One mustn't die to find Christ," Marik quickly retorted, trying to calm his nerves and become a master over his mind again, eliminating the animal instinct that rose from within.

A whisper enveloped his mind, making him sense the pause in time. On the battlefield, even the slightest hesitation could mean death. The big man noticed and grabbed the saber with his free hand. Blood pulsed through the big man's fingers through his grasp on the blade of the sword that now seemed embedded in his throat. A river of red began to drain down the sword toward his neck. The warmth of the waterfall of his own life source fell upon him.

Marik felt the big man try to yank the sword from him, which pulled him off balance just enough as the missile of death nearly hit its mark, ripping through his cloak, just grazing his ribcage as it passed through and slapped into a rock several yards away. His flesh was ripped open on his side, and it burned with fire momentarily. Then adrenaline washed over the pain as panic began to ensue. Just then, another barrage of arrows came. One blasted into his right thigh, through leather, muscle, and bone; another struck him in midsection, taking his breath. His vision narrowed to a small tunnel. *Must focus,* was his thought. Then, with what felt like one last shove of his sword, he fell forward for what seemed an eternity.

Chapter 29

HONEY FROM THE ROCK...

But the salvation of the righteous is from the Lord; He is their strength in the time of trouble. And the Lord shall help them and deliver them; He shall deliver them from the wicked, and save them, because they trust in Him.

—Psalm 37:39-40

Julia and the girls had been running now for what seemed days as they fled up the canyon walls to the sanctuary. They were not alone. Many others from the village were with them, fighting for air to fill their lungs as they pushed their bodies beyond their physical limits. Maria had fallen behind but told them not to worry but go on. There were others with her who were aged, some with handicapped limbs. They all struggled to flee to safety together. There had been no divine intervention this time, unlike the previous encounter with the papal guard. There had been no fellow Vaudois warriors to aid in their protection. It was if they had been forgotten by everyone, including God.

Some of the younger ones tried to help the elders up the steep terrain. They all had spent their lives here, so the only thing that was unfamiliar to them at this altitude was the pace at which they were climbing in order to escape the onslaught that pursued them up the mountain.

How far could they go before they could stop fearing that they might be followed to their sanctuary? Should they stop and find another route so as not to give away the holiest of places? Julia struggled with this thought as the fear and darkness tried to smother her mind. The vile images they had seen before escaping the village—friends, family, and neighbors being killed and tortured by the creatures who carried the symbol of the holy cross as their banner—could not escape them.

The girls were tiring now. There seemed to be no stamina left in their once-strong little legs. They could run and play all day in the alpine meadows, but something about the demonic force weighed on them all, forcing them to tire now as despair seemed to gain on them like the fog on the breath after an early-morning rain.

There were many caves in the fingers of the mountains that were their home, many of which Julia was familiar, so she chose one that was nearby that might provide some shelter from the cold rain that pelted them. They needed time to rest and regain some strength and warmth before fleeing farther up the granite monolith if they continued to be pursued. Besides, the rest who straggled behind needed time to catch up with them.

They gained the mouth of the cave, and she instructed the girls to begin gathering material to make torches as they moved just inside out of the weather. The respite from the icy winds instantly warmed her. She found a slab to rest on while she waited. The light was dim, but she could make out others finding their way to their temporary refuge. As if by instinct, they all knew where to go. It was the first time since beginning their plight that she had a chance to think of the others behind and of Jean Paul. Her heart quickened as a dark agony swept over her. She tried not to think of what might have become of him. It was evident that the army that now pursued them up the mountain had not been slowed at their entrance into the valley, which meant that Jean Paul's and his companions' efforts were in vain.

Then there was her little Jakob and his grandfather. There had been only one message from them, which arrived shortly after Christmas, saying that they had reached their destination and they were doing well. That was months ago. Were they still safe, or had they possibly tried to return, only to have been slaughtered like the others?

Her mind drifted as she tried not to despair. Marik was with them; in that, some comfort came over her. Would he ever return to the Vaudois, or was he like the shadow of a passing cloud over the peaks that towered above? Her heart was heavy. If he did return, dare she allow the truth of her growing interest in him be known to him, or would he only think of her as the mountain widower she was? He had sacrificed his own safety to find them, which in its own way gave her pause. The more she reflected back on it, the more she felt something for the passion this man had for God, which then caused her to want to know more of him. But then again, he too could be lying dead below, bleeding out the last ounce of passion for God and the Word they held so dear.

She felt her throat tighten as she choked back tears and pushed the pain away. She tried to lessen the weight of her sorrow by trying to recall Scripture, any Word of God that might make this darkness go away. The first thing that came to mind was Psalm 81. Before she knew it, she was singing the words softly as she rocked back and forth on her stone seat.

"Sing for joy to God our strength; shout aloud to the God of Jacob! Begin the music, strike the timbrel, play the melodious harp and lyre. Sound the ram's horn at the New Moon, and when the moon is full, on the day of our festival; this is a decree for Israel, an ordinance of the God of Jacob.

When God went out against Egypt, he established it as a statute for Joseph. I heard an unknown voice say: 'I removed the burden from their shoulders; their hands were set free from the basket. In your distress you called and I rescued you, I answered you out of a thundercloud; I tested you at the waters of Meribah. Hear me, my people, and I will warn you—if you would only listen to me, Israel! You shall have no foreign god among you; you shall not worship any god other than me. I am the Lord your God, who brought you up out of Egypt. Open wide your mouth and I will fill it.

"But my people would not listen to me; Israel would not submit to me. So I gave them over to their stubborn hearts to follow their own devices. If my people would only listen to me, if Israel would only follow my ways, how quickly I would subdue their enemies and turn my hand against their foes! Those who hate the Lord would cringe before him, and their punishment would last forever. But you would be fed with the finest of wheat; with honey from the rock I would satisfy you."

"With honey from the rock," she repeated, "I would satisfy you."

Just then, the girls came back in, carrying the torch material along with some of the other children from the village they had met up with. They were all carrying baskets of bread that the elders had asked them to grab on their way out of the village.

"Honey from the rock," she whispered to herself.

One of the men who had just arrived who had been escorting the children called to them all, "We must go deeper into the cave before we can make any fire to warm ourselves."

Julia nodded, and with the children, she started building the torches. As they hurriedly assembled the lighting material, some of the elders began to arrive. Julia questioned them as they entered about the whereabouts of Maria or Jean Paul. They had not seen Jean Paul since he left to defend the village, and her darkest fears felt confirmed that she would never see her oldest son again on this side of heaven.

Julia tried not to hound those arriving, but she tried as gently as possible to ask each person who arrived, "Have you seen either of them? Where were either of them last seen? Is he, is she still alive?"

They slowly, painstakingly made their way into the cave entrance, most trying not to make eye contact with Julia when she did ask, provoking her worst fears even further. Their faces told of the terrors they had just endured, and their exhaustion was ever more apparent. In desperation, she was nearly ready to abandon the safety of the cave and go back down to search for her son and her late husband's mother when a strong arm grabbed her from behind. She turned, and her eyes met the steely, glazed stare of Albert Jourdan.

"You'll only meet death down below, my dear," he said with the words of wisdom she had so often heard in the services he spoke at. "I'm afraid Maria is now home with the Lord, and she and her son have surely been reunited. In this we can take solace."

Julia's eyes began to water as she felt the tug of her Kristoff's love pull her down.

"Be strong, Julia. It is what Kristoff would have expected."

She nodded, knowing Albert was telling her the truth and sparing her the tale of what or how he knew what he was sharing.

"And my Jean Paul?" she asked. She knew the pain that she felt in her heart could not be any worse, any bleaker at this point. No other news could drive her any further into despair than she already was.

"I'm sorry," he started as her heart did manage to find a step farther into the dark abyss of sorrow. She felt her knees weaken as he spoke, "But I haven't seen or heard any news of Jean Paul."

"You what!" she said, not believing her own words.

"Nothing, my dear," he continued. "We took heavy casualties, but there was no mention of your son in the dead."

"Praise God in that small miracle," she said weakly.

"Yes, but I would not get my hopes up to high," he said as he shook his head. "Nothing was spared in the carnage." He put his arm around Julia and turned her to walk back inside.

"But there is a chance. The Lord has worked miracles before."

"Yes, we will keep him in our prayers for sure," confided Albert. "There is always that slim ray of hope . . . and chance."

They returned to the cave, where she sat back down on the rock with Albert until she had regained her composure.

"I'm going to call a council meeting with the others. We must speak to God and ask him for guidance. Are you going to be alright?" he said, putting his arm around her and consoling her as a father would his daughter.

"Yes, Uncle Albert, I'll be fine. Go on, they will need your presence. I'll stay here and wait for others—others who will need a kind face to greet them after their arduous journey from the hell below."

"Bless you, my child. You are stronger than your years would ever know." Then he rose and continued deeper into the cave, carrying one of the torches, escorting a couple who had just arrived.

Julia remained at the entrance waiting for others, coaxing them to rest before they moved deeper into the cave, giving the children more time to collect additional supplies. In between the refugees, she kept praying and thinking of her family who remained.

Finally, the last of the elders had arrived. The leader of the small group assured her there would be no more.

They rested just a short time. Then one elder stood and addressed the others, "Lord, give us strength." The others followed, and then they were off. A couple of men stayed behind to cover the mouth of the cave to camouflage it from anyone who might be scanning the ravine for obvious caverns.

Safety now lay in the depths of the mountain, where there was only one avenue for escape—the way in which they entered. Their fate, like never before, was firmly in God's hands.

Chapter 30

SURROUNDED

He himself shall also drink of the wine of the wrath of God, which is poured out full strength into the cup of His indignation. He shall be tormented with fire and brimstone in the presence of the holy angels and in the presence of the Lamb.

—Revelation 14:10

Lucier's rage spewed from the bowels of the dungeons like molten lava erupting from a volcano as he madly began gathering troops and deploying them throughout the city, searching for the escapees. He made it perfectly clear that he especially wanted Gabriel and the boy to be caught and brought back to the Sheol, dead or alive. He would not be made a fool of again. He quickly dispatched cavalry to the outer reaches of the city's limits to set up road blocks, lest they try to escape. He had them in his grasp once, but he mistook their meekness for weakness and was not prepared for what transpired. He was still not sure what did actually happen, but he was certain it was demonic in nature, for God was certainly on his side. What dark powers they practiced he didn't know or understand, but he would not be deterred from pursuing and destroying them for the sake of his family, the church.

The priests had warned him about the Vaudoisians, but he didn't really take what they said to heart. He had been through so many bloody battles and tragedies so dark and bleak that he held their rants and prophetic descriptions in a skeptical, humorous light.

But that was before tonight.

What he had just witnessed was not of this earth. There was no description in his mind that could define what happened in the dungeon. The only valid explanation had to be steeped in the satanic depths these people would lower themselves to in order to corrupt and permeate the Christian institution he protected and served at all costs. He tried to put some boundaries on his rage, lest his mind come unraveled. Was it their power that was making him feel this way? Was it their satanic forces working on his soul? He had to focus, erase these pathetic thoughts, and move on. He had the full force of the entire papal army at his command, most of which was stationed in Rome, but his Lyon guard was a full battalion large. If needed, he would use them to squeeze this city of its inhabitants until every single person was accounted for and premise searched, until every heretical soul was drained of every drop of its life blood.

It was now personal.

*   *   *

After Jakob was captured, Peter instructed Steffan to corral up the scribes and loaded them all into separate wagons, as they had decided beforehand. The first copies of the Bibles were still incomplete, needing only to finish out the last book, Revelation. Yet it was imperative to save what had been accomplished to this point. They divided up the mass of writings in hopes that at least one load of the precious cargo would make it to the rendezvous point, where they could reconvene with Arktos and complete their inaugural copy. Then they left Lyon for good.

Arktos and Peter quickly gathered their belongings and what was left of his staff who had not traveled with Marik and Waldo's family to Venice and with Steffan and the scribes. Meanwhile, Peter reminded everyone of the evacuation plan. They would all need to leave Lyon immediately because they were at risk of being discovered. He took aside the most trusted of his remaining staff members and instructed them to meet at the fallback location they had previously established in the great forest. For security reasons, he sent them ahead and told them to scatter into smaller groups, not to try leaving the city together.

Up till now, they had not yet seen or spoken with Gabriel, but Peter knew his most trusted sentry would have his back. He just didn't know where or how, but he had faith. That was enough for him at the moment. There were more than enough other things for him to be concerned with. The main one was the safety of Jakob and Arktos.

Anna and Jakob were quickly loaded onto the back of one of the horses from Peter's mounted sentries. They too mounted steeds and took off for the outskirts of town. They had just rounded the corner of the main market square when they could see from a distance the road block at the edge of town. Behind them, in their haste, they had caught the attention of other papal guards, who began to yell and blow their horns in alarm, which caught the attention of those at the blockade.

Things were going from bad to worse.

Just then, from the shadows of an alleyway, Gabriel appeared, with large, double-handled swords in each hand and a breastplate of gold with helmet to match. The symbols of the metalwork were dazzling but unknown. The morning sunlight caught the brilliance of his armor and gleamed with a radiance of unearthly quality. He stood between the fleeing party and the blockade, which was now turning to trap the Vaudoisians before they could escape. They saw the glowing warrior and did not hesitate to rush onward, with their attention on the mounted runaways, giving him little thought until he stepped into the middle of the road, directly in their path of destruction. Then he received the full fury of their charge.

His sword work was a flash in the eye. The blood that spewed forth was like a child's play in the fountains on summer days as it sprayed about, covering the walls that bordered the street. Blades whirled, blinding fury, metal to metal, flesh and bone destroyed until the being within escaped from the flesh pile that remained.

In the blink of an eye, the entire blockade guard had been destroyed. The guard that chased those in flight rushed madly onward, sensing the urgency, again disregarding the radiant being that stood waiting. Arktos and Jakob felt Gabriel's smile greet them as their horses flew by him. He half turned, still facing the onward-rushing troops, looking over his shoulder and nodding as they sped for the once-blockaded edge of town and beyond.

He winked and smiled and then turned to face the battle to come.

Their horses quickly took them beyond the site of the skirmish that ensued, but they could hear the cries and the din of metal to metal as they knew Gabriel had their backs. They dared not slow. They rode as fast as their horses could carry them till darkness began to fall. They never saw Anna's family. Jakob didn't want to think of what might have happened, but in his heart, he knew that they had most likely been caught by the blockade and taken back to the dungeons, for they were nowhere to be seen.

His heart sank for the small child who might well be orphaned, yet still alive. She clung to Jakob's back as their driver spurred the horse onward. She could hear Jakob begin to hum an unknown melody, and her mind seemed to melt in the notes that permeated through her body as she clung to him. Reality now seemed to slip away as they quickly raced onward. Her fears faded behind them as the dust from the road drifting across the fields that flew by in a blur of speed.

Blood dripped from the edge of Gabriel's helmet's visor onto little rivulets of pulsating veins. The armor's once-golden hue, now splayed with the crimson, had an amber sheen that throbbed as if alive. His mighty swords were one with each of his arms as the rivers of red melded one into the other. About him lay countless bodies hacked, sliced, and dismembered, all in the vain attempt to destroy his being—a being they had no idea of whence it drew its strength, its soul, to survive.

The armor rose and fell with the labor of his heavy breath. Killing was not light work, but with the rush of adrenaline, nothing becomes apparent until the din of battle ceases. Then, the beleaguered limbs, lungs, and spirit have respite enough to reflect upon the imagery beset upon them. Soaking in the brutality as the blood-stained ground absorbs the wetness of slaughter, the soul drinks in the gore in giant gulps until the wretchedness becomes one huge, cumulative ocular, guttural expulsion from which we try to hide, to bury, or succumb to. Our mind's eye is blinded by the fury and wants us to withdraw forever.

Yet Gabriel knew this scene too well, for it was yet just another battle in which evil must be destroyed for the glory of God to continue to exist. This was just one more macabre scene of death through which he must journey to meet his Maker and Lord again on the other side.

Perhaps he might slow the inevitable, but something inside told him he alone would not stop the darkness, for its presence was near. His hands momentarily relaxed their grips on the handles of the mighty blades he held. They hung down at his side, draining, spilling the life blood upon the earth.

He exhaled slowly and pressed his mind to erase all he saw before him. Then he inhaled deeply, trying to revive his weary muscles. He prayed for guidance.

He waited.

Soon, the thought of Abishai came to mind. Abishai was the son of Zeruiah, the brother of Joab from the Old Testament. He was one of King David's Three. The Three were some of the most elite fighting men in David's army, and Abashai was known for once killing three hundred enemy warriors with a single spear. The hairs stood up on the back of his neck as some of the greatest warriors ever flashed through his mind—soldiers in the Lord's service. Energy began to flow back through his body, and he could feel again. He was ebbing from that place where death is dealt from a distance—not personal, but removed— back to now. He felt the slight breeze from the south and started to notice movement around the perimeter of the road and buildings that surrounded him. He was becoming fully aware, reawakening to the present, when the cloud came over, and with it the feeling of despair lashed at his bulwarks of faith.

The pallid gloom of evil was near.

Gabriel raised his head, eyes focusing through his lowered brow, until his gaze met those of a distant dark figure.

Lucier.

Gabriel's hands renewed their grip upon the swords. He thought of Abishai, and steel raced through his veins.

Lucier stood without a weapon in his hand, but the movement continued about the periphery until finally Gabriel realized he was being surrounded by archers.

"Finally we meet," Lucier said with a sense of humor to his voice. "I must applaud your talents with the blade," he said, lightly clapping his black-gloved hands together in a mimicking gesture of praise.

Gabriel stood firm, now fully realizing his mistake of staying motionless on the battlefield. He slowly raised his swords to the protective position, one in front, one behind, blades erect toward the sky.

"Oh how I would love to battle you in a one-on-one duel, but you see," he said pausing to raise one hand to his chin while posing the other behind his back as if in deep thought, "I have much to do and many more heretics like yourself to dispatch before my day is done. I do love a good battle, though, so let's see how well your God protects you against odds—odds, say, beyond your grasp." He chuckled slightly.

Gabriel stood firm. Scripture came to his lips, and he began speaking in a whisper to himself as if to prepare for the flow of battle that was about to ensue: "The sun will be darkened, the moon will give no light, the stars will fall from the sky and the powers in the heavens will be shaken . . ."

Lucier's head nodded to the lead archer, whose hand was held aloft, and his hand dropped at the signal. A full regiment of archers had been summoned at Lucier's command upon hearing of the altercation at the attempted escape of the Vaudoisians from the city. They now lined the walls and rooftops of the adjacent buildings to the scene. A thousand missiles flew toward one target, sharpened points aiming for one soul, one life, one being.

The dark cloud overhead suddenly exploded, and a brilliant flash blinded the vision of all the marksmen aiming through their bows. The roar was deafening at the same time, and in the blink of an eye, the column of heat engulfed all, man, missiles, vision.

Then nothing.

Chapter 31

LAST BREATH

Therefore I urge you to take nourishment, for this is for your survival, since not a hair will fall from the head of any of you.

—Acts 27:34

Marik stood before an ancient tree, twisted and curved from centuries of exposure to extreme elements, fighting for every ounce of survival. Its bark was nearly gone. It was mostly gray-white flesh of wood, cracked and barren, looking more like old bones than wood. It sat atop the small group of boulders on the high pass like a sentinel, watching, waiting.

The clouds washed overhead, gray, with snow blowing lightly. He could not feel the cold; he could not feel the anguish. He stood numb, watching, looking for any sign of life. There were only a couple small branches on an outstretched limb that contained the remnants of leaves—tiny breaths of color in a stark landscape where life seemed void.

He tried to move toward it but was held captive in his place, by what he could not tell. He again forced movement but could do nothing. He could see the cold. His breath exhaled in small puffs of white that quickly flew from his face, chasing the clouds.

Suddenly trace amounts of moisture started to ooze from the tree, at first appearing as dark stains on the bleached bones. Then there were obvious signs of wetness as the cracks became rivulets of tiny streams running down the face of the tree onto the rocks below.

He watched as the tree wept.

The wind now wailed over the ridge, snow blowing sideways. The wailing became a sob as he could hear the voice of his wife screaming for the pain to stop. He was back in the room, close in the darkness, save for the lamp by the bed that shone upon the sweat-drenched body of the young woman. The birth was near, but her small frame could not handle the delivery. Each push sent her one step closer to the end until the wail became two. Then there was but one.

He felt the helplessness of the moment wash over him again.

The motherless infant died a few days later. There was no wet nurse in their village. They had sent for someone, but she arrived just as they lay the tiny casket in the ground.

Marik shuddered. The cold bit at his extremities until the ache felt like the cold granite he now fell upon. The wailing began to rip at his soul.

His heart ached from the utter sorrow, and again he tried forcing movement, anything, trying with all he had to reach the tree. He pushed with all his might. Then, resigned to giving up, he thought, *Move just one toe, just something to prove I'm not paralyzed.* With all his might, he painfully forced a toe to finally move. Out from under a rock nearby, the flow of one tiny silver thread of life trickled toward him. He reached out with a hand and touched the flow. A flash of pain raced up his arm to the back of his neck. He could feel the wetness on his fingertip, but the pain was nearly unbearable. As he opened his eyes, he could barely see dampness on his fingers and looked about him, realizing that he was now somewhere dark but not alone.

He tried to sit up, but the pain was too great. He was alive, but where? He could smell the dankness of wet clothing on the human body near him, but there was not enough light in the chamber to discern who or how many were with him. His head throbbed with each heartbeat. His hands were bound. He could not reach the pain in his side, but something told him there was nothing good about the pain that emanated from there.

Although the air was cool, he could feel sweat trickling down his face. *Fever,* he thought. *A sure sign the infection has begun.* Having spent time in the first Crusades, he was well aware of injuries and their potential outcome on a soldier. A puncture of any nature to the torso usually led to a slow death, if not instant. Some were fortunate when the missile struck a bone and was deflected but usually the infection from the impact was what killed.

He tried to stay focused and remember where and what he was doing before he wound up here in this state. Death and savagery were everywhere. He could still see the image of the large man in the hole and feel the sudden shift of his sword, then the archers nearby losing their attack, then pain and darkness.

Julia. His heart quickened. *I've got to still find them,* he thought to himself. He struggled at the ropes that bound his wrists again, but the captor knew his knots too well. The circulation was nearly cut off, and his hands were becoming numb the more he struggled. His feet were not tied, so he tried to stand, but the pain again reminded him of his condition, and he nearly lost consciousness, becoming nauseated from its force upon his body. He fell to his knees, and with his head bowed upon the floor, he began praying aloud.

"Dear God . . . dear, dear Lord . . . give me strength . . . give me the faith of Daniel, Lord, I need to survive this lion's den and get to those who need my help."

He panted now, his breath shortened from the pain in his side.

He could feel the warmth of wetness spreading down his side, to his leg. He knew time was now his enemy. He would be no use to the Vaudoisians if he didn't get help soon for his own wounds. He continued to pray silently as he sank further into despair, going in and out of consciousness.

It seemed like an eternity had passed when suddenly the door to the dark chamber flew open and blinding light flooded the room.

The body that had been lying next to him was grabbed and dragged out, still unconscious. Shielding his eyes against the blinding glare with his elbows, he tried to see what was happening. He did not recognize the person they hauled away, but over in the far corner, leaning against the wall, he thought he caught a glimpse of someone he did know.

Jean Paul?

Then the light was gone.

"All is lost," Jean Paul said from the corner in a near whisper. "Satan has won."

"No . . . you are wrong . . . you've got to fight," Marik spat as he tasted his own blood on his lip, as the pain was now near the blinding point. "We've come so far." He paused to try to fill air back into his collapsing lungs, his head bowed. Still, he forced all his strength to try to revive Jean Paul, if that was him, since he knew it was his only hope.

"Your grandfather is so proud of you and . . . and . . . you should see Jakob."

Marik could sense movement from the corner coming closer. Was it Jean Paul? If so, he had to make the connection before he lost all consciousness.

"I pray they are not to return here again. Please tell me they are not."

"Yes . . . it is him . . . praise God," he quietly whispered.

The urgency in Jean Paul's voice was a far cry from the despair of a moment ago. At least he was now up.

If only I can keep him captivated long enough to make him realize the urgency of needing to get help, he thought to himself.

"No, they surely won't come here. They are too busy with getting the Word written," he said with one final breath, and then he collapsed to the floor.

He could hear Jean Paul move closer and try to lift him, asking him more questions, but he was unable to muster enough strength to speak anymore. His lips moved, but nothing came out. His breath was labored. There was not much time. All he could do now was pray and try to remain conscious.

Jean Paul suddenly felt a strange courage flow back into his veins as he tried to get Marik to sit up. Then he realized, to his horror, that his friend had been hit. The stub of the arrow's shaft still protruded from his side. He was losing blood and likely wouldn't last much longer if the spear point was not removed.

Jean Paul only knew of one thing to do. He drove his knees to the floor and began praying, "Dear God, see our need. Why you have allowed these demons to destroy us I do not understand, but I will never understand all that you do. I pray that you show me guidance like never before. Please take away our pains, heal our wounds, and give us strength. I will take up the breastplate of righteousness for you, Lord. Let his will be done."

Then, as if by second nature, like breathing, he prayed the words to a Psalm that came to mind: "The Lord *is* righteous in all His ways, Gracious in all His works. The Lord *is* near to all who call upon Him, To all who call upon Him in truth. He will fulfill the desire of those who fear Him; He also will hear their cry and save them. The Lord preserves all who love Him, but all the wicked He will destroy. My mouth shall speak the praise of the Lord, and all flesh shall bless His holy name forever and ever . . . Amen."

Suddenly a flash of whiteness filled the room and the guard returned.

"The major wants to speak to you, boy. Seems he thinks you might have some valuable information we might need. Personally I doubt it, although I'll enjoy watching you suffer through the interrogation." He and the other guard chuckled as they reached for him, nearly tripping over Marik's body that now lay still upon the floor next to Jean Paul. "It's the least you can do before we put your heathen head on pike."

"I'll tell you anything you want to know if you see to it my friend here gets help," he said, glancing over to Marik as they began pulling him out the door.

They both laughed, "That bloke is nearly gone. He's not much for this world, and besides, from what I hear he deserves a slow death."

"That's right, after the number of soldiers he sliced up on his way up the mountainside, I ought to give him a good kick in his side there too . . . heretic sympathizer."

And with that, they slammed the door as they dragged Jean Paul off to his final moments with the major. The spark of life that Marik was able to reignite burned inside him, and the mere mention of his grandfather and brother carrying on the Word gave him the tiny sliver of hope he so desperately needed. He tried to catch one last glimpse of the chamber door, but he wasn't given the opportunity because they quickly turned a corner and were off.

He didn't have the chance to see the large shadow slip from behind a nearby column and enter the chamber. Nor did he see figure return, carrying the body that was quickly and silently loaded onto a cart and hastily driven off toward the lower reaches of the valley and beyond.

Jean Paul now only felt a distant passing of that courage that he had known. He closed his eyes and tried to hang on to that tiny flame of hope that flickered deep inside. There was going to be at least one more chance to find out if God was with him or not. Fight he must to the end, for his family and Marik if nothing else.

He owed him that much.

Chapter 32

BROTHERS UNITED . . .

Then the Spirit took me up and brought me in a vision by the Spirit of God into Chaldea, to those in captivity. And the vision that I had seen went up from me.

—Ezekiel 11:24

Darkness was quickly approaching as they finally stopped for the night to rest in a hidden hunting lodge deep in the dark woods Peter had used in his other life. Much to their relief, they found Steffan and the scribes already encamped and unloaded. The servants who had gone on before were already there as well, preparing the bedding for their stay. There was a small fire in the hearth with a large black kettle hanging over it, cooking something that reminded everyone of the hunger that had escaped their minds as they fled. They had ridden in the driving rain most of the day, and the warmth felt good. They peeled off layers of soaking wet clothing to dry and began to ladle bowls of the warm sustenance from the pot.

Peter had caught up with them later in the evening, just before arriving at the lodge. He had been nearly breathless from the chase the guard had given. He had made a false loop and now had doubled back to try to throw them off his trail. He knew they would canvass the area, but they should have been safe for the night and possibly longer. He instantly noticed the one person who was missing. He kept silent but somehow sensed the worst.

They had a sentry posted outside near the perimeter of the grounds even though they were well off the highways. Peter and Arktos still felt the need to be cautious. They feared being found by the guard that now patrolled the open roads. Even though the lodge was well hidden in the forest, nothing was certain. They were a good distance from Lyon, on the road to Chambery, but not far enough to feel entirely safe from the manhunt that now chased them.

Weary from the ride, they quickly found comfort in the lodge's safety. Jakob huddled close to his grandfather, with Anna nearby as they supped from their bowls of hearty broth. The small girl was beside herself with terror, but neither she nor Jakob complained. The meal and warmth were taking off the edge of the road. It was as if they understood the purpose for their journey, which would eventually become clear to all.

When they had finished with their meal, Jakob watched as one of the younger servant women from Peter's household came over and took Anna to her pallet, consoling her while she tucked her in for the night. The imagery of their journey to Lyon flashed back in his mind. He thought of home, Mother, Jean Paul, and the others. His heart ached for them—for the times before when there was no terror, no fear. He missed Gabriel already and wondered if the mighty warrior had somehow miraculously survived. He had hope, but he feared that was all. He thought of the countless lessons the extraordinary teacher had provided him. His lira was nowhere to be seen, but the music was still with him.

A small voice inside him beckoned a melody that brought immediate comfort. His eyes closed, and he breathed each note. As the sound reached his throat, the vibration hummed. Cascading waterfalls of flowers dipped in honey sweetly flowed through his mind. He saw high clouds drifting over the pastures of green while the sheep grazed below. He drifted from one valley to the next, sweeping down in great arcs through the passes. He flew wide around the Mt. Cruix up Quenten, swinging around the Rora to their home. Storm clouds were hanging low, but he soared on. The sweetness of the melody began to weep with minor chords of sorrow. Up ahead he could see two men on either side of their prisoner, and he paused in his flight. The notes now became the cadence of a chant, low, ancient. Through the door of distant reaches, he could see the face, pale with fear.

*   *   *

As the two soldiers carried their meager prisoner to his prearranged meeting with the major, they gave little thought as to who or what the people were who had garnered so much death and mayhem from the seat of the almighty on earth himself. They had seen so many battles over religions that it was all nothing more than one man's word against another's. This lot was no better off than the distant Muslim crowd they had vanquished back in Jerusalem in their recent campaign. As they drug Jean Paul's nearly weightless body effortlessly along, they gave little heed to the figure that stood in their path ahead. Nor did they realize as they approached that the figure seemed to give off a radiance that brightened the immediate surroundings. Dusk was upon them, but it seemed if a shaft of light somehow found its way over the mountain and into their path.

Jean Paul felt an eerie presence and opened his eyes, raising his head ever so slightly as they approached the figure, undeterred. Suddenly, something struck out and caused time to stop. The men holding Jean Paul captive had frozen, as if by some strange hand. He dropped to the ground since their grasps had loosened from the inability to continue to grip. From his knees he looked ahead as the brilliant figure walked toward them.

"Father . . . is that you?" he questioned as the image from the past flashed into his mind. Nothing was said as it stepped ever closer. Now within an arm's length, the figure bent and reached out a hand, as if to help Jean Paul to his feet.

"My son," the light spoke.

"Lord my God, Father, it is you." He grabbed the outstretched hand and leapt to his feet the best he could as the bindings fell from his hands, embracing the luminance.

"I told you I would be with you, and is it not true?"

"Yes, yes, it's true," he sobbed on the shoulder of the image of his father.

"You must go to the others and take them to safety. Do you understand?"

"Yes . . . yes I do, but—"

"Do not question why, for its God's will that you have been chosen to lead. Do not question but rather firmly accept what has been given."

"Yes, Father."

"You falter when doubt creeps into your faith, and each time, Satan extracts another pound of flesh for it. You must finally stand strong and once and for all realize that unquestionable love from the Father can never wane or die."

"Yes, forgive me for I have sinned, and it's true . . . the doubt . . . it did cause me to lose faith, to the point I thought—"

"Yes, you thought God had forsaken you and our people, but why else would we have been asked to carry on his Word if he wasn't going to be there for us in our time of need?"

"I just didn't—"

"Yes, you just didn't trust what you have been taught from the earliest days of your life . . . Why? Because it's our nature to question, and if we do not accept his ultimate love, his only Son, Jesus Christ, then we cannot fully be one with him and our faith is little more than a pebble on the bank of the flowing stream of life, never moving, never giving life to others."

"I have Jesus in my heart, Father and now more than ever before, I see the error of my ways. I only pray it has not cost the lives of others in vain."

Timothy W. Tron

"We all have a price to pay, some sooner than others, and someday your time will come as well . . . just not now. Now go, and don't stop until they are found, for the sanctuary protects all who seek its domain. And son, remember, the love of a father for his son never dies . . . never . . . never," he said as the light slowly faded.

Then, as quickly as it had appeared, the light was gone. The two guards collapsed on the ground. Jean Paul took off for the nearest escape route, finding his way quickly up the walls of the canyon that enclosed their tiny village, and was quickly gone from the hell that continued for the unfortunate souls left behind in the Vaudois, giving thanks to God every step of the way. His task was clear, and he now sought out the others, for there had to be some survivors. He prayed every breath, panting as he climbed, that God would deliver him to his family soon. With every breath he drew closer to God, asking forgiveness for his doubt.

*   *   *

Jakob fell asleep with the vision of his brother escaping the darkness in his mind, dreaming of his safe flight to the light. He could sense the others, each fearing their fate but lifting voices in unison in prayer to God. The voices comforted him and put his mind at ease. He knew of the sanctuary and that they would all find safety there.

He remained in peaceful slumber, not stirring. The fire slowly ebbed till embers glowed. The night sounds surrounded them with its voices, yet all slept soundly. Jakob flew on, drifting with the sounds. The song of the heavens comforted his weary young soul, and sleep was never more welcome.

Chapter 33

FEAR OF SELF

The pillars of heaven tremble, and are astonished at His rebuke.

—Job 26:11

Lucier had the entire area searched—every building, home, alleyway. Any place someone could hide was thrown open, overturned, and broken into, yet nothing was left of the mystic warrior who had defeated so many. In the days that followed, Lucier ordered a full sweep of the city, imprisoning all possible heretics. The first few innocent souls were interrogated, and from them, a list of potential followers of Waldo was constructed. The rest filled in as time went on. Some were even discovered to have in their possession what appeared to be chapters and verses from the Bible, translated into the common language. This was proof of the heresy at work he had been warned about. He would find them all, and then, when the time was right, he would bring them to the town square, where he would make an example of any who followed or supported the Vaudoisians and their Lyon leader, Peter Waldo. His embarrassment would become the fire that would consume his soul and the lives of any who would fall into his clutches.

Death for the sake of the Lord was upon Lyon, and mercy was not in the air.

Standing outside the exterior gates of Sheol with the light of day quickly fading into dusk, Lucier watched the rider approach—evidently someone coming with news. He stood, arms crossed, with guards on either side of the gate standing at attention. People hurriedly passed by, heads down, trying to avoid eye contact. The place of evil they passed only housed those with blackened souls; anyone associated with it was certainly an ambassador of death and darkness. Those standing outside it were of it and to be feared as much as the place therein.

The soldier dismounted, saluted the general, and then presented him with a sealed scroll. He returned the salute. The rider still standing at attention awaited orders

.

"At ease, soldier," Lucier said, looking approvingly at the rider, who apparently had just returned from the ongoing campaign in the Vaudois from the look of his dust-covered tack. "I trust your fellow warriors are faring well in their current conquests?"

"Yes sir, General, sir."

"Very well, take your horse and yourself inside and see the quartermaster, and let him know that I said for you to be taken well care of."

"Sir, yes sir," the soldier said, still without moving.

"Go now, and God be with you."

The soldier saluted then turned and stiffly walked into the inner courtyard of Sheol, disappearing from sight.

Lucier turned to follow but was halted by the screams of a woman who, with her children in tow, was being forcibly dragged through the front gate. Obviously she was one of the collected heretics who were being slowly gathered up today. *She wails as if being burned alive,* thought Lucier. *However will she act when she actually is?* He scoffed to himself at the thought.

"You butchers killed my husband. You will all burn in hell" she screamed between sobs of tears.

Lucier stopped at this. No wonder she was so distraught—but then again, they chose the path they were following, and with it came the consequences. She began quoting Scriptures, words from the Bible. How could she? *I shall not be swayed, but for the greater good, we must endure these painful recitations*, he told himself, trying to block out the woman's obviously painful rant.

He then turned to follow the path of the courier who had long ago gone inside when he saw the children at the shackled woman's feet. Small urchins with tear-stained cheeks knelt in prayer at her feet as she stood fastened to the ox cart near the corner of the enclosure as they waited their dim fate. His skin crawled as he felt stiffness in his throat rise from the depths of his stomach. *They can't be praying . . . not little children. Surely they do not realize what they are doing. They only mimic what they have been taught.* He felt himself transfixed and noticed the other guards in the area stopping as well. The tiny figures continued to pray as the bottom of their mother's dress lightly brushed the tops of their small bowed heads.

He felt compelled to do something but then quickly corrected himself, as if in battle, and shouted out, "Carry on . . . carry on." Then he turned, gesturing to the others to move along as well, returning to his chambers, where he closed the heavy oaken door behind him and pulled up a chair to the table where there was a lamp already burning with golden flame. He sat down with a great force and leaned his elbows on the table, resting his head in his hands. His figure cast long shadows against the whitewashed wall, moving in great throes of anguish as the lamp flame danced. *What am I doing?* he half-thought and prayed at the same time.

The darkness in his mind washed over his spirit like great waves on a rocky shoreline, crashing one into the other, pounding and unrelenting. He breathed heavily. He tried to push it out, but it ebbed further and further into his awareness. The fire crackled in the hearth nearby. The faint smell of smoke reached him and shook his frame with the memory long forgotten.

The long, windswept field appeared ahead of him as he rode, and then came the horror of seeing the thin smoke rising from the broken, charred home. His children lay still, unmoving, and silent. He knelt beside their tender, lifeless, burnt bodies, picking up the youngest girl and holding her, cradled in his arms, as if it would make him feel better, but the stench of death could not be mistaken, nor could he try to avoid the obvious or make it right again.

God had turned his back on him for some reason, and he would never forget it—not now, not after all he had done in the name of the Lord. He had slaughtered countless lives for the sake of Christianity, and now this. Evil could not be held in check; it spread across the land like the blight of some sickness, illness of the human soul, blackened by one tortuous moment after another. He knelt and laid the tiny, scorched body back in its resting place. Begging for God to take him, he didn't know how many hours or days had passed when he realized the blinding hunger and thirst he felt slip past the numbness of his tear-swollen face.

As he sat there, watching a sunrise, seeing the golden glow now upon the bleakness of death about him, he finally came to his senses and realized someone would pay. He didn't care how far, how long, or how hard he had to fight, but the demons who did this would pay with their lives, their mothers' lives, their children's lives . . . all of them. He would destroy every last one until their blood ran like rivers over their land, and then . . . then he would be relieved of his pain. It was pain that would never leave, for he felt that part of him was gone now—the caring, tender part of a father was stolen in the night, taken away forever. Now he didn't care if he lived or died. He would become the warrior he always feared—the one with nothing left to lose. He had lost everything, and nothing else mattered save for bringing restitution to his tortured soul.

"Stop it . . . stop it now . . . push it out . . . Father, please forgive me, for I have sinned." He shuddered in breaths of air as he came from the trance. *How far have I gone into the darkness? What have I become?* All these thoughts came to him as he thought of the mother and children and the bitterness of persecuting others who believed in the same God, believed in the same Bible, but were separated from what he was told only because they wanted to be closer to God of their own accord. *How far have I slipped into the hell from which those who started this all arose?* he thought again.

He paused in prayer, sitting in the silence of the early evening. When he felt as if he was somewhat back to his senses, he took a deep breath. Then he broke Major Crowell's seal on the scroll and began to read his report. The ink figures on the skin spoke words he didn't care to read, but he knew he must. It was his job—his mission—to carry on, to right the wrong caused so long ago.

Crowell had reported that the Vaudois of the Rora had been cleansed of all heretics, with much bloodshed on their part and very small casualties on the part of the papal guard. He went on to say how the other valleys were being searched as well, with little luck in finding any more concentrations of Apostle Speakers or inhabitants. It was as if they had all vanished after the first attack.

However, there was very little positive news to report about those who had been captured being converted to Catholicism. This was the supposed goal of the priests who had been sent along with the detachment, so they could say that they were not merely performing genocide but rather were on a mission to convert the heathens to a recognized religion. It was reported that they would either not speak at all or begin quoting Scriptures upon the final appeal by the priests before being killed if they would not convert. They simply would not move in their beliefs.

How futile; how utterly futile, he thought. *It's such a waste of life to die for that nothingness. These people must be crazed or so brainwashed by some roaming preacher heretic that they are under some spell to believe beyond the normal capacity for sanity. How could anyone be so blind to not see what they do is so senseless and without cause?* He continued reading the report, with its formalities of numbers, location, and number of soldiers in command and so on. He scrolled down the few names of those listed as captured. Nothing seemed to speak to him until he reached the name of Jean Paul, and he suddenly recognized the name. Then it dawned on him: this was some relation to the boy they had captured with that—that warrior who disappeared into nothingness.

Something was awry here. Something was not right.

The tiny children praying at the foot of their shackled mother with a sense of knowing—being something more than they would be if they were simple children; the child who was seemingly being protected by something other than a normal soldier. Something was different about it all. He just couldn't put his finger on it. If this were a battle strategy, he'd recognize it in instant, but this was something else. A source, a power far stronger than the darkness he held in the recesses of his heart, pulled at him. He could feel it but didn't understand what it was. Fear welled up inside until he had to crush it out again before he was consumed.

He must find one of these people and somehow question them himself. There would have to be one eventually who would succumb to his forces, and he would find out then what his adversary was up to. That was all there was to it—nothing more. He slammed his battle-scarred fist on the table and wadded up the scroll, throwing it into the fire. He didn't continue reading the part that spoke about how the refugees had fled the valley and escaped somewhere in the upper regions of the Vaudois where they could not be found.

He also failed to read about the part where the warriors from the neighboring Vaudois fell upon them as they began their march down the western slope of the mountains. They had nearly completed their sweep from east to west, searching as many valleys as possible and were on what was thought to be the last leg of their triumphant campaign when the mountain people attacked. They were unsuccessful at trying to return fire to those that had ambushed them since they were gone before they knew what was upon them. Their knowledge of the mountain terrain was so far superior that there would be no chase, no recourse to any such attack. Many of Crowell's men were slain before they could retreat to the lower reaches of the western Piedmont, where they regrouped.

Crowell was glad to escape that Godforsaken land, for only mountain goats and raptors could possibly live in that place. The heretics were expelled from the valley he had been commanded to attack, and that was all he cared about. There were countless other valleys, countless other crags where those crazed mountain people could hold up and carry on their insanity for centuries. He wanted nothing more to do with them. His unseen injury was part of the reason for the resignation, which Lucier failed to see as well. The last vestiges of the scroll were consumed by the flames, much like the spirit of those who had attacked, being slowly consumed by the fact that they were no longer facing an enemy like they had seen on the Crusades but instead armed warriors from another world.

These were people like their own families that they slaughtered only because they had been told to do so—because they believed in something different that couldn't be explained to them other than that it was unacceptable in the eyes of the papacy. To the richly robed priests of the higher authorities, these meagerly dressed peasants were demons of the faith and to be erased from the presence of the earth.

Now the army that barely once had a semblance of purpose sat without a leader, rotting, decaying, until it soon became a base camp for ruthless and savage, wanton destruction throughout the Piedmont and valleys of the western faces of the mountains that majestically faced its spewing of filth over the land with its flames fanned by the dark-hearted priests who remained, doing the will of God they could see from the blackened depths of their being.

The flame of the rage instilled by the faith of some could not be kept lit by those of none, for it was all the same and nothing at the same time. Only the humanness was obvious, and death, human or not, was forever.

Chapter 34

INNER SANCTUM

You are my hiding place and my shield; I hope in Your word.
—Psalm 119:114

everal days passed, but they did not feel safe leaving the cave. Their scouts had seen straggling parties of the marauding soldiers, mostly pillagers, scouring the remains of their Vaudois. Although they were all anxious to return to what was left of their homes, they also felt inhibition in knowing the horrors that awaited them. The elders had called several council meetings to bring their collective minds together as one.

They made camp in the deepest reaches of the vast cave. They now sat in a large circle, praying in unison, facing the inner ring and the firelight from the small source of warmth. Almost no one outside of the elder's council had ever seen them in enclave before, so the others sat outside the group, held captive by the scene that unfolded before them each time, learning as they watched.

The grotto had been chosen not by chance but by preconceived necessity. There was water and an avenue by which smoke could escape, allowing them to cook and stay warm, even though the ambient temperature in the cave was far more inhabitable than the outside temperatures could be in the hardest part of winter.

Julia and her girls—all she had left of her family—had followed the others into the inner sanctum, hoping to find solace in the company of other survivors. The sound of the prayers of the elders gave her and the others great relief and a sense of strength at the same time.

Their images from the fire danced upon the cavern walls in and out of the dark recesses, like spirits to a dance as they chanted: "Listen to my words, Lord, consider my lament. Hear my cry for help, my King and my God, for to you I pray. In the morning, Lord, you hear my voice; in the morning I lay my requests before you and wait expectantly. For you are not a God who is pleased with wickedness; with you, evil people are not welcome. The arrogant cannot stand in your presence.

"You hate all who do wrong; you destroy those who tell lies.

"The bloodthirsty and deceitful you, Lord, detest. But I, by your great love, can come into your house; in reverence I bow down toward your holy temple. Lead me, Lord, in your righteousness because of my enemies make your way straight before me.

"Not a word from their mouth can be trusted; their heart is filled with malice. Their throat is an open grave; with their tongues they tell lies. Declare them guilty, O God! Let their intrigues be their downfall. Banish them for their many sins, for they have rebelled against you. But let all who take refuge in you be glad; let them ever sing for joy. Spread your protection over them that those who love your name may rejoice in you. Surely, Lord, you bless the righteous; you surround them with your favor as with a shield."

They ended the chant and sat silently, heads bowed, continuing to appear as if in prayer.

No one spoke.

The only sound in the cave came from the fire, which might occasionally pop or hiss. Time passed as others drifted in and out of sleep as they watched, silent as well, for fear of disrupting the council's trance. There was a feeling of supreme reverence—a feeling of being more than their own, ages of precious love, timeless devotion, hovering, covering a blanket of soul over their collective whole. Wisps of smoke from the fire, hesitant to leave, drifted upward, forming fluid circles, drifting on transparent currents.

Julia didn't know if it was day or night. She only knew that her body had succumbed to wanting sustenance. Her motherly instinct knew that if she was feeling it, then her children would either soon be also having pangs of hunger or be fearful of asking. She was about to rise to go find something when an older lady, Aunt. Raviol, came by, passing out bread to the children. Then Aunt Raviol came over to Julia and offered her a handful of the luscious manna, freshly baked. She whispered her thanks, and Aunt Raviol continued emptying her basket as she went to the many weary and grateful patrons of her wares.

The elders had obviously prepared for the event and built a makeshift oven somewhere in the cave, far in advance of today. She was grateful for all she had and felt comfort in the fact that those that had died had been slaughtered as martyrs. Yes, they had been forced from their homes, but they still were able to find shelter and had elders with the foresight to plan for contingencies like these.

The bread melted in her mouth as she turned and continued to observe the council in action. Still silent, sitting in their circle, the elders began to stir, not rising but appearing to being pressed or pushed upon by an unseen force. Each one's countenance grimaced in and out of pain. Something began to work in each, moving around the ring, searching, looking, until finally, one of them spoke.

The voice was not one of their own. A powerful echo made of many voices erupted, "The time has come for a change for my people."

The elder's head was thrown back, and his body lay back upon the ground while his legs still sat in the crossed position. Arms splayed out to his sides, twitching spastically in spread-eagle fashion, the voice continued, "Do not fear, for I am with you always. I have given you many blessings, and many more will follow, but be not of yourselves, for that which you do is for all who follow. I am the Light, and the Light is for all to see. There will be many who will die for the light, but it will not be in vain if you continue to believe. The ears of many tingle of the Word that you keep, for in my name you go."

The elder who had spoken now began coughing in convulsions and appeared to have been greatly strained by the experience as the others realized and quickly came to his aid, leaving their positions. The elders had evidently achieved their goal and were now caring for their own, apparently accustomed to the event, while the onlookers had become greatly disturbed. The council members who were not attending to their fallen comrade gathered quickly and deliberated over the word they had just received. Then, just as quickly as it has transpired, they finished. Albert rose and addressed the other members of the Vaudois, trying to relieve the fears he could hear growing, while the remaining elders continued trying to revive and raise the elder from his reverse prone position.

"We all have heard the story. We all know our mission. It is no secret to us here why we are who we are." He spoke in long, purposeful prose. "The Word each of you have, each of your families continue to strive to pass on to the next generation, you have seen here today, is more than any of us singularly can possible preserve. Rather, will take all of us and our fellow Vaudoisians in the other Vaudois as well."

There arose a slight murmur from the onlookers, for they had never attempted to give the Word to the other Vaudois. Albert knew from what had been said that it was time to do this, as did the other elders, who now nodded in agreement.

Someone called from the shadows, "So we are to spread the Word beyond the confines of the Vaudois. Is this what you're asking us?" the voice questioned.

"Yes, it has been divinely requested," retorted Albert, "to which you were just witness, were you not?"

"Yes, Uncle" replied the voice. "It's just that we have never attempted to go beyond the granite walls that have protected us up to now."

"Yes, exactly. My brother, do you not realize it is not the stone that has kept you safe all these centuries since our visit from the prophets? I pray that you now realize . . . it . . . was . . . *God!*"

"Amen!" said the audience in unison.

"Forgive me, Uncle, for my ignorance," said the voice, and it was quiet.

"Be not afraid or ashamed of such thoughts, for they are expected and normal," Albert continued.

He knew this would be a radical approach, yet he now realized, as if shaken from a dream, that this was something they should have seen before now. Surely God had not created this chaos to force them to ask for guidance. Then the thought of Arktos and Jakob on their journey to Lyon to help the merchant get the Word translated and written down made it perfectly clear. There was no mistake. It was certainly the path they must now choose. As he stood looking around at the remnants of those that had survived the massacre below, he realized that there may even be parts of the Word that could be missing if those members who processed it had been eliminated. Only time and recounting of those remaining would tell.

"We must take this path that God has given us," he continued, "and not fear what we will encounter beyond these walls, for God is with us."

"And we will survive," came the strange voice from the opposite side of the chamber.

Julia heard it too. Something about it seemed familiar yet different.

"Show yourself, my brother," Albert spoke to the shadows.

Jean Paul stepped into the dim light of the council fire. The congregation gasped.

Julia couldn't get her breath at first as she rose to her feet. Then she burst out from her lungs what air should could muster. "My son . . . praise the Lord, my son," she cried out as she raced over, hugging Jean Paul as the others stood and gathered to her side, all embracing the mother and son as one.

"Thanks be to God!" Albert said as he looked toward the heavens from within the depths of their sanctuary. The reunion carried on for some time as tear-filled cries of jubilation filled the chamber.

"Thanks be to God!" the others repeated until the excitement calmed.

The void that followed turned into somber reflection as they all began intently listening as Jean Paul began to share with them the events that had transpired in recent days. He told of how he had been taken prisoner and should have died like the others, who all were mostly slain in the initial onslaught. He paused as they memory of seeing his fellow Vaudoisians die by his side welled up inside him until his eyes watered and his throat became tight with emotion.

He thought of the image of seeing his friend since childhood being beheaded, as if he were nothing more than an animal. There had been nothing he could do but watch. He recalled the eyes staring back at him, glazed, distant, and soulless, as the head fell with a dull thud on the ground. He fought to regain his composure as others put their hands on him, urging him to continue when the pain subsided.

It feels good to be back with my kindred family, he thought.

He continued on, describing his feeling of hopelessness when he was being marched to certain death—his thoughts of letting his people down, the loss of faith. And then suddenly, out of nowhere, came the vision.

"My captors had told me they were taking me to see the major one more time before they would then take great delight in killing me," he said with measured breath. "Then a bright light appeared, and I could see a heavenly being. The guards who held me froze, for it was evident they too could see this image. My first thought was of Father; perhaps he had not died after all. But then the more it spoke, the more I realized it was something not of this world. It had to be an angel. The heavenly being

243

said many things to me, but the thing that touched me most was when he said, 'The love of a father for his son never dies, never.'"

As if tired from trying to recall the event, Jean Paul slowly sat down while peering off into the distance, as if seeing the scene once more, trying not to forget any detail, however small it might be. The others gathered around him to hear him speak further

"It was then I realized that Father is with me—both of them."

Julia sat at his side now with her hand upon his knee, proud of her son but even more joyful of his presence.

"Were there any other words from the heavenly being?" asked Albert, since he and the council's interest had been piqued by Jean Paul's experience.

"Yes," he said, sipping from a skin pouch they had brought him to refresh his parched throat. "He said I was to lead our people to safety."

The council members all looked at one another and then turned to Albert. "Safety?" he asked Jean Paul.

"Yes, Uncle, he was very clear. He clearly said, 'You will take your people to safety.'"

The words drew the immediate attention of the elders, who had drawn near to hear the words. The mention of the need for safety caused them great consternation. The council reconvened back into a group, where they huddled to discuss this, for it was clear that although they had been asked to spread the Word, there was obviously more persecution in store in their future. Jean Paul's request from the heavenly guest was obviously an omen for what was to come. The irony of choice they faced did not escape them. They were supposed to spread the Word, but in the face of growing opposition or even death. It was the ultimate paradox.

The choice had been made. Their path had been chosen. Their fate was in the hands of God, and the Word was in theirs.

Chapter 35

THE GOOD SAMARITANS

But a certain Samaritan, as he journeyed, came where he was. And when he saw him, he had compassion. So he went to him and bandaged his wounds, pouring on oil and wine; and he set him on his own animal, brought him to an inn, and took care of him: . . . And he said, "He who showed mercy on him." Then Jesus said to him, "Go and do likewise."

—Luke 10:33-34,37

The darkness enveloped the room, save for the distant flicker of the fireplace, where a low flame glowed. He could smell the aroma of meat cooking over the fire and hear the occasional hiss of fat as it dripped onto hot coals. He realized his hunger for food. He tried to sit up, but the searing pain in his side shot through his body to the top of his head. Looking down at the source, he could see bandaging with dried blood stains. He felt queasy and eased himself back to the laying position as he draped the backside of his forearm across his forehead, feeling that his pulse was strong and steady. His mind was mostly blank. There was scant memory of what happened, other than the feeling of a distant cause. He needed to get back, but to where? Where was he? He could tell that he was only alive but for the grace of God and a blessed soul who thought he was too important to allow to perish—but who?

As he lay there trying to reconnect to memories that had been all but erased, the door to the dwelling opened, flooding the room with a blast of fresh air and light. A large figure stood in the doorway, nearly blocking the entire entrance. The being was huge. He slowly ambled into the chamber carrying a large load of wood that he dumped in a pile next to the stone hearth, causing an eruption of noise. He looked over at Marik and smiled.

"I see death has not claimed you today," his deep voice chuckled as he stood back up and stretched out the massive back that cracked from the force of muscles pressing it back into its natural shape.

Then the flash of the face came to him—from the grave, his sword, the moment of pain, then darkness. He could see the unhealed wound on his caretaker's neck that he had so long ago inflicted. Again, the questions arose with no answers. Why did this adversary not kill him when he had the chance? The wound in his side was deep, he could tell, but he could also feel his strength returning, and for that he knew he owed this man his life—the life he tried to take. The scene now played back to him, as if in slow motion; his fearless ride, slaying anyone in his path as he rode to the Vaudois, searching for survivors in the wake of the utter massacre. Then came the image of the man he ran through with his sword, falling face down into the grave where his keeper stood, stoic, ready to die, and the image of him holding him at bay with the tip of his saber on the big man's throat. There were words, but he couldn't recall them, other than knowing he had threatened the man, who didn't seem to fear dying. Then he recalled the missiles of death striking him repeatedly and the fall into darkness.

Why was I spared? he thought, turning painfully on his side and watching the big man as he went about his duties of preparing a meal—something he had obviously been doing unbeknownst to Marik during his apparent recovery.

"Sit up. You can try feeding yourself today," said the big man with his back turned, stirring something in a large black pot that hung on a wrought-iron arm extending over the fire next to the spit where the meat hung that Marik had noticed earlier.

"It's about time . . . for a while there I thought you were going to go on to the other side."

He finished pouring some liquid into a wooden bowl, which he then carried over to Marik, handing it and the wooden spoon to him. Then he backed up and watched to see if his patient would for once be able to take sustenance on his own.

Marik dipped the tip of the spoon into the dark broth and touched it to his parched lips. It smelled of a rich broth, with a mint-like, herb aroma that seemed to soothe his pains instantly just from the smell. He could see little leaves floating on the surface of his bowl. The broth tasted good, and he slowly began sipping it from the spoon, allowing the medicinal aspects of the fluid to begin working. Meanwhile, the big man watched and grinned, obviously satisfied with his success. Then he turned and began preparing his own meal.

Eventually the big man sat and ate at the table in the center of the room, joining Marik in his meal. He made grunting noises as he supped on his food, apparently showing his satisfaction at the taste or else just carrying on in the custom he was used to performing. Neither spoke as they ate.

Marik wondered to himself if he was a prisoner in this place. He did not find any sign of bondage or shackles anywhere near the bed where he had obviously spent a lot of time in the recent past. Yet with the wound he felt in his side, there was little chance he would be able to go anywhere fast—at least not for a while.

Feeling strengthened from his meal, as he sat the empty bowl upon the edge of his bed, he finally broke the silence. "Your name?" The big man did not turn from his food but continued on enjoying his solo feast.

"Your name, sir—who may I thank for saving my life"

He paused, half turning, and then blurted out with a mouthful of food, "Your God." Then he continued chewing, returning his full attention to the slab of meat in front of him.

"Marik . . . my name is Marik . . . and your name please?"

He didn't slow his consumption, again speaking with his mouth full, not turning. "Berg."

Marik paused, reflecting on the irony of the moment. He was experiencing kindness from a total stranger, one whose life he had considered ending in his fit of rage, his blindness of purpose, other than for revenge upon the helpless people he saw murdered each step of the way on his attempt to return to the Vaudois. Yes, the memory was returning.

"Thank you . . . Berg, for saving my life. For that I will forever be in your debt."

Berg humbly nodded his large mane of hair as he continued, not speaking, but obviously acknowledging that Marik had recognized his sincere generosity. The herbs began to ease Marik's pain, and he once again felt the need for sleep. He returned to his pallet, pulling up the hides that covered his body, providing warmth.

"Thanks be to God, and thank you, Lord for sending Berg," were the last words he heard himself whisper as he drifted off to a restful sleep.

The recovery had begun. Redemption was near.

Chapter 36

LONG JOURNEY HOME . . .

The plunderers have come, on all the desolate heights in the wilderness, for the sword of the Lord shall devour from one end of the land to the other end of the land; No flesh shall have peace.

—Jeremiah 12:12

In the days following their slim escape from Lyon, Peter knew too well that their current hiding place would not keep them out of harm's way for long. They had to move, but to where? He had several scouting parties sent out, all reporting back that the roads were being patrolled by the guard, quite heavily. This would make their flight to safety even more difficult.

However, there was an even bigger problem.

One of the scouting parties that had gone out to the lower reaches of the Piedmont to search for the best route to enter the mountain ranges to reach the Vaudois found an alarming discovery: a large papal army camped at the base of Quenten. From their report, it would be physically impossible to make it to the pass that led to the upper reaches of Quenten. The entire valley was covered, and passing through it without detection was improbable. They could try to camouflage themselves in wagons, pretending to be peddlers, but they would likely be searched, since blockades had been set up on all the roads leading to any mountain pass.

The only other option would to be travel south, making the southern pass at Rouga, and then return north and attempt to make the valley from the east before the winter snows began. The timing would be crucial. Being unable to reach the upper Vaudois before winter would be suicide. The gravity of their situation made Peter feel the need to confide in Arktos, for he knew the terrain near his Vaudois better than anyone, and if there was a back way in—one that they might be able to travel even if weather became bleak—he would know. The elder had been working with Steffan and the scribes soon after arriving, and they had finally completed the first edition. All that would be left to do now would be to make the unending copies. When the way was determined to be clear, he would dispatch them to various locations to continue the mission, but first he had to speak with Arktos, for their future depended on it.

He searched the grounds around the lodge for some time, finally finding the old man seated behind the barn on a stump, whittling on a cane he had cut from a sapling. He seemed to be in deep thought as Peter approached, but he quickly stopped when he heard the footsteps nearing, looking up while still holding blade to cane. His clear blue eyes under his snow white brow smiled at his host. Over the past year, they had come to know one another quite well, and a lifelong friendship had grown, one that would carry them both to their graves.

"Good morning, my friend. What brings you to my side?" Arktos said, smiling and then returning to the work on his staff.

"Blessings to you as well," Peter returned, finding an old bucket near the back wall of the barn and picking it up to use as a seat near Arktos.

"The mourning doves are telling me it's going to be a fine day today," the old man said, as if speaking to himself.

"Good . . . we could use some sunshine in our lives."

Arktos looked up from his work, catching the inflection in his friend's tone. "Something bothering you, brother?" he asked with a furrowed brow.

Peter shook his lowered head and sighed. "It seems we are in quite a predicament."

Arktos was silent, knowing it was time to listen. He sat still, waiting for more.

"We're blocked from entering Quenten from this side, and it's likely we won't be able to make the Vaudois from the east before the winter snows start."

Arktos nodded his understanding in silence but without the face of one that was worried.

"The papal guard is camped at the base of Quenten, across the entire Piedmont valley" he said, now with a bit more stress on the fact as to why they were blocked, but still no change in Arktos's demeanor. He waited for a response that matched his concern, but there was nothing.

When he finally couldn't stand it any longer, he had to ask, "You know something, then, don't you? There is a secret entrance you know about and it's all going to be all right . . . that's it, isn't it?" Peter now said, smiling.

Arktos returned to his work on the stick but said nothing.

Peter knew that for some reason he was either wrong or he had overstepped his place with the elder. "Forgive my brashness, my friend. I only find solace in knowing we will be safe from harm and that you are returned to your people safely."

Continuing to whittle without raising his head, he replied, "Peter, my beloved friend . . . God has chosen our path. However painful . . . however sad . . . however dangerous, we are to only give ourselves to him and then follow."

Peter was silent, now with his elbows resting on his knees as he sat looking forward into the depths of the forest beyond their sheltered refuge. The mourning dove cooed. Somewhere in the distance, they could hear another answer.

"There is no secret entrance, then, is there?"

There was a long pause. "No," Arktos softly replied as he continued with his actions on the wood.

Peter understood his peace, at least on the surface. He was still learning, trying to reach the depths of sanctity the old man seemed to be able to effortlessly go to whenever he wanted. He was certainly the student in all aspects of anything having to do with Christianity when compared to Arktos. He was a man unlearned in theology or the priesthood, but he could easily be the leader of any or all. His lifetime of memorizing and living the Word of God had created a man who was the personification of the teachings of Jesus, if not the embodiment of the apostle Paul himself. He sat, laying his face in his hands, reaching out to God in prayer as they sat. The gentle whisk of the blade on the wood, the wind in the trees, and the subtle coo of the dove were the only sounds.

Peter prayed to God for forgiveness, for in his mind, it was his fault that the people of the Vaudois were now in danger. The initial attack that had been thwarted by some miraculous event was likely made possible due to his men searching for the Vaudois. They had certainly been followed. Now, with the army camped at the base of Quenten, they were either preparing for another attack or had returned from one. In either case, the future did not bode well for the people he had searched for, found, and now discovered to be more special than he could have ever imagined. As with anything human, his hand in the mix of the natural flow seemed to have caused a disruption that, otherwise left to its own devices, would have continued on for centuries more. He begged for God's forgiveness again and again.

Finally, after a pause, he felt compelled to ask, "Father . . . please . . . please show me the way for you are the truth . . . the light." He was silent for some time before looking up.

"Amen," said Arktos, pleasingly gazing upon him as he realized the old man had been watching.

The gesture warmed his heart. There was a comfort there he had little experience with before knowing these people, yet he gained more of every day that passed in their presence.

"Thanks be to God," he replied, smiling back.

Since the day he had heard the story of the peoples who spoke the Word of God and their meager existence, living like Jesus had required of his disciples, he felt the calling. When he decided to give up all his worldly possessions and use his former wealth for a cause that would in essence ruin the life he once knew, he had no idea the change his heart and soul would experience.

"You know there is a way that would be much easier," answered Arktos.

"Huh?" replied Peter, not believing his ears. "What do you mean . . . easier way?"

"I mean, we can go through the Piedmont, straight up the pass to Quenten . . . we can be like David when he walked past King Saul and his armies."

Peter shook his head in disbelief "I'm sorry . . . I . . . I just don't see it."

"Trust in the Lord."

"It's—it's suicide. They'll capture us all and then . . . we . . . we'll never finish our writing," replied a flustered Peter.

"My son . . . trust in your faith. Have I not taught you these past few months the strength in believing? Have you not seen with your own eyes the power of God through those who have and will always be one with the Lord? I ask you . . . do you truly believe Jesus died on the cross for us as suicide . . . or was it something he had to do for us . . . so that we may live free of sin? Do you see?"

Peter sat thinking, knowing what Arktos meant, but to test his faith in such a bold maneuver would either destroy their mission or . . . or prove to him beyond belief that he was now part of something far greater than anything he had known. The church had professed the greater power of God, to be feared, to accept their guidance and protection, but this—this acceptance, allowing God to work in and through you was an aspect of belief that was like learning to swim. You either learned or you drowned.

"Yes . . . yes, I see and yes . . . I must trust in him"

"Good, then when you decide it is time for us to leave, let me take care of getting us through the Piedmont."

Peter nodded in agreement, looking down as he spoke. "Yes, my brother."

There was a pause in the discussion, which Peter noticed. His eyes trailed over to the old man, who now sat back on his perch, looking to the heavens with eyes closed. There was concern written across his face.

He spoke, eyes still shut "Peter . . . my brother."

"Yes, Arktos, I'm here."

"Pray for those in the Rora, in all the Vaudois . . . I feel a foreboding of darkness in my heart."

He paused again, sitting in the same posture, reflecting, not speaking, and appearing to be receiving something.

Peter knew better than to interrupt and waited for more; however, he was soon disheartened when Arktos continued, "The Spirit tells me that many may have perished and now are home with our Lord in glory."

He turned back to his stick, silent in action. No other words came forth. He turned his attention to the object at hand, something that was now, something to occupy the mind from idle thoughts. Unthinking, he carried on with his task, facing nothing and looking at everything.

Peter sat stunned from the sudden revelation. He realized that somehow the old man knew the fate of his people but reluctantly accepted his word.

It was all he could do.

Chapter 37

THE LIONS OF THE WORD

A mountain of God is the mountain of Bashan; A mountain of many peaks is the mountain of Bashan.

—Psalm 68:15

Jean Paul stood at one of the highest peaks on Quenten, looking down at the vast army that made camp at the entrance to the main valley. From up here, they were almost as small as specks of dust, but he could discern great numbers. There were too many to fight. Even if all the neighboring Vaudois warriors could be summoned, there would not be enough.

There was nothing left to do but to follow the advice of the messenger in his vision and move his people to a safer location. All they had left was the upper regions of the Vaudois—the place so remote that even their knowledge of living at the highest elevations would be tested. There would be no wood for fires, air would be scarce, and warmth would be a premium. Yet there was no place else to go. *Closer my God with thee*, thought Jean Paul.

The air had begun to cool down in the last few days and whipped at his clothing as he stood studying his adversaries below. They would need to move soon if they were going to move at all, for the seasons were short up here, and the snows would soon blanket the land. The scouting parties returning from their village reported atrocities so vulgar, so horrific, that they advised against anyone returning. Besides, the chance of being discovered was ever present due to the continued bands of scouts being sent out by the guard, trying in vain to capture the few refugees who had escaped their wrath.

His people had been weakened in numbers but not in spirit. They were accustomed to hardships, but this was the ultimate test of faith. Jean Paul met with the elders that evening and made arrangements for their departure the following day. They would retreat up to the higher reaches. There they would find their last bastion of hope: the sanctuary of the elders. There they would also find ancient dwellings made of stone that could be repaired and readied for the harshest winter they would have experienced in years. It was their only option. They would prepare a last defense, in case they were found, and there they would fight to the last man, woman, and child, for the last breath of all would be the last Word of God.

Albert was in attendance at the meeting that evening. He sat silent until near the end of the discussion about the logistics of the move were complete, and then he spoke.

"My fellow Vaudoisians, brothers . . . sisters . . . children of God, we carry with us the most precious thing known to mankind. Yet there are those who try to destroy us for some reason—one I have yet to understand, for what we speak, we speak of the truth . . . nothing more." Everyone nodded in agreement at this.

"We must find ever more people who can help us in this cause. I ask the council in addition to this move that we send some of our most knowledgeable out to the neighboring Vaudois to teach the Word, for I fear we have already been to protective and waited too long. You see, we never thought we might be hated for the Word we have kept all these centuries. We never thought mankind would be so influenced by Satan that he might want to destroy the Word. We just never imagined such a world as this."

One of the other elders said, "How will they move when the guard is looking for people to arrest?"

"We will move during the darkness of night, my brother," replied Albert, "sleeping in caves by day or by the cover of friendly persons to our cause."

"I see more risks with each new turn," replied the other elder.

Jean Paul stood up at this point, having heard enough hesitation. His youth spilled out into his lips, and with a fervent breath he said, "Let me remind you of the Maccabees."

There was silence.

"When the Maccabee's followers received information that Lysias was surrounding the fortresses, they and all the people begged the Lord with laments and tears to send a good angel to save Israel. The Maccabee was himself the first to take up arms, and he urged the others to run risks as he did and to come to the aid of their brothers. They dashed out at once, ready for action. While they were still near Jerusalem, a horseman in white garments and wearing full body armor made of gold appeared to them and led them. All together they praised the merciful God, and their souls were strengthened. They prepared themselves to attack not only men but also the fiercest animals and even the iron walls. They proceeded in battle order, having a heavenly ally thanks to the Lord's mercy toward them. Charging like lions against their enemies, they took down eleven thousand foot soldiers and sixteen hundred horses, and they put all the rest to flight."

When he finished, no one spoke.

"For you see, God is with those who live by his Word, and my fellow Vaudoisians, we are keepers of this Word, and as such, we have kept his Word for centuries. For us to be protected by the angel in white, all we have to do is believe and to accept him wholly. It's not enough to just memorize the Word, but like my grandfather taught me, but I failed to realize until it was almost too late, we must also feel the Word in our souls."

With that they all nodded to Jean Paul, each realizing the change in his demeanor and the obvious change of soul since the start of this journey. Yet the change, the adversity, all at once, was too much for some to grasp, so they sat in silence for fear of saying the wrong words—all but one.

Albert stood and walked up next to Jean Paul.

He stood facing him. Then he reached down and grasped both of his hands. "I knew your grandfather since we were boys tending sheep on the upper slopes of this great mountain we call home . . . I felt the loss of a son when you father died . . . and I recognize a leader when I see one. Like Arktos, you, my son, are not only my friend but someone I will follow."

With that, he embraced Jean Paul as the other elders quickly rose and gathered round, accepting him into their fold, for now, even though his age was young, his soul was one with the enclave.

Chapter 38

GRACE

I will wash my hands in innocence; So I will go about Your altar, O Lord.

—Psalm 26:6

Anna followed the butterfly gingerly from flower to flower, edging ever closer as she walked. Jakob trailed behind, intrigued by the games the child could invent. They were in a meadow glen deep in the woods, where they had become one with their new surroundings. It had been several weeks since they first arrived at the hunting lodge, but they were learning to enjoy their new home.

She held out her hand to the gentle insect as it seemed to sense the invitation from the innocent one. It fluttered briefly above the golden flower, lightly on the soft breeze and then landed, ever so fleetingly, upon the child's outstretched finger. Delighted in her accomplishment, Anna looked back at Jakob, who she knew had been following, and let out a short burst of laughter. The butterfly lifted off, swayed by the current that flowed past, and wafted along to the next bright spot in the meadow. She laughed and ran after it. Jakob continued to watch and follow.

The edge of the opening was completely surrounded by dark woods, with ancient oaks overhead. A stream ran along the length of one side, where Anna now ran, chasing her tiny friend, who lifted up higher in the flow then back down again, over and over. They soon found themselves along the creek bank, where there was an endless supply of opportunities for discovery for children their ages. Here in this place, they could forget all the realities of life and be free spirits again.

Jakob looked into the clear, fast-flowing waters. The motion of clear fluidity played in his mind. Water that once flowed past his mountain home in raging torrents now gently flowed past, gurgling over rocks and laughing in their ears. Sparkles of sunshine flickered over the water as they ran past, time being of no consequence. The shadows of the trees bent over and back as the day's light passed overhead. They shared a lunch of berries and bread on an open rock near the creek, each sharing recollections of happy days of their young lives. Then they raced off to explore new adventures.

They did not realize the time that had passed until the coolness of evening began to whisk over the backs of their necks. Anna was far ahead of Jakob, continuing her downstream wandering. Jakob was about to call to her to remind her that they should soon be returning when he noticed the bright flash of light in the distance. It was a glancing light off of something metal. His warning senses alerted, and the hair stood up on the back of his neck.

Not a moment must be wasted, he thought, as he raced ahead to catch the girl.

Unaware of the danger, she merrily danced onward. Jakob's feet could not carry him over the rough terrain of the wooded landscape fast enough as his heart raced in his ears. As quickly as the flash, he heard the scream of her voice as he realized the danger was real. Then he rounded the curve in the bend of the creek bed to find two papal guards, one with Anna in his grasp and the other laughing as he pointed at her with an outstretched sword, lifting her dress. Anna's face was white with fear. The innocent air had gone, and the look of anguished fear was in her eyes. Rage erupted in his soul that felt as if he would vanquish their faces from this world forever. He felt a primal rage, one he knew better than to allow to surface.

She caught a glimpse of Jakob coming into sight, and the acknowledgment of his presence gave notice to her captors as they turned to look.

Jakob froze.

Anna, in her moment of despair, didn't hesitate. She had seen this before, and she called to Jakob, for it was their only chance in her young mind to save them. As a plea to God, she screamed "Jakob . . . sing . . . sing, Jakob . . . sing to the Lord"

The soldiers laughed, and the one with the sword started to advance toward Jakob.

Knowing in his heart she was right because of the hours of training he spent with Gabriel, he felt something was right for once. He pushed down the fire within and beckoned forth the spirit—the connection to the beyond he had been taught, the bridge to Heaven. As if on cue, he began, gently, as if the brook's melody lifted his voice. He began, and the melody that rang along that creek bed soon found the ears of the battle-hardened warrior who advanced toward him and not long after his vengeful companion.

What seemed like an eternity later, Anna came running free as the men didn't hesitate to race for their freedom.

Anna and Jakob didn't look back. They didn't need to. In their young hearts, they knew they were freed by the grace of God, and they never questioned the act.

Behind them, the two soldiers would never recall the day they were lost in the woods, searching for something they would never be able to speak of again. That part of their minds and their lives was erased forever by something they had never heard and likely never would again due to their blackened souls.

Chapter 39

CANCER

And the Lord said to me, "The prophets prophesy lies in My name.
I have not sent them, commanded them, nor spoken to them; they
prophesy to you a false vision, divination, a worthless thing, and the
deceit of their heart."

—Jeremiah 14:14

The reports that had flowed in following the initial attack upon
the Vaudois to His Excellence were glowing, expounding upon
the virtues that were being exalted on the valley's inhabitants.
However, in the months that followed, little in the correspondence
described the embittered people who were found or left behind. The
tortured confessions elicited by the priests, with Torrinto as their chief
persecutor, were far and few between. It seemed these people were
resolved to die rather than to admit their sins, which, according to
Torrinto and company, were nothing more than failing to convert to
Catholicism. In and of itself, this was admission enough to be labeled
a heretic.

Pope Lucias III stood before his congregation who had gathered for
the commemoration of all the faithful departed mass. The audience
in attendance had broken all records for any previous mass. The clergy
had been hard at work gathering the faithful for the service that would
precede the year-end Christmas celebrations. Lucias did not disappoint
those in attendance either, putting on the display and pageantry that
had become synonymous with his holy office. There was a dual purpose
for the solicitation of the faithful to attend, however. The message today
was meant not only to uplift the spirit but to also benefit the morality

picture the papacy wanted to paint, from their point of view. There was a battle of souls, and the papacy did not intend to loosen its grip.

Lucias III spoke of the sacrifices of those during the first Crusades who had given their lives to protect Christianity, the papal crown, and Christians the world over. The speech elicited great emotion from those in attendance. There were many veteran warriors of that noble cause gathered today. This had been purposely choreographed to add an electric pulse to the mass so that all could share in the spirit.

His Holiness paused, letting the crowd gather themselves, for the next point was the dagger he meant to deliver to the heart.

He spoke slowly and distinctly now, making sure each word could be heard from his platform high above the congregation. His sermon now turned inward, toward the embattled peoples closer to home. He began by describing how Satan can turn even the most devout Christians into heretics, changing their minds and eventually their souls so they become unrecognizable in the Lord. He spoke of how their contempt for the church had led them astray and to begin teaching as false prophets, forgoing the God chosen institution that was the Holy Roman Church. The more he spoke, the more intense his voice became, rising in pitch. The veins stood out on his temples as sweat began to stain the crimson sash that decorated his ornate robe.

He painted a picture of the Vaudoisian people as crazed lunatics who only half understood who God was, pretending to be priests and converting innocent Catholics to their heretical cause. Then they were brainwashed into becoming their slaves and concubines, bearing more of their heathen children to live in the caves and continue their wicked, sinful cult. The crowd was now awash in hysteria, frothing the words back, spilling out anger, fists lifted, shaking at the air.

He had performed beautifully, working them into the maddened frenzy. "The heretics must be destroyed," he shouted, "lest they join the ranks of their brothers of Islam, who threaten our Lord and Savior, Jesus Christ!"

The crowd was now on its feet. A roar erupted echoing the sentiment of His Holiness. The aged, wrinkled lip, wet now with perspiration and spittle, grimaced back at the throng.

Knowing the limits of time, he quickly changed course so as to not lose the heightened awareness of the moment. He raised both arms to quiet them now, pausing, as if to rein them back in, forcing the flame of anger to now direct itself to the passage from the Bible, where the Word of God would confirm his words. He closed by quoting the book of Jeremiah, when Jeremiah spoke of the vision he had seen: "And the Lord said to me, 'The prophets prophesy lies in my name. I have not sent them, commanded them, nor spoken to them; they prophesy to you a false vision, divination, a worthless thing, and the deceit of their heart.' Therefore thus says the Lord concerning the prophets who prophesy in my name, whom I did not send, and who say, 'Sword and famine shall not be in this land'—'By sword and famine those prophets shall be consumed! And the people to whom they prophesy shall be cast out in the streets of Jerusalem because of the famine and the sword; they will have no one to bury them—them nor their wives, their sons nor their daughters—for I will pour their wickedness on them.'"

He bowed his head ever so slightly, so as not to lose the papal air, and prayed, "Lord, I pray for the lost souls. I pray for the priests performing their rites in the land of the wicked, and last, Lord . . . I ask for God to strike the false prophets down where they stand, all their men, all their women and children, sparing no one, and Father . . . in the name of the Father, Son, and Holy Ghost . . . save the Holy Roman church in all its glory, forever and ever . . . Amen"

The chorus of bishops then served the Eucharist to the congregation in mass while the pope was escorted off to his chambers. He was drained from his performance. The long walk to his room seemed almost too far. Upon reaching his lavish abode, he summoned the chamber boys to help him get undressed and cleaned up. He collapsed upon the divan, limp, trying to push the burning fire out of his mind so peace would come.

The troubles that lie to the north had not been extinguished as he had hoped, for he could feel it seething, like an open wound. He had worked the mass beautifully today, though, fueling the fear of the future and fire of the past into one.

It had to be done.

The unknown element capable of prophesying bothered him to his core. The reports coming back from Torrinto in secret disturbed him, causing sleepless nights, which only added to his anguish. The suspicion that these obstinate, poor, illiterate mountain peoples could accurately and miraculously recite portions of the Bible, if not the entire Bible, was bewildering at best. When the entirety of the Nicaea council's compilation was considered along with the Gnostic Gospels, there was no human way it could be put to memory.

Yet, as time passed, the suspicions were appearing to be confirmed, bit by bit. The truth was difficult to obtain.

Torrinto and his interrogators were having great woe in extracting anything that would substantiate this suspicion in a court of law, since most the wretched pilgrims would remain mute even unto their untimely deaths. The few recitations were observed were done in secret, while they were hiding or while undercover.

Yet, there it was: the fact that they had preserved the Word of God of their own accord—a Word not compiled by mankind but that was given to them reportedly from the sources themselves. What would it do to the power of the papacy should it become known? Or worse yet, what if the unknown Word produced an entirely different view of the hereafter or the road to perdition? His stomach churned; there were too many unknowns.

Then there was the other, more-distressing side note: the fact that the books these people quoted were exactly as they had received them, unfiltered and encompassing all of the writings and teachings that followed the ministry of Jesus and his disciples. This Word they possessed gave a power that bound them to one ruler, but a ruler who was not of this earth. That in of itself sent a shiver of terror of down the papal spine, causing him to shudder at the thought.

The oration he evoked today would stir the hearts and minds of his faithful, refueling their fire and hopefully their spiritual passion. He knew the longer the heretics lasted, the stronger they would become. Yet his force had grown complacent. The last report of the military operation was of a lengthy bivouac encamped at the base of the mountain stronghold where the heretics called home.

What must I do to light a fire under them to get them to return to pursuing these people to the very end? What fear must I strike in their souls so they will feel the darkness ebbing closer? His mind whirled as plans to put an end to this cancer overwhelmed all other thoughts *I will find a way, for I am the embodiment of heaven on earth, and if it is my will, it shall be done!*

Then black-veiled thoughts of wickedness crawled into the mind of His Holiness, blocking out any hope of his redemption. He chose the path, as God allowed, and something most vile and contempt began to fester inside him. The sanctity of the papal throne would be eroded by it so that mankind would soon be forsaken by an age of darkness. The darkness would envelop the continent into an abyss of despair that might have otherwise been prevented were a stronger man on the throne.

Feeling an urgency to act, the pope summoned his scribe, who arrived almost immediately with scroll and pen in hand.

"Take this down," he said, motioning to the scribe to come closer. "This must go to General Lucier."

The scribe began preparing the text and paused, waiting for words to begin. "Honorable General, I bequest thou find adequate substance relative to the matter we spoke of at hand, enough to begin the purge of this sin from our domain, for all matters of equal importance will await the outcome of this task. I trust you will be successful, for it is God's will you carry, and I will pray that all demons standing in your way will be vanquished once and for all. Carry this with you if any should question your mission, for the Holy Crown of the church stands behind your actions. His Excellence, Pope Lucias III."

The scribe stood, sealed the scroll with the ceremonial wax, and allowed His Holiness to press his ring print into its seal for authenticity. Lucias motioned for him to leave, sending him out with the order, "Send it immediately." The scribe met the courier at the door, where he took the message and was off.

Lucias felt even more drained but somehow also a bit more relieved. He reclined on his divan. As the chamber boys mopped his pallid brow, he closed his eyes and prayed, trying to calm his frazzled nerves. Around him was the opulence of golden vessels, gold-inlayed woodwork, gilded chalices, gold-leafed paintings encrusted with jewels, and centuries of obsessive wealth. This air of sanctification was preserved for only the most holy of humans, the man who now prayed for guidance. He was blinded through his closed eyelids and would never see the true light.

As he lay there, helpless in his own divine suffering, others, far, far away, lay in their own putrid stench of death while Holy Roman priests inflicted the wrath of God upon them until they cried out in final anguish for it to end. Some begged for forgiveness of the sins of those performing the ungodly act, achieving a level of spirituality few would know, least of all their persecutors. The pope could not see and was unable to reach this level, although his office proclaimed he was the embodiment of it. Sorrowfully, Pope Lucias would never reach that level of faith because of his edicts that would soon come back to haunt him. His place was enthralled in the depths of the soul from which nothing survives, longing for the place from which it shall never return.

In the far northern reaches of the upper Vaudois, the white blanket of winter had enveloped her people in the quiet solitude. A crushed flower lay wilted upon the newly fallen snow, and the angels wept

Chapter 40

HOPE

Behold, the eye of the Lord is on those who fear Him, on those who hope in His mercy.

—Psalm 33:18

Marik awakened to the sound of wood being moved around on the fire. As he sat up, rubbing his eyes, the golden glow of the young woman he saw struck him with a sudden gasp of beauty his sullen eyes had not seen in countless days. His formidable beast of a host and the shadowy, whitewashed walls of this chamber were all he had known since arriving at this unknown destination. Her auburn hair was pulled behind her in a long braid that nearly reached to the floor, draping across the back of her handmade woolen dress that showed gentle curves in all the right places.

She paid him no mind as she attended to the food she was preparing, but she kept his image in the periphery of her eyesight.

He felt his side. The wound was nearly healed now, but his strength felt distant. The pain was gone. Only the faint itch of scarring was left.

He spoke first, asking, "Where is my friend Berg today?"

Not turning from her task while her hands kept moving, stirring the broth, she reached for the bowl and answered, "Gone."

Marik stiffened at the sound. Noticing his change in demeanor, she continued, "Only for a short while." Her dialect sounded faintly familiar, but he couldn't place it in the few short words she had said.

"My name is Marik . . . and yours?"

"I'm Berg's sister, Kelcey," she replied, turning toward him and placing the bowl on the table in front of where he sat. "I will be attending to you until he returns. Then he and the elders will hold council and decide your fate," she said with an air of confidence, as if to let him know that he was not a welcome visitor. He had sensed that since he became conscious days earlier. He wanted to talk more, but he felt he had already pushed his welcome beyond her capacity for tolerance.

"Thank you for the food and for your family's hospitality," he said, head bowed as he slowly rose. He reached for the table as he shuffled over from his pallet. "I cannot begin to—"

"Don't thank me," she interrupted him before he could continue, "for I would have had left you to die—especially after I heard what you did to Berg . . . or rather I should say tried to do," she said with a scowl on her face and a chuckle in her voice as she collected her cooking utensils and moved toward the door.

She cracked the heavy door open and turned. "Let's just get one thing straight," she said, turning to look him in the eye, which he tried hard to do as he squinted into the bright light of day beyond the door. "Berg heard something, felt something, I don't know what, but you are only alive today because of that; nothing more."

Before he could respond or agree, she turned and slammed the heavy door, causing dirt to shake loose from the rafters, dusting him and his soup with tiny particles from above. He laughed to himself, and once again, he dove into the dark soup he had come to know as the food that had been instrumental in saving his life.

Kelcey would come and go for days afterward, each time opening up to longer discussions with Marik but never staying long, She was only there to provide him the sustenance she had obviously been ordered to do until her mountain of a brother returned. As the days passed, he slowly learned who his providers or captors were. They were from the clan of Hugh, also known as Huguenots. They had inhabited the upper reaches of Piedmont on the western side of the Alps for as long as they could remember. He had heard about them but never met any of them in person. They were ancestral supporters of King Hugh Capet of the Franks.

They, like the Vaudoisians, felt that the Catholic Church was trying to hoard the Word of God and that each man should be allowed to study and preach the Word of God himself, relying upon God for salvation and not payments to the church to ensure his final redemption. They had begun to severely criticize the church for practices they felt were becoming more ritual than spiritual, in particular the sacramental rituals and what they viewed as an obsession with dying and the dead. They felt more vehemently than the Vaudoisians that the rituals, images, saints, pilgrimages, prayers, and hierarchy of the Catholic Church did not help anyone toward redemption. To them, the church needed a purging of the corruption and impurities. To many, it was becoming painfully obvious that the pope was ruling the church as if it were a worldly kingdom. There was a veil of spirituality up front, but in reality, behind the scenes, the church exacted a pound of flesh for each soul it claimed to clear for redemption. The clan of Hugh was searching for a reason to break away, and that excuse was about to unfold before them.

Days later, Berg finally returned. Marik was sitting outside the shelter of his uncertain prison as Berg and a few others rode up in the late-morning hours, obviously weary from the road. The air was chilled, but it felt good to Marik after being confined to the little hut for so many weeks in recovery. The horses blew tiny puffs of steam out their nostrils as they walked past. All dismounted and made their way to the stables while Berg walked over to Marik after handing his lead off to another who was heading for the stables as well.

"'Tis good to see your safe return," called Marik as the big man approached.

"'Tis good to be back home," he said in a weary tone.

"I've much to ask, but again, I want to thank you for all you have done—you and your clan."

Berg nodded in return as he turned to sit heavily on a crate next to Marik. Then he leaned back against the wall of the structure and exhaled in a long breath. Closing his eyes, he folded his hands across his massive chest, which now bore light armor fixed in place with heavy leather strappings. He and his companions had obviously been out on some sort of mission that had put them in harm's way.

"So I hear from Kelcey you've made great progress," Berg continued.

Marik smiled, although Berg could not see. "Yes, she has been very kind. But . . . how did you know? Did you not just arrive from the road?" he said, looking in Berg's direction.

"We passed her on the road as she and some friends were headed to market in the next village."

"Oh, I see. Did she tell you of all the trouble I was for her?"

Berg chuckled. "No, I didn't hear that, which, to be honest, I was expecting. No, not that . . . but I did hear something else."

Marik's eyebrows rose at the notion that he had actually somehow managed a glimmer of friendship with her when all the time he knew she secretly hated him.

"I hear you've also been asking about us," he said in a slightly accusatory tone, opening his eyes in Marik's direction.

"I only wish to know more about the people who saved my life," he quickly retorted.

"Understood . . . I guess I would be the same," Berg said, turning his head back, looking straight ahead and resuming his restful pose, as if napping.

"Berg," Marik said after a slight pause, "tell me . . . what made you save my life . . . when it was obvious you clearly did not have to do so?"

There, he had thrown it out there now. All during his recovery, the question, once he regained consciousness and was aware of what might have transpired, had eaten at him until it became the object of most of his thoughts. He had to know, no matter what the cost.

The big man did not answer or stir.

For a moment Marik thought Berg had drifted off to sleep and was resolved to leave it at that. Regardless of why, he was forever in debt to this Samaritan's deed. But then, as if awoken from a dream, Berg replied, "It was what you said."

Marik looked in his direction. Berg's face still looking forward, but now his eyes were open again, as if he was looking off to some distant place.

"What words? I don't remember any words," Marik asked honestly, for there he had no memory of that exact moment in time. The pain, anguish, and countless amount of blood he lost from the wounds he suffered in the moment afterward had erased most of that fateful day.

"You said to me, '*One mustn't die to find Christ.*'" Berg turned and looked at Marik, who was now sitting with an awestruck look on his face. He didn't know what to say.

Berg continued, "You had me at your sword's tip, pressing against my throat, and were probably an instant away from taking my life, but then you said that . . . You paused to speak words that only a Vaudoisian or Huguenot might speak, and you said them in the heat of battle. It was then I realized something was wrong. Something about who I was serving was not right, and my self-imposed exile from my clan was obviously the wrong path. All of that suddenly became so vivid; there was no hesitation in what I must do. I instinctively grabbed your sword, the only thing I could do, which surprised you enough for me to gain the momentary upper hand. I had no idea the archers were there, and you were upon me before I realized you had been hit. They came to check on us and see if I was alright, telling me of your charge up the valley and the death you delivered as you rode.

"I listened to them, hearing the tale of someone who was driven by something—someone that had the sake of others in mind and someone who was on a mission. We looked down at your dying, bleeding body there in the bottom of that grave, next to the slain body of the comrade I had only recently known. A sergeant at arms came up and verified the success of his archers. He directed me to pull you out of the hole and take you down to the holding cell they had created in the little village up ahead. They wanted to try to pull information out of you before you died. Your actions had made you a target of suspicion, and they needed to know more.

"Sometime later, I finally got you down to the holding cell and deposited your body there, leaving you with the guards in charge. I told them they had better hurry with their questioning since it was obvious you didn't have long to live. I returned to my makeshift campsite and sat by the fire, thinking.

"I knew there was something more I must do, so I returned to the jail with the idea of liberating you from your captors, only to find your cell unguarded. I took it as a sign and brought you here to safety, where we still very nearly lost you."

"All because I said those few words?" asked Marik, now in total astonishment from the tale he had just heard.

"No." Berg shook his large mane of hair. "No, it wasn't just those words, my friend." He paused, looking at his former adversary.

Marik smiled back, for to hear of his near-death experience and miraculous liberation from the captors who would have certainly put him to death from this man, and to now hear him call him a friend, warmed his heart. He knew Berg would be a friend forevermore.

"It was far more than that," he continued, "for I knew in my heart, God had sent you. It was as if he spoke through you to me in that instant as I was standing there in that grave with your sword at my neck." Pausing, he looked down, as if struggling to find the next words. "You see, there is a passage in the Bible where Jesus was speaking, and it reminded me of the words you spoke that day. It goes something like, *'I am the resurrection and the life. The one who believes in me will live, even though they die.'*"

Marik's heart sank. Images of the people of the Vaudois came flooding back to him like the long-lost memories of loved ones who had gone on before. He could hear their recantations of Scripture, long passages, one after another. The faces of Jakob, his grandfather . . . and his mother all came rushing back in a fury of spirit that caused his face to flush with pain. He bowed his head as tears gathered in his eyes.

"My brother, have I hurt you?" asked the gentle giant with compassion.

Marik shook his head no. He couldn't make words just yet; his throat was too choked with emotion to respond. In his heart, it all returned, full volume, overflowing all else. He knew in that moment he had to return—to find what was left, if anything.

Finally, he regained his composure enough to respond, "No . . . no, you haven't caused the hurt, my friend, for that infliction is due to another. My heart longs for those I fear did not survive that fateful day we met. Your tale only reminded me of why I was there that day and those who I never was able to reach." His voice cracked at the last, and he bowed his head again as water droplets fell from his chin.

They sat in silence for a spell, both men reflecting on the past and what it had to do with them now. Snowflakes fell gently; the air was getting colder with each passing day.

Berg finally broke the silence. He explained to Marik that the council would meet soon, and they would then decide his fate. Since the day he had arrived on the stretcher, it was mandated that he would have to stand at the council and be tried either as an enemy or friend of the clan. Berg tried to convey to Marik that he had been spared by God for a reason and not to worry.

It was easier said than done, but Marik went along with the big man. He had no choice. The next day he and Berg were called to council.

Marik knew that the council could either brand him as an enemy or accept him as one of their own. Part of him felt he needed to talk, but Berg's story might be enough to sway their opinion and vote. He did not want to overstep the boundaries of his host, for it was he alone who had allowed Marik to survive to this point. The tale of his survival, being plucked from the tragic fate that awaited, and then being nursed back to health was almost too much for him to bear alone. He knew there was a God and felt he had been spared for a reason. Why he had been brought here as part of God's plan was not yet obvious, but he was beginning to get a clearer picture with each passing day.

They arrived at the council, which was located in the lodge at the end of the village. There was a central fire pit each speaker stood in front of when he or she spoke. The meeting had already begun and continued as they entered. Berg escorted Marik to a low bench along the wall near the pit but away from the light of the council fire. All heads and eyes were on the current speaker. Hardly anyone noticed their arrival. The aged, white-haired man who stood before them now was the main elder of the council. He spoke of fighting that had been reported from the recent scouting party. Marik realized that was where Berg had gone on his recent trip.

The speaker described how the papal army had taken it upon themselves to attack helpless mountain peoples—good, God-fearing Christians. His voice rose with each tale of horror the party had encountered. They found village after village burnt out and destroyed, with the population either mutilated or entirely missing. There were a few warriors who tried to repel the massive force, but their number was so small and the force so large that they stood little chance, if any, of protecting themselves.

He then began talking about the corruption of the church and the church's departure from a force for salvation to becoming an oppressor, which turned it into the demonic force that allowed it to perform such horrors. He talked of how now was the time for his people to consider their path—where they should go from here. They as a people had found much fault with the church since the time of King Hugh, and their disdain was growing with each passing report. They might have already entirely separated themselves if it were not for the fact that they still relied upon the Catholic priests for the Word of God.

The statement hit Marik like a ton of rocks. His head began to spin.

Had he heard correctly? Was the only thing keeping this band of Hughs from being free was the Word? He had to speak now. It was imperative, yet he held his tongue for fear of stepping out of bounds during the somber proceedings.

Berg looked in his direction, noticing the agitation on his face. Having spent time bringing Marik back to life, there were some things about his demeanor he had learned along the way. Instinctively, he arose. "Speaker Galack, I would like to interrupt if I may?"

The council turned to the giant of a man.

It was rare for Berg to speak at a council meeting. He was a man of action, with few words, so when he did ask to speak, it was usually of major importance.

"Go ahead brother . . ." said Galack, motioning.

"I feel there is something we may learn from the man God asked me to save," he said, turning with his outstretched arm pointing to Marik.

He felt all eyes turned upon Marik. Knowing the gravity of the moment, he slowly stood, clearing his throat.

"Honorable Huguenots," he began, "I come to you by what can only be described from my perspective as a miracle." He paused to add gravity to the next statement. "I have heard your discussions about the plans and future of your clan and have suddenly realized why God spared me and brought me to this place."

Galack's eyebrow raised, as if the statement might have come from one who spoke freely, without thought. Not knowing Marik's true nature, he had no way of knowing his sincerity.

"I believe there is something you need to know. First, let me give thanks to God the Father, for what I am about to speak is only due to the glory of God."

He paused, thinking of all that had transpired. He had seen so many miracles, so many revelations, and a people so precious that they could only be still in existence because of the hand of God. He reflected on Arktos's first hesitation to share with them. This gave him pause now, but something urged him on, for this was a moment that could not wait. Clearing his throat, he continued, "The fact I need to share with you is that the written Word now exists in your language—one that you may possess for your own keeping."

An eruption of voices filled the council chamber.

The mention of the God's Word being available for all caused even the most stringent follower of protocol to lose his bearing, forcing Galack to begin slamming this spear upon the ground in great resounding thuds repeatedly as he tried to regain control. Finally, after several excited minutes, the council was back in order. Galack faced Marik now to question him on this last statement so he could know the merits of it.

"How is it possible that the Word, up to this point protected by the Holy Roman Church, could be available to the common man?" he began his interrogation. "How is it possible that the Word of God can even be understood and interpreted by untrained, uneducated laymen such as ourselves?" All eyes now peered at Marik for an answer.

Without faltering, he answered, "My brothers in Christ, I share with you a story of valor, faith, and countless sacrifices that have made something that heretofore seemed implausible possible." He again hesitated before continuing, but this crowd, knowing what he did about their predisposition for intolerance to the Catholic empire and the circumstances that led Berg to save his life, made him feel compelled to share what he knew—all of it.

"I start by telling you how insignificant my role in all of this was. I was only sent to find a people who had preserved the Word of God through centuries of time. Little did I know how much my life would change after my encounter with these storied people."

He could feel a stirring in his heart as he spoke. He carried on with purpose in his voice now. "What I found was entirely greater than a people who could recite the Word of God, verse for verse, book by book, but something much, much deeper. I found persons who were and are the epitome of everything and anything Christian. They live and breathe the words they carry beyond a level of comprehension by even the most scholarly priest."

He now began to pace as he spoke, seeking the eyes of all who dared to peer into his as each sat rapt by his oration. "You see, they walked in the way; they did not just speak the word. To carry on something so precious, preserved through centuries by careful memorization and recantation by a people who could be considered as close to resembling the teachings of the apostle Paul himself, full of piety and humbleness, glorifies God in and of itself."

He now stopped dead in his tracks and turned toward Galack. "But in reality, my lord, they may also being counted as your comrades in arms because even as we gather here tonight, they now suffer and are possibly vanquished forever."

His voice faltered now, eyes turning downward. "This I speak to you now with a heavy heart, for I fear their demise was due in part to the mission I was sent upon to help create the object of your jubilation just minutes ago."

His head now bowed. He stood silent as all felt his pain.

Galack waited until he felt the time was right. Then he spoke in a commanding tone, "We will stand with our brothers in *Christ!*"

With that, the entire council burst into a roar, all stomping or beating upon the ground in a great throng of passionate agreement.

Marik looked toward Berg through watery eyes and saw the same in the big man's face as the roar continued. He put his hands on his face and wiped away months of anguish, moving them down his chin as he raised his head toward the heavens. He gave thanks to the one above and prayed for the people of the Vaudois.

God knew they needed it.

Chapter 41

FRUITION

To the present hour we both hunger and thirst, and we are poorly
clothed, and beaten, and homeless.

—1 Corinthians 4:11

Since the day of their close encounter with the guards in the
forest, Anna and Jakob kept close to the lodge, never venturing
out of eyesight. They fearfully divulged the mishap to Arktos
and Peter, but they did not get the response they had expected; neither
grew angry or upset.

Soon thereafter, though, work began on preparing to move once more.
The weather had been growing steadily cooler with each passing day, and
soon winter's icy chill would be on them. Time was of the essence.

Scouts returned with reports of possible avenues of safe travel. All the
options were considered with everyone's safety in mind. Peter and
Arktos spent hours discussing plan after plan, with the elder often
retiring long before his younger comrade had given up reviewing maps
and charts. Peter wanted to know every possible escape route, every
possible turn in the road, not leaving anything to chance. He knew the
old man had faith and was merely humoring him for the most part, but
it bothered him more that he could not just leave things to fate. His
faith was nothing like the ancient Vaudoisian's, and it never would be.
This much he realized, but he couldn't help desiring to walk in Arktos's
footsteps.

When the crisp morning came that Arktos announced to him it was time to go, he gave in to the old man's intuition and ordered the wagons readied for departure. They would prepare all day, resting a while, and then begin their journey under the cover of darkness the following evening. Steffan and the scribes had already been dispersed randomly many days before to various undisclosed locations to continue the work. The timing was no mistake. They took nothing for granted and wanted as little attention drawn to their departure as possible. If any of the scribe wagons were discovered, they would be found alone, and the bulk of the work would not be lost or the mission compromised. So far, everything seemed to be going smoothly. There had been no reports of any of their parties being detained or spotted up to this point.

The plan Peter had devised for their escape to the Vaudois was to send out three small convoys of wagons with only a couple of undercover armed men escorting each, knowing that small traveling family bands were not uncommon. A large contingent of their full accompaniment would be obvious and would surely jeopardize the mission. Like their scribe detachment, they would travel small and inconspicuously. Arktos, Anna, and Jakob would remain together, with Peter himself leading a second, and the third would be comprised of his trusted house servant Amesh and his family. They would try to converge nearly at the same time at the crossroads that met at the upper Piedmont, where their trek into the mountains would begin.

That evening a thick fog blanketed the region, obscuring all who traveled upon the open road. The cautious travelers welcomed the additional camouflage, and with trepidation, they set out for their final destination. Their journey would take them mostly over rural stretches of roads where, for the most part, the only thing to fear were bandits. The papal guard had been nowhere to be seen in recent days; there had not been any patrols. They made good time the first night, and as each small party made camp by the morning sunrise, each group's leader led the others in a prayer for their first night's safe journey. They then welcomed sleep as they spent the day off the road, biding their time until it was safe to move again. Peter had estimated that, barring any unforeseen troubles, they would make it to the crossroads after three nights.

As the sun rose from behind the towering peaks of the Alps in the distance, the fog from the night began to lift. Mourning doves cooed their greetings to one another. As Peter looked down at the handwritten words that covered the pages of the book he held in his hands, he welcomed the dawn with the Word of God—the Word he was now able to read on his own.

This was the first time he had a chance to embrace the work they had done. The leather-bound volume smelled of the fresh ink that beautifully played across the Far East paper he had been so fortunate to find. The supplier promised unlimited supplies, and he welcomed the transaction. Here now, sitting in the outdoors with all of God's creatures around him, he could feel a strength that seemed to pulsate through his soul as he read the Scriptures as he wanted, turning page after page, stopping when and where he desired. This was what he had searched for all his life. Now their future rested on fate. They were days away from their perceived safety. For now he took it all in, for if it were gone tomorrow, he would have lived to at least seen this heaven-sent blessing he held in the palms of his hands.

The pages seemed to glow with the growing morning light. Peter couldn't help think of how many others would soon come to find this feeling of unbridled spirituality. How would they react to holding the Word of God? How would they take to being told where, when, and how they could worship when all it took was the ability to read it from the book themselves? In his heart, he knew the change was coming. In his being, he could feel the changes taking shape. Would he live to see it though? He closed the book and tried to rest. The night's journey had been uneventful, but he was tired and needed rest.

Must empty my mind, he told himself as he leaned back on his pallet. *God's will be done.* With that, he closed his tired, burning eyes and slowly drifted off to a fitful slumber.

It was one night down and two to go.

Chapter 42

UNTHINKABLE

Therefore Sheol has enlarged itself and opened its mouth beyond measure; Their glory and their multitude and their pomp, and he who is jubilant, shall descend into it.

—Isaiah 5:14

Flames danced high in the night sky, carrying with them sparks from the embers below the feet of those who were engulfed in the raging inferno below. A few screams escaped their bodies before the flesh melted into oozing blobs, running down charred skeletal remains. Their dying cries blended with the wails of those left behind who watched in horror at the massacre unfolding in the town square.

Devilish shadows danced on the nearby walls as one by one, more human fuel was added to the fire. Before the bound bodies were thrown upon the fiery bed, they were matter-of-factly asked, "Do you confess your sin, denounce your beliefs in Satan, and wish to convert your soul to Catholicism?" Most responded with placid stares of conviction while others screamed that their tormentors would burn in hell as their last breaths were sucked from their lungs by the massive heat into which they succumbed.

It had been weeks since any reports from the troops stationed at the upper Piedmont had reached Lucier's desk, so he sent a courier to inquire of Major Crowell as to what had transpired. When the courier returned empty handed and with the report of the major's seemingly unannounced retirement, he went into a fit of rage so severe that many thought he would lose his mind. A few days afterward, he received another letter from a courier from the pope with the orders to begin what Lucier felt was needed all along. Being the good military man he was, he had awaited his marching orders from the top. Now with the holy blessing from His Excellence and the feeling of divine guidance from above, he unleashed the pent-up vehemence that had been held inside, under pressure, growing more and more rancid with each encounter until it spewed forth and soon became reality.

First he would send a new commander and regiment to the Piedmont to regroup those troops that remained. The man he put in charge, Major Apollyon, was a legendary crusader who was known for his ruthless, bloodthirsty conquests. His father had been a bishop in Turin before dying an untimely death due to an unknown illness. His father, a devout man of God, had died even though Apollyon had prayed unceasingly. To him, God had turned his back on his father. This had turned Apollyon against the church for a time, providing sufficient vengeance for anything godly, and created a warrior with no boundaries. He was a perfect comrade in arms or one's worst enemy.

Lucier sent the major and his contingent out immediately, since time was of the essence. The weather was changing, and if his reports were correct, the heretics were still within reach even though the snows were beginning to cover most of the upper mountainous passes. He would join Apollyon in a few days and lead the final assault, once and for all, crushing this uprising before its sickness infected any more of his Christian family. Before he would depart to do so, there was one last task he had to complete: the beginning of the end.

He turned is indignation toward Lyon, pouring forth a vengeance so bitter with a fury so savage, one could have mistaken him for the devil incarnate. From the depths of the burning abyss, loathing ruthlessness erupted, flowing out into the streets of city. Those who had been rounded up in the house-to-house search were being dragged from their prison cells in one last dramatic display of the supremacy the Roman Catholic Church held over its rebellious subjects. Their convictions would become their death sentence, for any who vowed to not convert to Catholicism or who held beliefs outside of the church—synonymous with those of the Vaudoisians—was labeled a heretic.

There were but a couple hundred found. Most had escaped upon hearing of the crackdown. Many headed for obscure regions out of the reach of the guard. Others had stayed, not believing the church could become the monster they now witnessed in the square. Lyon, once considered by many to be one of one of the most civilized cities in all of France, was now displaying all the attributes of hell on earth, the convulsions of barbarism of yesteryear.

The acrid smell of smoke and brimstone filled the air.

Horrified citizens peered from dark-shuttered abodes as firelight flickered in their eyes, reflecting images of Hades' inferno. Sheol had become the hell on earth for which it was named, and the intestines of the infested cauldron erupted into the being of mankind. The scene was so inexplicably horrific that one could only stand to watch the procession of men, women, and children from the bowels of the unholy prison and into the fire in mere glimpses of time. Their fate had been prescribed by their choice of spiritual path, and they were being led to their deaths by those with no hopes of knowing a soul of their own.

With blankness of spirit and steeled visions, disconnected beings only moved from one endless task of brutality to the next, savoring the intake of burning juices that temporarily ease their anguished sufferings. They would awaken to the next light of day knowing the vilest form of life still existed: their own. The atmosphere was suffocated by a tumultuous spiral of morbidity, death, and collective despair, each feeding upon the other until the darkness enveloped everyone who would allow it to, extinguishing even the dimmest flicker of light. Death welcomed many this night. Into her eternal arms they gladly stepped, fearing not, knowing faith would lead them through to the other side . . . where all was naught.

The bishop and several of his priests had gathered to pray for the lost souls who escaped within the flames into the black night sky. One of the priests climbed upon the back of a wagon and began to read to the few who dared to gather a passage from the Bible he felt appropriate for the moment at hand. The words read aloud at the macabre scene of death and sanctity were meant as prayers but echoed a haunting lamenting of woe to come, "Outside is the sword; inside are plague and famine. Those in the country will die by the sword; those in the city will be devoured by famine and plague. The fugitives who escape will flee to the mountains. Like doves of the valleys, they will all moan, each for their own sins."

Few listened because the screams and crackling inferno covered up the misguided clergy's well-meant guidance.

The flesh had been severed, the blade had been struck, and the hemorrhaging had begun. Nothing could stop it now. The seething bitterness had reached a point of no return, and only the complete annihilation of a belief, of it perpetrators, could sate the thirst for vengeance by the ones who would topple their own kingdoms for sake of trying to save them. Blood would run as freely as the mountain streams from whence the purest of faith had supped.

Purity of heart was all that could save them now.

Chapter 43

MANY HILLS TO CLIMB
BEFORE I REST

Woe to those who call evil good, and good evil; Who put darkness for light, and light for darkness; Who put bitter for sweet, and sweet for bitter!

—Isaiah 5:20

A family of deer played in the road near the forest's edge as evening approached. The moon was already aloft, nearly full, waxing in the crisp night sky. The buck was the first to hear. He lifted his head from its predatory stance apart from his young son's gaze and flicked an ear toward the sound of the wagon approaching. He exhaled out a bark of warning to the others, stamping his front legs forcibly. They bounded into the shadows of the wooded sanctuary nearby as he stood his ground, watching.

From the bend in the curve, Jakob could see the buck standing in the middle of the road and then trot off, chest held out, snorting his warning, head high as if to say, "This is my land . . . but I will allow you to pass." They had plenty of fresh game to eat. It was salted down in the barrels they carried as part of their cargo. Had that not been the case, one of the armed guards in their party would have taken aim with their long bows and taken him down.

Jakob watched the beautiful creature vanish into the winding path of sheltered woods from which he came and thought back to his homeland—vast, ancient, partially wooded, with twists and turns so varied, so random that one could barely believe anyone could find his way more than once, let alone twice. His mind drifted back to a time when his father, Jean Paul, and he had gone on his first hunting trip.

They had set out to pursue a herd of wild mountain sheep far in the upper reaches of their mountain home. The animals were very wary. They were intelligent and cunning, knowing every move of even the most remote creature in their realm. Yet his father, from years of experience, quickly taught them how to creep up on the elusive beasts. Before they knew it, they were close enough that they could see the breath of the animal and smell his odor.

On this particular day, they had left their home long before daylight and climbed high into the upper reaches of the Vaudois, where the trees would not grow and the air was bitingly thin. It was Jean Paul's turn to try his bow today. He had practiced for weeks with the new weapon and learned to shoot well enough that his father felt he was ready to try it on a real, live target. Jakob had only been brought along to watch and learn, for he was still unable to pull the bow.

They all sat silent, pausing for the right moment. Kristoff waited for the wind to change. Then he motioned to Jean Paul, who stood behind a boulder some twenty paces away, to strike. The youth stood, arrow already prepared, and pulled the string taut.

Jakob had stayed close by his father and watched his father's motion. Then he looked back at the large ram whose head came up at the sound of Jean Paul's movement. In his excitement for his brother to shoot, he instinctively jerked his leg, causing a small rock to fall down the slope below them. The rock then hit another and another until a crash of stones could be heard clear across the valley. The arrow never hit its mark, for the animal's reaction to the inadvertent mishap of Jakob's foot was instant, and the entire herd was out of range before the disgusted Jean Paul could even let out a disgusted, *"Jakob!"*

Kristoff laughed as Jean Paul came around the narrow footpath with his scowling brow directed toward his little brother. "I believe God has blessed the goat today," he said, chuckling as he patted Jakob on the shoulder as he stood.

"But Father . . . I asked you not to bring him. He's too young."

"You were too young once," he said, smiling.

"I'm sorry, Jean Paul," murmured Jakob with his head down, feeling bad for letting his brother down.

"It's alright," he replied back, knowing his father would rather him set a good example than to continue to berate his little brother for spooking the prey.

"Besides," Kristoff continued as they began their slow descent toward home, "it leaves us the opportunity to hunt this fine fellow again someday . . . and who knows, Jakob, it might be your turn next time."

Jakob smiled at the memory as the wagon just entered the sheltered shadows of the dark woods, which blocked out the moonlight that filtered through its weave of branches overhead. The memory of his family brought brief, momentary comfort. The crashes of deer running away in the woods nearby returned his mind to the sheep that had scattered on that day so long ago. On their hunting trip on that day, they returned home with plenty of other wild game. In the forests below, they found wild pheasants, which his father took down with several quick shots. Later a couple of small deer ventured into their path, and Jean Paul was able to shoot one, redeeming his value as a hunter—value his father had never discounted. It had been a memorable day, one that Jakob would cherish forever.

*   *   *

Traveling at night lent an eeriness to their journey. They were traveling without torchlight, relying on the moon and stars above. The leafless branches of the dark limbs above looked like giant fingers grasping for souls who entered their dark lair below. The little light that filtered to the roadbed below made it nearly impossible to see, let alone navigate, yet they traveled onward, hoping the other side was not far. All along their inner fears were heightened with every turn in the road, every sound in the woods.

For this party, the sound of the woods abated, only to be replaced by another crashing roar from another direction. The sound was definite and growing stronger with each pulse.

Suddenly from behind them came a thundering regiment of cavalry, led by Apollyon and his attachment of knights of the papal guard. They were followed by several hundred armed soldiers, also on horseback. The first instinct of the guards escorting the caravan was to take cover, but Amesh, Peter's most trusted servant, quickly reminded them of their disguise and told them to act as meekly as possible.

Time stood still as the darkness approached. The guards second guessed Amesh. The warriors' instinct to survive was nearly impossible to suppress. They still had time to prepare even as the distance between them diminished with each stride of the oncoming horses.

They had not yet been spotted, since they were watching the horde approach from the cover of the woods. The riders' armor gleamed in the bright moonlight. Amesh pulled his cart to the side and motioned for the others to follow.

Youth's impertinence in battle often overwhelms the advantage of speed. The young guard's steel had not been battle tested like his brethren, who held their blades in check.

There was the flash of moonlight bouncing off the metal. The onrushing throng was so indifferent, so unthinking, and reacting to something like this was only natural. All the eyes of the party were inexplicably drawn to the sound that followed: the flash of the sword leaving its scabbard.

The voice of steel grating from its restraint instantly rang a mental alarm within the army, causing the first wave to flinch. Without hesitation, they all presented weapons. A thunderous wave of death engulfed the tiny band, slaying and slicing each being that came into focus.

Amesh raced for the cover of the nearby stand of trees, only to be felled from behind by a battle axe square in his back. He was dead before his limp body hit the ground. The others scattered, some crawling under the wagons, only to be dragged and quartered on the spot. Their severed bodies were then hung in the nearby trees for others to witness as they passed, as a sign of conquest from those gone before.

Young or old, it did not matter.

Apollyon had learned from countless battlefields that a trail of fear was as good a weapon as a strong broadsword, so he used every ounce of flesh that remained to display the grisly vestiges of slaughter. When the grotesque display of humanity was complete, he spurred his steed forward, ordering his troops onward, leaving nothing but the dead in his wake.

There was no life spared. It was over in a matter of seconds. All who breathed the words of the Father met their Maker in that shadow of the night. Their journey was done.

The forest grew strangely still.

*   *   *

Jakob felt something peculiar at the calm, but couldn't place the thought. Uncomfortable, he edged slightly closer to his grandfather, reaching for the old man's hand. He grasped it tight and closed his eyes.

He needed prayer—and now.

Arktos could tell something was bothering Jakob, knowing the boy's gifts; he relaxed, allowing the horses to follow the road, and closed his eyes in prayer with him while his hands held the reins loosely in check.

Nothing could be said. Nothing could be prayed that wasn't heard immediately by the members of the third party who believed, as did they. Their message was immediate, for they were already home.

They rode on the rest of the night through the shadowed forest, reaching a river near dawn. For safety's sake, they would wait for daybreak before trying to ford the river. Once again they made camp off the road, back in the cover of the heavily wooded surroundings. As the sun began to paint peach colors across the azure blue sky, their beds were made, and their weary bodies tried to rest.

Arktos sat by the small fire, finishing the last of his breakfast while the others retired. He looked into the low embers as a small curl of smoke lifted, briefly hovering before disappearing. *Only one more night's travel before we meet up with the other two caravans*, he thought to himself. Over on the edge of their tiny camp, one of the guards Peter had assigned to their group stood sentry. Arktos thought of his assignment and wondered if the soldier knew what fate awaited him. Obviously Peter wouldn't have assigned someone to them unless he trusted him without question—someone who also believed in their cause.

He wondered to himself if all of this would come down to simply a battle of flesh and blood. How much warfare could they stand? How many would die for their belief . . . and why did it have to be this way? So many useless but meaningful thoughts flooded his mind. Would there be anyone left of his family?

He reached inside his woolen tunic, finding the archaic fish hook. He felt his smooth solidness of the ancient bone, which reminded him of the reason it was in his possession to begin with. A people's existence depended upon him. A precious gift had been endowed upon them to maintain and preserve, and it was as much a part of them as they were a part of the mountains they inhabited. There was so much to lose, yet so much to gain.

When it all began to close in on him, as now, when there seemed nowhere else to turn, he would return to the one thing in his life that brought peace to his soul. He began speaking the Word. One word would begin and then the others would follow, but all would hold meaning to the here and now. It was an unconscious act, led by the Spirit.

The Word of God rang true as he closed his eyes and spoke, "Be strong and courageous; do not be afraid nor dismayed before the king of Assyria, nor before all the multitude that is with him; for there are more with us than with him. With him is an arm of flesh; but with us is the Lord our God, to help us and to fight our battles. And the people were strengthened by the words of Hezekiah king of Judah."

Somewhere in the distance, another tired party bedded down for the day, unaware but hopeful, for their reunion with their brethren was close at hand. The day would bring solace, while the shift of darkness continued, and storm clouds began to form at the peaks of the mountain range to their east.

Sleep came and was welcomed by all.

Chapter 44

PRESERVATION

I was watching in the night visions, and behold, One like the Son of Man, coming with the clouds of heaven! He came to the Ancient of Days, and they brought Him near before Him.

—Daniel 7:13

A scene of bitter irony unfolded as the children of the light moved, casting long, moonlit shadows across the snow-covered terrain. With one labored step at a time, they slowly advanced up the mountainside, their future uncertain. They prayed in unison as they marched, each gathering strength from the others. Young and old, they bent toward the steep incline, helping one another. The freezing cold air meant nothing; their spirits were lifted beyond what their bodies could feel. Their plight was purely one of preservation—not of themselves but of the gift so long ago bestowed. They desired to keep it alive for another generation to learn, to share, and to worship. Not even the most rancid cancer that was now growing in the hearts of men below their mountainous realm could squelch its fervor.

Miraculously, they had recovered much of the livestock from the hillsides surrounding their burned-out village remains. They were moving them and what little belongings that were left in the shadows of darkness up the mountain, to the higher, more-obscure valleys where they sought refuge. Recent snows had slowed their ascent, but these were a rugged people who were used to the hardships; no one complained. They moved en masse, leaving no one and nothing behind. They traveled in the night, taking precautions to keep from being seen by any of the wandering, rogue warriors who were left in the wake of the recent massacre.

Divine guidance watched over them now as their footsteps were covered with the new-falling snow. There was a purpose in the direction they marched. Long ago the elders had made contingencies for if and when this day would come, and it was in this last bastion of hope they sought refuge.

Jean Paul and Albert led the contingent to the hidden cavernous fortress that would become their temporary home for the long winter ahead. This is where they would survive until the snows melted, allowing them to rebuild their lives and their farms and continue in their faith as they had always done.

That was their plan.

There was ample room inside for sections of the cave to be used as corrals for the livestock. The rations were small, but with time, they might be able to stealthily recover some of their supplies from the lower Vaudois that they would need to make it through the long winter. There would be losses, but with care, they would survive.

Once everyone had reached the confines of their new sanctuary, the council chose the most robust elders and young student escorts to depart for the neighboring Vaudois to begin their missionary work of teaching the others. They would have to leave before the winter snows blocked the passes completely. There would be no time to spare, for their task would be hard, and their journey would be arduous. Those who were chosen rested for only a day and then departed, again under the cover of darkness. Those who remained were left to feel as if they were on the voyage with Noah, with all the animals living under the same roof. But the arrangements were only temporary, and most felt it was a humorous change, one they would make the best of, regardless of why they were now here.

Stores of salted food rations, along with stockpiles of kindling, lamps, wool, and other supplies, were already there waiting on them when they arrived. This cave, like the previous one, also had ovens built into the rock walls with vents escaping out to allow the exhaust from cooking and heating fires to be maintained. Several crevices in the upper reaches of the cavern allowed light to enter during the day through filtered levels, bouncing from one granite wall to the next, creating a soft glow within. There was also an ample supply of fresh water from a small stream deep within the interior of the cave, which flowed unabated year round. The entrance was obscured by a series of turns in the pathway leading up to it, along with boulders, which blocked its view from direct sight from below. It was the ultimate sanctuary, and for now, they needed the reprieve.

Julia and the girls found an alcove that fit their needs perfectly. They built pallets from woolen skins they had managed to bring along the way. Weary from the night's march, they lay down to rest after having a bite to eat. The girls recited Scripture they had recently learned before nodding off while Julia stayed up, resting against the stone wall of her new home. She sat watching the lamp's light flicker against the walls, making the shadows dance in a slow waltz. The soft echo of a sheep bleated somewhere in the barn section of their cave, reminding them of their shared quarters. She closed her eyes and took in a deep breath. Over in the corner, she could hear Rebecca, her youngest daughter, breathing in the syncopated rhythms of sleep. Angela, the older of the two, lay next to hear, her arm wrapped lovingly over her little sister. *Both were younger than Jakob,* she thought to herself.

She hugged her arms against her body, reaching back and pulling her shawl up over her shoulders, knocking off the slight chill. The cave was much warmer than the outside, yet there was an occasional chill that floated past as the memories of her loved ones who were with her only in memory. She could not look up and see the stars in the sky, but she knew in her heart Kristoff and his mother were there, reunited once more.

Oh, my sweet Kristoff, she thought. It seemed as if eons had passed since he had died. Jakob looked just like his father, and when he was around, she could take solace in seeing Jakob's bright, smiling face and easily remember Kristoff. Her heart ached for them both. She wondered where

Jakob and his grandfather might be at this moment and thought of all the special things that made each of them so dear to her.

She began to hum a song she would often hear Jakob singing to himself as he worked or played. She would often find him, off in a corner or under a tree all by himself, singing aloud, unaware of the world around but fully engaged in whatever activity he might be performing at the time. The more she thought of him, the more something became obvious—something she had not really noticed before: he always seemed to be either singing or humming to himself. He rarely was mute, but when others were around, he would be silent, listening, learning, and watching. Her throat tightened as she could feel the pain of missing him well up inside. She tried to comfort herself by thinking of one of his favorite songs and began to hum it softly to herself, not wanting to wake Rebecca.

The melody came easily to her lips, as her mind drew his image. A comforting warmth spread over her being.

Chapter 45

THE CROSSROADS IN TIME

The Lord is my strength and song, and He has become my salvation;
He is my God, and I will praise Him; My father's God, and I will
exalt Him.

—Exodus 15:2

They awoke the next evening to a misting rain. The air was cold and heavy, making one's breath easily visible. The crossing had been without incident, and soon the banks of the river were a distant memory. Jakob sat in the back of the wagon with Anna as nightfall began to darken the skies. She sat looking out the back, silent, watching, the grayness making her face an ashen color. The pallid calm face made him feel uneasy.

He purposely shifted his gaze to the objects around him. He noticed he was sitting near a case that looked familiar, and upon further investigation, he realized was the case of his lira, which he had not seen or played in quite some time. He lifted the lid and peeked inside, reassuring himself that the time he spent with Gabriel learning the music was not a dream. Sure enough, there it was the beautiful instrument, smooth and golden in color. He raised the lid a little farther and noticed something was engraved on the inside of the lid—a figure that was not legible but something he recognized from somewhere before. He paused and then closed the lid.

A flood of thoughts came rushing back to him, like being shaken from a dream. First he saw the image on the doorway of the inn where they stayed upon their initial journey from the Vaudois. He went farther back to another place. He did not know if it was a dream or reality, but it was a place he had seen. It was a cavern with a stone slab table . . . light from above . . . then there it was, near the stone altar, the symbol again. Somewhere from the depths of the cave came a haunting melody he was forced to follow. It was a song he recognized, like the symbol, but one he could respond to, and he began to sing along. As he walked farther, the golden hue of the lamplight flickered upon the cavern walls, reflecting the face of his mother, sitting in repose upon blankets near the wall and his sisters lying nearby, both fast asleep. He quietly walked as he sang, moving closer to her figure.

The feeling of Jakob's presence was overbearing. Julia did not want to lose the sensation. She paused before opening her eyes but felt compelled to do so.

Slowly as she squinted, something came into focus. She was awake with her eyes wide open, and there before her was her son. Dear God, it was him! Jakob's image was before her. As the light from the distant torch flickered through the body, she could see his outline. It was vaguely ghostly.

Her emotions welled up deep inside. *Is this his apparition? Has he died?*

There had been no word, no messages, and now this.

Tears blurred her vision of him, but she continued to softly sing, trying not to lose what might be her last sight of him forever. She was shaking with a passion so fervent that she could barely whisper the words. The image wavered on the sea of cascading tears that flowed from her eyes; she couldn't stop. His lips moved as she could feel him singing along.

Nothing could make her stop; she couldn't if she wanted to.

Jakob's heart ached for his mother, who now sat before him and wept soulfully, but there was nothing he could do—not from here. Yet he felt as if he could reach out and touch her, the vision so real. The melody rang true. The song of his heart was beating as one with hers.

As the final verses came to an end, softly, gently as the distant sunset falls into the earth, so did her image drift off into the hazy mists of moisture that engulfed their wagons as they approached the shadow of the mountains.

He wasn't aware when Anna silently moved closer to him, hearing him singing. She knew something was going to happen. She had seen enough to know that something always seemed to occur when his voice rose in song. However, this time her assumption appeared to be wrong. Only his demeanor changed from dreamlike to melancholy. She gently placed her arm around his shoulder and held him close.

The rain fell upon the wagon's canopy above like the teardrops of his mother, and he cried.

Chapter 46

FEAR NOT

Then an angel appeared to Him from heaven, strengthening Him.
—Luke 22:43

eter nervously waited at the crossroads for any sign of the other two caravans. His own party was pulled to the side, off the road and out of sight, so as to be obscured from passersby, all keeping to the shadows. The sky was beginning to lighten, even with the heavy cloud cover and dense fog. Their scheduled arrival would have put them all at this point well before daylight, causing his elevated unrest. In the distance, a lone rider approached, appearing out of the fog bank like a spirit.

The man approached, putting his hand upon the sword at his side before pulling up several yards apart from Peter. It was not uncommon to be ambushed by thieves on the open road, and it was apparent Peter was up to something.

Peter raised his hands above his head to show he was unarmed and to try to relieve any fears this stranger might have. "I mean no harm, my friend. I only want to ask you what or who you might have seen upon your recent journey."

The stranger paused, contemplating the woods nearby, searching for others who might be waiting in the wings to attack. His horse stirred, agitated at the pause in their travel and sensing others nearby.

"I mean it, with the Lord as my witness. I pray you please let me know of any sightings of my fellow travelers upon whom I now wait."

His head jerked back toward Peter at this, and he pulled the reins tight on his horse, spurring him gently forward within reach of Peter. Now his sword was now drawn but not in a threatening manner.

"You speak of others, but only God knows of their souls now, my friend," he replied. He talked with his sword moving in erratic motions at each word. "Yes, I have seen something so vile, so repugnant, I fear it will forever be etched into my mind. May God have mercy on their poor, wretched souls."

Peter's heart sank. The plan to separate was his, for fear that traveling as one large group would put them at risk of being found, yet now something horrible had happened.

"What . . . ?" The words seemed difficult to form. "What did you see exactly?" he forced out, not really wanting to hear the response but knowing he had to do so.

"Bodies, parts . . . flesh and entrails strewn from one side of the road to another; flesh stripped from their bodies and pulled taut over wagons, with animal parts intermixed with the rancid smell of blood and death all perpetuated into the air," he finished with the backside of his free hand over his mouth, as if the recalling of the sight was about to make him sick once more.

Peter himself was becoming nauseous. A sick feeling bent him double. He was losing all hope. The most precious thing in the world might now be lost. *Would it have been any different had I been with them?* he questioned himself. He felt his knees weaken, his mind spinning.

"Sir, are you all right?"

Peter raised a hand as he bent over double, sick with anguish, fear, and anger all boiling into one feeling. Seeing their leader doubled over while the mounted, armed man sat there was too much for a couple of his most loyal guards, who came rushing from their hiding spot in the bushes, only to startle the horse, causing the rider to lose his balance and nearly be thrown.

Peter, realizing the perilous situation, he forced his stature erect, "Hold on, hold on . . ." he yelled.

The guards stopped their advance, blades still drawn. The stranger had now swung his horse to the opposite side of the road, ready for their advance, prepared to fight, his sword at the ready.

"Everyone just calm down," Peter said, again trying to regain his composure. "They're just trying to protect me. It's alright."

The air was thick with tension as each man watched the other for any betrayal of Peter's request.

"Sir, I am Peter Waldo of Lyon, here with my guards. We were on a mission and have prearranged a meeting with two other caravans at this spot. You have brought us horrific news as to possibly why the others have yet to show up." He bowed his head. "It saddens me to think all may have been lost."

"I understand," he replied, taking his cap off in a reverent manner.

"Was there by chance any sign of an old man or young boy and girl . . . anything?"

"Sir, I wish I could comfort you in your time of pain, but honestly, the brutality was so severe, I could not discern much. It was hard to tell man from beast, such was the butchery."

Peter's head remained down, and his heart sank. The other guards walked up now, their broadswords returned to their sheaths. All tried to comfort their lord, who now had fallen upon to his knees, head and hand in prayer.

The stranger dismounted and joined in leading them: "God stands in the congregation of the mighty; He judges among the gods. How long will you judge unjustly, and show partiality to the wicked? . . . Selah. Defend the poor and fatherless; do justice to the afflicted and needy. Deliver the poor and needy; free *them* from the hand of the wicked."

"Amen," whispered Peter, his head still bowed, wetness upon his cheeks.

The stranger's horse let out a low grunt as his ears cocked back toward the cloud bank that blanketed the road behind them from the same direction he had just arrived. There came a sound from the midst, but no image appeared—only the creak of a slow-moving object.

It appeared as a gray shadow from the fog, slowly, piece by piece, first the horses and then the wagon itself.

Peter stood. Everyone turned to see Arktos slowly appear, sitting on the driver's seat and smiling ear to ear from his snow white beard. It was a sight Peter thought he'd never be so glad to see again.

"Thanks be to God," he said as he rose and made his way toward the long-anticipated travelers.

"You act as if you've seen a ghost," remarked Arktos with an air of humor.

"You don't know the half of it, my friend," a grateful Peter responded, rushing up to the old man and embracing him with a force that jarred him nearly from his seat.

Arktos could see the drying emotion on the face of his friend.

"I see you have been worried, my brother."

"All is not well," he responded, slightly stepping back. "The rider here just brought us horrible news that I at first thought to be of you, but thanks be to God, at least you were spared . . . As for Amesh and the others, I pray God will find their souls home with him."

"I'm truly sorry," Arktos said, bowing his head in remembrance of their fellow comrades.

The stranger, approached, hat still in hand, leading his horse behind him. "Sir, if I may?"

Peter turned, facing the unknowing messenger.

"I have studied for years in the monastic ways of Christianity. Only recently, after witnessing the change in an institution I had once thought God's deity on earth, I decided to choose to follow another path, which now seems to have intersected with yours. I do not fully know of your mission, but I sense there is something here with which I may be able to assist. The brutality I just witnessed and the horrors I have just escaped in Lyon—all are pointing me to another land, another way, for I am certain *that* is not the Christianity I know and love."

"Horrors in Lyon?" questioned Peter.

"You have not heard?"

"No, we have been away for some time trying to stay one step ahead of the papal guard, I'm afraid."

"'Tis a good thing, for all of Lyon has become Sheol itself, with General Lucier burning all who would not succumb to the auspices of the church."

"Lord in heaven!" Peter gasped.

"May God have mercy upon those poor souls," answered Arktos.

Jakob and Anna had poked their heads out of the canopy behind Arktos at this, and the little girl's face immediately distorted into fear and horror as tears welled up in her soft blue eyes. The others noticed, and

Jakob realized poor Anna's parents probably never had a chance. She said nothing. She just turned back in the direction they had just come from and wept for her family. Nothing could be done. They could only comfort the now-orphaned child. Jakob rejoined her and tried his best to ease her suffering.

The stranger continued on, "What is worse, the horror I saw was done by those sent out from that hell on earth, which means they could be anywhere or at least very near."

"Yes, exactly. We should get off this road at once, for we have to be near the encampment of the papal troops," replied Peter.

"You are only a mile from their position now," said the stranger. "And sir, if I am to join you, allow me to introduce myself. I am Dabria of Lyon."

"We are pleased to meet you, Dabria, and thank you for arriving when you did. We unfortunately now know the fate of our other brothers, as well as those poor souls left behind in Lyon."

"Enough talk; let us get on now," commanded Arktos, who became quite anxious to continue moving after hearing all that had transpired. "I don't plan on becoming an ornament for this demonic army we are about to meet," he said, slapping the reins on the horses as the wagon jerked into motion once more.

They bivouacked not far away and allowed Arktos to prepare for their passage through the heavily guarded pass that would lead them to their homeland and beyond. Their faith was in his hands. Yet their faith was about to be put to the ultimate test . . . for faith got them here, and faith would lead them home.

Chapter 47

INTO THE LIGHT

Then he opened his mouth in blasphemy against God, to blaspheme His name, His tabernacle, and those who dwell in heaven.
—Revelation 13:6

Lucier and his small contingent of guards left long before dawn for the base camp of Quenten, where Apollyon would be waiting. The smell of burnt flesh still permeated his nostrils as the fresh air of the countryside seemed to invigorate his mind.

They rode at breakneck speed, for their urgency was forced by the impending storms that now enveloped the peaks of the mountains to which their adversary would take shelter. If nothing else, they would make the camp by late morning and then attempt to begin the final campaign against these heretics.

The farther they rode, the denser the fog became, as if the mountains were being shrouded from view on purpose.

With a singular purpose in mind, Lucier fought off all his natural battle instincts for the sake of making the Vaudois before the snows blocked their passages. There was no report for him to know that there would be nothing there for him to find. The dense cloud that now lay upon the ground was becoming like the one that shrouded the rational thoughts of a superior mind until only the stream of self-righteous purposefulness remained. They flew blindly onward into the mist. Blindly, their faith became obscured, until there was only the cancer of self that remained.

Major Apollyon had arrived at the base camp the day before. His men were only slightly tired from their ride. The brief encounter with the small band of militants they had met on the road had rejuvenated their spirits and made for some entertaining butchery along the way. They quickly began regrouping what was left of the previously trained guard and dismissed all those who were not registered as regulars. The rogues who had joined of their own account were forced to leave or were taken down immediately by force. They were subjugated by the very blades they had used upon the helpless beings they had slaughtered, raped, and pillaged under the guise of being part of the papal force. Those who took over were not far removed from the same, yet it was all a matter of who was ordering the death to be delivered. The papal crown wanted it to be known that this was their realm of control and theirs alone.

Knowing Lucier would soon be joining them, Apollyon whipped the men back into order, along with his subordinates, quickly arranging the forces back into a recognizable army that could hold its own with any force of like or greater strength. He knew Lucier would want to move as quickly as possible since the weather seemed to be deteriorating with each passing hour. All blades were sharpened, horses reshod, and armaments restocked so that when the call was made, they would move out at once.

By later in the morning, they had achieved all that had been asked, and they were now lingering in their encampments, adorned with their armor, battle gear, and prepared mounts. Some cooked meals over fires while others lounged about in their tents. All had performed the standard military hurried preparations. Now they simply waited for their marching orders, which each expected at any time.

The fog covered the encampment so much that even the mountains above were nonexistent in the shroud of gray. There was no sun—only grayness to the day, if it could be called that. A mist hung in the air, with cold, visible breaths upon every mouth that spoke.

It was in this blanket of whiteness that the wagons carrying Arktos and Peter's party slowly, quietly rolled by, some easily within sight of the army's posted sentries. Yet, not one alarm was sounded. There was not a flinch of a horse's ear. No one detected the caravan of spirit that floated by.

Some thought they heard a distant melody faintly echoing from a distant shore. A sweetness of the sound made one think of another place and time. Those who heard the muted strains of the lira instantly drifted off to their homelands, families, or distant pasts, walking hand in hand with loved ones, seeing faces of old, or reliving memories of a beautiful time gone before. None realized, their trance or saw the padded wheels of the wagons, wrapped in woolskins, as they silently bound past and up the entrance to the Vaudois.

As quickly as they appeared, they were gone, vanished into the mist and disappeared from sight, to begin their ascent to the place where their voice would once again be protected by the fortresses of granite within.

Or so it seemed . . .

Lucier had not seen the caravan or witnessed its disappearance into the cloud bank, but something told him there was something amiss when he and his detachment rolled into the camp. Men stood around as if bewitched, none realizing where they were or what they were doing. It wasn't until he had the trumpeter sound the alarm that any realized he had arrived.

Apollyon threw back the tent's flap, roaring out, furious that Lucier had not been announced, and approached the general with full salute.

"What in God's name is going on here?" demanded a furious Lucier.

Before answering, Apollyon yelled at his sergeant at arms, *"Why the hell wasn't the general announced?"*

All he received back was a blank stare at first and then a curt reply: "Sir, General Lucier is in the camp."

Disgusted, Apollyon returned his attention to the general. "Sir, we have been awaiting your arrival. The men are prepared; we are ready to march at your command."

Lucier was still upset with the lackadaisical feeling he noticed upon arriving at the camp. He realized there wasn't much he could change, but something nagged at him; something wasn't right. "Have your sentries been alerted to any travelers on the road leading to the passage?"

"I have not had any up to now, but I will ask for a full report immediately," Apollyon responded.

Apollyon again turned to his sergeant at arms and asked for a report. The sergeant quickly sent men off to retrieve a full, up-to-date report. Apollyon motioned for Lucier to join him back in his tent, where they could await the report and go over the plans he had prepared for the final assault.

Lucier, still heated, hesitated, looking around at the fog that engulfed the entire area. He could only fume that there couldn't be a better cover for someone who was trying to sneak by, but then again, this was a fully armed camp, with sentries posted all along the entrance to the passage. *Perhaps I'm being too paranoid*, he told himself. He passed it off as just being an old worrisome soldier and walked inside Apollyon's officer tent.

The general's aged intuition was wiser than he knew.

As they slowly ascended the base of Quenten, Arktos felt his spirits lift with each passing stone. They slowly rose above the cloud bank that had protected their stealthy entourage through the encampment of a full regiment of the papal guard. As they gradually climbed, the air grew clearer and crisper until snowflakes began to fall all about.

Jakob and Anna poked their heads out of the wagon, each seeing the joy in the falling whiteness, reaching their small hands out to touch the frosted heavenly flakes. Jakob's lira had played in his hands like an old friend. The melodies he had learned from hours of instruction from Gabriel flowed effortlessly from his soul, enveloping them all in its beauty and love, with the heavenly host of angels watching from above. Their journey was not yet complete, but their path was becoming clearer each day. Today was one to be remembered.

The farther they climbed, the heavier the snows began to fall. Fearful that they might not make their destination, Peter tried to quicken the pace. Arktos sensed his urgency as he rode up on horseback.

"My friend, did I not tell you to have faith?"

"Yes, and I have and did, but now there is the obvious I have to deal with. We can't afford to be stopped by a snowstorm when we are so close."

Arktos stopped his wagon and peered into his good friend's eyes from the depths of his sky blue eyes as the edges of his lips curled into a smile. "Faith, my brother . . . faith," he reminded Peter once again.

Peter paused, realizing there was a reason he kept repeating himself. From where he sat on horseback, he could barely see the passage to the upper Vaudois ahead. He wasn't sure of the way, since he had only heard of the valley, seen Marik's report, and been told of the pathway by Arktos, so he was once again forced to listen to the aged mountain spiritual leader. Without him, they would not reach the Vaudois or the people and Word he sought to protect.

"Yes . . . I'm sorry. You are absolutely right. It's just that with the snow and the altitude, I'm worried we won't make it."

"Yes, I know," came the gentle reply.

"You obviously know that we can make it, or else you would also be more diligent about your pace."

"Actually," he paused and looked skyward, "I don't." He smiled a whimsical smile. "But I have all the faith in the world that we will," he said with a wink. With that he cracked the reins on the team, which lurched in gear as they continued onward.

Peter only shook his head and had to smile. "May God be with us," he said to himself as he fell in behind the wagon as they continued onward and upward, into the whiteness, into the light, leaving the darkness far, far below.

Chapter 48

THE WILL OF GOD

Then justice will dwell in the wilderness, and righteousness remain in the fruitful field.

—Isaiah 32:16

Around midday, after only a couple hours of intense discussions and planning, Lucier and Apollyon emerged from the officer's tent. The dense fog from earlier had started to finally burn off, but the air was more chilled than before.

They were met at once by the first sergeant, who had just returned from his information-gathering mission.

The sergeant snapped to attention. "Sir, orders to report."

"Go ahead, Sergeant," Apollyon responded, returning the salute.

"Sir, there were no reports of anyone seeing anything other than one or two stragglers along the road. There were no caravan or wagons as you mentioned."

"Very well then, thank you for your earnest report." He began to turn and noticed the sergeant had not moved. "That will be all, Sergeant," he said, motioning with his head for him to carry on.

"Sir, there is something else."

Lucier heard the tone and immediately strode over to the pair.

Apollyon replied with hesitation, "Go on . . . out with it."

"Sir, the men swear they saw or heard nothing, but—"

"But what?" Lucier blurted out without hesitation, wanting the words to come quicker.

"General Sir, the men found . . . after further investigation fresh . . . wagon tracks," he said, biting his lip. He realized the oddity but couldn't understand it either.

"Did I hear you correctly?" Lucier replied, looking now at Apollyon, growing angrier with each second.

Apollyon turned to his trusted officer. "Tell me again—you saw fresh tracks but nobody, absolutely no one, heard or saw *anything!*"

Straightening to attention, the sergeant at arms felt as if he had only the known facts to report. Withstanding any emotion, he had to report what was found. "Sir, that is correct. I verified it myself. As unfathomable as it sounds, I too could not believe it until I saw it with my own eyes."

"May God damn their souls!" shouted Lucier, slamming his fist down on the map table at his side. The crash of his fist echoed off the distant mountain walls as a warning to all who heard.

"Ready the men at once," barked Apollyon. "There's not a moment to spare."

"Sir yes sir," he retorted, saluting and spinning on his heels, quickly disappearing. A light wind picked up, blowing the papal flags that hung above the commander's tent. With the skies growing steadily darker, snowflakes began to fall—lightly at first and then growing in intensity.

Lucier stood outside the tent, cursing under his breath as snowflakes began to accumulate on his eyelashes. They had pursued them this far, and now the weather was going to make things even more challenging.

315

He stood glaring at Apollyon, who readied his forces as well as anyone could. It wasn't his fault, yet the fire within the general's being was burning with an unquenchable flame. He wanted to lash out at the enemy, but there was nothing there. It was like a shadow, visible but unreachable.

His men had learned to fear the glare that was meant for another. The blood of battle would not sate this hell within him. He and the pope's souls were one and the same, both tortured—one from a scar so deep that only the gates of Hades would awaken his reconciliation while the other's tainted vestments would never be cleansed on this side of the Eastern Gates. The faith of the virtuous few would be tested by the power from the seat of Rome itself until even by the smallest of chances that a faith held from the heart, from the Word itself, would survive and create a gift that would last for centuries to come. The battles had yet to begin, and one was about to start.

Finally, after what seemed like countless hours, they set out, marching up the pass toward an unseen enemy, to pursue them into oblivion from where they already existed. Rora would be their first objective. Although it had already been destroyed, Lucier wanted to see for himself that it was gone. From there they would spread out, flooding the neighboring valleys and destroying everything until the job was complete. The great purge of heretical beliefs would be complete, and the sanctity of their faith would remain whole.

As they moved slowly up the base of Quenten, Lucier couldn't help feel a sense of adulation. At last, free of the confines of the city, back on the battlefield, he was at home. He knew somehow the heretics were not far ahead. Soon the blood would flow and his suffering would ease, albeit incompletely. At least for a short time, he would be free of the demons that haunted his soul. This was his glory.

The snowflakes grew larger the farther the regiment moved, and soon they found their footing becoming more challenging. Yet onward Apollyon pushed his men, unfettered by the bitter cold. His heartless pursuit was perfectly fitted for the battlefield, and like his boss, he was finally back where he belonged. Their drive overrode their intelligence for caution, and into their fate they rode.

Farther up the mountainside, Peter feared their faith would not be enough to keep them going. The snow had steadily fallen, and now large drifts were growing at every turn. Each time he knew the next would bring them to a dead end, but the farther they traveled, the more jovial Arktos became. It was obvious the old man was in his element. The ravines and gorges through which they passed were like the many wrinkles upon the backside of the old man's hand. He knew them from one end of the Quenten to the other, and if there was anyone alive who would find their way home in a driving snowstorm, he would be the one that could do it. Their wagons slowed them down, though, with their considerable loads, so that they sometimes barely made a walking pace. In spite of this, they confidently drove onward, bent toward the fury the mountain threw into their path.

Chapter 49

HOMECOMING

Now it had happened as they were coming home, when David was returning from the slaughter of the Philistine, that the women had come out of all the cities of Israel, singing and dancing, to meet King Saul, with tambourines, with joy, and with musical instruments.

—1 Samuel 18:6

For two days, both parties, the fleeing and the pursuers, struggled up Quenten's rugged terrain, the aggressor gaining with each step on those being pursued.

It was near evening on the third day when they rounded a last ridge, bringing Arktos and Jakob's farm on the edge of Rora into full view below.

Snow swept across the landscape, blanketing the charred remains of all that remained. Nothing moved. Peter pulled up even with the wagon where Arktos and Jakob sat. Both sat stunned, looking blankly at the desolation below. Their solid rock structure of their homestead still stood, but it was obvious there had been a fire from the blackened eyes of windows that remained, empty and sullen.

Arktos bit his bottom lip. It all became clear—the foreboding he had seen. He hadn't wanted to believe it, but after their deliverance through the child's gifts, one after another, he knew to expect it. But to actually see it before him . . . it was just . . . just . . . The gravity of the moment encompassed the entire party.

Jakob grabbed his grandfather's shoulder. "What have they done? When?"

The boy couldn't understand. In his mind, they had snuck past the forces below. He was sure they would return to their Vaudois, to meet their family once again, and then together they would all retreat to a safer place. In his young mind, that's the way he had seen it. He couldn't connect his vision with the reality he now saw. His mother in the cave, her tears . . . Too many questions flooded his thoughts now, overwhelming him. His eyes watered, yet he kept strong.

"Where will we go now, Grandfather?"

"There are places. We will survive. We must," he said, not looking away from the sight of the place where he raised a family, where countless memories were created. He could see his son as a young boy, running through the tall summer grasses, laughing and spinning as he chased the sheep in play. He recalled the days they had worked hand in hand, building, adding on for the new family that was coming. Memories, like the snowfall that now covered the rooftop below, were collected and blown from one thought to the next. Now it was all . . . all gone.

"We will survive my son . . . We will, we must," he whispered as his voice choked with emotion.

He reached up and cracked the reins, and they began their descent into their precious Vaudois. The cathedral spires of granite that towered above them shadowed over their little party that made its way to a home without a homecoming. They had returned, but there was nobody left to return to.

Arktos halted the wagon outside the front door of their former home. As he climbed down, it was obvious he felt his many years in the weary bones. Everyone watched as he tearfully entered the home, only to return a short time later empty handed. There was only a shell. Nothing had been spared. The snow swirled in little eddies about his feet. The now-barren apple tree where he had spent many a summer day was broken. Shards of limbs were all that remained. His favorite bench was broken, with only remnants visible under the blanket of white. That was all that was left of any sign the place had once been inhabited. No one said a word, as he slowly climbed back up to his wagon seat.

He cracked the reins, and the rest of the party fell in behind. There was nothing to say, for the words had been erased for now.

In what seemed as a funeral march, they slowly and methodically made their way from their homestead, past the other many small farms, and into the village of Rora. Nothing had been spared; everywhere they looked showed the results savage destruction.

Ahead the most gruesome discoveries awaited.

They rode past the morbid displays of brutality, the nearly unrecognizable human heads on pikes outside the village walls, vestiges of a frugal defense from a force so overpowering that their efforts were in vain. Patches of hair remained on some. They were touching remembrances of friends and relatives who suffered when their end came. Now all that was left of their beings were the frozen grimaces of deathly stares. Snow-covered mounds of bodies littered the roadway here and there. In some places the limbs reached out as if calling for help. Peter began to wonder if any had survived, so total seemed the death toll.

Onward they journeyed, Arktos leading as if a purpose drove him on or a thought. He was silent, facing forward, not looking at the remains that littered the roadside.

Then suddenly, from behind them, they heard the trumpet call.

Ice ran down Peter's spine as he halted and turned to see, not wanting, not believing.

There on the ridge above sat the papal army they had so cautiously avoided that foggy morning, two days ago. The darkness of the evening was already grasping the footholds of the massive summits that lined their Vaudois, but now it seemed to crush the air from his lungs. "My

God . . . what have I done?" he whispered out loud through nearly frostbitten lips.

Arktos stopped his wagon and slowly lowered himself to the ground. He began walking back toward the edge of the village, back to where the futile force had once before sacrificed all. Peter called to him, but he walked onward, ignoring the calls of those behind.

God had put him here. It was his time. He marched toward something so black, so demonic, but he cared not, for he breathed every breath of faith left in his heart. He walked in cadence with the Scriptures that now erupted from his spirit into the air, filling it with the voices of many from the mouth of one.

"Then I saw an angel standing in the sun; and he cried with a loud voice, saying to all the birds that fly in the midst of heaven, 'Come and gather together for the supper of the great God, that you may eat the flesh of kings, the flesh of captains, the flesh of mighty men, the flesh of horses and of those who sit on them, and the flesh of all *people,* free and slave, both small and great.' And I saw the beast, the kings of the earth, and their armies, gathered together to make war against Him who sat on the horse and against His army."

The thundering horde began to slowly drive toward them now, the earth shaking with their force.

The old man continued onward, straight toward their path, praying and not wavering.

Unexpectedly, a call from the other side of the village erupted in a great roar. From behind Peter came an earth-shaking horde of Huguenot warriors, some on horseback, others running, all shouting, "Glory be to God!" as they ran. In the lead he thought he recognized a rider on a horse that looked a lot like a horse he once owned. But it couldn't be . . . The snow blew heavily now. The scene was surreal.

Marik? he thought. *It couldn't be. Who are they? Where did they come from? They are obviously not inhabitants of the Vaudois. They all seem to be seasoned warriors. They are all dressed in animal skins, most without armor, but they are all large, massive-chested soldiers, undeterred in their charge.*

A blur sped by him at the instant as Dabria joined in the charge, his sword drawn. Peter could hear him shouting something as he passed, but he failed to discern what it was because of the sound of the masses engulfing everything around.

They all met in a mighty clash at the base of the ridge, where Apollyon's force had charged upon seeing the oncoming force. The snow at the base had accumulated to the point now that it was knee deep to their horses. The men on foot behind were stalwart in their motions, unable to maneuver quickly as the larger, beastly horde crashed down upon them from the snow-blown pasture.

The major was in the lead, his broadsword cutting swathes through the vigilant swarm, severing flesh from bone. He was a force of swirling death with each blow. He charged headlong into the enemy, living for the moment. Not far behind him, Lucier was likewise spewing forth his vile testament to hatred and loathsomeness. Each was in an embittered battle with an unknown enemy yet grateful for the taste of blood.

Berg stayed close beside Marik as they charged headlong into the demonic throng. They had marched all day and the night before to reach the farthest end of the Vaudois through a pass Marik had found when he and Steffan took the high ground when they first encountered the great battle on their first visit. Although they had traveled many strenuous miles to reach this point, the rush of adrenaline that pumped through their veins now buoyed them into battle. Their spirit was one. They fought for God.

As they drove battle axes, broadswords, and pikes into their victims, they shouted, "For He put on righteousness as a breastplate, And a helmet of salvation on His head; He put on the garments of vengeance for clothing, And was clad with zeal as a cloak."

The papal force had seen frenzied warriors before, but nothing like this—nothing like the united voice they carried as they cut down row upon row of armored guards.

Lucier could see the tide was beginning to turn and searched the battlefield for Apollyon. The soulless hellion was surrounded by three of the rouge warriors. Lucier tried to work his way through a throng of his own, busting through, knocking one to the ground and crushing his throat under the hoof of his horse, uncaring, reaching out for his faithful comrade.

He saw a mountain of a man, larger than the rest, barreling straight for Apollyon. By the flight of his horse, he could see the approach was not random but calculated. He was too far away to shout a warning. In the din of battle, the screams, thrusts of air from bloodied lungs, drowned out any hope of communication in the literal sense. Brute screams of agony were all that were recognizable.

Berg recognized the rank of the man who was now taking down so many of his clan members and had enough. He would put an end to his being, even if it meant losing his own. He charged.

At full gallop, his horse leapt over the bodies of his dead brothers who lay at the feet of the mighty destroyer. The giant broadsword held overhead came down with a crashing force as it shattered Apollyon's left shoulder, forcing a grimaced burst of anger to erupt from his mouth. Unfazed, Apollyon swung instinctively with the other arm and caught Berg's rib cage with the slice of his blade. Pain shot through Berg's side as warmth spread down his pant legs.

Apollyon waited with a left shoulder barely intact as blood gushed through what was left of his armored shoulder. They both swirled, turning to face one another, each parlaying those attempting to dismount them. Those who did not have adversaries in their faces paused to watch the dramatic scene unfolding before them.

They charged again. Berg held his reins between his teeth as he held his broadsword in one arm and his battle axe in the other. His drive was direct and swift. There was no border to leap; his path met the major's head on. Their weapons met with a slap of steel on steel. Berg's thick-edged blade stopped the major's blade cold with his own as they drove their horses together, each beast's chest armor clashing into the other's. In that brief instant, blades in check, Berg swung the impressive battle axe fully into the back of Apollyon's neck with all his might.

Apollyon froze. His horse staggered backward, reeling from their initial impact. Blood began frothing from Apollyon's grimacing mouth. He started to smile a macabre, morbid grin just before his head rolled off his shoulders, bouncing off his horse and onto the ground. What seemed like minutes later, his body collapsed what would have been head first onto the back of his horse. The beast wouldn't know the spur of his master again.

Berg turned, only to see Lucier halt his charge. The general, seeing the death of his major, instinctively realized the lost momentum and fatalism of the moment. He called a full retreat, at which point the entire remnant of the guard began to contract to the base of the ridge where they had first entered the Vaudois.

The snow that had accumulated in drifts slowed their progress as they fled for the ridge to escape. Their enemy, now close in pursuit, drove them beyond their physical limits. Unlike before, their inner fear pumped their weary limbs, void of oxygen, cramping in pain. Some fell in the anguish of starved muscles, only to have the blades of their foes driven into their vitals. They suffered only a brief minute longer before peaceful rest overcame their plight.

The once pure white snow was littered with the bright red crimson of so many bodies, many hidden in the drifts, with the red-splattered crystals surrounding the holes in which they slept the eternal sleep of the damned.

Jakob, fearing for his grandfather's safety, stood in the wagon, wanting to help but unsure how. Anna reached up and squeezed his hand. She began humming the song she had so often heard him sing to himself. Unaware, he joined in, and together they sang in unison. "God is our refuge and strength, an ever-present help in trouble. Therefore we will not fear, though the earth gives way and the mountains fall into the heart of the sea, though its waters roar and foam and the mountains quake with their surging. Selah . . ."

Peter stood between Arktos and Jakob, the two he had so long sought who had now made the mission of spreading the gospel to all a reality. He was hoping, praying that somehow God would save them. It hit him like an unseen tidal wave from behind—like a strong invisible wind, pushing him slightly toward Arktos, who now stood with his back to him, facing the theater of death in the foreground. The little hairs stood up on the back of his neck. Something surreal, a power untold, was spreading. He could feel it.

Arktos stood watching the battle, near the wall where months earlier his own grandson had made a final stand. Around him remains of skulls gaping open jawed, calling for no one, silent in their deathly gaze.

Undaunted, he stood his ground.

His hand reached for the ancient fishing hook that still hung around his neck. Feeling its presence, his mind thought back to the glorious days of the apostles and their gifts and message given to all. He felt something deep inside yet outward at the same time. The Spirit reached through him again as the words leapt from his lips. As the wave of light, power, and heavenly energy burst through him, without thought, as one breathes, so did the Word of God come forth.

"Then the beast was captured, and with him the false prophet who worked signs in his presence, by which he deceived those who received the mark of the beast and those who worshiped his image. These two were cast alive into the lake of fire burning with brimstone. And the rest were killed with the sword which proceeded from the mouth of Him who sat on the horse. And all the birds were filled with their flesh."

From above, it first sounded like a low-frequency rumble. Then it built into a crescendo, a giant crash. Then a thunderous roar began to grow, building with each additional crash. The granite tower above the ridge was now ablaze in a blinding fury of whiteness that was crashing down toward the fleeing papal guard. Horses, riders, running soldiers— all were consumed. Where there was once an army, there was now emptiness. A silken white blanket once again folded about the ridge, blocking all escape.

The annihilation was all but complete. The papal forces were suffocated by the mountain of snow that engulfed the ridge and all those who were upon it. Some fortunate few on the edges of the ridge, not directly under its massive weight, tried to wriggle free, but they were quickly fallen upon by the Huguenot warriors who remained. Blades were thrust into bodies that would never fight again, until there were no more. The brutal scene was repeated over and over until the massacre was complete.

A collective sigh was heard as the earth recomposed itself. The massive weight of the avalanche crushed everything, and the groans of its victims below were subdued into nothingness.

All was still.

The soft white flakes from the sky had stopped, and the clouds near the peak broke as the sunset's golden hue reflected off the neighboring peaks, giving a heavenly aura to the scene below.

Jakob and Anna climbed down from the safety of the wagon and joined Peter's side. Jakob could see his grandfather, now kneeling, head bowed, obviously in prayer. They slowly made their way to his side. Souls lost, whether good or bad, needed the prayer of salvation, and the aged Vaudoisian offered them up to heaven above. The rest of the little band joined him until soon all the remaining Huguenot warriors gathered around them, all honoring the elder, all kneeling in reverent prayer upon reaching the growing throng. From the back of the small army strode an obvious leader, who made his way to the front.

Galack stood before Arktos, and after allowing his presence to be known, he excused his interruption and introduced himself to the reticent spiritual leader. Arktos looked up and motioned for Galack to join him at his side, which he did. They all then prayed as one, Huguenot and Vaudoisian. They were one in spirit and now, one in mission. Whether the elders had foreseen it or not, the evangelic spread of their Word had begun. The world needed what was once given by God's only Son and needed it now.

Peter was humbled by the scene beyond words. As he too knelt near Arktos, Anna, and Jakob, he felt a hand touch his shoulder. He looked back toward the hand to see the face of his long-lost friend and faithful companion, Marik. He immediately stood, and they embraced in a hug that evoked memories of others now gone, others missing, and others for whom they struggled onward.

The tearful reunion gave a healing power. All who watched were moved.

All who survived would become witnesses, and the Word of the Lord would live on from this day forward

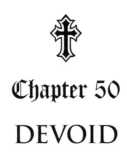

Chapter 50

DEVOID

Then hear from heaven, and act, and judge Your servants, bringing retribution on the wicked by bringing his way on his own head, and justifying the righteous by giving him according to his righteousness.

—2 Chronicles 6:23

On the other side of the ridge, the massive snow bank shifted, exposing the body enough to relieve the monumental pressure that had trapped it heretofore. Weakly, slowly it moved, until the face was free, able to breathe. It lay motionless, life ebbing to and fro. He was unrelenting, fighting to survive. Not even death could keep him hostage. The darkness was devoid of his presence for now.

Lucier struggled. His painful, labored movements took him merely a few feet, but his will was driven by the blackened heart within. Once he was totally free, he collapsed and prayed to God, thanking him for his deliverance. He vowed to avenge the death he saw as wrongful.

He was the only survivor of the papal army, for God still had a purpose Lucier would painfully realize someday but not before many more would fall to his wrongful retribution. It would not happen before innocence was put asunder for a cause that would leave a scar upon mankind and the Christianity they shared.

As Lucier crawled down from the mountain to heal and recover, he was not alone. Far off in the shadows lingered one who would not fear his wrath—one who waited with purposeful mission.

Dabria bided his time, for he knew to appear too quickly would arouse suspicion. He would wait until there was a need. He had waited this long for the darkness to come within his grasp; he could ill afford to lose the opportunity again.

Here, alone in the wilderness without the protection of his army, he was but a man, wounded, hurting, and vulnerable, body and soul.

Darkness lived on, but God's will would be done.

Chapter 51

THE LIGHT SHINES IN THE DARKNESS

For you were once darkness, but now you are light in the Lord. Walk as children of light.

—Ephesians 5:8

In the days following the battle, Galack and his men tended to their wounded. Berg's injury was mostly superficial, but it needed bandaging as well. He and his Huguenot brothers buried their dead the best they could in the nearly frozen ground. Not all were found, including Dabria, the wayfaring stranger who joined the caravan just prior to their passage up Quenten. Those they feared were buried under the snow would be eulogized as one—brothers in spirit who died for the ultimate cause. They would all be missed.

The harder task awaited. The survivors had to tell the families of those who were deceased of their journey's end, regardless of how they died. No one looked forward to that day; they never did. Yet, the burial of the dead continued. Berg and Marik worked side by side. They joked about the irony of the scene since only a few months earlier, this was how they had met. Now they were brothers in faith.

The papal army dead who could be found, who weren't buried under the avalanche, were gathered into a large mass grave and set afire. Those entombed in the ice would have to wait until spring. Their battle was at its end. The black smoke rose to the snow-filled sky, making a grayness of spirit to the eye. Prayers were offered up for all the dead. They also gave thanks for the miraculous gift God provided them by allowing them to defeat the overwhelming force. They realized God's will had been done.

Marik and Peter spent a lot of time catching up on all that had transpired when time allowed. With each new minute they were reunited, it was obvious to Jakob and Arktos that Marik had changed. Something about him was different. He was kind enough before, but now there seemed to be a grace about him, a feeling of wanting to do more that showed with every action, every word. Days later, Peter would explain Marik's near-death experience to them. Between his recounting and Berg's retelling of the story, it was obvious God had been at work in countless ways.

The weather was closing in on the mountain, and to Arktos, it was apparent they would never make it to the upper reaches of the Vaudois where he knew the survivors would have escaped to, if there were any. His heart ached to know, but he knew it was not worth the risk. Resolute to wait, he urged Galack and his clan to return to their homelands now, before it was too late.

The resources that were normally stockpiled for their farm and the village had disappeared from countless days of plunder and what little the former residents could glean before their escape to higher ground. Galack realized that it would be nearly impossible for Arktos and his family to remain, so he invited them all to join them in their villages on the other side of Quenten, where they could share winter quarters and learn more.

The old Vaudoisian realized God had brought the Huguenots into their world for a reason, and he gladly accepted their newfound friend's hospitality.

As they made their way through the nearly blocked pass, Jakob looked back at the shell of a home that had once been all he knew. The snows swirled in a fury of white that soon blocked the image from sight as their caravan began its trek. Once again, he was leaving behind all he had ever known, his memories, his home, his Vaudois. This time, unlike before, there were no loved ones bidding them a fond farewell.

He could only imagine his family as he motioned an empty good-bye to the nothing on the ridge below.

Their precious Vaudois once again sat empty . . . waiting for the souls it had known for an eternity to return. It waited in God's time now.

Above them, in the highest habitable reaches of the mountain, the core of the Apostle Speakers survived. They had dispersed many to the neighboring valleys to begin teaching, memorizing, and spreading the Word. Elder Jourdan was blessed to find all of the Word had survived somehow, if not by the grace of God, for he knew it was God's will. Even to the most faithful it was a testament to their belief and faith. They had safely remained in their mountain sanctuary, continuing the tradition they had done for so many centuries now. They had been chosen for a reason. It was apparent, perhaps not to themselves, that their spirit was not the only gift from God, but that through the Word, there would be many blessings to flow.

As darkness grew across the land, the light would continue to shine in the darkness.

Lux lucet in tenebris . . .

Bibliography

Books:

Joseph Visconti, *The Waldensian Way to God, English.* (Maitland, FL: Xulon Press, 2003), 576.

J.A. Wylie, *History of the Waldenses.* (London, England: Church History, 1985).

Alexis Muston, *The Israel of the Alps: A Complete History of the Waldenses and Their Colonies.* John Montgomery, Translator. (Paris, AR: Baptist Standard Bearer, 2001), 572.

Giorgio Tourn, *The Waldensians: THE FIRST 800 YEARS* (1174-1974). Camillo P. Merlino, Translator. Charles W. Arbuthnot, Editor. (Torino, Italy: Claudiana Editrice, 1980).

Internet:

http://www.waldensiantrailoffaith.org/history.html

http://www.Orthodoxwiki.org

http://www.ChristianHistoryTimeline.com

http://www.Biblegateway.com